THE
INFLUENCE

THE
INFLUENCE

BENTLEY LITTLE

CEMETERY DANCE PUBLICATIONS

Baltimore

❖ **2013** ❖

Cemetery Dance Publications
132-B Industry Lane, Unit #7
Forest Hill, MD 21050
http://www.cemeterydance.com

The characters and events in this book are fictitious.
Any similarity to real persons, living or dead,
is coincidental and not intended by the author.

Second Cemetery Dance Hardcover Printing, December 2013

Trade Hardcover ISBN: 978-1-58767-419-8

Printed in the United States of America

3   5   7   9   10   8   6   4   2

Cover Artwork & Design © 2013 by Elder Lemon Design
Interior Design by Kate Freeman Design

For Judson, my brother

ONE

KARMA? WHAT A CROCK OF SHIT.

When his sister Alma and her husband Jay had needed a co-signer so they could buy a house in Mesa, Ross had been there for them. He'd even ponied up $5,000 he couldn't really afford in order to help with the down payment. And when his brother Rick's pothead son Kevin was arrested for attempted arson in Texas, Ross had cabled the boy the money for bail *and* paid for Rick's plane ticket to Austin, as well as a significant percentage of the lawyer's fees. Not to mention the loan he'd given to his Aunt Melissa when her husband ran off with his secretary, or the "presents" he'd given to far-flung relatives who'd fallen on hard times, or the many instances when he'd picked up barely known offshoots of his family tree at the airport and given them a place to stay.

So when he lost his job at Air Research, Ross naturally thought that everyone would be there for him. But when a year passed and he still couldn't find another job, when he began gently hinting that he could use a little help to tide him over, his brother and sister suddenly started making themselves scarce. And all of those other relatives? Conspicuously absent.

Even his parents.

So much for the idea that sending out good stuff brought back good stuff in return.

It was his cousin Lita who finally came through for him.

He hadn't seen Lita in probably ten years, although they'd been close as children. She'd lived in New Mexico, but every summer, her family would come out to Phoenix for a week or two. They'd spend hot afternoons in air-conditioned movie theaters, and have evening picnics by Canyon Lake or the Salt River. They would always set aside one morning for the zoo and botanical gardens, and one day they would always spend at the amusement park Legend City. It was vacation-as-routine, but to Ross, as a child, there was something comforting about that. He knew what to expect and he looked forward to it. Lita did, too.

He'd been in seventh or eighth grade when Lita and her family had stopped coming, at an age where he didn't want to acknowledge that he even *had* a family, let alone spend time with them. Even so, though he'd never admitted it to anyone, he missed her, and the subsequent summers had never seemed as magical or fun. He'd seen her periodically after that—at her mother's remarriage, at their grandmother's funeral—but while they spoke and were cordial, the closeness they'd once shared was no longer there.

So it was a surprise when, one early October morning, out of the blue, she called to check up on him. She'd heard from her mom, who'd heard from Ross' mom, that he'd lost his job and had been out of work for the past year, and unlike the other selfish, self-involved narcissists who called themselves his family, she actually seemed concerned. He didn't want to burden Lita with the full extent of his financial problems—his savings were practically gone, his unemployment checks were scheduled to stop soon, and he was going to have to sell his condo (if he could in this market) and move to a smaller apartment in a cheaper area of the Valley because he couldn't keep up the payments—but under her determined questioning, he buckled, confessing all.

"I have an idea," she told him when he was finished.

"Yeah?" he said wearily.

"You should take a few months off and come visit." There was a teasing quality to her voice that he remembered from childhood and that made him feel as though no time had passed and they were both ten years old. She wasn't joking, however, and while her approach was playful, her intent was to give him some financial breathing room. She suggested renting out his condo in order to earn some extra money to help keep up the payments. That way, he'd still have the place when he *did* find a job. In the meantime, he could spend a few months in Magdalena with her and her husband. They had over an acre, and there was a shotgun shack on the property where they'd lived while they were building the house. He was more than welcome to use it.

Ross demurred. "Thank you," he said sincerely. "That's very generous of you. But I can't—"

"This is me you're talking to."

"I still need to look for work," he told her. "And I don't think I'll find too many engineering positions in…Where do you live? Magdalena?"

"What are you talking about? We have train tracks not twenty miles from here. Joking! I know what kind of engineer you mean.

And I also know that you're not pounding the pavement for a job like that. You're emailing resumes. You can do that from here. We have internet access."

"I have to show up in person to get my unemployment."

Lita was silent for a moment. "Okay," she said. "You're off the hook. For now. But the offer's open. When your unemployment runs out, come on over and take a break from the rat race. We've got plenty of space, and we'd love to have you. And I'm serious. Think about renting out rather than selling. This is just a temporary setback. You don't want to lose everything you've worked for just because of a little bad luck."

He was touched. As much by the reconnection as by her genuine kindness and generosity, especially in comparison with the rest of his family. "Thank you," he said simply.

"I have an idea," she suggested. "Why don't you come down for a visit? A weekend. We haven't seen each other in ages. It would be good to catch up."

He immediately thought of twenty reasons not to go—starting with the price of gas—but to his surprise, he said yes. He wanted to see Lita again. And get to know her husband, whom he'd only met once. And maybe he *would* take a sabbatical from real life, drop out of society and live off the grid for a couple of weeks. It would give him a chance to think about the future, to make plans without a gun to his head.

"All right!" Lita said, and she said it the same way she had when she was a little girl. He found himself smiling into the phone. "Got a piece of paper?" she asked. "Let me give you directions…"

Magdalena was a small town in southeastern Arizona, only a desert mountain range away from Mexico and closer to the New Mexico border than to Tucson. Getting to it was far more difficult than it should have been in this MapQuest world, but then again the information superhighway had been paid much more attention to in the last few decades than had real highways, so perhaps it should not have come as a surprise. Past Benson, past Willcox, Interstate 10 was clear all the way to New Mexico, according to the road signs. But, following his cousin's directions, Ross pulled off on the anonymously marked "Exit 96" and took the bleached two-lane blacktop south.

Ten miles in, he passed an abandoned gas station, and twenty miles further on, he saw a small hill atop which someone had erected a giant white cross, although there was no other trace of human habitation.

Somewhere along the line, the pavement seemed to have faded away, and Ross was not sure if he was now travelling down a dirt road or over asphalt that had been retaken by the desert after battling the sandstorms that hit disproportionately this section of the state.

There were no signs indicating that any town lay ahead, nothing even telling him how many miles to the Mexican border. He'd been off the highway for an hour and was about to take out his cell phone and try calling Lita to make sure he was on the right track (that is, if he could get a signal out here), when ahead, at the base of one of the low rocky mountains that blocked the edge of the horizon, he saw a flash of reflected sunlight. It disappeared as the road dipped, then reappeared as his car topped a small rise. There was more than one glinting object, and he realized that they were probably the metal roofs or water towers of a town.

He was still many miles away, but as he drew closer, he saw darker objects between the bright flashes, buildings, and, eventually, a white "M" on the sloping brush-covered side of the chimney-peaked mountain directly behind the town.

Magdalena.

Lita and her husband really *had* dropped out of the rat race. This was about as remote a location as she could have found anywhere. And while there was something admirable about that, and while the rugged desert was undeniably beautiful, Ross felt an odd twinge of discomfort. He was a city boy, Phoenix born and raised. To him, the wilderness was somewhere you visited on vacation, not the place where you lived. Still, though he might not want to reside here permanently, it might be a fun spot for some R & R while he sorted out his options.

He slowed the car. Referring to Magdalena as a "small town" was giving it the benefit of the doubt. More of a village or hamlet, it appeared to have one main street, the road he was on, which dead-ended past what looked like an old adobe church and seemed to turn into a hiking trail that wound up the side of the mountain. What he supposed was the downtown consisted of a handful of small businesses and houses, in addition to a slightly larger market with an independent gas station in its parking lot.

Ross glanced down at the directions on the seat next to him. Lita had said her home was down the second dirt road on the right. He turned on the road, passed a shabby beauty salon, three or four ramshackle houses, then was back in open country, where, three miles past a cattleguard, just where she'd said it would be, he saw an old-style metal mailbox with the number 11 stenciled in black on the side. Following her instructions, he turned left at the mailbox and drove down a rutted dirt driveway to a surprisingly new ranch house that seemed completely at odds with the surrounding community. To the left of the house was a corral and, beyond that, a long low building that resembled a barn. Lita and her husband, apparently, were ranchers.

Ross parked next to a dusty pickup in front of the house. He'd promised to be here for lunch, but he'd left later than he'd planned and the journey had proved longer than expected. It was now after two. He hoped they'd eaten already and hadn't been waiting on him.

Lita emerged from the house, alerted by the slamming car door as he alighted from the vehicle. She greeted him with an excited squeal, running up and throwing her arms around him in a big hug. Dave, her husband, stood shyly on the porch.

Lita had barely changed in the decade since he'd seen her. Her hair was shorter and lighter in color, but even a life lived outdoors had put no wrinkles on her face, and he was suddenly conscious of the fact that he'd chubbed up quite a bit in the past year.

"It's so great to see you!" she enthused. She nudged his belly with an elbow. "Put on a few pounds, I see."

"Junk food'll do that to you. Junk food and stress."

"Speaking of food, I'll bet you're starving. Or did you eat on the way?"

"No. The trip was a little longer than I thought."

"I should've warned you about that. Come on in." She led the way up the porch steps. "You remember Dave."

Ross shook hands with Lita's husband, who smiled and said, "Nice to see you again."

The two of them *had* eaten, but Lita had made gumbo and kept it warm in a crock pot. Dave, a big man, said he was hungry again and joined Ross as he ate. Lita drank iced tea and reminisced with Ross about places no longer there, like Legend City and the below ground movie theater in Los Arcos mall. Laughing at the memory of their visit to South Mountain's Mystery Castle, where the tour guide had forbidden an overly curious Ross from asking any more questions, she admitted that she'd never had a subsequent summer vacation as fun as the ones she'd spent with his family.

"Why did you stop coming?" he wondered. "I never understood that. Money?"

She shrugged. "Maybe. Partly. But my parents weren't getting along much then, and it was kind of the beginning of the end. They got divorced when I was fifteen, and after that I lived with my mom and the problem was definitely money."

"I missed you," Ross said.

She smiled, put her hand on his. "I missed you, too."

She asked about the rest of his family, his parents, his brother and sister, and he told her the truth, the unvarnished version.

"I never liked your sister," Lita admitted. "That's why I always hung out with you and your brother. Although him I could take or leave, to be honest with you. Maybe because he was older than we were. He always seemed like he was doing us a big favor just by gracing us with his presence."

"That was Rick. Still is."

"Remember that time you two got in a fight and you sprained your wrist?"

"I remember."

"What was that thing you always used to say when you were trying to be tough? 'I'll kick your ass to pay for Friday?'"

Ross laughed.

"What did that even mean?"

"I have no idea. I just thought it sounded cool."

"It made you sound like a *dork!*"

"Well, what about you?"

"What about me?"

He tried to come up with a corresponding embarrassment for her but couldn't do it under pressure and gave up, laughing. "All right. I was the dork."

Ross was glad he'd come, and after finishing his late lunch, he was taken on a tour of the house and property by Lita and Dave. It was indeed a ranch and even had a name, the L Bar-D. Dave, who'd grown up in Sonoita, the son of a cattleman who'd gone broke and made a midlife career change to become a postal worker, dreamed of owning a herd of cows. At the moment he and Lita had only a horse, a goat, several hives of bees, which provided the organic honey they sold, and a coop full of chickens, which supplied the eggs from which they received most of their admittedly small income.

"But we don't need much," Dave insisted. "We live simply."

Beaming, Lita took her husband's hand. "And happily."

The shack where they'd lived while the house was being built, and where Ross would be sleeping, was to the left of the chicken coop and much cuter than the word "shack" had led him to believe. A prefab structure they'd bought and put together themselves, it was basically set up like an efficiency apartment, with a counter separating the small cooking space from the living/sleeping area, and a closet-sized bathroom containing a toilet, a sink and a narrow shower. Lita had kept the place up—like a guestroom, Ross supposed—and he had to admit that it was pretty nice. He even had a view of the open desert through the front windows.

Lita nudged him with her elbow. "Admit it, Rossie. Not a bad place to stay, is it?"

No one had called him "Rossie" since he was a kid, and hearing it now made him feel old.

"It's nice," he admitted.

Despite his initial reservations, Ross enjoyed the weekend. He thought he'd be bored, but while the pace of life was slower than in Phoenix—*much* slower—it was relaxing. Besides, Lita and Dave had DirectTV and internet access, so it wasn't as though he was completely cut off from the real world. Monday morning, as he prepared to depart, he actually felt sad to be leaving.

Lita poked her head through the open car window as he was about to go. "Promise me, if things don't work out, if you run out of money, if you don't find a job before your benefits expire, if you just need a place to clear your head, that you'll call. I'm serious. Your shack will be sitting here waiting. And, as you can see, we have plenty of room. It'd be good for you."

"Thanks," he said. "I had a great time. And I appreciate everything you've done. Both of you."

"Promise me," she repeated.

He smiled at her. "I promise."

TWO

ROSS KEPT HIS PROMISE—AND MUCH SOONER THAN HE'D intended.

Despite the state of the economy, despite all of the personal setbacks of the past year, he'd honestly thought he had a shot at getting hired by McDowell Industries, an aerospace firm based in Houston. They'd accepted his resume two months ago, and while he hadn't been called for an interview, the personnel director had phoned himself and assured Ross that he was on the short list. So it was quite a blow when, the day after Halloween, he received a generic rejection, a one-line email notifying him that the position had been filled.

The unexpected news caused him to take stock, and Ross decided that if he was going to take advantage of his cousin's offer, he should do so sooner rather than later, while he still had money coming in and could pay some of his own expenses, before he became a complete leech and freeloader. The prospect still didn't sit well with him, but being able to contribute made it a lot more palatable, and in the back of his mind was the idea that he could get some sort of part-time or seasonal job in the area—manual labor or a service position—that would enable him to pull his own weight.

At least he didn't have a huge debt hanging over his head. Another supervisor, Alex Yoon, who'd gotten laid off the same time as Ross and who had also not yet found employment, had been using his credit cards to see him through the past year. Now they were all maxed out, and he couldn't even make the minimum payments. A financial advisor had told him that the only option left was personal bankruptcy.

Ross was not in that bad a shape.

Yet.

He informed everyone of his decision several weeks prior to implementing it, hoping it would spur his parents and his siblings to help out somehow. But they only congratulated him, as though moving into a shack out in the middle of nowhere was the equivalent of finding a great new job. He shouldn't have expected anything different, and it was his own fault for thinking his family might actually give a damn, but the reaction still left him feeling angry and disappointed.

As it happened, he didn't have as many personal possessions as he thought he had. Friends helped him move the furniture to a storage unit, along with a couple of boxes of books, games and CDs, another couple of boxes filled with pots, pans, plates and kitchen utensils, and several garbage sacks filled with various odds and ends. In his car, coming with him, were most of his clothes, a few books, his laptop, a small microwave, his toolbox, a lamp and some necessities that he knew Lita's guest house didn't have. After dropping a condo key off at the realtor's, he met his friends at Roundtable Pizza, where he bought them what was either a late lunch or an early dinner—"Linner," Trent dubbed it—and unlimited pitchers of beer to thank them for their help.

"When're you coming back?" Patrick asked.

Ross shrugged. "When I get a job, I guess."

"So…never?" Alex said.

They all laughed, but underlying the humor was a depressing truth, and a sense of melancholy pervaded the proceedings after that, no matter how hard they tried to ignore it. Eventually, everyone left, and Ross drove out to Chandler to spend the night at his parents' house before hitting the road in the morning. They'd made up the couch for him but had not gone to any extra effort to make his final night a special one. It was Saturday, so his mom baked meat loaf, the way she always did, and it was as bad as he remembered. He ended up eating mostly side dishes, white bread and creamed corn, just as he had as a kid. Neither his sister's family nor his brother's had been invited over to say goodbye, and after dinner he sat in his parents' living room while his mom and dad watched *Jeopardy* and then a *CSI* rerun and then went to bed.

He left early, not bothering to wake his parents, not bothering to say goodbye, hitting McDonald's for a quick junk food breakfast before heading out on the highway. He felt a little down as he headed into the pre-dawn darkness and the last lights of Phoenix disappeared behind the low desert hills in his rearview mirror. But the sun came up soon after, rising quickly, clear and bright, and a weird feeling of liberation overcame him as he passed Picacho Peak, heading south.

By the time he reached the outskirts of Tucson, he was filled with a renewed sense of optimism. He raced past a freight train, chugging slowly on tracks that paralleled the highway. He wasn't merely leaving behind his old life; he was starting a new one. This wasn't a retreat. It was a beginning. And if it so happened that he never found a job making as much money as he had at Air Research, if he ended up eking out a living doing manual labor or working the land, well, that was okay. He would survive. He might even thrive.

He didn't know what the future would hold.

And for the first time, that prospect was not frightening to him but exciting.

He'd told Lita he was coming today, but he'd also told her that he'd arrive mid-afternoon and not to save lunch for him, he'd grab something on the way. In Tucson, he found a Target, where he looked for something he could bring to his hosts as a thank you present. Nothing struck his fancy, but he stopped off at a nearby Bookman's, where he browsed for an hour or so before picking out a Southwest cookbook and a boxed set of Beatles CDs that he thought Lita and Dave would like. For lunch, he ate at a Subway in Benson that was adjacent to the gas station where he filled up, and it was shortly after two when he finally drove down the dirt road into Magdalena.

As before, the directions to Lita's ranch were on a piece of paper on the seat next to him, but this time he didn't need them. He remembered the way and turned down the second dirt road, passed the beauty salon and houses, went into open country and turned in at the mailbox, going up the narrow drive until he reached the L Bar-D. He pulled up in front of the main house rather than the guest house, figuring he'd better check in first, but before he could even get out of the car, Lita was on the porch and waving him forward. "Park by the shack!" she called.

Ross nodded, started the car again and drove around the house and several yards down, stopping on the side of the small building.

Dave emerged from the guest house, where he'd been installing a new water-saver showerhead, just as Lita ran up. It was clear almost instantly that the two of them had been fighting—

about him?

—but they were both friendly and welcoming, individually if not together, and Dave helped him unload the heavier items while Lita brought over supplies such as paper towels and bottled water from the main house. The living room/sleeping area was larger than he remembered, which was good, because he'd brought quite a few things. He told Lita and Dave to just pile everything in the middle of the floor and on the counter, and he'd find a place for it. From the Bookman's bag that he'd taken from the front seat, he withdrew the cookbook and Beatles CDs that he'd bought in Tucson. "Here," he said, clumsily handing them over. "A little thank you present for letting me stay here."

"You didn't have to—" Lita began.

"All right!" Dave said. "The Beatles!"

She shot him a look of disapproval.

"And I want to pay rent," Ross said. "Each month, I'm going to—"

"No," Lita and Dave said together. They looked at each other, and something like a smile passed between them. "You're our guest," Lita told him, "not our tenant. We invited you here. We're not taking money from you."

"But—"

"No buts, Rossie. Discussion over."

He recognized that voice from when they were young and knew it was futile to argue with her. "Thanks," he said sincerely.

"We'll leave you alone, let you get settled. I'll give you a shout out when dinner's ready. You can eat with us or take it back here to the shack, whatever you want."

Already he felt awkward, an intruder in their lives. "Do you need some help?" he asked. "I'm not a great cook, but if you want someone to—"

"I can handle it." She smiled. "Just get yourself settled in. We'll sort out the details tomorrow. And thank you for the cookbook. You didn't have to go to all that trouble, but it was very thoughtful of you."

"The CDs, too!" Dave called as they headed out the door. "The Beatles," Ross heard him say as they walked back to the house. "A boxed set!"

He spent the rest of the afternoon putting things away, checking his email every other minute and walking around, pacing. He felt restless, unsure of what to do with himself, and thought he had probably made a huge mistake in coming here. He was not a rural/country/wilderness kind of guy; this wasn't the place for someone like him. He wasn't going to sit in his room and write a novel, wasn't going to set up an easel and paint a picture of the surrounding scenery. He was an engineer, for God's sake. He worked on projects, with other people, in a crowded office, and even his leisure activities involved city life. But out here he couldn't go to movies or clubs or concerts, couldn't hang with his friends at a pizza joint or do any of the things he usually did.

At least he had his computer.

He played *Plants vs. Zombies* and *Angry Birds* until Lita stepped into the yard and announced that it was time to eat. Glancing through the window, he was surprised to see that the day was gone and it was dark already. Walking between the two buildings, he could see the lights of town in the distance, slightly downslope, though the road to the ranch had seemed flat. Above, an amazing array of stars filled the sky, so thick in spots that they appeared to be clouds. He hadn't noticed such details when he'd come up for last month for the weekend, and it hit him that he was no longer a tourist. He lived here. For now, at least, this was his home.

He had never felt more alone.

Unsure of the etiquette involved, he knocked on the kitchen door and waited for Lita to open it before going inside. "Don't be so formal," she admonished him.

"I wasn't sure—"

"If there's something you're not supposed to see," she said, "the door will be locked. Otherwise, just come in. Our house is yours."

Sitting at the kitchen table, Dave reddened.

"Well, uh, thanks," Ross managed to get out.

"Welcome to my world," Dave said wryly.

Lita smiled. "He loves it."

Neither of them were quite sure to what she was referring, so they did not respond as Ross sat down awkwardly at the table across from Dave.

Lita had made chicken enchiladas, from a recipe in the cookbook he'd given her. "But it's not exact," she warned. "I had to change a few things because we didn't have all the ingredients. As you might have noticed, out here we can't just run down to the local supermarket if we need something."

"Now that you mention it, where do you get your groceries?" Ross wondered.

"We make a monthly run over to Willcox for the things that'll keep," Dave said, motioning toward the open larder to the right of the refrigerator. "Beans, rice, detergent, what have you. There's a small grocery store in town for some of the day-to-day stuff, but a lot of things we barter or buy from neighbors."

"Or pick up at the farmer's market," Lita offered, bringing over a plate of enchiladas.

"Or pick up at the farmer's market," Dave agreed. "We sell there, too."

"There might not be as many choices as there are in a big city," Lita conceded. "But we eat a lot healthier now than I did when I was growing up. A lot more fresh food and homemade items." She touched her husband's shoulder, their earlier fight—whatever it was about—obviously over. "It suits us."

Ross nodded and bit into the food she'd put in front of him. "Delicious," he proclaimed, and meant it. "Thank you. And thanks for the cookbook."

They ate. And talked. About things in general, about nothing in particular. It was nice, pleasant, and time flew by, but eventually they finished eating, and Ross looked through the window at the shack across the yard. The lights were on in the small building, but around it, all was black. It made him feel depressed to realize that this was where he lived now, in what was basically a studio apartment surrounded by a lot of nothing.

The feeling must have shown on his face, because Lita put her hand on his. "What are you thinking?"

"To be honest," Ross said, "I don't know how long I'm going to be able to take this. I've been here for, what, four hours? And already I'm lost. I don't know what to do with myself."

"Culture shock," she told him. "I felt the same way when I first came here. But you'll get acclimatized pretty quickly. And once you get used to it, you'll wonder how you ever ran in the rat race."

"Maybe. But right now, I'm looking at a lot of free time."

"You can go online, look for work."

"That's a whole hour out of the day." He leaned forward. "Dave. I was wondering if you have some jobs I could do around this place, something I can help you with. Not for payment," he added quickly. "But to, you know, pull my weight."

"Not really."

"Come on. There must be something I can do, some sort of busywork you could give me."

"We-l-l-l," Dave said slowly, "We will be selling at the farmer's market on Thursday. I'm a little behind on fixing a section of roof on the coop, so you could help out by collecting eggs for me. That'd definitely save me some time."

"Done." Ross paused. "How exactly do you collect eggs?"

Dave laughed. "I'll show you tomorrow morning."

"Okay." Another pause. "You ranchers get up at, like, four, don't you?"

"Not us. We get up when we get up. I usually eat breakfast, catch up on the news and maybe get out there around eight. "

"That's more my style."

"In summer it's earlier because it gets so hot, but right now…" He shrugged.

"Perfect."

Ross wasn't a big dessert guy, but Lita had made some sort of lemonade pie in honor of his arrival, so he felt obligated to have a piece. It was delicious, and he told her so, and she explained that the lemons came from one of the trees behind their house. It turned out that, in addition to an extensive garden, she and Dave had several fruit trees on the property: lemons, oranges, apples, persimmons.

Dinner had stretched to well over an hour, and Ross excused himself, pushing his chair back from the table, not wanting to overstay his welcome. Lita seemed disappointed and asked him to stay, so they could continue to catch up on old times, but he told her that there would be plenty of time for that. Besides, Dave wasn't asking him to stay, and the last thing Ross wanted was to be a point of contention between them, particularly if he *had* been the source of the argument they'd had before he arrived. "I'll see you guys tomorrow," he said.

"Goodnight," Lita told him. "You want me to call you for breakfast?"

"No, I'll just make myself some cereal. I can't be coming over here for every meal."

"It's—" she began.

"I'm not much for breakfast, anyway." He nodded toward Dave. "I'll be up by seven and ready by eight. Should I just come over here or..." He trailed off.

"I'll stop by and get you."

Ross nodded. "Sounds good. " He took his leave and waved as he stepped out through the kitchen door, the way he'd come in.

He'd left a light on in the guest house, but surrounding the structure was nothing but darkness, an inky emptiness that engulfed the world beyond for as far as his perceptions stretched. It made him feel small and uneasy, and that feeling did not abate as he entered the guest house and closed the door behind him, sealing himself in. He thought about watching TV, but there was nothing on, so he IMed a couple of friends and spent the next hour chatting online, describing his first day of exile, before going to bed early, feeling sad and lonely as he fell asleep listening to the clucking of chickens in front of the overwhelming silence of the desert.

Ross awoke in the morning feeling better. He wasn't sure if it was because he had something to do today or because he was already starting to get used to this place, but he was almost cheery as he poured some milk and Raisin Bran into a bowl, and made himself coffee. The television helped, too. Watching the *Today* show, the way he usually did, seeing crowds of people begging for the attention of the weatherman as he walked outside the studio, made Ross feel more connected to the larger world, although when he heard that the next segment was an interview with the Muppets, he shut off the TV. There was nothing more embarrassing than seeing a well-respected reporter who ordinarily questioned heads of state about important world events pretend to interview a puppet, and force himself to laugh at the stock replies issuing from the unseen man working Miss Piggy or Kermit the Frog.

He brushed his teeth, then opened the drapes. Dave was already carrying a toolbox and ladder toward the chicken coop. Ross opened the door and hurried after him. "I thought you were going to come and get me."

"I was. After I took my supplies out, I was going to see if you were up."

Ross wasn't sure he bought that. He had the distinct impression that Dave did not want him along, but there was no overt opposition as he quickly put on his shoes then followed his host over to the coop.

Dave had already leaned the ladder against the side of the building, had climbed up and was near the top, placing his toolbox on the barely sloping roof. An oversized plastic pail filled with patching materials lay at the foot of the ladder. "Could you hand that up to me?" he called down.

Ross picked up the pail by its metal handle—it was heavier than it looked—and used both hands to push it to shoulder level, where Dave took it from him. "Thanks."

Dave placed the pail on the roof next to the toolbox, then climbed down. "Follow me," he said.

The chicken coop was much bigger on the inside than it appeared on the outside, and the adjoining yard, behind the building, was as big as a baseball diamond. Both were filled with pacing, clucking hens far too numerous to count.

"How many chickens do you have?" Ross asked.

"A hundred."

"Wow."

"It's not as much as it sounds. We could really do with a hundred more, but we just can't afford it. The guy I bought the animals from, he has a free-range farm out past Willcox, and he has over five thousand layers. We'd be making a *very* comfortable income if we had that many birds. I'd probably have to hire a man or two to help me out." He shrugged. "But of course, we don't."

"So what do you want me to do?" Ross asked.

"Collect eggs."

"Okay."

"If they were caged, it would be a lot easier," Dave admitted. "You'd just walk down the aisles and pick the eggs up from the grates. But we don't believe in that. It's cruel. Chickens raised that way have no life at all. They can't even turn around. They're stuck in the same position for their entire adult life. They're just egg machines. But as you can see, our chickens have litter to scratch around in, and in the yard here they can get down in the dirt to fluff up dust around their feathers, which, believe it or not, helps control parasites. We also don't cut off their beaks, although a lot of places do, even so-called 'organic farms,' because chickens like to fight. But, so far, we haven't had any trouble."

"So how exactly do I do this?"

Dave pointed to tubular structures lining the walls. "Those are nesting boxes. That's where they lay the eggs—for the most part. There are also a couple of other places I'll show you where you're likely to find a few. Anyway, you pick up one of these baskets here, get a scoop of feed out of this barrel, throw the feed out, and when the birds go for it, pick up the eggs and put them in the basket. When the basket's full, bring it over to the house, drop it off, then come back, get another basket and keep on going.

"We store the eggs in a root cellar next to the toolshed on the other side of the house. It's kind of a natural refrigerator. Before we put them in there, we clean them, inspect them, carton them, then take them down."

"Then you sell them?"

Dave nodded. "There are standing orders for big customers like the store in town, and they'll come in throughout the week to pick up their eggs, but a lot of our sales are at the farmer's market." He held up his hands in a gesture of completion. "That's about it."

He walked with Ross through the filling of the first basket, but the process was pretty simple, the chickens cooperative, and Ross filled the second basket on his own while Dave worked on the roof of the coop. There was something oddly relaxing about egg collection. A Zen thing, he supposed. Presidents and people in power always made a big show about doing manual labor on their time off: clearing brush, chopping wood. He'd always assumed that was for effect, an effort to show the yokels that they weren't just pointy-headed intellectuals but deep down were simple, honest hard-working folk like themselves. It had always seemed phony to him, contrived. But having been initiated into the rural experience himself now, he understood how simple, repetitive work could help clear the mind, could offer a welcome respite from the overthinking of modern life.

For lunch, Lita made them all a frittata with some of the eggs he'd collected and with vegetables from the garden that she'd canned at the end of last season. It was delicious, and he took a plate of leftovers back to his shack, intending to heat them up in the microwave for dinner.

"I'm glad you came," Lita said before he left. "I'm glad you're staying with us."

Ross thought about his dwindling bank account, the final unemployment checks coming up, and his condo, which, hopefully, the realtor would be able to rent out or sell. "Me, too," he said.

THREE

OVER THE NEXT FEW DAYS, ROSS DEVELOPED A KIND OF routine. He'd wake early, make himself breakfast, then go out and gather eggs. He was on his own schedule, didn't need to wait for Dave to invite him or help him, and after one or two hours of collecting, he'd take all the eggs he'd amassed and bring them over to the house, where he'd help Lita clean them, sort them and place them in cartons.

He didn't love working with chickens, but he got used to it, and it gave him something to do, even though, at odd times throughout the day, he would have flashbacks to his former life, what he thought of as his *real* life, thinking: *I should be in a staff meeting right now* or *I should be on break, heading to Starbuck's with Alex* or *I should be mapping out specs for a new flight control system*. It was ridiculous, the 180 his life had undergone, but he did not allow himself to dwell on it for fear of becoming mired in self-pity.

Following the completion of his "chores," as he jokingly called them, Ross would have lunch, sometimes by himself in the shack, sometimes with Lita and Dave, and in the afternoon, he'd go online, make phone calls, send out resumes and look for work. Evenings were spent watching TV, playing online games or emailing friends, though he took dinner with his hosts, both because he felt obligated and because Lita was a far better cook than he was.

On Thursday, they went to the farmer's market to sell. He set his alarm for five, but Lita and Dave were already up, Lita gluing labels onto the last jars of honey, Dave carefully packing the egg cartons and honey jars into larger boxes along with protective layers of bubble wrap. The market didn't open until nine, but they were ready to go by six-thirty, and they ate a leisurely breakfast together before counting out money to put in the change box, loading a table and chairs into the back of the pickup, and heading off to town, three abreast in the truck's small cab.

After a bumpy uncomfortable ride on obviously shot shocks, they arrived in Magdalena, where the last section of street in front of the church was blocked off with two sawhorses, though that was probably unnecessary since Ross doubted there was much traffic here even on a busy day. Leaning out the window, Dave motioned to a cowboy-hatted septuagenarian standing next to the sawhorse on the right, and the old man pulled it aside to let the pickup through. Dave parked at the far end of the farmer's market next to a Native American family setting up displays of jewelry and leatherware on a sheet-covered folding table, and the three of them got out of the cab.

Looking up at the adobe church at the end of the street and at the adobe building behind the pickup truck, Ross felt as though he was no longer in Arizona. He'd been born and raised in the state, but unlike California or New Mexico, which both had heavy Spanish influences, Arizona had always seemed to him very *anglo,* more cowboy-and-Indian than the rest of the Southwest, less Mexican. Magdalena, however, felt like it belonged south of the border. Even its name stood out from those of its more American neighbors: Willcox, Benson, Bisbee, Douglas, Tombstone… *Magdalena.*

He had never felt farther from home.

Ross helped Dave unload and set up the table and chairs in front of the down tailgate, while Lita carefully unpacked the cartons of eggs and jars of honey and began arranging them for display. Dave pulled out a large wooden sign with the words "L BAR-D RANCH ORGANIC EGGS AND HONEY" written on it, using bricks and two-by-fours to prop it next to the table.

According to Lita and Dave, the farmer's market accounted for a significant portion of their admittedly small income, but Ross could not see how. Even if every family in town bought from them today, they couldn't make more than a hundred dollars or so. How could they survive on that?

He helped separate the various types of honey, as well as the brown eggs from the white eggs. Additional sellers had arrived while they were setting up, and Lita said, "There's still another ten minutes before we officially open. Want to take a look around?"

"Sure."

Dave stayed at the table while Ross and Lita walked down the street, looking at the various stalls. Before this, if he'd ever bothered to think about this area of the state, he would have assumed it to be barren, godforsaken desert. So it was something of a surprise to see such a large variety of locally grown produce being sold, not to mention baked goods, jerky, tamales and cheese. He actually bought some turkey jerky and a quart of unfiltered apple juice, while Lita stocked up on onions and garlic. Looking back, he saw that several other sellers were buying honey or eggs from Dave.

The last stall they visited— the first stall, really, since it was closest to the sawhorses blocking off the street—resembled a larger version of Lucy's psychiatric booth in the *Peanuts* comics. A sign above the booth announced "MUSHROOMS!" in bright rainbow letters. There was a cute little girl in front of the stand who couldn't have been more than five. Dressed in a long granny skirt and looking like a baby hippie, she was chanting: "Farm fresh mushrooms, piccadilly pie! Farm fresh mushrooms, piccadilly pie!"

"What's piccadilly pie?" Ross asked the girl.

She giggled, turning away. The woman behind the stall smiled. "She made it up. She just likes the way it sounds. We do have farm-fresh mushrooms, though. All organic."

Ross was not a big mushroom fan, but the woman and her girl seemed nice, so he looked at the display out of politeness. Lita smiled at the woman. "Hi there, Hattie."

"Hi yourself, Lita."

"You have any of those Portobellos?"

"Of course I do. How many do you want?"

"I'll take three for now."

"Coming right up."

Lita paid for the mushrooms, which were placed in a small bag, and the two of them headed back to where Dave was waiting as the little girl chanted behind them. ""Farm fresh mushrooms, piccadilly pie! Farm fresh mushrooms, piccadilly pie!"

They arrived back just as a rotund man in a priest's collar stopped by to examine a carton of eggs.

"Good morning, Father," Lita said, stepping around the table.

The man smiled kindly. "Good day to you, Lita. And to you, too, David. I trust this is your new guest?"

Word, apparently, had spread.

"My cousin, Ross," Lita introduced him. "Father Ramos."

"A pleasure to meet you," the priest said, extending a hand.

Ross shook. Father Ramos' grip was dry and surprisingly firm.

"How much are you going to set me back this week?" he asked Dave.

"For you?" Dave grinned. "The same price as everyone else. Three dollars a dozen."

The priest laughed. "I've said it before. You would be an asset to our congregation. May I expect to see you this Sunday?"

"You never give up, do you?"

"It's part of the job description. So how about it?"

"We'll take it into consideration," Lita told him, smiling.

"A man cannot but try." He looked at Ross. "You are welcome as well. All are welcome."

Ross nodded his thanks for the invitation without committing himself. He was not a churchgoing person, never had been, but he liked Father Ramos and did not want to hurt the man's feelings. The priest paid for and picked up his eggs, said "Peace be with you" to all of them, then moved on to the Native American family at the next stall.

Ross looked over at his cousin. "If I remember correctly, you used to go to church every Sunday. In fact, when you stayed with us, *we* had to go to church, when we should have been out playing. You don't go anymore?"

"I'm not Catholic."

"What are you?"

"Nothing. I *used* to be Methodist, and, you're right, we did go to church every week. After what happened with my parents, though, I kind of got turned off religion. It's hard to believe in an all-good, all-powerful God when you see bad things happen to good people and good things happen to bad people."

"I've always been a heathen," Dave said helpfully.

Ross laughed. He nodded toward the adobe church at the end of the street. "So is that Father Ramos' place?"

"Yeah," Lita said.

"Looks like it's the only church in town."

She waggled her hand back and forth in a maybe-yes-maybe-no motion. "Sort of. There's some sort of wacky hardcore fundamentalist sect that meets in different people's living rooms, but I think Father Ramos has the only *official* church in Magdalena."

"He seems like a good guy," Ross observed.

Dave smiled. "And a good customer. I don't think he knows the meaning of the word 'cholesterol.'"

Ross glanced around at the slowly growing crowd. "So Magdalena really *is* like one of those little towns where everyone knows everyone else."

"I guess so," Dave conceded.

"Is that good or bad?"

"A little bit of both," Lita said.

Another man was approaching, a tall guy with a thick black beard, wearing a battered straw cowboy hat.

Lita nodded at him. "Here comes Jackass McDaniels, our resident handyman, plumber, roofer, electrician, everything."

"I think he can hear you," Ross whispered.

"Oh, that's his name. At least, that's what he calls himself and what everyone else calls him. I'm sure his parents didn't name him that, but—"

The man held out a rough hand. "Jackass McDaniels, jack-of-all-trades. Pleased to meet you...?"

"Ross," he said. "Ross Lowry."

Lita put a hand around his shoulder. "My cousin."

"Well, any cousin a Lita's is a…friend a mine?" He shook his head. "No, that don't sound right. It's somethin' like that, though. Anyway, you need any work done on your house or your car or you just need an extra hand to help out, give me a holler. Lita and Dave know where to find me."

"Okay." Ross nodded.

"Whatcha got here today? Got some of that clover honey? That's my favorite."

"Not the right season," Dave said. "We have some mesquite, though. Sweet and fresh."

"Gimme a jar." Taking a wad of cash from his front pocket, the handyman peeled off a five, handing it to Lita before taking the jar of honey Dave passed to him. McDaniels held up the container. "You know, I have a buncha these jars sittin' around the house. You want 'em back?"

"Of course," Lita said. "For each one you bring back, you can have a quarter off your next purchase."

"Why dintcha tell me that before?"

"We thought you knew."

"Well, now I do." McDaniels grinned. "I'll bring 'em next week." He tipped his head toward Ross. "Nice t'meetcha."

Ross smiled as he walked away. "Jackass McDaniels, huh? Who's that behind him, Dickhead O'Malley?"

Laughing, Lita hit his shoulder. "Knock that off!"

A beefy, angry-looking man with a clear sense of entitlement was striding through the sparse crowd toward them, making a beeline for their table. A smaller, Hispanic man followed subserviently in his wake, pulling a wagon.

"Cameron Holt," Dave said. "He has the big ranch to the north of ours. Hey, Cameron. How's it going?"

The man ignored him. "I'll take six dozen white eggs and a dozen brown eggs."

"That'll be twenty one dollars." Dave reached back into the bed of the pickup to meet the order, while Lita collected the money.

Waiting patiently behind the rancher in the closest thing they'd had to a line so far was an elderly woman holding very tightly to the arm of an even older man, obviously her husband. When Holt left abruptly, leaving his underling to pick up the egg cartons and pack them into the wagon, the woman stepped forward, pulling her husband with her.

"Hello, Mrs. Ford," Lita said with genuine warmth. "And Mr. Ford."

"How are you today, dearie?"

Ross had never heard anyone outside of an old movie call anyone "dearie" but the affectionate term came effortlessly and naturally to the old woman, and she and Lita chatted unhurriedly for several minutes before Mrs. Ford bought a small jar of honey. Throughout the conversation, her husband had not said a word, had merely looked around blankly. She was still holding tightly to his arm, and after saying goodbye and telling Ross that she was pleased to have met him, she turned her husband around and led him away. "Come on, Del," she said. "Let's buy some bread."

"He has Alzheimer's," Lita said sadly after they left.

"He's had it ever since we moved here," Dave pointed out.

"I know. I just feel sorry for Ms. Ford. She's such a nice lady."

A couple came walking up the street, a middle-aged man and woman who would have looked more at home shopping high-end stores in Scottsdale than trudging down a dirt road way out here in Magdalena.

"Our local royalty," Lita whispered. "Paul and Heather Coburn. Heather *Cox*-Coburn," she corrected herself. "He's an internet tycoon. She used to be a model. Last year, she was on *The Real Housewives of Houston*. They just moved here in September...well, not exactly *moved* here. They bought up a lot of land, built a gigantic house and threw themselves a housewarming party. They flew in celebrities and business bigwigs but didn't invite anyone local. It was on *Extra* and in *US Weekly*. Since then, they come out for a month or so at a time. I think he fancies himself another Ted Turner.

"They never buy anything from us," she added.

Sure enough, the couple walked past, looked down at the table, then continued on. They didn't buy anything from anyone, Ross noticed, and for some reason he was reminded of couples in old movies, who strolled down avenues just to be seen.

The farmer's market was scheduled to go on until one, but it was clear to Ross after the first hour that his presence was not really needed. There was seldom more than one customer at a time—a pace either Lita or Dave could easily handle alone—and since he was here in town, he decided to walk around and check out the local businesses. Until now, he'd only seen Magdalena from a car window, and briefly at that. So he took advantage of the opportunity to do a little exploring, walking down the dusty street past a dingy laundromat he had not noticed before, and a closed fix-it shop whose narrow window space was piled high with toasters, typewriters, blenders, mixers and various obsolete household items.

The grocery store was open, and Ross walked inside. Walking down the aisles, he understood why Lita and Dave didn't do much shopping here. Aside from the fact that it was dark and depressing, the store's shelves were poorly stocked, mostly with things like Spam and Hamburger Helper, and the refrigerated case in the back was nearly empty, although he did see several L Bar-D egg cartons. The balding old man behind the counter seemed hostile and suspicious, and though Ross had originally intended to buy a can of Coke or something, just to help the place out, when he caught the glare the old man was giving him, he decided to leave without buying anything.

Amazingly, he was already halfway through the town. On this side of the street there was a closed post office, a feed and grain store, a combined blacksmith and machine shop… and that was about it. On the opposite side of the street, a bar he had not noticed before was housed in a skinny building shoved between an empty storefront and a consignment shop. As he passed by, he smelled cigarette smoke and heard Mexican music wafting from the bar's dark interior.

Most of the other businesses on this side of the street were closed—although whether permanently or only for the day it was hard to tell—but around the corner, he remembered, was the beauty salon.

It occurred to him that he could probably use a haircut.

Not that he had any important interviews lined up.

Still, it was important to maintain standards, and it was probably a good idea to remain prepared. Just in case.

The beauty salon was open, though empty of customers, and Ross went in, a bell jingling above the door as he entered. An older, heavyset Hispanic woman got up from a pink chair near the back to greet him. A younger, slimmer, considerably more attractive version of the woman—obviously her daughter—remained seated, reading a *People* magazine.

"Excuse me," Ross said, looking around. "I was wondering if there was someplace in town for a man to get a haircut. I didn't see any barber—"

"Right here," the older woman said. "Men, women, children: we do all."

"But is there a—"

"There is only us. Do you need a shampoo, a trim? Have a seat. Market day special. Six dollars."

Six dollars? The price list above the cash register said that men's haircuts cost fifteen. They must be really hurting for business, Ross thought. Which was only logical. He had no idea how many people lived in the outlying areas, but the town itself was smaller than a subdivision in a regular city. It must be nearly impossible to make a living cutting hair here. Especially when, judging by the people he saw at the farmer's market, many of the locals probably cut their own.

"Sure," he said, moving over to the chair the woman indicated.

The younger woman had stood, putting down her *People* magazine. "Don't you have an appointment, Mama? Isabel?"

"That's not until… Oh. Yes."

Ross was not sure if the mother really *did* have another appointment, if the daughter wanted to be the one to cut his hair, or both, but the thought that an attractive young woman was purposely maneuvering to work on him because she might be interested got his attention. He smiled at her in the mirror, and she smiled back. There was no ring on her finger, he noticed as she draped a protective sheet over him and fastened it around his neck.

"How do you want it?" she asked, lifting the hair on the top of his head, and was there a sly sparkle in her eye as she said those words?

He explained how he wanted his hair cut, and she went to work. Her body pressed softly against his as she leaned forward, and beneath the sheet, his penis stiffened. *Really*? he thought. He looked at himself in the mirror, realizing how pathetic his life had become.

The bell over the door jingled again, and he glanced over to see a mailman, or, more accurately, a mailwoman—mail *carrier*—walk in and drop a stack of catalogs and envelopes on the counter near the door.

"Thanks, Jeri!" the mother called.

The postal worker nodded in acknowledgement before heading back out to the street.

The mother's supposed customer—Isabel—hadn't arrived by the time his hair was finished, Ross noticed. The daughter spun him around in the chair. "How's it look?" she asked. She gave him a hand mirror and spun him around slowly so he could see the back of his head.

He'd asked for a slightly shorter version of the haircut he already had, but the stylist had obviously followed her own instincts and had taken off far too much. He forced himself to smile. "Looks good," he lied.

He paid, leaving a two-dollar tip that wasn't really deserved.

"Jesus Christ!" Dave said when he returned. "You're bald!"

"He looks fine," Lita said, walking around him in a circle as she examined the haircut. "He kind of has that Rotary Club, Chamber of Commerce, Kiwanis vibe."

"Kill me now," Ross moaned.

They both laughed.

"Was it the mom or the daughter?" Lita asked.

"The daughter."

Dave shook his head. "Always go with the mom."

Like most of the other vendors, they started packing up around ten minutes before the farmer's market was scheduled to close. There hadn't been any customers for nearly twenty minutes, and no new people had arrived.

"How much did we make?" Dave asked as Lita counted up the cash.

"Three hundred, give or take."

Ross saw Dave's pained grimace but said nothing as he helped fold up the table. He was right: they *weren't* making enough to live on. How long would it be before they had to throw in the towel, sell their ranch and try their luck in the workaday world?

They finished putting everything away, then got into the cab of the truck and drove slowly down the street between the other vendors who were packing up and getting ready to go.

"Did you have fun?" Lita asked.

"Sure!" he said with exaggerated enthusiasm.

She jabbed him with an elbow. "Smart ass."

"No. I did. Kind of. I mean, it was nice to get out of the house. And I got to meet some of your neighbors. By the way, that Cameron Holt seems like a real piece of work."

On the other side of Lita, Dave nodded. "He is. But he has the biggest ranch in the valley, wields a lot of power, and the rest of us kind of have to tiptoe around him."

"Why does everyone call this a 'valley?'" Ross wondered. "It's not."

Dave chuckled. "You're right. And I do it, too. I'm not sure why." He thought for a moment. "Maybe the people who founded the town came over the mountains—" He pointed out the driver's window. "—and after coming through there, this flat area looked like a valley to them."

"But there's no mountains on the opposite side. There's just… desert."

"They have to call it something, I guess. I could say Cameron has the biggest ranch in the *area* or the biggest ranch in the *region*.

But it doesn't have the same cowboy poet ring as biggest ranch in the *valley*."

"So, this Cameron. Are you guys on good terms or what?"

Dave shrugged. "I guess."

"*I* don't like him," Lita said decisively.

"I don't either," Ross said. "The dude definitely gave off a vibe."

"He's a consistent customer," Dave said. "That's all I care about."

"I was wondering about that." Ross decided to broach the subject. "Do you guys have *enough* customers? I mean, do you sell enough honey and eggs to survive?"

Next to him, Lita and Dave shared a look.

"For the moment," Dave said without elaborating.

They drove in silence for the rest of the trip home.

FOUR

CAMERON HOLT USUALLY WATCHED FOX NEWS WHILE HE WAS eating breakfast, but those assholes were going on about immigration again, talking about closing the border and deporting all the illegals, and he got so angry that he had to turn off the TV. How the hell did those politicians and talking heads expect him to bring in his beef without illegals? The ranch was closer to Mexico than it was to any city in America, for God's sake, and there was no way in hell any white man would put up with the shit he needed to dish out in order to make sure his cattle were branded and fed and foaled and rounded up and driven to market on time.

If those fuckheads in Washington would bother to come out and talk to an actual rancher for once, they might discover how the world really works.

Besides, it was their illegality that made his cowhands so valuable. Not only did they work cheap, keeping costs low and profits high, but if they didn't obey him, he could hold the threat of deportation over their heads. And if any dared to defy him or tried to call his bluff, they were out. Because he could always find more to take their place. They were hard workers, these Mexicans, almost all of them, and they were plentiful.

He glanced out the kitchen window at the dusty corral and the barn beyond. It was a hard life out here and most Americans were soft. They couldn't hack it. His wife sure as hell couldn't. That bitch Debbie had taken off after only two years, and now she was living in some apartment in Los Angeles, probably spreading her fat thighs for every swinging dick that came sniffing around. Well, fuck her. The ranch was doing a hell of a lot better without her than it had with her.

Cameron finished his eggs and coffee, left the dishes on the table and, hitching up his pants, went outside. He saw immediately that one of the steers had somehow gotten around the fence and was eating grass by the side of the barn, and he bellowed at the top of his lungs that someone better get his ass over here right now or heads were going to roll.

Three cowhands came speeding around the corner of the barn. He wished they were Keystone Cops chaotic, clumsily falling over each other, so he could laugh at them, but they were quick and competent, each carrying a length of rope that they lassoed around the animal to help them drag it back to its pen. Angry that the steer had escaped and angrier still that the cowhands were so easily able to take care of it, Cameron grabbed a switch from a nail on the side of the barn and whipped the backs of the workers as they passed in front of him. "Useless!" he yelled. *"Perezoso!"*

It turned out that two more cows had wandered away (some asshole had not locked one of the gates—and there would be hell to pay for that once he found out who), so Cameron got on a horse himself and led a crew to track them down. One was actually off his property and on the road, standing confusedly before a cattle guard, while the other ended up munching weeds in a ditch from which it took all four men to drive the steer out. He wasted half the morning bringing back those two strays when he should have been taking care of other business, and he gathered all of his workers together when he got back, ordering them not to take time off for lunch today, reminding them that they were one phone call away from being deported, and warning them that anyone who left any gate open in the future would be beaten and then fired.

He himself did go inside for lunch, making some microwaved macaroni and cheese, washing it down with a brew and watching a Headline News show on the kitchen TV while he ate. He had just finished when there was a knock at the front door. "Come in!" he bellowed, too lazy to walk out to the front of the house. *"Entrar!"*

Moments later, a young brown face peeked nervously around the corner. "Senor?"

Cameron frowned. "What is it?"

"Melquiades say he know who left open gate. He say it Ramon. But Ramon gone. We no find him. Melquiades think he run away."

"Good," Cameron said. But it wasn't really good because now he would have to find another cowhand. Things would be gearing up pretty soon before the spring roundup, and he was going to need every man he had.

The boy who'd come to deliver the message was about to leave when Cameron told him to wait. He looked the kid over. Slim and somewhat effeminate, he couldn't have been more than fifteen or sixteen. Cameron wasn't sure, but he thought the boy was Jorge's

47

son. Jorge was one of his most loyal workers, had remained last year even after Cameron had beat him nearly senseless for stealing oranges, a crime it turned out he didn't commit. If Jorge had stood for that, he surely wouldn't make a fuss over...

Cameron closed the kitchen door and pulled the windowshade.

He wasn't a homo or anything. He just needed a little release. With Debbie gone, his supply had been cut off, and as men in prison knew, when women were scarce, things sometimes needed to be taken care of using whatever else was around.

And this one didn't look like he'd mind a little Sandusky.

"What's your name, boy?" he demanded.

"Rudolpho."

Shit. It wasn't Jorge's kid.

That's what was the matter with all these fucking wetbacks: it was almost impossible to tell them apart. He remembered this one only because of that stupid name. *Rudolpho*. Like Rudolph the Red-Nosed Reindeer. If he recalled correctly, this one was older, nineteen or twenty, and when he'd first come over, before Cameron had knocked some sense into him, he'd been prattling on about a wife and kid he'd left back home in Mexico.

Damn.

Cameron had wanted someone younger.

Still, beggars couldn't be choosers.

"Turn around and face that wall," he ordered in Spanish. "And drop your pants."

There was hesitation, a frightened pause, and that was all Cameron needed to get hard. He shoved the kid, making him bend over and clutch his ankles as he pulled down his own pants. The height was off—it would have helped if the kid were a few inches taller—but Cameron grabbed the boy's waist, bent his knees a little, positioned himself and thrust. There was a short sharp cry, then silence as Rudolpho grimly willed himself to take it. Cameron started pumping. Knowing there was pain beneath the stoicism made him finish faster, and with a loud grunt, he came, spurting deep.

He pulled out.

This was the difficult part, the embarrassing part—afterward. Feeling disgusted, Cameron pulled up his underwear and pants and left the room. He wanted to clean off, but he didn't want to see the boy or talk to him, and he waited until Rudolpho had left, until he'd heard the screen door slam, before taking a hot shower and scrubbing down hard. He wondered if the kid would talk.

Maybe he should have him killed, Cameron thought.

But the feeling passed, and by the time Cameron was through showering and drying off, he felt fine. He put on new underwear before pulling his old jeans back on, then slipped on his shirt, socks and boots, and walked out onto the porch. He saw Rudolpho standing by himself near the barn. The little swisher didn't seem any worse for wear, and Cameron wouldn't be surprised if the kid would be up for it again.

He'd probably choose someone else next time he felt the need, though.

Maybe he'd even hire a maid. The house was a fucking mess, and it would be nice to have a woman again.

Maybe he'd hire a couple of maids.

He could afford it.

Rudolpho limped into the barn, obviously in pain, and Cameron smiled, feeling pleased with himself.

Life was good.

FIVE

"So," Dave asked as they ate dinner, "what are your plans for the holidays?"

"I don't know," Ross admitted. "I haven't thought about it. Why? Do you need me to go?"

"No!" Lita put a hand on his shoulder. "Of course not!"

Dave laughed. "Exactly the opposite. If you're going to be here to hold the fort, we thought we might get away for a few days, visit the family."

"Sure," Ross told them. "I'll feed the chickens, horse, goat, whatever you need me to do."

Lita kissed his cheek. "Thank you! That would be wonderful! That is the best Christmas present you can give us!"

"You know," Dave said, "every New Year's Eve, there's a sort of community get-together, and we have, like, a big potluck at one of the ranches. It's your basic New Year's party. Drinking, music ... drinking. It's a lot of fun. We'd love to have you with us."

"Maybe," Ross said. "We'll see."

For Christmas, Lita and Dave drove to Las Vegas to spend the holiday with his mom and dad, who had retired there. Ross could have gone back to Chandler to be with his own parents, but Rick and Alma had that covered. This year, he actually had an excuse not to see his family, and he took advantage of it, telling them that he needed to remain in Magdalena to take care of the ranch, although he did call them early in the morning to wish them Merry Christmas. Long about noon, however, after finishing his chores, he started feeling a little lonely, despite the various football games and marathons on TV, and as he reheated the roasted chicken and rosemary potatoes Lita had left for him, he found himself wondering what the daughter from the beauty salon was doing. He should've gotten her name, he thought, then chastised himself for being such a loser that he was spending his Christmas day fantasizing about the girl who'd given him his crappy haircut. He considered calling or texting some of his friends in Phoenix, but they were probably all with their families, and he didn't want to disturb them.

Maybe he *should* have gone to his parents' house.

No. That was the one thing he'd gotten right, and he spent the rest of the afternoon listening to tunes and reading the Steve Jobs biography that Lita and Dave had given to him for a present.

It was unseasonably warm for December, and that night he sat outside, drinking beer and looking up at the stars. The chickens seemed unusually quiet, their background clucking lower in volume than usual and occasional rather than constant. Several times, he thought he saw something in the sky, something black and silent, gliding over the ranch, bigger than a bird, yet smaller and lower than an airplane. The temperature had dropped, but he remained outside, looking up, trying to figure out what the flying thing was, until he saw its strange shadowy form pass directly overhead and realized that he didn't *want* to know what it was. Feeling uneasy, he went inside, pulled the shades over the windows and turned on the TV, watching the end of *The Sound of Music* as he tried not to think of what might be in the sky above.

He dreamed of monsters. He was on a flat arid plain, hardpacked dirt with no rock or vegetation, that stretched endlessly in all directions. There were creatures in the air, creatures on the ground, abominations whose like had never before been seen or imagined, and they were all after him. He had come from nowhere, was going nowhere, and his only purpose was to avoid the monsters and survive.

In the morning, Ross awoke to a bright, cloudless, unseasonably warm day. The concerns of last night seemed foolish and childish as he went out to feed the chickens, but he still could not help glancing up every once in awhile—just to make sure the sky was clear.

SIX

Lita didn't want to go out on New Year's Eve. She knew why Dave wanted to do it. Magdalena was a *small* town, and if they hoped to survive with their little business over the long haul, they had to not only cultivate relationships but be seen as part of the community. This year, though, Ross was here, and since he'd decided not to go, she thought it would be more fun to buy a big old tub of ice cream, stay in and order some movies on demand.

Dave was adamant, however, and she put on her most western-looking skirt and blouse, dragged out the cowgirl boots she wore exactly once each year, and brought out the lemon pie she'd made earlier in the afternoon. She'd made an extra smaller one for Ross, and she brought it over to him in the shack. "You sure you don't want to come?" she asked. "Last chance."

He shook his head, smiling. "Don't worry about me. I'll be fine."

Lita sighed. "I wish I didn't have to go either."

"You could stay." He gestured around the room. "I have an exciting evening planned. I intend to eat your pie, watch the *Curb Your Enthusiasm* marathon and be in bed by ten."

"That's so sad!" She laughed. "You're not even going to stay up until midnight?"

"Nah. New Year's has never been a real holiday to me anyway. There's no gifts, no feast, just…bad TV."

"Well, I'll be thinking about you."

"With envy?"

"Actually, yes," she admitted. "See you tomorrow."

"Have fun."

By the time Lita walked back up to the house, Dave was ready to leave. The party this year was at Cameron Holt's—yet another reason she didn't want to go—but a lot of friends would be there, some of whom she hadn't seen in awhile, and as they drove down one dirt road and then another on their way to Cameron's ranch, she gradually grew more enthusiastic about the evening. The desert was dark, and long before they arrived, a line of white headlights and red taillights could be seen winding like a snake toward their destination, which shone like a beacon in the blackness.

The parking area in front of the house was full, so people had started pulling off the edge of the drive and parking in the weeds on the side. Dave pulled behind a dented white pickup that Lita recognized as Vern Hastings' truck, and Vern and his wife Rose got out. Vern gave a short wave, and the two of them headed up the drive without waiting.

"Typical," Lita said disgustedly as she handed Dave the pie and held tightly to the doorframe before stepping out onto the uneven ground.

The music was audible even from here, but she didn't recognize the song and couldn't tell if it was live or recorded until the tune changed to "American Farmer," and it was clear that it was not Charlie Daniels singing. She turned to Dave. "Cameron hired a band?"

"I think Jim Haack's boys started a band with a couple of their friends. It's probably them."

"They're not bad," Lita said.

Holt's foreman, Jorge, was standing on the front porch, directing guests around back, and Dave waved a greeting. "He's making you work on New Year's Eve?"

Jorge shrugged and smiled, but Lita could see the resentment in his eyes. She felt sorry for Jorge. And for all of Cameron's workers. The man was clueless, heartless and pretty much an all-around bastard. She was surprised he kept any workers at all. If she were Jorge, she would have defected to another employer a long time ago.

They turned the corner. The Haack boys did indeed have a band—Tumbleweed Connection, according to the name written on front of the bass drum—and they were set up in a corner of the back patio where a line of small speakers put out surprisingly loud and surprisingly clear sound. Quite a few couples, including several senior citizens, were dancing to their version of "Act Naturally."

Cameron and some of the other big ranchers were clustered around a keg that had been set up on the opposite side of the patio, laughing loudly at some private joke that was no doubt offensive to three-fourths of the other people there, and Dave immediately started toward them.

Lita grabbed his hand. "No," she said. "Uh-uh."

"We'll just stop by and say hi. We'll put in an appearance, then move on. It *is* his party."

"David..."

"We have to. These are our customers." He nodded toward Vern Hastings, backslapping people by the open pit barbecue. "And our competition."

"All right," she reluctantly agreed. "We'll put in an appearance."

But Cameron and his buddies, Jack Judd in particular, were already half-drunk and in a garrulous mood, and instead of the quick hello she'd expected, they got drawn into a discussion about the prospects of turning the valley into wine country, making Magdalena Arizona's version of Napa. It was an endlessly looping debate, made even more interminable by the fact that the ranchers were downing beer like it was water.

Lita escaped as quickly as she could, leaving Dave with Cameron's crew (although he'd definitely hear from her about it later. What happened to the 'moving on' he'd promised?) and heading toward friendlier territory. Darla and JoAnn were hanging out with Lurlene from the laundromat, and Lita joined them next to a picnic table filled with various pretzels, crackers, chips, dips and salsas. Everyone asked where her cousin was—they'd all heard that Ross was staying with them—and Lita explained that he hadn't wanted to come.

"Is he cute?" JoAnn asked. "I heard he was cute."

"He is, actually. But why are *you* asking?"

"Yeah." Lurlene nodded toward JoAnn's husband. "Ain't your man keepin' you satisfied?"

"As a matter of fact, no, he isn't." They all laughed. "But I was asking for my sister."

"Becky's back?" Lita asked, surprised.

"She will be. Back and single. I'm just trying to keep her options open."

Lurlene put a hand on Lita's arm. "Honey, don't let your cousin anywhere *near* Becky."

"That's not funny!" JoAnn objected, but the rest of them thought it was, and the wild Becky stories started flying.

Lita paused to get a drink—the nonalcoholic punch, for now—and by the time she returned, Lurlene had wandered off. Since Darla had been sick in the weeks leading up to Christmas and they hadn't seen each other in awhile, there was some catching up to do, and the three of them did so, staking out a corner where they could talk privately.

Dave eventually extricated himself from Cameron's circle and began to mingle, gradually working his way over to Lita. He gave her a quick kiss, and she was surprised to taste nothing stronger than beer on his lips. "Having fun?" he asked her.

"Actually," she said, "I am."

"See?"

"What about you?"

"Not so much," he admitted.

They both laughed.

Father Ramos was there at the party, parked at the dessert table, but his presence wasn't the deterrence to bacchanalia that Lita wished it had been. He was in his most jovial, convivial mood, gladhanding everyone, and while conversation in his immediate vicinity was cleaned up considerably and those nearby, the Mexican workers who formed the backbone of his congregation in particular, were on their best behavior, alcohol was still being consumed in copious amounts. She could tell that, instead of toning things down as the evening wore on, the faithful were going to end up reveling as hard as the heathens, although perhaps making up for it by being more contrite in their confessions the next day.

As in previous years, things started to get rowdy by about ten.

Somewhere by the barbecue, two men got into a shouting match loud and serious enough that others had to speed over and separate them before the argument escalated. Lita saw a woman bent over a corral fence, loudly vomiting. Behind her, one young man she didn't recognize was thrusting his hips in her direction, pantomiming having sex with her, while a group of friends, including Lee, the stockboy from the grocery store, and Boo, the mechanic, laughed uproariously.

It was all downhill from here. She knew what was going to happen. As midnight approached, the firearms would come out. To herald the arrival of the new year, redneck ranchers and Mexican cowhands, united for that one magical moment, all of their differences pushed aside, would shoot their guns into the air, whooping and hollering. It was pure luck that no one had been injured or killed yet by one of their bullets plummeting back to earth, but as far as she was concerned, it was only a matter of time, and she wanted to make sure that she and Dave were gone by the time this year's idiotic ritual was enacted.

Dave had gone off with a couple of other organic farmers who wanted to check out Cameron's barn and see how the other half lived. She found the three of them chatting with Jorge in front of a narrow pen housing a milky-eyed and shockingly overweight veal calf. In broken English, the foreman was trying to defend Cameron's indefensible cattle raising practices, but she could tell that he didn't believe what he was saying. Neither did his audience, who kept asking him how livestock could be treated so inhumanely.

"Tell to Senor Holt," Jorge kept saying. "Tell to Senor Holt."

Lita grabbed the sleeve of Dave's shirt, tugging on it. "I want to go home," she told him.

He looked at his watch. "It isn't even eleven yet."

They'd talked about this before, and she looked straight in his eyes to make sure he understood. "I'm tired, I'm cold, I want to go."

He did understand. He nodded. "Okay."

It *was* getting cold, and Lita wasn't sure why she hadn't brought a jacket. Stupid. Dave bid his friends a happy new year, and the two of them walked out of the barn into the night air. A sharp breeze had sprung up in the last few minutes, and Dave put an arm around her shoulders to stave off some of the chill. A few other people—families with kids, mostly—were also starting to leave, getting out before the shooting started and things got out of control.

By the corral, Cameron and one of his buddies had already cornered Doris Stiever, the part-time gas station cashier whose husband was deployed in Afghanistan. She let out a shriek that would have been a cry for help if she hadn't been drunk, but was playful and flirty because she was.

"Let's go," Lita said primly.

Dave nodded, and they said goodbye to the people on their way as they headed back toward the front of the house. On the drive, a Jeep and a pickup were both attempting to turn around without hitting each other. Farther up the lane, green palo verde trees glowed red with the taillights of departing partiers.

Vern Hastings' truck was still parked in front of theirs, but whoever had pulled in behind them had left, so it was easy to back up and pivot about. Although everyone else who was leaving early had turned left, toward town, they turned right, into the desert, toward home. The land was dark but the sky was bright, filled with both a full moon and, incongruously, a visible field of stars.

Something swooped low over the top of the pickup.

Dave slammed on the brakes, nearly driving them into a ditch. "What the hell was that?"

Lita didn't know, but she had seen it too, a shadow that passed over the windshield, briefly blotting out the moon and stars, and she'd felt an instinctive terror, an inner recoiling that raised goose bumps on her arms and left her shivering. Like Dave, she twisted her neck sideways and ducked her head down in order to look up through the windshield, but it was gone, whatever it was, and there were no dark shapes moving across any portion of the sky.

She straightened up, glancing over at Dave, who looked back at her with a confused expression. "That was weird," he said.

She nodded.

"What do you think it was?"

"I have no idea."

"A vulture?"

Lita shook her head. She might not know what it was, but she knew what it wasn't, and it was neither a bird nor a plane nor anything she had seen before. It was strange, and she didn't like it, and though she'd been granted even less than a glimpse, just a suggestion of darkness more sensed than seen, she hoped she never saw it again.

She shivered as Dave put the truck into gear and continued on toward home.

They made it back without incident. Later, after showering together, they made love to see in the new year, and in the middle of it, from far away, she heard faint popping sounds.

At the party, the guns were going off.

SEVEN

I T HAD BEEN OVER THREE HOURS, AND HIS KNEES HURT SO MUCH that he doubted he would be able to stand without rolling onto his side first and then pushing himself up with his hands, but Father Ramos remained kneeling, hands folded in supplication as he continued to pray. It was good that his knees hurt. They should be bloody. His legs should be broken. He should be in constant torturing pain for the rest of his life.

He had been there.

He had seen it.

He was a part of what had happened.

He closed his eyes even more tightly, squeezing out a tear and letting it roll slowly, unobstructed, down his cheek. He asked for God's guidance, but heard nothing back, felt nothing. No ideas implanted themselves in his brain, no helpful advice was presented to him. Either God was deliberately ignoring his entreaties or—

There was a voice.

Father Ramos stopped praying, silencing the words in his head and listening for sounds in the stillness of the church.

It came again, a word.

"Hector."

His heart pounded so hard he thought it was going to burst. The ecstasy he'd always assumed he would feel should the Lord actually speak to him directly did not materialize. Instead, he was overcome with terror, a paralyzing fear that rooted him in place, even as he heard his name called again.

"Hector."

He should have run from the party as soon as it happened. He should have fled this town and never looked back. But that was animal instinct, gut not head. That was a human reaction. For while, as a man he might want to flee, as a priest, he knew that he could not. God was everywhere and He would know where he went and what he did. The right thing to do, the only thing to do, was exactly what he had done: remain and pray on it. If he was to be punished, so be it. If Magdalena was to be wiped off the map, its memory erased from the world, then that was what would be. It was the Lord's decision to make, and whatever He chose would be right.

Father Ramos thought of Sodom and Gomorrah and how, when the angels visited Lot, the people of the town demanded that Lot surrender the angels to them. The people were struck blind, and the next day their cities were destroyed.

Was that what would happen here?

"Hector."

He was sobbing, and was dimly aware that he'd wet his pants.

There was another sound in the empty church. A shuffling noise behind him, as though something large and barely mobile was shambling slowly across the concrete floor toward the front of the church. The priest closed his eyes even more tightly, so tightly they hurt, his lips mouthing a fervent prayer.

The shuffling grew closer.

He turned quickly, letting out a cry so sharp and frightened that he startled himself. But there was nothing behind him. There was only the voice, coming from nowhere, coming from everywhere, saying his name. *"Hector."*

"What do you want?" he cried.

Laughter was the response. Not the loud, eardrum-bursting laughter he would have expected, but a low sibilant snickering that seemed to emanate from the building itself, swirling and echoing around him until it graduated from stereo to surroundsound. He was enveloped in cold, an icy dampness settling over him and chilling him to the bone. He expected an accompanying revelation, assumed he would now be told what was in store for him, but—

It was over.

The church was empty save for himself, and the abandonment left him as devastated as the revealing of punishment would have. He fell forward onto the floor, filled with anguish and despair, sobbing in remorse for what had happened and in fear for what it could bring.

Jorge ran breathlessly into the kitchen from the side porch while a still-hungover Cameron was eating breakfast. "Senor Holt! Senor Holt!"

Cameron shot him a withering look. "How many times have I told you to knock first, *pendejo?* This is my home! You can't just run in here whenever you feel like it."

"But Senor Holt! The cows! They are dead!"

"What?"

"The cows are dead!"

His head was pounding, and he wanted to be angry, but there was a triphammer of fear in his chest as he stood up and followed his foreman out the door. *All* of his cows couldn't be dead, he knew. Although he realized with dismay that he would not be surprised if they were. None of this surprised him, in fact, and the most frightening thing about what was happening was that he'd somehow suspected it.

He thought about the party last night and shivered.

All of the cattle *weren't* dead. But six of them were, and they lay in the yard next to the house in an almost perfect circle, touching head to tail, their legs pointing in toward the center of the circle like the spokes of a wheel, their spines curved to form the outer ring. It was an eerie, otherworldly sight, but he expected nothing less. He glanced around at the gathered crowd and realized that they were looking to him for reassurance. Their faces held nearly identical expressions of confusion and fear. A couple of workers were missing, and though he wanted to believe they were busy elsewhere on the ranch, he had the feeling they had fled.

More men would run away if he didn't nip this in the bud, so Cameron pushed aside his own fear, put on his toughest face and ordered everyone back to work, telling them in his pidgin Spanish that he was going to call the vet and have him do an examination to find out what had killed the animals. If the meat wasn't contaminated, they were going to butcher the cows this afternoon.

A few of the men crossed themselves—not a good sign—and though Cameron wanted to yell at them, berate them for being ignorant superstitious peasants, he did not. Partly because he did not want to drive them away.

Partly because he understood their fear.

He glanced involuntarily at the smokehouse, then looked quickly away. He couldn't tell from here whether the door was still locked, but he wasn't about to go over and check, not with his workers hanging around. He didn't want to remind them. The last thing he needed was for the rest of them to run off.

He ordered Jorge to make sure the men stopped lounging around and started doing what he paid them to do. Then he walked back into the house to call the vet.

Was this the beginning of an epidemic?

Jose Gonzalez had barely hung up the phone when it rang again. The fourth call this morning. It was another rancher, Cameron Holt this time, with an almost identical story. Holt, too, claimed to have lost six cows, which put the total right now at twenty-four.

This was scary.

In rural areas such as the desert surrounding Magdalena, outbreaks weren't usually so sudden or spread out, and already he was wracking his brain trying to determine what it could possibly be. In the back of his mind was the nagging specter of a man-made pathogen, an airborne biological weapon that had escaped from some secret lab.

Even though it was New Year's and he was supposed to have the day off, the veterinarian promised to come out to Holt's ranch as soon as possible, and he quickly cross-referenced the symptoms that had been described to him, using both the textbooks on hand and several dedicated websites. He found nothing promising, and by the time he got to the first ranch—Cal Denholm's—Jose was worried enough that he put on a surgical mask.

The six steers were lying on the dirt, bodies stretched out and arranged in the shape of a rectangle, two forming one long side, two another, and one each creating the short sides connecting them. Denholm had said nothing of this, and the sight, while bizarre, eased Jose's mind. The animals had been deliberately placed—they certainly could not have died and fallen this way by accident—and that meant human involvement. Poison, most likely. In his mind, the chance of an airborne pathogen diminished greatly.

More confident now, he strode over to the bodies and bent down to examine one. The eyes, he saw, were milky and occluded. He was about to ask Denholm if he'd noticed that before the animal died, or if he'd noted anything unusual in the steers' appearance or behavior, when sudden movement near the lower portion of the steer's face startled him and made him yank his hand back.

From the cow's mouth slithered a creature unlike any he had ever seen, a terrible wormlike organism that thrashed in crazed death spasms as soon as it emerged fully into the air. Initially a sickly greenish color, it quickly dissolved into a gray gluelike mess on the dirt.

"What the fuck is that?" Denholm shouted, stepping back and away.

The other animals started moving. Their legs trembled and jerked, their heavy bodies shuddered, and then suddenly those wormlike creatures were everywhere, wiggling out from both ends of each steer, thrashing about as they hit the air, dissolving into slime once they were fully exposed.

The rancher and his cowhands watched from afar, having backed up several yards. Jose, too, moved away. On an intellectual level, he was fascinated by what he saw, but on a human level, he was repulsed and frightened in a way he had not been since childhood. Part of him wanted to stand here and observe, while part of him wanted to run away as fast as his feet would carry him.

Intellect overrode emotion, and he remained in place, watching, until it was all over. From the emergence of the first creature to the dissolving of the last, not more than three minutes had elapsed. It was a frighteningly quick episode, and when it was done, the dirt was wet with sticky gray goo and the six steers were little more than hide-covered skeletons. Whatever those wormlike organisms had been, they'd hollowed out the animals' insides.

In his bag, Jose had tongue depressors and petri dishes, and he used one of the wooden sticks to scoop up some of the gluelike residue from the dirt. He had no illusions that he would be able to identify its origin, but he wanted to examine the substance anyway. He'd also send a sample off to the lab he used in Tucson. They should be able to provide him with a detailed chemical analysis, although he had absolutely no idea what that would show.

"What the hell happened?" Denholm said. They were the first words any of them had spoken since the dead steers had started convulsing.

Jose usually tried to give comfort to the owners of his patients, to provide them with hope even when he was unsure of an outcome. But this time, he was forced to be honest. "I have no idea," he said.

It was the same at the other three ranches, though in each case he arrived too late to see what happened to the animals' corpses. Strangely, descriptions of the witnesses were different at each location. At Joe Portis' place, yellow spiderlike creatures had spilled from the cattle's mouths and anuses, again dissolving once encountering air. Jack Judd's cows expelled multi-legged things that vaguely resembled centipedes, and at Cameron Holt's, bright red moths flew out of the animals, falling instantly to earth as sticky gray gloop.

Jose took samples at each location.

From the positioning of the bodies, he still believed that someone was involved, that a person had deliberately arranged the cattle into specific shapes, but he had to admit that he had no clue as to how or why. And the presence of those creatures pretty much threw his poison theory out the window.

He had never encountered anything like this.

He was not sure *anyone* had.

And as he headed back to his office, he kept glancing at the seat next to him, where his petri dishes sat in his black bag, to make sure that some new monster didn't emerge from the collected slime to attack and kill him as he drove.

EIGHT

HAVING FALLEN ASLEEP IN FRONT OF THE TELEVISION AND then gone to bed early the night before, Ross awoke with the dawn on New Year's day. He'd been planning to make himself french toast but found that he didn't feel like going to such effort. Instead, he heated water for oatmeal in the microwave, poured himself some orange juice and turned on the TV. It was what he usually did on this morning—eating breakfast while watching the Rose Parade—but something seemed wrong today. He felt listless and low. Even the parade floats looked less colorful than usual. Outside, the sky was leaden, high clouds blocking out both the sun and any trace of blue, the monochromatic grayness mirroring his mood.

The feeling did not dissipate as he went out to feed the chickens and collect eggs. The hens, too, seemed unusually subdued, making very little noise and pecking at their food in a desultory fashion. There were probably half as many eggs to be gathered as on a usual day and when he took them over to the house, the doors and drapes were closed. Ross left the egg basket on the back porch then returned to the guest house. He thought he might go online and do…something. But his laptop was unable to access the internet. That was probably to be expected so far from civilization, but he had had no problem until now, and, on impulse, he tried to access the internet using his cell phone.

The message *No Signal* appeared on his screen.

The TV continued to come in fine—all channels, as far as he could tell after a quick check—and he was able to use the land line and call his parents to wish them a happy New Year's, so there was probably nothing major wrong, only a temporary glitch. But building on his already gloomy mood, the lack of internet access bothered him, and he felt distracted and unsettled as he played previously loaded games on his computer for the rest of the morning until Lita invited him over to the house for lunch.

Ross could tell something was wrong when Lita called around dinnertime. There was a strange hitch in her voice, and when he walked over to their house (the Big House, as he'd started to think of it), both she and Dave were seated on the couch in the living room. Usually, around this hour of the evening, Lita would have been cooking, but there was no smell of food from the kitchen, and neither of them looked as though they had any desire to eat. Indeed, Dave seemed stunned, almost in shock as he stared blankly at the coffee table in front of him, nodding listlessly in response to Ross' greeting.

Ross stood there awkwardly, unsure of what to do or say, uncertain as to what was going on, and it was Lita who filled him in, taking him into the kitchen, away from Dave. "We got a call about a half hour ago," she said quietly. "Dave's parents were killed in a car crash."

"Oh my God."

She nodded. "Some drunk conventioner from Des Moines driving a rented SUV. Head-on collision. Neither of them made it to the hospital."

He didn't know what to say. What *could* a person say at a time like this that wasn't trite and ineffectual?

A bitterness crept into Lita's voice. "The drunk driver, of course, survived."

"I'm so sorry," Ross said. "Is there anything you want…I mean, what can I…?"

"We have to go to Las Vegas. We could be gone for awhile," she said. "A week, maybe. I don't know. Do you think—"

"Don't worry about it," he assured her. "I'll take care of everything. I'll even sell at the market if you need me to."

"I'm not sure we'll have enough *to* sell, based on what you brought in today." She touched his shoulder, spoke softly. "Thank you, though. I'm glad you're here. I don't know what we'd do if you weren't."

"When are you leaving?" Ross asked.

"In the morning. I'm driving, but I want him to get some sleep. I'm worried about him."

Ross nodded.

"I was wondering…" She seemed hesitant.

"What?"

"If we could borrow your car. The truck's been making some weird noises, and another long trip might—"

Ross cut her off. "Of course," he said.

She threw her arms around his shoulders, giving him a grateful hug. "Thank you."

They returned to the living room. Dave seemed slightly more alert, though definitely not his normal self. He looked up at them as they entered. "She told you?"

"Yeah. I'm sorry..." That sounded lame. "For your loss." That sounded lamer. He stood there awkwardly, not saying anything more, hoping that silence would be more effective at expressing his feelings than his words had been.

Dave looked at Lita. "Is it all right?"

"Yes," she assured him. "He'll take care of everything."

"We're sorry to do this to you," Dave apologized.

Ross waved him away. "You have more important things to deal with right now. In fact, I'm going to leave you two alone, so you can...do...whatever you need to do." *Stupid!* He glanced over at Lita. "Unless you need me for something."

"No, you go on." She tried to smile, but just looked sad and tired.

"Okay, then. I'm there if you need me, though. Just...give me a call." He left before he embarrassed himself, and after making a sandwich for dinner, he watched the national news, turned off the TV, checked his email, turned on the TV, tried to play a video game, walked restlessly onto the porch, then settled down to watch a *Doctor Who* DVD. The lights went off in the Big House around nine, and he waited a half-hour to make sure he wasn't needed before going to bed himself.

Exhausted by the stress of the day, he fell asleep instantly.

In the morning he awoke early, while it was still dark, hoping to see them off, but they'd already gone. Lita had left a note taped to his screen door, telling Ross that he could use their house while they were gone and to help himself to anything in the kitchen. She said there were instructions for him on the kitchen table, and when he went over to the Big House, he found that Dave had provided a feeding schedule for the horse and the goat, as well as detailed directions for monitoring the bees, and watering the garden and the fruit trees.

It was another bad day for egg harvesting—he collected exactly ten—but whatever was wrong went far beyond poor egg production. The chickens themselves seemed…different. If he told anyone about it he would sound crazy, but several times he thought he caught some of the hens peeking at him from behind a wall of the coop. Watching him. *Spying* on him. That made no sense, of course, was probably not even possible, but it creeped him out nevertheless, and he hurriedly fed the fowl and collected all the eggs he could find before bailing.

He was afraid of the bees, so he stayed away from them. They'd survive for a day without being scrutinized, and if Lita and Dave weren't back by tomorrow evening, he'd check on the hives the following morning. He was also afraid of the horse and goat, he was embarrassed to admit, and without his cousin or her husband around to run interference for him, he threw the hay over the fence in the horse's general direction and dumped the feed in an area where he knew the goat would find it. He had no problem watering the garden.

Along with instructions, Dave had left him a list of the customers who might come by during the week to pick up their standing orders, and one of them arrived that afternoon, Ben Stanard, the old man from the grocery store. He was no less hostile out of his natural environment, and Ross actually experienced a small sense of satisfaction when the store owner demanded twelve dozen eggs and he told Stanard he could only have six.

The old man glared at him. "My order's for twelve."

"Sorry." He felt like smiling, but he didn't.

"Where's Dave?" Stanard demanded. "Let me talk to him."

"He and his wife are out of state right now. Family emergency. I'm in charge until they get back."

"We had a deal."

"I'm sorry, but there's a production problem. I have no control over that."

The store owner frowned, spit on the ground, then walked over to the handtruck where Ross had stacked the egg cartons. "This is bullshit," the old man growled as he loaded them up in his SUV. "Dave's gonna hear about this!"

This time, Ross did smile. "Have a nice day!" he called out.

Lita called in the evening. She sounded tired. The funeral, she said, was going to be held on Wednesday. She thought they would probably be back by the weekend. It was only a preliminary estimate, but with the life insurance and the assets, and the fact that Dave was his parents' only child, she said they could be getting something close to a million dollars.

He was silent, stunned.

"Are you still there?" she asked.

"A million dollars?" he said incredulously.

"They had a lot of insurance." There was sadness in her voice but also an audible relief, and Ross realized that, egg problems or not, Lita and Dave would probably now be in the position to have the ranch they always wanted.

"So what's happening there?" she asked. "Is everything all right?"

He described his day.

After Ben Stanard had left that afternoon, Ross had gone into the cellar on the side of the house to do inventory. There were more eggs stored there than he realized (he probably *could* have given the store owner his full order), and quite a few jars of honey. He told Lita now that he wanted to sell at the farmer's market on Thursday—if she and Dave would trust him with the truck—and she gave him permission to go ahead, though he could tell that she didn't care one way or the other. He understood. There were far more important things on her mind at the moment. He didn't want to bother her with details, so he assured her that everything was fine here at home, then told her to make sure she got enough sleep before he hung up.

In the morning, he forced himself to check out the bees. In his note, Dave had said that if Ross carefully followed all of the instructions, the bees would neither swarm nor sting, and, indeed, that was the case. He was too untrained to be able to extract honey or even tell if honey was being produced, but the bees themselves were fine, and that would suffice until Dave returned to take over.

Again, the chickens acted odd, and this time one of them actually pecked his ankle. The pain was immediate and much greater than he would have expected, and instinctively Ross reacted by kicking the animal, sending it squawking away, flapping its prodigious feathers. He felt bad about that until he looked down at his ankle, pulled up his pantleg and saw blood, a trail of it dripping down his skin and into his sock. Angrily, he looked up, but the attacking bird had blended into the pack. Good thing for it; because he would have kicked the animal again if he could find it.

Ross tossed out the rest of the feed, dumping it in a pile rather than sprinkling it across the yard, and postponed egg collection until he washed off his wound and put a couple of Band-Aids over the surprisingly deep gash. When he did return to the yard, he found only two eggs, one unusually small and one extraordinarily big. Neither looked like anything that could be sold, and though he didn't really want to touch them, he picked both up and took them to the root cellar, leaving them in the basket. Dave could check them out when he returned. Maybe he could figure out what was wrong.

Ross finished his chores and had an early lunch, making himself a sandwich and washing it down with some Beck's.

He felt weird and ill-at-ease. It was daytime and his computer was on, but the ranch still seemed creepy. He was all alone here aside from the horse, the goat, the bees and those freaky chickens, and he was far enough away from town or the nearest house that, as the movie tagline said, no one could hear him scream. So if he tripped and conked his head on a rock, or if he choked on his food and suffocated, there'd be no one to rescue him.

Tripped or choked?

That wasn't really what spooked him, was it?

No. It was something less tangible, and for some reason he found himself thinking about Christmas night, when he'd seen— or, more precisely, *felt*—that big black thing swooping low and silent over the ranch. Goose bumps popped up on his arms, and he decided to call Alex, knowing he'd feel better if he had someone to talk to.

His cellphone battery was dead, though he'd just charged it last night, so he used the land line in the shack to phone his friend. The news was not good. Just as Ross had had to abandon his life in Phoenix in order to survive, Alex was planning to move to Salt Lake City, where he'd found a job as an IT supervisor for a small company that made rubber floor mats.

The news made Ross depressed. "Kind of far afield, isn't it?"

"I won't have to declare bankruptcy."

"But you're an engineer."

"So are you."

Ross looked out his window at the chicken coop. "You're right."

They spent the next hour commiserating, catching up on the doings of their other friends, glumly appraising their respective futures, and by the time he hung up, Ross no longer felt afraid. His apprehension had been stupid and childish, nothing more than a symptom of cabin fever, and he decided to take the pickup and drive into town. There wasn't much to do in Magdalena, so he ended up going into the bar, where the only other patron was Jackass McDaniels, the handyman, who remembered him from the farmer's market and invited Ross over by patting the stool next to him and saying, "Sit your ass down, bud. Any cousin a Lita's… ah, you know the drill."

Ross ordered a beer and asked the question he'd wanted to ask since meeting the man. "So is your name really Jackass? Your parents didn't name you that, did they?"

The handyman shrugged. "Might as well've been my name. That's what my old man called me. My momma always called me Chester—that's my given name—but my daddy never called me nuthin' but Jackass. When the old bastard died—praise the Lord—I decided to sort of reclaim the word, make it good. You know, kinda how the blacks did with n—"

"I get it." Ross held up a hand. "So is your mom still alive?"

He shook his head sadly. "Died a couple a years ago, God rest her soul. But she was good up to the last. No oldtimer's disease or cancer or nuthin'. She just died in her sleep, peaceful like, and there wasn't none of that wastin' away or loss of memory. It was a good life, and she went out on top." He drained half his beer glass in one chug. "How about you? Momma and daddy still alive?"

"Yeah."

"Not that close, huh?"

Ross was surprised. "You can tell?"

"Got a sixth sense about these things. People with daddy issues can always spot a fellow traveler. Want to talk about it?"

"Not really."

"Okay." McDaniels finished his beer and ordered another.

Ross nursed his drink. "So, have you always lived here?"

"Magdalena born and bred."

"And was your dad a handyman, too?"

"Nah. A farmer. And a shitty one at that. We lived in a trailer in the middle of a dead field where he was always trying to grow cotton. He grew *some*, I guess, and we raised enough animals to kinda eke out a crappy existence. But after he keeled over—heart attack—my momma and I sold the land to Holt, who was trying to expand his ranch at the time. A lot of other people at that end of the valley already sold, so we were pretty much the last holdouts. Momma was tough, and we ended up gettin' some decent money. I was of age then, and I convinced her to buy a little plot of land up close to the mountain here, and me and a few buddies put up a house, plumbing, wiring and all. I was pretty good at it, so I just kept on. That's how I became a handyman. Now I can fix or build just about anything." He nodded at Ross. "You're...what? Some kind of scientist?"

"Engineer."

"What're you doin' here?"

"I can't find a job."

"I thought that was a good racket to go into, engineering. I heard there're lots of jobs available."

"You heard wrong."

The two of them talked for awhile about how hard it was to make a living these days—"Although, I'm pretty sure it always has been," McDaniels said—and then Ross got up and said he had to go.

"Well, nice talkin' to you," McDaniels told him. "And if you or your cousin ever need some work done…you know where to find me."

"Here."

"Most afternoons."

Ross drove back to the ranch. He decided to prepare early for the farmer's market tomorrow and get things ready, so he put the sign and the folding table in the truck, boxed up a dozen jars of honey and counted out ten egg cartons, about half of the amount in the cellar. On a whim, he decided to check if the hens had laid any more eggs, and when he went out to the coop, he was surprised to find that they had. He collected nearly two dozen, in fact, all of them normal looking. As it was getting late, he took them down to the cellar and left them in the baskets, intending to sort them tomorrow. Not only had none of the chickens attacked him this time, most of them had been hiding, and while that was definitely weird, he was not complaining. It was better than being pecked.

The fear returned after nightfall. He'd left a light on in the kitchen of the Big House to let potential burglars know that someone was home (as though a burglar would drive all the way out here on that horrible dirt road in the middle of the night to steal Lita and Dave's TV), but that single light somehow made the house seem creepier than darkness would have. He closed the drapes in the shack to block all views of the world outside, but it made him feel claustrophobic, and he found that not being able to see outside made him think there *was* something out there. So he partially opened the drape on the front window, enough to let him see if anyone—

anything

—was coming, and he popped in a DVD of *The Larry Sanders Show* in order to take his mind off the morbid track on which it was headed.

The comedy was distracting, but not distracting enough. He was always aware of his isolation and the night outside, and even as he was laughing at Gary Shandling's neurotic self-obsession, Ross kept glancing toward that partially exposed window. He didn't know what he was afraid of, exactly, and wasn't sure what had put him in this mood, but his mind kept drifting to that black thing he'd seen in the sky and the way the hens had *spied* on him before that one had attacked him, and he wished Lita and Dave would hurry up and come back.

He'd never been a devotee of Ben Franklin's philosophy. That "early to bed, early to rise" aphorism had never made much sense to him, but since coming out here, Ross always seemed to fall asleep before ten o'clock. It was probably the lack of things to do at night—he understood now why those pioneer families on the prairie would go to bed soon after the sun went down—and tonight he was grateful that he was starting to doze in front of the television. He didn't want to be awake when midnight rolled around, and though he was no longer watching, he left the TV on for company as he got ready for bed, using the remote to turn it off before curling up and pulling the covers over his head.

He slept through the entire night, undisturbed.

And dreamed.

It was the most realistic dream Ross had ever had, so real that even for a few seconds after he'd awakened, he still thought it might have happened.

He was here, in the shack, and Lita had come back from Las Vegas alone, leaving Dave to tie up all the bureaucratic loose ends resulting from his parents' deaths. Ross was lying on the floor when she walked in, on his back, reading a magazine that he held up at arm's length.

Lita said nothing as she closed the screen door behind her, and when he put down the magazine and glanced over at her, Ross saw that she was naked.

"What are you doing?" he said, panicking.

Smiling, she said nothing, striding across the room until her bare feet were on either side of his head. She squatted over his face. Her vagina was gorgeous—pink and perfectly formed, the delicate slit framed by roseblush labia—and she dipped lower, lightly brushing his mouth, her sweet juices dripping onto his lips.

He awoke with a powerful erection, a tent-poler that raised the covers above him. His lips *were* wet and tasted slightly salty, and it took him a moment to realize that he'd bitten his bottom lip and it was bleeding. It had all been a dream. Patting his lip with the palm of his hand, Ross saw a small spot of red, and he continued to dab at the cut with his palm until the bleeding had stopped.

The sun had risen, and white light seeped into the room from cracks in the drapes. He'd overslept. Getting up, he still had an erection, and he pushed down on it, trying to get it to go away. She was his cousin, for God's sake, and he felt shamed and disgusted by whatever part of his brain had concocted that cockamamie scenario. The erection disappeared as he took a cold shower, and he washed, dried off, got dressed and chugged a glass of orange juice before heading outside to quickly feed the horse and goat. The chickens he'd see to later.

Glad that he'd packed the boxes ahead of time, Ross loaded them into the cab of the pickup, honey on the floor and eggs on the seat next to him. He should have asked Lita where they kept the money box, but he probably had enough ones and fives in his wallet to make change, and he found a notepad and pencil with which to tally up sales.

He drove to town. As before, the street was blocked off, and though the cowboy hatted senior manning the barricades didn't know him from Adam, the old man must have recognized Dave's pickup because he pulled one of the sawhorses aside and waved Ross through.

He wasn't as late as he thought he'd be. Most vendors were still setting up, and he pulled next to the Native American family, who had their table out and were arranging their jewelry and leather goods. With no one to help him, Ross dragged his table out of the truck's bed on his own, unfolding the legs and righting it before taking out the sign. He'd forgotten to bring the bricks and boards that Dave used to prop the sign up, so he leaned it against the pickup's bumper. It couldn't be seen from afar, but Ross assumed that by this time, most of the market's patrons probably knew where the L Bar-D table was. Besides, if they didn't, the display of honey jars and egg cartons should make it pretty clear what was being sold.

He arranged the jars and cartons on top of the table.

Jackass McDaniels stopped by with some old honey jars to trade in. Ross didn't know what to do with them, so he told the handyman he could bring them back next week, when Dave and Lita would be back.

"Nah," McDaniels said. "You take 'em and give 'em to Dave when he gets back. He can credit me next time."

McDaniels didn't buy any more honey, but he hung around and shot the breeze for a few minutes, leaving only when other customers started to arrive. The priest didn't come by this time, but neither did Cameron Holt, and though Ross didn't recognize most of the people who stopped by, he did recognize Anna Mae, the old woman whose husband had Alzheimer's. When she worriedly asked after Lita, Ross carefully explained where she was and that she would be back next week.

"Oh, that's terrible!" Anna Mae kept repeating, genuinely distressed.

"I'm sure they'll be very touched by your concern," he told her.

There wasn't much to sell, so he ran out of eggs early, honey soon after that. Once he'd packed up the table, sign and boxes, and made sure the money was safely tucked into the front pocket of his jeans, he took a quick tour of the other vendors' displays.

He walked by the mushroom stand, saw the little granny-skirted girl. He smiled at her. "Hi."

"Dick suck mushroom! Pickaninny pie!"

Shocked, he faced the child. "What did you say?"

She giggled, turned away, and ran behind her mother, who was standing behind the booth, frowning at him.

He still wasn't sure he'd heard what he thought he'd heard. "What did you say?" he asked again.

The girl shook her head, refusing to answer.

"Stop badgering her!" the mom ordered. "Either buy something or leave. In fact, no, you can't buy anything. I won't sell anything to you. Get out."

"I—" Ross began.

"I know why you're sniffing around here!" the mom screamed. "You think I don't? You're using her to get to me! I know what you want!" She lifted her skirt to reveal dirty blood-stained underwear.

"Lady, you're crazy," Ross said and walked away as the woman screamed after him.

"What a bitch."

At the sound of the voice, he looked to his right, where a dark-skinned young woman with long black Pocahontas hair was standing behind a table covered with an assortment of large individually wrapped cookies in the shapes of various household items: couch, table, refrigerator, television. Approximately his own age, she was dressed casually in loose jeans and a Decemberists t-shirt, which instantly put her in his good graces. She smiled at him. "You must be Lita's cousin. I'm Jill."

"Ross," he introduced himself. He did not remember seeing her before.

Jill nodded toward the mushroom booth. "What's with her?"

"I don't know," Ross admitted, "but—"

"A lot of crazy things have been happening around here lately? Believe me, I know."

The girl was still chanting. "Dick suck mushroom! Pickaninny pie!"

Ross tried to ignore her. "Why? What's happened to you?" he asked.

"Nothing much," Jill said. "I was attacked by Puka, the golden retriever I adopted at birth and who has never so much as growled at a squirrel. Right after he bit me on the leg, he ran away, and he hasn't come back since. Although I have a new friend: a snake took up residence on my front stoop this morning. I had to sneak out the back door to get out of the house. I'm just hoping it's gone by the time I get home. Oh, and my friend Jenny called me up last night and told me she hated me. She wouldn't tell me why, and she won't answer the phone when I call, or return any of my texts."

"Wow."

"Yeah."

"My tale of woe is not quite as bad, but I *was* pecked by a chicken." He was tempted to mention that black flying thing but decided against it.

"And that crazy mushroom woman screamed at you after her daughter said racist obscenities."

"That, too."

"It's a weird world," Jill said.

A customer strolled over, wanting to buy one of the refrigerator cookies, and she excused herself to help the man. Had Ross walked away, that might have been the end of the conversation, but she was attractive, and she seemed nice, and he noticed that she wasn't wearing a ring.

Pathetic.

It *was* pathetic, but it kept him there. He motioned toward her cookies after the customer left. "Those look amazing," he said.

"Thank you."

"Can you actually make a living with this? I mean here? In Magdalena?"

"Oh no. I have to have a day job."

"Which is?"

She shook her head. "You'll laugh."

He laughed. "No I won't."

"You just did," she pointed out.

"Sorry. But I wasn't laughing at your job. I was laughing at the idea that you *thought* I would laugh at your job... Never mind. Forget it. You don't have to tell me if you don't—"

"I'm a telemarketer."

"Hmm."

"I guess that's better than laughing."

"No, I'm just surprised. You don't look like a telemarketer."

"What does one look like?"

"I don't know. Older. Grotesquely overweight."

Jill laughed.

"You definitely have the voice for it, though." Ross looked around. "Where do you work? Do you commute every day? Because I don't see any calling center here in town."

"I work out of my home."

"I didn't know they did that."

She shrugged. "It's another way to save money: no brick-and-mortar. There are five of us in my unit. We all log in to a central exchange where we're monitored, and everything we need shows up on the screen." She smiled wanly. "It's not something I'm proud of."

"What do you sell?"

"Do you really care?" She looked at him skeptically.

"No," he admitted.

A woman with her young son in tow walked up and bought two cookies. Ross bought a cookie, too, a TV set. He wanted to talk to Jill more, but some friends of hers came over to chat, and he waved goodbye as he excused himself.

He ate the cookie on the way back to the ranch. It was delicious.

That evening, Lita called and said they'd be back on Saturday. She sounded worried, and he asked what was wrong, but it turned out to be nothing. She was just concerned about her horse, and he reassured her that all of the animals were fine.

"Do you think you could take him out for a run?" she asked. "He needs daily exercise."

"That's not going to happen," he told her. "Besides, you'll be back in a few days."

Now her tone sounded amused rather than worried. "Are you afraid of my horse? Are you afraid of Mickey?"

"I don't know how to ride a horse," he said defensively. "I don't know how to put on a saddle or any of that."

"You're afraid," she teased.

"Fine. I'm afraid."

Lita laughed. "I'm glad I called. You cheer me up."

"I'm happy my cowardice amuses you."

She hadn't talked to Dave about it yet, had only been toying with the idea in her own mind, but Lita told Ross that once they received their money, they might be able to pay him for the chores he did around the ranch, hire him on as an official ranch hand. He didn't want to argue with her over the phone, so he didn't respond to her suggestion, but there was no way that was going to happen. He felt like enough of a freeloader already, even with the chores, and the charity of payment was more than he could put up with, no matter how awful his financial state.

Lita promised to call again tomorrow, and before hanging up, Ross told her how much they'd made today at the farmer's market. "You didn't have to do that," she told him.

"I wanted to," he said. "Not that I don't love sitting around here by myself all day."

She laughed. "I hear you."

There'd been a trace of light in the west when Lita called, but the night outside was now full dark. He hung up the phone. He hadn't told his cousin everything about the farmer's market, and he found himself thinking about the chanting little girl and her mom with the bloody underwear.

Dick suck mushroom! Pickaninny pie!

Feeling uneasy, he turned on the television, but the DirecTV was out, and there was only snow and static on the screen. Turning on his laptop, he found that he could not connect to the internet. The room was well-lit, but the blackness of the windows made him nervous, and he closed the drapes, made sure the door was locked. Leaving the TV on, in case the satellite came in again, he put on a They Might Be Giants CD and looked through a trade magazine that he'd brought with him from Phoenix but hadn't yet had time to read.

He finished the magazine, moved on to the Stephen King book he was reading.

An hour passed. Two.

When it became obvious that the DirecTV was not coming back on, Ross decided to call it a night. Leaving on only the light in the bathroom, he took off his clothes, got into bed in his underwear. He was hard for some reason, and he tried lying on his back for several minutes, then tried moving onto his side, but his erection would not go down, and he soon realized that if he ever hoped to fall asleep, he would have to take care of things. Pushing off the blanket and pulling down his underwear, he began to masturbate, thinking about Jill, imagining her naked.

Concentrating hard.

So he wouldn't think about Lita.

NINE

I T WASN'T POSSIBLE.

Anna Mae woke up with the dawn—and Del wasn't in bed next to her. She sat up, confused, thinking maybe she was still asleep and dreaming. She always set up the railing on his side of the bed at night so he wouldn't fall out, and even if he had been able to crawl over her it would have been impossible for him to do so without waking her up. There was no way he could be out of bed.

Yet he was.

She heard noises coming from the kitchen.

The sounds of someone making breakfast.

"Del?" she called hesitantly.

Although he'd done it every weekend for the first forty years of their marriage, it had been years since he had been able to make breakfast for them. Even before the Alzheimer's struck, his arthritis had been so bad that he had simply not had the manual dexterity to manipulate cooking utensils or even pour milk. Now, however, she smelled pancakes.

What was going on here?

Anna Mae got up, pulling her nightgown closed around her neck. Had someone helped Del out of bed, taken him into the kitchen and started making breakfast? It didn't make any sense, but it was the only possibility she could think of. She glanced around as she walked toward the bedroom door, looking for some type of weapon, just in case. Leaning against the side of the dresser was the cane she'd bought her husband that he never used, and she picked it up, holding the handle tight, prepared to whack someone with it if she needed to.

From the kitchen came the clinking of silverware. Walking slowly, trying not to make any noise, Anna Mae moved down the hall, past the bathroom, past the linen cupboard. Gathering her courage, lifting the cane above her head, she stepped into the kitchen doorway.

And saw Del.

"Anna Mae!' he said, smiling happily as he poured orange juice out of a pitcher and into a cup.

She screamed.

Del rushed forward, a look of concern on his face. "Are you all right?"

This couldn't be. She felt like fainting. The husband standing before her had not existed for over a decade, and seeing him like this was like seeing a ghost. He put a hand on her shoulder, the way he used to, and she nearly melted. This was something she had never expected to experience again outside of a dream. It was the answer to her prayers. A miracle. But it was a miracle that frightened her, and while this was a good thing that had happened—a *great* thing—she could not help thinking it was a thing that was not supposed to be.

Anna Mae looked into her husband's eyes. She didn't know how an outcome that was so right could seem so wrong, but it did.

"What's the matter?" Del asked, and while his voice sounded older and more cracked than it had the last time he'd been lucid, the familiar cadences were there.

She started crying.

His fingers touched the cheeks under her eyes, wiped away the tears. "It's okay," he said. "I'm here."

He *was* here. She had her husband back. It might be wrong, and it might not last, but for now he was hers, and she threw her arms around him and, through her sobs, whispered into his ear. "I love you. I love you."

"I love you, too," he said.

"Paul!"

Where *was* he?

Heather Cox-Coburn stormed out of her studio and into the main hallway, looking for her husband. *The View* was over, she'd finished her workout, and he was supposed to be there to bring her a mid-morning green drink. It was bad enough that he was forcing her to spend an entire month out here in the asshole of America, but to ignore and forget about her this way was really unforgiveable. Heather strode down the hallway toward his office. He was probably sitting in front of his damn computer. He wasted half his day either on that machine or on the phone, constantly monitoring his company, although his business ran fine on its own—and if it didn't, there were people in place who would make sure that it did.

"Paul—" she said angrily, walking into his office.

He wasn't there.

She looked around to make sure he hadn't keeled over from a heart attack, then walked back out of the room just as her cell phone rang. She expected it to be Paul and was about to give him an earful, but it turned out to be Tyra Banks. Yesterday, Tyra had invited her out to LA to attend a taping of her show, and Heather had jumped at the opportunity. Paul had objected, saying they were supposed to be on vacation, but *he* certainly wasn't on vacation, and if he was going to spend all day online or on the phone or video conferencing with his investors, she should be able to spend a week with her friends.

Heather was afraid Tyra was calling to cancel, but it was nothing so drastic. She just wanted to make sure that Heather packed a bathing suit because they were going to be spending a few days at the beach house.

"Thank God," Heather said. "I'm getting tired of staring out at this godforsaken desert."

Tyra laughed. "I told you you shouldn't have quit the biz."

Heather heard a noise behind her and turned to see Paul standing at the end of the hallway.

She knew instantly that something was wrong.

It was the way he was standing, the stiffness of his legs, the cocked angle at which he held his head. He was wearing what looked like pajamas, though she wasn't aware that he even *owned* pajamas. "I'll have to call you back," she said into the phone, clicking off without waiting to hear her friend's goodbye.

Paul stared at her silently.

"I've been looking for you," Heather said. She tried to summon up some of the anger she'd felt a few moments prior, but her husband's appearance threw her off balance. She felt nervous rather than angry, and she remained in place, not wanting to walk down the hall to where he stood.

He started toward her.

"You were supposed to bring me my green drink," she said, still trying to pretend that everything was normal, nothing was wrong. "I understand if you were busy, but at least you could have sent someone around to give it to me. You know I need to replenish after my workout."

He was still walking up the hallway. There was a dullness in his face that she did not recognize, a slack expression that made him appear almost retarded. She moved back a step involuntarily.

"I want to sell balloons," he said.

"What?" She experienced a moment of cognitive dissonance. Wasn't that what it was called when two things didn't go together and made no logical sense? Something like that. Whatever the term, she was experiencing it now, and she looked into her husband's blank face and had no idea how to respond.

"I sold it this morning."

"What?" she repeated dumbly.

"Everything. The stocks, the trademarks, the—"

That woke her up. "You did *what*?" she demanded.

"I'm selling the house, too. The houses. All of them."

She was about to yell at him, when he stopped directly in front of her. A cold wave washed over her skin, summoning goose bumps, as she saw the slow smile spreading across his slack features.

"I want to sell balloons," he said.

⚜

"Mama?"

Maria's heart was pounding as she looked from the lottery ticket in her hand to the numbers on the screen.

No.

It wasn't possible.

"Mama!" she called again, louder this time.

They'd opened the salon on New Year's Eve day and New Year's day—a lot of women wanted to get their hair done for parties, and some of the men liked to start off the year with a fresh cut—and in preparation, they'd closed the day before and she'd driven over to the beauty supply shop over in Safford to stock up on what they needed. While there, she'd gotten a Powerball lottery ticket at Circle K, a spur-of-the-moment purchase made when she bought herself a Diet Coke for the trip home and the clerk told her he was out of ones, would it be okay if he gave her eight quarters?

She'd taken the Powerball ticket instead.

Now it looked like she'd won.

They were millionaires.

"Mama!" she yelled.

"I was in the bathroom," her mother said, walking in. "What's—" She took one look at Maria's face and, somehow, she knew. "*Madre de Dios*! she cried.

"Double check for me," Maria said, her breathing tight. "Make sure."

Leaning over her shoulder, her mother looked at the ticket in Maria's hand, then at the numbers on the screen. "Aaaaaiiiieee!" she screamed, throwing up her hands.

This couldn't be happening. Things like this did not happen to people like them. It must be a mistake. She was looking at last week's numbers, or someone had typed in the *wrong* numbers, or...or...something. They couldn't have won—she glanced at the winning amount at the top of the page—six million dollars.

Six. Million. Dollars.

Maria suddenly felt dizzy. If she wasn't sitting down... she would have had to sit down.

Inside her head, she could hear the pulsing of blood through her veins. It sounded like salsa music, a rapid syncopated beat.

It was a miracle.

Her mother thought so, too. She was crossing herself, praying in Spanish,

Maria put down the lottery ticket, afraid to hold it in her hand, afraid she might accidentally tear it, afraid her sweaty fingers might rub off one of the numbers. They couldn't afford to take any chances. She placed it carefully on the desk, then grew worried because she was no longer holding it. She almost told her mother to take it, but her mama was clumsy and who knew what might happen?

Maria picked the ticket up again, breathing deeply, her heart pounding. "We have to turn this in," she said. "As quickly as possible. We can't let it sit here or leave it around the house. We have to turn it in, get the money and put it immediately in the bank."

"And we can't tell anyone," her mother said, whispering.

Maria stood. "We need to go right now."

"Go where?"

Maria turned the ticket over, reading the fine print, trying to figure out how to redeem their winnings, not something she'd ever thought of before because they had never won anything. There was a phone number and a website—

They were already on the website!

Stupido. She clicked on the instructions for claiming a prize. For an amount up to a hundred dollars, she could redeem her prize at any retailer that sold Powerball tickets. For larger amounts, she could send in her ticket or bring it in person to the lottery headquarters in Phoenix. A person correctly picking all six numbers including the Powerball number—

her!

—had to bring the ticket to lottery headquarters and had to agree to participate in a press conference and use her likeness for publicity purposes…

Maria stopped reading.

"Pack up what you need," she told her mother. "We are going to Phoenix, and we are staying at an expensive resort."

"We can't. We have to open up the salon. Maybe we can close for one day, but tomorrow we need to open."

"Mama, we never have to open again. Don't you understand? We're rich. We can do whatever we want to do. We can live wherever he want to live."

Comprehension dawned in her mother's eyes.

Maria smiled. "*Yes*, Mama."

"I want to live in California."

"Then we will. Now pack up a suitcase. We're going to collect our money."

Her sister seemed different.

JoAnn returned to the living room with two cups of coffee. Becky looked pretty much the same, her appearance had not changed, but she was quiet, subdued, not her usual brash and abrasive self. Accepting the coffee, she sipped it silently, and JoAnn wished Lurlene, Darla and Lita were here. She knew what they thought of Becky, and this would show them that her sister really had grown up. Handing Becky the coffee cup, she could hardly believe it herself. This was the meeting she usually *told* people had happened, not the one that really did, and for the first time in recent memory, JoAnn was glad that her sister had come to visit.

They talked for awhile, innocuous conversation about relatives and work. There was no argument for once, no shouting, and they finished talking on the same even keel as when they started. That was a miracle.

Done with her coffee, Becky put the cup down on the low table in front of her and stared for a moment out the window. Ordinarily, she would be unpacking by now, but this time she made no effort to take her suitcase into the guest room or even get off the couch.

She glanced nervously around.

"What's the matter?" JoAnn asked.

"I don't know." Becky sat down, fidgeting.

"You okay? You ain't on drugs or nothing, are you?"

"No," Becky said, annoyed. "I don't know, I just..." She shook her head, suddenly stood. "I gotta go."

"You just got here!"

"Something's wrong," Becky said, moving closer to her sister.

"Then tell me about it. You can talk to me. Is it a guy?"

"No, I mean something's wrong *here*. I could tell even on my way down. As soon as I got close to town, I felt...I don't know... weird. I almost turned around right then and there."

JoAnn thought about New Year's Eve and her blood ran cold.

Becky was staring at her. "You feel it, too, don't you?"

"No. No, I don't." But she was still thinking about New Year's Eve. She realized that she'd expected there to be a lot of gossip about that night, but there hadn't been. She wondered why. It was as though everyone was afraid to mention it, afraid to bring it up, and the fact that Becky sensed something meant that they probably *should* be scared.

And yet…she wasn't.

"I'm going back home," Becky said. "I can't stay here." There was a pause. "I think you should come with me."

JoAnn was touched. Becky lived in a one-bedroom apartment on the crappiest street in Casa Grande, and for her to invite JoAnn to stay with her really meant something. It was a personal sacrifice that, before today, JoAnn would not have thought her sister capable of making. "Nah, I can't," she said.

"Weston, too. Both of you should come with me."

Becky really *was* scared. She had to be, to invite Weston. The two of them had never been able to stand each other. JoAnn felt a wave of love for her sister.

"There's something wrong, Jo. I feel it. Something bad's going to happen."

It already did.

"I'm serious!" Becky said angrily, reacting to the expression on JoAnn's face. She was starting to sound like her normal self. "Despite what you think, I'm not some flake. I don't go around…I don't *do* stuff like this. But it's like…like…like one of those people who has a premonition, who tells everyone to stay off the plane and then the flight goes down, killing them all. I can *feel* it, Jo. Something's wrong here!" She seemed almost ready to cry.

JoAnn put an arm around her sister's shoulder. "Maybe you should go back," she said. "If you feel this strongly, it's probably not a good idea to stay."

"What about you?"

JoAnn thought about it, and despite her sister's fears, despite what had happened on New Year's Eve, she actually felt…better.

In fact, she felt more optimistic than she had in months. Both personally, with Weston, and at work, things were going well. Very well. And she expected them to improve even more. New Year's Eve had been horrifying, but it was as though that had acted as some sort of catalyst. That had been the low point and now things were looking up. As strange as it might seem, as illogical as it was, she felt happy, happier than she could remember being in a very long time.

"Well?" Becky demanded.

JoAnn smiled at her sister, gave her a big hug. "Call me when you get home."

TEN

Ross was in Lita's kitchen, borrowing milk for the Pasta Roni he planned to make for lunch, when the phone rang. He debated whether or not he should answer, but it could be Lita or Dave. It might even be an emergency. They might be stranded on the highway somewhere. Maybe they'd tried to call his cell or the line in the shack and been unable to reach him.

He picked up the phone. "Hello?"

"Hello. Is this Ross?"

He didn't recognize the woman's voice. "Yes," he said.

"This is Jill. From the farmer's market?"

"Oh, hi!" Ross was happier to hear from her than he was willing to admit. He'd thought about her several times over the past two days, and he'd found himself hoping that he'd see her at the market next week. While they hadn't exchanged phone numbers, she obviously knew Lita's, and he was impressed that she'd made the effort to call him.

"Are you busy?" she asked.

"No, not at all."

"Do you have time to talk?"

"Sure." He put the milk back in the refrigerator.

"I mean tonight."

He smiled. "Are you asking me out on a date?"

"I guess I am."

Ross thought about that for a second. He didn't recall seeing any restaurants, and there definitely wasn't a movie theater in Magdalena. "Is there anywhere around here to *go* on a date?"

She laughed. " No. Not really. But I thought I'd invite you over for a home-cooked meal. We could talk, get to know each other..."

"That sounds great," he admitted.

There must have been an implied caveat in his voice. "But?" Jill prompted.

"How about a rain check?"

"Oh." She sounded disappointed. "Okay."

"Lita and Dave are getting back today, and I should really—"

There was the sound of a car pulling into the dirt outside.

"Hold on, I think they're here now." Ross looked out the window.

"I'll call back later," Jill said.

"I can still talk. You don't need to—"

"I'll call back later."

He was sorrier to say goodbye to her than he had any right to be, but he hung up the phone and went out to greet Lita and Dave. They were both getting out of the car, and they both looked tired. Lita gave him a wan smile. Dave nodded solemnly. Ross didn't know what to say—asking about their trip seemed too trivial, and they were probably not in the mood to discuss anything heavy right now—so he simply helped them carry their bags into the house then left them alone. "I'll come back later," he said. "When you're settled in."

Outside the shack, four hens were standing sentry in front of his door. They had somehow escaped from their enclosure and glared at him belligerently. He felt an irrational flash of fear as he looked at the animals, arrayed in an almost perfect semi-circle and facing outward.

This wasn't right.

He considered shooing them away, kicking out at them as he went into the guest house, but he knew that no matter how much money they had coming their way, Lita and, especially, Dave, would not want him to damage any of their laying hens. Ross was too afraid to pick them up, however, so he hurriedly returned to the house to get Dave, who quickly got a box out of the shed and took each of the birds, one by one, feathers flying, back into the enclosure, while Ross stood near the front door to make sure none of the chickens tried to run away.

"I wonder how they got out," Dave mused. "The gate was locked, and I don't see any breaks in the fence." He turned to Ross. "Egg production still down?"

"To almost nothing." He explained about the odd eggs he'd stored in the cellar and described the overly aggressive behavior of the birds.

"Yeah, I thought they were acting a little weird, too. We'd better keep an eye on them." Dave clapped a hand on his back. "Thanks for all your help, Ross. Seriously."

"No problem," he said. He'd offered his condolences after first hearing about the death of Dave's parents, and he thought it was appropriate to do so again, after the funeral, but Dave was already striding across the yard toward the Big House.

Later, Ross thought, and walked into the shack.

Outside, he heard the hens squawking, their agitated voices blending together in a way that sounded almost like human conversation.

Jill called back after an hour and a half, and she talked to Lita, who came over to the shack and told Ross that he was going out on a date tonight. "I talked to Jill," she said. "It's all arranged."

"What?" He shook his head, confused.

"I was afraid you might try to weasel out of it, so I accepted on your behalf. You'll meet her at her place at six. I have the directions."

"Weasel out of it?"

"I know you." She leaned against the doorjamb, a smile playing across her lips. "So...do you like her?"

"I barely know her."

"You could do worse," she said.

He thought of the summer after fifth grade, when Lita's family had come to visit and they'd gone to Big Surf, which boasted a wave-making machine that created waves in its lagoon just like those of a real beach. On the sand, he'd seen Shauna Boyd, a girl from his class, lying on a blanket next to her older sister, getting a tan. Shauna was a little bit chubby, and some of the boys made fun of her for that, but Ross had a crush on her, though it was not something to which he would ever admit. Seeing her in a bathing suit, he thought she looked wonderful. His brother Rick, having seen where he was looking, burst out laughing. "Break out the harpoons!" he cried. "Whale ashore!" Ross had felt sick to his stomach, but he hadn't been brave enough to defend Shauna, and he'd even forced himself to smile at Rick's joke so his brother would think he was cool. Lita had scowled at Rick. "Jerk." She put an arm around Ross' shoulder. "Go talk to her. Apologize for your brother."

"You could do worse," she added.

But he hadn't been brave enough to approach her, and Shauna had hated him until she moved away in eighth grade.

He'd been grateful for Lita's intercession, though, and her understanding, and he smiled at her now. "Still looking out for me, huh?"

"Always."

An image flashed in his mind, the image from his dream: Lita, squatting over him, naked. He looked away, his face hot with shame, wondering how and why he could even have thought of such a thing.

"Lita!" Dave was calling her from the Big House.

"Coming!" she called back. "Six o'clock," she told Ross. "Her place."

He left a half-hour early, not secure enough in his knowledge of local geography to risk setting out any later, though Lita told him when she handed over the address and directions that it was less than five minutes away. It took him about ten minutes to navigate the dirt roads that led to her small house, and, as a result, he arrived with twenty minutes to spare. He contemplated driving around for a bit, but figured he'd probably been seen already through the windows. Leaving after that, even if only for a little while, would seem weird, so he pulled into her driveway behind the battered Ford Econoline already parked there.

Jill lived in a small cul-de-sac just east of Magdalena's main street, in the shadow of the chimney-shaped mountain with the white "M" on its slope. There were five houses arranged in a semi-circle, and hers was one of three facing away from the mountain, looking out over the desert. He hadn't realized that the road had climbed, so gradual was its slope, but now that he was here, he found that he could look down upon the church, off to his left.

Jill *had* seen him, and she emerged from the house just as he was closing his car door. It occurred to him that he should have brought some sort of gift, a bottle of wine maybe, but it was too late for that now and, feeling embarrassed, he greeted her empty handed.

Jill gave him a quick friendly hug. "Welcome to my home," she said. "Come in. I hope you like pasta."

"Sure. Of course. Who doesn't." He cringed inwardly at his own awkwardness. "I would've brought something—" he began.

"I invited *you*. Remember? You don't need to bring anything."

"Still…" He followed her inside.

Jill's house was small but creatively furnished. Like the other four residences on the cul-de-sac, it had on the outside a prefab look, almost like one of those double-wide trailers, but inside she had used the limited space wisely and decorated her home with an imaginative hodgepodge of styles and colors: an old steamer trunk being used as a coffeetable sat in front of an orange 1950s couch, next to which stood what appeared to be a fake streetlamp. There was supposed to be a dining room—although it was little more than a wide passage connecting the living room with the kitchen— but as might be expected from someone whose hobby was baking cookies, Jill had made it into *part* of the kitchen, equipping it with a freestanding butcher's block on which sat a well-used rolling pin, and a Hoosier cabinet with a built-in flour sifter. Though the area opened onto the living room, the lines of demarcation were clear.

Ross looked around admiringly. "Nice place," he said.

"Don't bullshit a bullshitter."

"No, I'm serious. It's very creative. Even when I *had* a place to live, it didn't look this nice. I have no imagination." He examined a cactus growing in a giant pop-art Planter's Peanuts container. "You could be an interior decorator."

"Thank you," she said, honestly appreciating the compliment. She smiled. "I think I was right about you."

The air smelled of garlic and herbs, and Jill led him through the doorway into the heart of the kitchen, where a huge pot of red pasta sauce was simmering on the stove. "I figured I might as well make enough to last awhile," she explained. "Since I'm going to all this trouble. Not that you're trouble," she added quickly. "I just meant—"

He laughed. "I know."

"Here. Sit down." She pulled out a chair from the table in the center of the kitchen.

"Do you need some help?" he asked. "Is there anything I can do?"

"No. I prefer to be a Lone Ranger. Sit."

Ross sat down, watching as she put a pot of water on the stove for the pasta and then started making a salad. He could have felt guilty, probably should have felt guilty, but he didn't. It was comfortable here, easy, and for a first date, he felt remarkably relaxed.

"Any more snake sightings?" he asked.

"That one on my front step? I haven't seen him, but he's still around somewhere. Hopefully not in the house. A crow slammed into my bedroom window this morning, though. He didn't crack it, but he was stunned enough to fall on the ground, and when I peeked out to see what had happened, Puka, my still-missing dog, zoomed out of nowhere, grabbed the crow and hauled off into the hills." She smiled. "So what's new with you?"

They talked of Magdalena, and the conversation came easily. She seemed genuinely unnerved by odd events she saw going on around the town—the subject that had inspired their initial contact.

He had to admit that he, too, had some questions, but, her concerns went much deeper, and Ross wondered if she was religious.

"The thing is," she said, "I think something happened, something to precipitate all this. I don't know what, don't know when, don't know how, but even with some of my friends it's like they're keeping something from me, like they all know something they've sworn to keep secret."

"Come on. You don't think that sounds a little paranoid?"

"Maybe," she admitted. "But just because you're paranoid—"

"—doesn't mean they're not out to get you?"

"Exactly." Jill put down the knife with which she'd been cutting tomatoes and looked to her left. "Oh. I almost forgot. Would you like some wine?" She picked up a stemmed glass and a bottle of pinot.

"Yes, thank you," he said.

"Sorry," she apologized. "I'm a terrible host. Can you tell I don't do this much?"

"Not at all," he said in an extravagantly exaggerated voice, and they both laughed.

Ross took a sip from the wine glass she handed him and nodded his approval. She took a sip of her own and went back to making the salad.

"So, did you grow up here?" he asked.

"No. Magdalena is one of those places where… I think the only people who want to live here are the ones from somewhere else. Most of the people who are actually *from* here end up leaving. I don't know too many local kids whose goal is to remain in Magdalena."

"So where are you from and how in the world did you end up in *this* town?"

"The same way Dave and Lita did, probably. No, maybe not. I think Dave's family knew about it because of the agriculture thing. But I saw an article in *Arizona Highways* about spring wildflowers in southern Arizona, and I came down here with my boyfriend at the time to take pictures. We were both in college— Mesa Community—and we were both art majors, both taking the same photography course. The actual wildflower drive shown in the magazine was closer to Sierra Vista, and we went there, but we had our camping gear and ended up exploring some of the dirt roads in this part of the state, and we happened across Magdalena. I'd never heard of it before, and I just thought it was so cute and so...so completely unspoiled. We ate lunch at the bar, and the burgers were great, and I just kind of fell in love with the place. We went back to Mesa, and Craig and I broke up soon after that, but Magdalena kind of haunted me, and after I graduated from MCC and then ASU, I decided I'd like to live out here, be a starving artist. Of course, I didn't even have enough money to do that, so I lived at my mom's house and worked for a few years after graduation. Various jobs, nothing permanent. I saved my money, and by the time the housing market crashed in 2008, I had enough for a down payment, and I bought this place. I was working as a telemarketer at the time and, amazingly enough, I was good enough at it to earn a pretty decent commission. I'd been painting all along, but I never sold anything, so I needed to have an income.

Obviously, there weren't any jobs around here, so I asked if I could keep my telemarketing job, though I'd actually been hoping I could quit. I was already working from home, checking in online, so they didn't care, and I moved to Magdalena...and here I am." She smiled. "Long story, huh?"

"How long have you lived here?"

"Going on five years now."

"And how'd you start with the cookies?"

"I don't know. I've always been into baking, cooking, what have you. A couple years back, I started making little…sculptures, sort of, out of my cookies. I'd experiment with different forms, give them away to friends, and someone suggested that I should sell them at the market, so I did. I don't make a fortune, but I pay for my space, and it gives me the opportunity to try out new ideas every week. I usually try to have a theme. It's fun, you know? Relaxing."

"Do you still paint?"

"Oh sure."

"So…can I see some of your paintings?"

She shook her head, her face flushing as she turned away.

"Why not?"

"Maybe when I know you better."

Jill had continued to cook while she talked, tossing the salad, draining the pasta, and now she plated the dinner and brought it over to the table. She was a good cook, and between her food and Lita's meals, Ross realized how deprived he had been growing up. "Home cooking" to him had always meant his mom's dry pork chops and overdone meatloaf, but he understood now that there were home cooks able to create dishes as good as those served in restaurants.

Like Lita, Jill was one of them.

Dinner was leisurely, relaxed, and though Jill offered to uncork another bottle of wine, Ross switched instead to water. The roads back to the ranch might be dirt and deserted, but he was such a lightweight that drinking even a moderate amount of alcohol could end up with him spinning his wheels in a ditch.

Jill seemed to have a pretty large DVD collection, and he expected the date to be a variation on the traditional dinner and a movie, but she seemed to have other ideas. After they finished eating, she put the dishes in the sink, telling him she'd take care of them later. "Let's go for a walk," she suggested.

"A walk?"

"Yes. An after-dinner stroll. Don't tell me that you don't like to take walks."

"No, I do," he said quickly, though he couldn't remember the last time he'd actually done it. In Phoenix, his condo was adjacent to a charmless business district, and Lita's place was so remote that, while he'd walked around the ranch doing chores, he had never even thought about strolling around the neighborhood—not that there was a neighborhood. "Is there anyplace *to* walk?" he asked. "I mean, we're kind of out in the middle of nowhere."

"I walk to town all the time."

"That's at least a mile!"

"Come on. You're not afraid of a little exercise, are you?"

"No," he said, but he hoped they wouldn't be walking all the way into town. That seemed a little far. He had a sudden flashback to when he was a kid and his whole life had been spent on foot. At the age of nine, he'd been on a rock-hunting kick, and he remembered getting up early one Saturday, before his parents were awake and going out on an expedition. He'd walked down the street, rock pick in hand, looking through neighbors' front yards for fossils and petrified wood. He'd found nothing more than a few pieces of slightly shiny, reddish gravel that he misidentified as jasper, but he'd incorporated the pieces into his next batch of rocks for his tumbler, and they'd actually polished up nicely.

Back then, every foray into the neighborhood had been an adventure, and he wondered when walking had lost its allure for him.

Probably when he'd learned to drive.

It was dark out, and Jill disappeared down the hall for a moment, returning with a flashlight. She flipped the light on and off, making sure it worked. "All right," she said. "Let's go."

They walked outside and headed down the lane, sauntering slowly. She pointed out a type of purple flower growing in abundance by the side of the road, shut off her flashlight to show him phosphorescent bugs dotting the sides of the ditch, and he thought he could understand why she liked to walk, what she saw in it. Ahead of them, down the slope, the lights of Magdalena made the town look much bigger than it actually was.

They held hands, like schoolchildren, and it was nice. He liked her. More than he had liked anyone in a long time. He liked being with her, liked walking with her, and he was glad they hadn't stayed inside and watched a movie.

Twenty minutes later, they reached the town, the road they were on meeting the main street in front of the church. They turned right, heading toward the small downtown. Jill sighed. "I don't know where we're going to get our hair done around here," she said.

Ross pointed toward the salon. "There's a—"

"Oh. I guess you haven't heard."

"Heard what?"

"Xochi and Maria? The mother and daughter who run the place? They won the lottery."

He wasn't sure if she was speaking literally or metaphorically. "The...actual lottery?"

"Yeah. They won six million dollars."

"Holy shit."

"They closed the place up, and they're not coming back. So we're down two beauticians." She toggled her hand back and forth. "Sort of."

Ross laughed, running his fingers through his too-short hair. "Tell me about it."

They had no destination in mind, but they walked down one side of the street and up the other. The bar was open, but inside it sounded rowdy, and they passed on by. He wished there was a regular restaurant in town—a hot cup of coffee and a warm piece of pie sounded good right now—but there wasn't, and with no place to stop, the two of them headed back into the darkness of the desert toward the small cluster of lights that was Jill's neighborhood.

It was cold, and he wished he'd brought a jacket, but Ross said nothing. He'd come across wimpy enough as it was. She was still holding his hand, and on the way back, her fingers rubbed lightly against his. He remembered seeing a Michael Palin travel show about the Himalayas, and in one tribal village, the girls would dance with the boys in a kind of public ceremony, and if a girl rubbed her finger on a boy's palm, it meant she wanted sex. Jill was doing that right now to him, and the feeling was electric. It was as though the nerves in his hand connected directly with his penis, and he walked all the way back to her house with a very pleasurable erection.

Inside, she made coffee to warm them up, and put on some music, romantic piano music that he didn't recognize.

They ended up kissing on the couch, making out like high schoolers, and soon he was grinding against her as her legs spread wide and her crotch pressed up against his. Moments later, they were in the bedroom and their clothes were off. It happened quickly, and he barely had time to wish that he'd showered for his date before she was frantically slipping a condom on and guiding him inside her. It had been awhile, and he wasn't sure he'd be able to hold out, but he didn't have to. She came even more quickly than he did, and as soon as she finished, she was whispering in his ear, coaxing him to climax. Which he did—and she did again—powerfully.

They lay there, spent.

"Wow," she said.

Jokingly, he pumped his fist in the air. "Got her on the first date."

"Let me assure you, this is not a regular occurrence."

"Hence the condom drawer."

She slapped his shoulder. "I'm serious!"

"I know," he said, laughing. "I'm sorry."

"It's been a long time for me," she admitted.

"Me, too."

They were silent for a moment.

"So," Ross said finally, "*now* can I see some of your paintings?"

She nodded, gave him a quick kiss. "Yes," she said. "You can."

ELEVEN

CAMERON HOLT STRODE INTO THE VETERINARIAN'S OFFICE with his fists clenched. He was angry but determined to keep himself under control and not make a scene, despite the fact that Gonzalez had not returned any of his calls and had been ducking him for nearly a week. Rye Callahan was in the waiting room— Cameron had seen one of his pigs in the trailer out front—as was an old Mexican guy with a scuzzy dog on a leash, but he strode past them, ignored the receptionist and pushed through the swinging door to the back, where Gonzalez was stuffing his face with a breakfast burrito.

The veterinarian looked up, startled, as Cameron barged into the room. He swallowed quickly. "I am still waiting for lab results—" he began.

"My cattle are dying! Four more today! How long does it take for your goddamn lab to run a blood test?"

"It's not just a blood test, it's—"

"You should know *something* by now! You should at least have a general *idea!*"

The two men faced each other, and Cameron saw something flicker across the vet's features: fear. He was afraid, not of Cameron but of what was happening, and Cameron knew that Gonzalez knew that he knew.

"I found out what you did." The vet crossed himself.

"You superstitious old woman!" Cameron had promised himself that he wouldn't yell, but he couldn't help it. "It's your job to cure sick animals and prevent diseases, not listen to local gossip."

"God is mad at you."

"Jesus fuck!"

Gonzalez crossed himself again.

"Knock that shit off," Cameron ordered. "My stock is dying. There's a disease going around, and we need to stop it before it wipes out my entire herd. And my neighbors'. It's not magic or evil spirits or—"

"God."

"Listen, asshole. If you think killing animals is God's will, then why in the hell did you become a vet, huh? You're thwarting God's plan. Every time you cure a sick animal, you're going against His wishes and getting rid of the sickness that He gave those animals. Is that what you believe? Because if you do, you're already going to hell, and you might as well just do your job and find out what's killing my cattle. If you don't, and you actually understand that this is all bullshit, then stop fluttering around like some frail old Sunday school teacher and get busy. Either way, *get to fucking work.*"

Gonzalez did not respond.

Cameron frowned. "Did you even send that stuff to a lab?" he demanded. He suddenly had the sneaking suspicion that the little beaner was lying to him, and the thought made him furious. He was tempted to just sweep his hand across the counter to his left and knock all of Gonzalez's veterinary implements to the floor, but he restrained himself.

"Of course," the vet said.

"God didn't tell you to pray about it instead?"

"I told you. I am waiting for the results. As soon as they come in, I will let you know. Yours are not the only animals that died, you know. I collected samples from all of the affected ranches."

Cameron didn't believe him. What the vet said was logical, reasonable and might very well be true, but it sounded like a lie to him—or, rather *felt* like a lie—and Cameron stepped forward, putting his finger in Gonzalez's face. "*Get* the results. Today. If I don't hear from you by tomorrow, I'm coming back. I can't afford to have any more of my animals die. If they do, it'll be your fault, and you'll pay for that."

The threat was strong, the moment was right, and Cameron strode out, back to the waiting room, where a worried-looking old woman with an orange cat in a cage had joined Rye Callahan and the Mexican guy. The cat was whistling, an odd birdlike sound that made the hairs on the back of Cameron's neck stand on end and for some reason made him think of the red moths that had flown out of his dead cattle. All four people, including the receptionist, had obviously heard the shouting from the other room, and they stared at him silently as he walked past them.

He pushed open the door and headed into the parking lot, trying to ignore the freakish whistling of the cat. But the tune stayed with him, stuck in his head, and by the time he drove back to the ranch, he was whistling it himself.

⌀

Cameron Holt was the last straw.

Jose Gonzalez had been thinking about leaving Magdalena ever since he'd learned what had happened New Year's Eve, but it was Holt who made up his mind for him. No job was worth this risk. Not just the physical risk, but the risk to his soul. God was angry at Magdalena, and the sooner he got out of here the better. There was always need for a good livestock vet. He could get a job anywhere there were farms or ranches. He didn't need to stay here. Sure, he liked the area, and he'd made a lot of friends, but things were going bad, and they were going bad fast.

On a practical level, his cell phone reception, which had been hit and miss, was now almost exclusively miss. WiFi no longer seemed to work, and even the DSL line in his office was out more often than not. He'd been relying on dial-up for his computer, which was slow under the best of circumstances, and in the case of looking up information for medical emergencies, of which there'd been more than a few the past week, was almost completely useless.

There was a *power* here that was interrupting all of these devices.

The same power that was creating monsters.

For it was not only the ranchers who were affected now. The problems were spreading. He'd seen pets in the last few days that exhibited symptoms and behavior he had not only never encountered before but had never *imagined* before, pets that were not merely ill but that had been transformed: a suddenly hairless German shepherd that had given birth to a macaw, a rabbit whose ears had fallen off and been replaced by horns.

Maybe he could have gotten a jump on all this, maybe he'd had the opportunity to nip it in the bud, but Holt was right; he hadn't sent in the samples to be analyzed. He couldn't. Because the petri dishes had fallen on the floor once he'd gotten them back to his office. Or, to be more accurate, they'd *jumped* to the floor. Returning from the bathroom, he'd arrived just in time to see the last petri dish spring off the counter where he'd placed it and fall to the floor, its gray goopy contents spilling out and joining the gelatinous mess from the other samples that had slopped onto the tile. The entire thing quivered as though it was alive and filled him with such revulsion that he'd reacted without thinking, holding his breath so as not to breathe what might very well be toxic fumes and pouring a bottle of alcohol on the blob in an effort to kill it. The mass dissolved into a smoky liquid, and he quickly left the room, going to the supply closet and putting on gloves and a surgical mask before returning to clean up the mess with a mop and bucket that he threw in the dumpster immediately afterward.

He'd intended to go back and get some more samples from the bodies of the cattle that had not yet been burned, but then he'd found out what had happened, and he'd been afraid to return. He'd been ducking Holt and the other ranchers ever since, and, knowing this day would come, he had started thinking several days ago that maybe it was time to leave Magdalena.

Now he knew that it was.

He was a doctor, and he was ethical, so he saw all of the patients that had been brought in—even Mrs. Miller's spooky whistling cat, for which he had no explanation or advice—but as soon as he was through, he told Janine to go home, closed up the office and headed to his house to pack his bags. He felt bad about not telling Janine the truth, letting her think that they were just taking the day off, but he didn't want *it* to know that he was leaving.

Whatever *it* was.

He would make it up to his receptionist, though, after he was out of here and safe. He'd send her a severance check and a recommendation. Not that a recommendation would be of much use to her here in Magdalena. But she was smart and had ambition, and maybe this would spur her to move on and look for work elsewhere. Hell, maybe he'd even invite her to work for him once he found a place and got settled.

But first things first.

He needed to get out of here.

He closed up the office and spent the next two hours loading up all of his books, medicine and medical equipment. Back at the house—a house he was renting from Cameron Holt's buddy Cal Demholm—Jose packed his clothes and most important personal belongings. It was nearly dark, his van was full, and there was still a lot of stuff to go, so he paused to decide what to do. He'd intended to just take off and make a clean break, but he saw now that that wasn't going to be possible. It would take three, maybe four, trips to haul all of his possessions away, and the smartest thing to do might be to wait until morning, drive over to Tucson and find a storage unit, then return with a U-Haul and get everything else. He could live in a hotel for a few days while he decided where to go next.

A tap on his window made him jump.

Jose looked up to see a bright red moth the size of his hand fly into the window, flutter away for a moment, then hit the glass again. It looked like a larger version of the moths that had emerged from the bodies of Holt's cows, but this one did not disintegrate. Indeed, it continued trying to get into the house, flying into the window again and again and again. Its mindless determination made him decide that it was better to leave tonight and come back tomorrow when it was light. The moth scared him, and he picked up one last box of books and carried them out to the van.

The moth hit him in the head.

There was a burning sensation where it struck his ear, as though the creature were made of molten metal. Jose cried out, dropping the box and putting a hand to the side of his head. His ear felt hot and sticky to the touch, and his hand when he looked at it was red with blood. Quickly, he hopped into the back of the van, leaving the box on the ground. He slammed the door shut before the moth tried to attack him again, and scrambled over his piled belongings until he reached the front seat.

Where a yellow spiderlike creature jumped up from the floor and attached itself to his arm.

Screaming, he tried to bat it off, but the thing's legs were digging into his skin, holding on, and its small flattened head was bent over, its fanged mouth biting into his flesh. Blood was running down his arm in multiple rivulets, dripping onto the seat. Jose used his other hand to grasp the creature's midsection, and though the pain was tremendous and he could both see and feel pieces of skin tearing off, he yanked it up, pulled it out, and held it away from his body, trying not to let the thrashing head or any of the wiggling legs touch him.

It looked like one of the spiderthings that had come out of Joe Portis' cattle, only this one hadn't dissolved after encountering air. It was very much alive, and he smashed it onto the top of the dashboard as hard as he could, again and again, until it stopped moving and two of its legs had broken off. He considered opening the door or window and throwing it outside, but was afraid that something else might get in, so he dropped it on the floor and squished it with the heel of his boot, gratified to hear a crunching sound as he ground it into the worn dirty carpet.

Breathing heavily, Jose stared down at the shattered body, wondering if it had sprung from one of the samples he'd taken. Maybe some of the gloop had leaked onto the floor and this had emerged from that.

He didn't know, and he didn't care. A week ago, he'd been happy, successful, and perfectly content. Now he was battered and bloody and fleeing for his life. God was punishing Magdalena, and he wasn't going to hang around to see how things turned out. Checking the front seat and the floor to make sure there were no more surprises awaiting him, Jose pulled out his key, started the van and drove away. Once past the edge of town, he pulled to a stop, opened the driver's side door and used his boot to scrape what was left of the creature out of the van.

He slammed the door shut, put the van into gear and sped down the dirt road, through the desert, praying that nothing else attacked him as he put Magdalena in his rearview mirror.

TWELVE

FOR THE TWELFTH DAY IN A ROW, FATHER RAMOS AWOKE WITH a headache and the memory of a nightmare. He opened his eyes slowly, bracing himself. As always, the pain behind his temple was so powerful that it hurt even to move his head, so he remained completely still on the pillow, praying without putting his hands together, begging for relief before attempting to sit up.

There was a lightning flash of agony, followed by unbearable pressure on his brain.

He wanted to cry out but dared not, because he knew God was watching and this was the punishment he was meant to endure.

He thought of last night's dream, in many ways the most horrific one he'd had because, while it was less overtly fantastic than the others, it seemed more real. In it, Cameron Holt, who was not Catholic—or even religious, as far as Father Ramos knew—

had come to the church for Confession. But in the confessional, instead of admitting his sins, Holt, laughing, had pulled down his pants and defecated. Before anything could be done about it, the rancher had withdrawn a knife that he'd brought with him and stabbed himself in the stomach. He'd obviously planned to commit suicide, but, just as obviously, he had not anticipated how much it would hurt, and his piercing cries of agony echoed in the church as Father Ramos scrambled out of his booth and tried desperately to open the other side of the confessional. Holt had done something to jam the door, however, and Father Ramos used all of his strength and weight to break the door open. Holt was still screaming—a sustained shriek that should not have been able to come out of that mouth—and he was crumpled on the tiny floor of the confessional, his limbs twisted like those of a contortionist crammed into a small box. There was blood everywhere, and excrement, and with a final cry so loud that Father Ramos thought his eardrums would burst, Cameron Holt passed out. Father Ramos managed to pull him from the booth, but he saw instantly that there was no hope. The rancher had not merely stabbed himself, he had *slit* his stomach open, and organs were spilling out along with blood, falling through the sliced flap of skin and muscle. Holt opened his eyes, and for one last coherent second, he stared into Father Ramos' face. "You killed me," he said, and died.

The dream still disturbed him, and he tried not to think of it as he slowly, *slowly*, swung around, put one foot out of the bed, then the other and, ignoring the pain, stood. He moved with effort, wincing at every step, and though the pain in his head lessened a little as he made his way toward the kitchen, it did not go away. He wondered if he should see a doctor.

Maybe he had a brain tumor.

He didn't really think that, though, did he?

No.

Because the headaches had started after *that* night—which made it even more frightening to him than a brain tumor because it involved the fate of his very soul.

He had no appetite, something *very* rare for him, and for breakfast he drank only a small glass of orange juice that he used to wash down the Advil he hoped would temper his headache. Sitting there, eyes closed, the pain did gradually subside to a dull throb, and he was eventually able to leave his quarters, prepare for this morning's mass and put on his vestments.

Ordinarily, unless it was a religious holiday like Easter or Christmas, he could expect about a third of the church members to show up for services, although some of the others might trickle in for confession later in the week to atone for their absence. Last Sunday, the pews were virtually empty, only three families arriving, for a new record low. It was because of what had happened on New Year's Eve, he knew, and he expected the same today. But when he entered the chapel from the vestry—

the church was full.

Father Ramos stared out at his parishioners, caught completely by surprise. The church had *never* been this crowded before. Every seat was taken, some with parishioners he did not even recognize, and he wondered for the first time if what had happened had been a roundabout way for the Lord to increase the size of His flock here in Magdalena.

The idea made him feel more confident. He conducted the mass with assurance, his voice strong, and the worshippers were more involved than they ever had been before, with every last one of them taking communion.

All because of New Year's Eve.

It was the very definition of a blessing in disguise.

He told himself this.

And he tried hard to believe it.

After the last service, after the final parishioners had gone, Father Ramos took off his vestments and retired to his quarters, intending to make himself an egg sandwich. His appetite had returned full force—his stomach had been growling so loudly during communion that he was sure people had noticed—and he grabbed a handful of cashews from the nut bowl on his way to the refrigerator, popping them in his mouth and chewing loudly. *Lesson to be learned*, he thought. *Never skip meals.*

He opened the refrigerator, took out a half-full jar of mayo and put it on the counter next to him, then grabbed the small carton of eggs he'd previously hardboiled for just such an emergency. Something seemed wrong, and for a brief flash of a second he thought they were experiencing an earthquake.

Then he realized it was the egg carton.

It was *thrumming* in his hands.

Immediately, he put the carton down, flipping open the top. The eggs inside were bobbing up and down like oversized jumping beans, a sight so crazy and inexplicable that he wasn't sure at first how to react. Gooseflesh had broken out all over his body. He watched the bouncing eggs and was suddenly afraid that one of them would crack open and *something* would come out. It made no sense—the eggs had been boiled—but he closed the carton quickly, threw it in the trash and immediately sealed up the Hefty bag lining the trash can. Holding it at arm's length and moving swiftly, he dumped the entire thing in the garbage can outside and closed the lid tightly. His heart was pounding, and he imagined the eggs continuing to bounce, eventually breaking out of the carton, tearing through the Hefty bag, jumping out of the garbage can.

By nighttime, they might be hopping toward his living quarters.

The thought was intolerable.

The dump was closed on Sunday, but Tax Stuart, who owned and operated the small landfill, was a friend and parishioner, and Father Ramos started to call him up to ask him to open it today as a favor, but he stopped dialing after the first three numbers and put the phone down. He would have to explain that it was an emergency, and Tax would ask him why, in order to make sure he was not dumping illegal chemicals or toxic waste, and Father Ramos...didn't want to have to explain.

There was another site where people abandoned cars, where they left discarded appliances and threw old paint containers, an unofficial spot past Saguaro Hill, and he decided to take his trash there. In fact, he intended to leave the garbage can there as well. He knew it was wrong to use the desert as a dumping ground, and he would pray for forgiveness after he was done, but, he rationalized, it was farther away from town than the actual landfill, and the more distant the better. Maybe the eggs—

or what was inside them

—wouldn't find their way back.

He took a deep breath.

After that...

He needed to go out to Cameron Holt's ranch.

He needed to see *it*.

Father Ramos steeled himself. The idea had been in the back of his mind ever since that first night of prayer in the empty church—

"Hector"

—and he had resisted it until now, fearful of God's wrath. But he was a man of the cloth, and if anyone had the responsibility to directly confront what had happened, to face what Holt was hiding in his smokehouse, it was him.

After checking to make sure the church was empty, Father Ramos put on his gardening gloves and carried the garbage can out to the station wagon. He didn't want to lay it down in case the lid fell off, but he didn't have to; when he put up the back seat, there was enough space in the rear well for the receptacle to stand upright. He deposited the garbage can at the dump behind Saguaro Hill, wedging it carefully between a rock and a rusted washing machine to make sure it would not easily fall over, then drove west, down the series of increasingly narrow dirt roads that led to Cameron Holt's place. He slowed the car as he approached the ranch. A chain was pulled across the road in front of the cattle guard, and from the center of it hung a No Trespassing sign. Beyond the cattle guard lay a dead cow, its bloated form covered with gray slime that encased it like a shell.

He pulled to a stop, staring through the windshield at the cow, thinking, not for the first time, that God was punishing them for what they'd done. He understood why Holt had put the body in his smokehouse, knew the fear and panic the rancher had felt—they had *all* felt—but the priest wondered now if it might be better to provide a proper burial, to show respect and remorse.

Isn't that what God would want?

He wasn't sure, but thought that if he could just get into the smokehouse and look at it, he might be able to figure out the best course of action.

It was impossible to continue driving up the blocked road, and he tried to decide whether he should honk the horn and wait for someone to show up, or ignore the sign, get out of the car and walk to the ranch. The decision was made for him as Cameron Holt himself came striding down the dirt lane. Father Ramos got out of the car, wondering if the rancher had some sort of security setup, a camera or a motion-detector, that let him know when someone had arrived. "Mr. Holt—" he began.

"Go away!" the rancher ordered. "This is private property!"

"I just came to see—"

"I know what you came to see." He stopped on the other side of the chain. Cradled in his arm was a shotgun. "Get off my land."

"Technically, this isn't your land."

"*Technically*, my property line is a good twelve yards back from where you're standing. This cattle guard does not mark my property boundary."

"I'm sorry, Mr. Holt. I didn't come to fight."

"I know what you came for." He shifted the shotgun in his hand.

Father Ramos took a deep breath. "I think we are being punished." That seemed to strike a chord, and he pressed on. "Maybe we should bury—" He wasn't sure how to refer to what was in the smokehouse. "—him...her."

"*It*," Holt said firmly, "and I intend to do no such thing."

"Why not?"

He could tell that the rancher had no answer, no real reason for his actions, but the determination was nevertheless set in stone. "Stay off my property, Father."

For the first time, it occurred to him that maybe the consequences they were suffering were not God's doing. "Just let me look," he said. "That's all I ask. I won't touch. I won't do anything. You'll be right there with me."

"No."

"It might have happened on your property, but it happened *to* all of us. You have no right to—"

Holt raised his weapon. "Leave. Now."

The threat was not idle. Father Ramos had no doubt that Holt would use his shotgun and feel no remorse afterward. He would have liked to believe that this was a result of what had happened on New Year's Eve, part of the ripple effect, but he was pretty sure that it was all Cameron Holt, that the rancher would have behaved this way regardless.

Reluctantly, he withdrew, walking back to his car. He would try again tomorrow, and the next day, and the next day…

But for the moment, all he could do was pray.

Which he did, silently, with his hands on the steering wheel, all the way back to the church.

THIRTEEN

ROSS ANSWERED HIS PHONE ON THE SECOND RING.

"Mr. Lowry?" It was Jamie Wong, his realtor from Phoenix, and she was calling with impossibly good news. Not only had she found someone who wanted to *rent* his condo, but another prospect was interested in *buying* it. At the full asking price.

Ross' head was spinning. Full price was $175,000. He could live off that amount for two years, easily. Three or four if he was extremely frugal. He could even get an apartment back in Phoenix if he wanted.

But he didn't want, he realized. Not only was he getting used to life in Magdalena—he was starting to like it. Sure, it was only temporary and eventually he would have to move on. And he did not want to be a third wheel to Lita and Dave. But he'd gotten into a groove here, and it was fun working on the ranch.

There was also Jill.

That was most of it. He liked her, and he wanted to see where this might go. It had been awhile since he'd been involved in a relationship, and while this wasn't a relationship yet, it had the potential to be, and he needed to give it a chance.

Lita and Dave had gone to Willcox for their monthly supply run, but he was too excited to keep the news to himself, so he tried to call his parents to tell them he had a buyer. Once again something was wrong with his cell phone reception, despite all of the bars showing on his screen, and though he attempted to call four times, even going so far as to wander around the yard facing different directions, he was unable to hear anything but silence.

Vowing to pay back Lita and Dave for all of the calls he'd made in the past week, he used the land line in the shack. He spoke to his mom, who seemed to think that this meant he was returning to Phoenix. There was relief in her voice, as though he'd been doing something wrong or shameful by living out here in Magdalena, and he sensed disapproval in the mention she made of his cousin.

Ross said goodbye and hung up the phone, his enthusiasm dissipated. Count on his parents to throw a wet blanket over any good news that might come his way.

He considered calling Jill to tell her the good news, but thought that might be a little too much too soon. Since he'd been planning to call her tonight anyway, he decided to tell her then.

He let Lita and Dave know what the real estate agent had said as soon as they arrived back.

"Does this mean you'll be leaving us?" Lita sounded dismayed.

Dave clapped a hand around his shoulder. "We need you around here, buddy. Don't bail on us now."

"Actually, I was hoping I could stay awhile longer." He felt embarrassed. "Not forever. Just until I find a job…"

"Of course!" Lita assured him. "We love having you here!"

"We're thinking of expanding," Dave said. "Now that we have some money. Eventually, I'll probably have to hire another person, but I thought, at first, the three of us could handle things. Until we get settled and figure out exactly what we need."

Ross was relieved. "Great," he said.

Lita smiled. "Then it's settled."

"I do need to go back to Phoenix for a few days," he told them.

"What are you going to do?" Dave asked. "Rent it out or sell it?"

"I think I'm going to sell. I need the cash, and I don't think I want to live there again anyway."

"If you rent it out, you'll have a steady income," Lita pointed out. "Plus the market is depressed right now. If you hold onto it, prices may go up."

"I'm not sure that's true. The neighborhood's been going downhill for awhile now, and I don't think that's going to change. This is the same amount I paid for it; I might not get this chance again."

"Will this get rid of your debt?" Dave asked.

"With a lot left over."

"Then go for it."

He left the next morning, after breakfast. He offered to leave later, after feeding the chickens and collecting eggs, but Dave assured him that he had things under control and told Ross to go.

He'd been gone for only a couple of weeks, but the city seemed more crowded than he remembered. And dirtier. As he approached Phoenix from the south, Camelback Mountain was little more than a hump outlined in gray behind a wall of white sky. Wind from a passing truck blew a plastic grocery bag into the front of his car, where the top of it fluttered above the edge of his hood for several miles before deserting him for a Lexus. It was weird seeing so many vehicles on such wide highways after traveling down narrow dirt roads with his the only car in sight, and it made him feel surprisingly ill at ease.

Ross had arranged to meet Jamie Wong at her office at two. Though he was nearly a half hour late, the real estate agent was still there and waiting for him, and she showed him two printouts detailing the financial pros and cons of both renting out and selling. Politely, he let her give her presentation, then told her that he wanted to sell the condo—her choice as well, since she'd be making a commission. The realtor expressed surprise that someone was willing to offer full price for a place in *that* neighborhood in *this* market but suggested that they not look a gift horse in the mouth. Ross sat there as she called the prospective buyer, who said he would meet them at the condo tomorrow morning. Jamie hung up the phone and told Ross that, if all went well, they could sign the papers in the afternoon and the money would be transferred into his bank account within five business days.

His cellphone worked here, but when he tried to call Jill, all he got was static. It was the same thing when he placed a call to Lita, and he gave it up. He'd be back the day after tomorrow anyway.

He stayed overnight at his parents' house, after meeting his friends for dinner. Alex was moving to Salt Lake City in two weeks, so they had an early going-away party at Yossarian's, a burger joint/bar in Tempe that several of them had frequented during their college days at ASU. It was still popular with students, though the clientele ran more toward jocks these days, and they were forced to leave early before a drunk and belligerent Trent got into a fight with a pair of steroid abusers from the Sun Devils. Patrick and Trent had carpooled, and while neither of them had brought along a designated driver, Patrick was closer to sober and got behind the wheel.

"Again?" Trent called through the open window. "Tomorrow night?"

Ross laughed. "We'll see."

After Trent and Patrick left, with J.D. and his latest girlfriend following immediately after, Alex asked Ross if he wanted to meet for lunch.

"Sure," Ross said. "If I'm finished with all the real estate stuff in time."

"Because I have a proposition for you."

"I'm not moving to Salt Lake City."

Alex laughed. "We'll talk. See you tomorrow. Garcia's. Noon."

"I'll be there. Or I'll call if I won't."

It was after nine when he arrived at his parents' house in Chandler, and, to his surprise, they were still awake. They seemed to be waiting for him, and from the expression on his dad's face, it was not to offer him a warm welcome and hearty congratulations. He ignored those signs, however, overlooked the restrained greeting, and told his parents that the sale was a lock, only signatures were needed to make it official. Sitting down on the couch, he talked about how it was nice to see his friends again, and how it was too bad Alex was moving to Salt Lake City.

That was his father's cue to jump in. "Why can't you get a job like that?"

Ross knew what this was about. And he was proved right as his dad began to lecture him about staying in Magdalena, while his mom nodded her agreement. They didn't have a counterculture bone in their bodies and, to them, living on his cousin's organic ranch was tantamount to joining a commune. This was nonsense, his father told him, and he needed to stop playing at being some sort of hippie and start seriously looking for a job. Ross didn't bother to remind his dad that he *had* been job hunting. For over a year. And despite the fact that, until he'd been laid off, he'd been far more successful than either his brother or sister, not to mention far more stable, he'd gotten much less support from his parents than his siblings had, either monetarily or emotionally.

But his parents saw him as some fuzzy-brained freeloader who had no desire to work.

Ross walked out in the middle of his father's lecture, not wanting to argue. Ignoring his dad's demands to "Get back here! Right now!", he closed and locked the door to the hall bathroom and took a long, lingering shower. By the time he got out, as he'd hoped, his parents were in the bedroom, their door closed. He didn't know whether they were asleep or not, and he didn't care. He was just glad they weren't in the living room. His mom hadn't bothered to make up the couch for him, so he got a sheet, pillow and blanket from the linen closet and did it himself, making as little noise as possible so they wouldn't come out and lecture him again.

He fell asleep watching David Letterman.

There was silence at the breakfast table in the morning. He tried to smooth things over by talking about how he'd be in pretty good financial shape once the condo sale went through, but his father would have none of that. "What I was trying to tell you," his dad said, "was that you need to stop pretending to be a farmer and get back to looking for a job. Things change fast in the engineering field, and you've already been away from it for a year."

Ross met his gaze. "You think I don't know that?"

"Then why aren't you out looking for work?"

"I am, Dad. Every day. My resume is on about a million sites, I keep up with openings and hiring calls…"

"You can't do everything through a computer. You have to be out there, pounding the pavement, showing your face, going to personnel departments so companies get to know you."

"Sure. And I'll put on my cufflinks and my hamburg—"

"Don't you get smart with me, young man!"

"I'm not looking for a job in 1950, Dad. This is the way it's done today."

"You're lazy. That's your problem. I don't know why you're out there on a farm instead of here in the city—"

Ross leaned across the table. "You want to know why? Because I was out of money and couldn't afford to keep my condo. I almost had to walk away from it and let the bank foreclose, but now, fortunately, I can actually sell it. Lita offered me a place to live. You didn't, Dad. Neither did Alma or Rick, despite all I've done for them. You're all a bunch of… Forget it." He stood. "I'm leaving."

His mother was scowling at him. "Don't you talk to your father that way!"

She was still lecturing him as he walked out the kitchen door and into the living room. His one suitcase was already packed, and he picked it up, shouted out a terse "Goodbye!" and headed out to his car.

He drove.

He had nowhere to go and no place to be until he was to meet Jamie Wong and the buyer at his old condo at ten, so he ended up at a McDonald's in Mesa, where he sipped refill after refill of coffee as he read each useless section of *USA Today* and *The Arizona Republic*. Where was he going to sleep tonight? he wondered. He didn't want to go back to his parents' house. And he certainly wasn't going to call his brother or sister. Could he make it back to Magdalena? Maybe. But he was thinking of seeing his friends again this evening—who knew when he might see them next?—and he decided to splurge and stay at a cheap motel. He had money coming in. He deserved to celebrate.

Ross arrived at the condominium before Jamie Wong and the buyer. He still had a key and let himself in. The place smelled musty and dusty; the air felt warm and heavy. He walked from room to room, opening the shades as he did so. The condo looked bigger than he recalled, partially due to the lack of furniture, partly because he was used to the much smaller confines of the L-Bar D's guest house. He walked back out to the kitchen, admiring the abundant counterspace.

There was a knock on the doorframe, and Ross turned to see a smiling Jamie Wong standing on the welcome mat with a squat heavyset man: Burt Abbey, the man who wanted to buy his condo. Ross had left the door open, and he waved to the two of them. "Come on in."

He disliked Abbey on sight.

These things happened. It wouldn't affect the sale, but it was a good thing that the realtor was there to act as a go-between because, despite the polite smiles, he could tell that the feeling was mutual, and if there were only the two of them negotiating, the deal would probably have fallen apart instantly. As it was, their natural antipathy kept the meeting short, and after a cursory walk-through and the realtor's point-by-point reading of an inspector's report, papers were signed, and the three of them parted ways, with Ross promising to stop by Jamie's office later in the afternoon to finish things up.

He drove to Garcia's and into the parking lot the same time as Alex, who honked and waved. The two of them pulled next to each other and walked into the already crowded restaurant, where a slutty looking waitress led them to a table next to a group of elderly women. They'd been talking about nothing in particular, rehashing their criticism of Trent's stupidity from last night, but as soon as the chips and salsa arrived, Alex got down to business.

"I've been in contact with the floor mat company," he said. "Getting up to speed with their systems and what have you. I found out that they're planning to expand and, get this, start making mats for railroads and airline cockpits. They outsource all of their machinery design, oversight and implementation, and what I was thinking—if I can get them to go for it—is that you could look over their needs assessment. From your own base, online. You could check in with their people, look into available equipment and…consult. I know you don't know anything about floor mat manufacturing, but the plant retrofitting's actually not all that different from the Boeing project we worked on, and I figure you could adapt pretty easily. You know how to do this. And you're good at it.

"Obviously, it wouldn't be a real job. There's no benefits or anything. You'd be a contract worker for this one assignment. But it might lead to something else. At the very least, it would keep you in the game, allow you to update your resume."

"That'd be great," Ross admitted.

"There's no guarantee, and the pay might be shit, but if I can convince them, can I tell them you're interested?"

"Sure."

"Then email me your resume when you get back. As soon as I hear something, yay *or* nay, I'll let you know."

"Thanks," Ross said gratefully. "I owe you one."

"Don't thank me yet. But, yes, you do owe me one."

They both laughed.

Since he was in the city and had the opportunity, he shopped at Target after lunch, picking up some necessities, then hit a few computer and electronics stores. He checked into a motel off Black Canyon Highway, then watched TV in his room for awhile before meeting his friends for dinner. This time, they didn't go out. Instead, they hung out at Patrick's place, where they ate Taco Bell takeout and played X-Box games.

In the morning, he woke early, scarfed down some muffins and bagels from the motel's free continental breakfast, then got a cup of coffee to go, and hit the road.

He made it to Magdalena by noon.

It felt good to be back. The ranch seemed like home to him now, and there was comfort in the sight of his small shack with the desert stretching out behind it. Lita had prepared lunch—ostrich burgers—and he joined her and Dave in the kitchen of the Big House, where he ate two burgers gratefully.

"How're the hens?" Ross asked.

Dave shook his head, discouraged. "They still haven't been laying well. I don't know what's wrong. Honey production's off, too. I'm not sure if there are environmental factors we're just not registering, or…I don't know."

"Ironic, isn't it?" Lita said when Dave excused himself to go to the bathroom. "Now that we've inherited money, our whole operation here's falling apart. A week ago, this would have ruined us. Now, I guess, we can just buy some new hens. Bees, too, I suppose." She shook her head. "It's weird the way things turn out."

Dave returned. He'd finished eating, so he didn't sit back down. He nodded toward Ross. "I was going to go out and do the rounds again, see if I could find some more. Want to come with me?"

Ross stood up from the table. "Sure."

Lita sighed in mock exasperation. "I guess I'll do the dishes. A woman's work is never done."

Ross accompanied Dave outside. They headed over to the chicken coop and the yard, but neither of them found any eggs, and both of them were assailed by angry, overly aggressive birds. It was Dave who finally swung his basket, hitting a hen and knocking the animal over. "Let's get out of here," he said.

They both exited through the coop after hanging their baskets on hooks. "I think they're getting worse," Dave said, discouraged.

"Do you think it's some kind of disease or..." He could think of no other alternatives since he knew next to nothing about raising chickens.

"Come here," Dave said. He led Ross around the side of the house to the cellar, checking to make sure Lita wasn't watching them through one of the windows before opening the cellar door. "I want to show you something. I haven't told Lita anything about it, so I'd appreciate it if you kept this to yourself."

Ross was intrigued. "Sure thing." He followed Dave down the steps. There was a foul odor in the enclosed space, a fetid stench that did not decrease in rankness with the opening of the bottom door and the letting in of fresh air. "Oh my God!" Ross pinched his nostrils shut, gagging.

"I know," Dave said, holding a hand over his own nose. "I put a couple of air fresheners down here yesterday, but they just got swallowed up. Don't worry, you'll get used to it in a few minutes."

Ross didn't think so, and he didn't want to be down here for even *one* minute, but clearly something was up, and he was anxious to see what Dave had to show him.

Just inside the doorway, along the left side of the wall, was a shelf on which sat various tools and jars. Dave picked up a ball peen hammer and carried it to the table in the center of the room, where oddly shaped, sized and colored eggs sat in a box. Next to the box, on the wooden tabletop, were scattered pieces of broken eggshell and what looked like dried blood.

"Watch," Dave said. Gingerly—

nervously?

—he picked up a large egg from the box and placed it carefully on the table, holding it in place with a finger to make sure it didn't roll as he tapped the egg lightly with the hammer, cracking it. He stepped back as the crack grew of its own accord. Within seconds, a tiny claw had punched its way out of the shell, and a moment later the shell was in pieces, a slimy black lizardy creature writhing amidst the fragments. It had a thin body, clawed appendages and an oversized head with beady red eyes and a permanently open mouth.

The hideous thing stared up at them, screaming.

Dave hit it hard with the hammer, smashing its head.

A smell like raw sewage emanated from the blood and brains that spilled out. The horrible stench in the cellar grew stronger, and Ross gagged, staggering back. Dave was gagging, too, and seconds later, both of them were bolting up the stairs. Miraculously, neither of them threw up when they reached the top, although each of them stood in place, bent over, breathing heavily and gulping in the fresh air.

Dave glanced over at the house to make sure Lita wasn't watching them. He exhaled heavily, straightened. "The thing is," he said, and Ross heard real fear in his voice, "they're all different. As far as I can tell. No two seem to be alike. I discovered it yesterday morning when I brought the six eggs I'd collected down to the cellar. One of them broke open immediately, and an insect came out. Not any insect that I've ever seen before, but kind of a wasp crossed with a scorpion. A big one. It came at me, and I batted it down and squashed it on the floor with my boot. Scared the hell out of me. But I cracked open another egg, wanting to see if it was the same. It wasn't. It was a freakish little thing that looked like a rat's head on top of an overgrown silverfish. And it made a sound like a baby crying. This morning, I picked one at random, checked again, and it was kind of a snake. Only…it kind of wasn't." There was a long pause. "My chickens are giving birth to monsters."

The words hung in the air.

"I don't know why this is happening," Dave said, genuinely confused. "Or how it could."

He looked to Ross as if for answers, but Ross had none to give. For some reason, he found himself thinking of that black thing he'd seen flying through the night sky. And Jill's missing dog. And the little girl at the farmer's market.

Dick suck mushroom! Pickaninny pie!"

Jill was right. There *were* a lot of crazy things happening around here lately.

"So what do we do now?" Ross asked.

"I don't know."

"What about…?" He gestured toward the open cellar door.

"I'll take care of it."

"What did you do with—"

"The other ones? I ended up burying them. At first, I thought about taking the bodies to the vet to see if he could figure out what they were and how they got into my hens' eggs, but I found out he left town, he's gone. I thought about burning the bodies, but with the smell that bad, the smoke might be toxic. Besides, I didn't want Lita to find out about it right now. It's…a stressful time. So I buried them out past that tree there. Deep. So the goat wouldn't try to eat them."

"And that's what you're going to do with this one?"

He shrugged. "I guess. But I'm saving those other eggs. I need to show them to somebody. Maybe one of the other ranchers. See if they know anything about it, if it's happening to them, too."

"So should I…?" Ross gestured toward the house.

"Keep her occupied. Keep her in the house. Keep her away from the window." Dave sighed. "Give me twenty minutes." Bracing himself, taking a deep breath, he once again started down the cellar steps.

Ross headed for the house.

FOURTEEN

Lita hadn't seen Darla since New Year's Eve, so she dropped by her friend's house on her way to the store. Jackass McDaniels was there, repairing the Ingrams' rain gutters, and she called out to him as she walked up to the front door. She should probably have Dave check their own rain gutters, Lita thought. It had been a mild winter, but that didn't guarantee anything, and by the time the monsoons rolled around this summer, they'd be too busy with gardening and ranch work to take care of small details like the gutters.

Jackass waved down at her from his perch on the ladder. "Hey there, Lita!"

"Hey yourself!" she called back.

"Still got your freeloading cousin living off you?"

She smiled, shaking her head. "*Now* I understand how you got your name!"

He laughed, and she waved as Darla let her into the house.

Ordinarily, Darla was grateful for visitors. As a stay-at-home mom in a family with one drivable vehicle, an old intermittently working Ford pickup, her options for social interaction were limited, so she talked on the phone a lot, was diligent about updating her Facebook page, and was always very happy when someone dropped by. But today she seemed nervous and unusually taciturn, almost as though she resented Lita's presence and wanted her to leave. It was a very uncomfortable vibe, and rather than accept the perfunctory offer to sit down, Lita lied and said that she was in a hurry and had just popped in to say hi.

"Oh," Darla said, and did not elaborate.

"I'm sorry I haven't called since we got back from Las Vegas, but we've been really busy, and after what happened to Dave's parents, it's been like an emotional roller coaster."

Darla was staring out the window as though looking for someone. She nodded absently. "Mmm-hmm."

"I guess I should've called before coming over," Lita said, edging toward the door. "Maybe I'll come back at a more convenient time. I have to get going anyway."

"Okay," Darla said.

Outside, Lita waved again to Jackass, who was still on the ladder. He, at least, seemed the same as always, and that made her feel better as she got in the car and drove away. On impulse, she decided to stop by JoAnn's and see what she thought about Darla's odd behavior. JoAnn lived close enough that she often saw Darla on a daily basis, so she'd probably have more insight into their friend's state of mind. And since this was her day off, she should be able to check in on Darla and get back to Lita pretty quickly.

She turned down the narrow lane that ended at JoAnn's ramshackle house, thinking, not for the first time, that if someone ever opened up a coffeeshop in town, that person would make a fortune. Magdalena needed a place where people could gather and talk that wasn't a bar.

Weston's truck was gone, but JoAnn's beat-up Jeep was in the carport, and Lita parked right behind it. JoAnn was certainly in a good mood. She came out of the house before Lita had gotten out of the car, grinning widely, country music blaring loudly from the open door behind her. "Lita!"

"Hey." She tried on a smile, but it didn't fit right.

"You headin' to the market?"

"Actually, I am. But I thought I'd stop by and see how—"

"That's great! Think you can give me a ride? I need to pick up a few things and Weston don't want me drivin' until he gets that front tire fixed on the Jeep. There's a spare on there now, but it's bald, and he don't trust it."

"Uh, sure…" Lita said.

"That's great! I'll be right back!" She ran into the house, shut the music off, and came flying out seconds later, purse in hand. "Let's get outta here!"

Slightly bewildered by her friend's manic energy, Lita got back in the car and started the engine.

"I was gonna walk, but since you showed up and were goin' there anyway…"

"No problem," Lita said.

"So. How are things with you?" JoAnn turned in the seat to face her and stared, waiting for an answer.

"Uh, fine. But I stopped by Darla's before I came over, and she *didn't* seem so fine. I was wondering what's up with her. Have you noticed anything…strange?"

"I ain't seen Darla much, actually. Been too busy. Weston has about all the jobs he can handle, and I been promoted at work. This weekend, we're actually buyin' a new freezer! Can you believe it? I think it's gonna be a good year."

"Yeah? I'm glad to hear it. But I'm worried about Darla." *And you, too,* Lita thought. "She didn't say anything, but something's wrong. I was wondering if you could look in on her. Or give her a call. Today, if you can. Then call me and tell me what you think."

JoAnn nodded, but…

But Lita didn't think she would do it.

That was a weird thought. Had JoAnn and Darla had a falling out? Maybe they had and, subconsciously, she was picking up on the signals.

No, Lita decided. It was something else. Both of her friends were acting strange, and she watched and listened to JoAnn as they shopped at the market, looking for some kind of clue, some indication that would tell her what was going on.

Back at home, Dave and Ross were acting oddly, too. Almost conspiratorial. Was she just being paranoid? Her period was due any time and her hormones were swirling, so it wasn't out of the question, but she didn't think that was the case.

What was the case, then?

She didn't know. The entire day was crazy. Everything was all topsy turvy, and she felt anxious and unsettled. She didn't want to confront Dave—he was having a difficult enough time right now without her piling on—so she cornered Ross in the yard, quizzing him. He said Dave was worried about the chickens and the eggs they were laying. She already knew that, and while she didn't think Ross was lying, she still had the sense that he was keeping something from her.

That night, in bed, Dave was more charged up than he had been in a long time. They'd been in a lull lately, even before he'd gotten the news about his parents, but tonight he came roaring back. He felt bigger and harder inside her than he ever had before, and while that was great, he pounded away with such ferocity that it hurt, and afterward her crotch was so sore that it was painful even to roll over and go to sleep.

But sleep she did, eventually, and she dreamed that all of her friends and family were planning a surprise birthday party for her. Only…when she walked into the room and they jumped out and yelled "Surprise!", they were standing behind a black birthday cake with black candles, and the smoke from the candles coalesced above their heads into the shape of a terrible horned demon.

FIFTEEN

DYLAN DIDN'T REMEMBER MR. NOODLE.
    Darla ate dinner silently as Tom and Dylan talked enthusiastically about who they thought would be in the playoffs this year. She felt sad. When he was younger, she and her son had done everything together: making beds, making lunch, dusting the furniture, reading books, playing games. She'd been there for every moment of his life, had suffered through *Teletubbies* and *Barney*, had sung along with *Sesame Street* songs and laughed with him at the slapstick antics of his favorite character, Mr. Noodle, on *Elmo's World*. Today, she'd discovered that he didn't even remember Mr. Noodle. It had come up casually in a conversation, and when he'd stared at her blankly after she'd made the reference, Darla realized for the first time that all of those special moments they'd shared, all of those memories she thought they'd been building, were

completely one-sided. *She* had memories. He didn't. And she had never felt so depressed in her life.

Still, she looked at him across the table and realized how lucky she was, how lucky she and Tom both were. They had a great kid, a wonderful family, and God had blessed them. It was churlish of her to worry about and obsess over such a small and ultimately insignificant matter as Mr. Noodle. But finding out that he'd forgotten about the *Elmo's World* character was symptomatic of a larger realization: Dylan was growing up.

Darla experienced a profound sense of loss. They'd done so many things together, but there were so many things they *hadn't* done, things he was too old to do now, and she wished that every year of his childhood could last five years so they would have time to do it *all.*

Now that he was ten, he was moving away from her emotionally, toward Tom, and while that was the way it should be, she still didn't have to like it.

In fact, there were a lot of things she didn't like.

She'd found herself distracted lately. Yesterday, for example, she was pretty sure Lita had stopped by to see her, but when she tried to recall the visit, nothing came to mind. She could not for the life of her remember why Lita had come over or what they had talked about or how long she had stayed.

Something was wrong. Something had been wrong for awhile now. Things had not been right since…

She didn't want to think about it.

Except she could think of almost nothing else.

Darla had never been religious, but she was seriously considering going to Father Ramos' church. He seemed like a good man, a nice man, and from what everyone said, he had a handle on what was going on here. Maybe he could explain to her what was happening.

Explain what was happening?

That wasn't really why she was thinking of going to church, was it?

No.

She'd had the fear of God put into her.

She'd heard that phrase all her life—*the fear of God*—but until now had not really known what it meant. The New Year's party had changed that, and everything that had happened since was just further confirmation. Like the Wizard of Oz, God was great and terrible, and those who incurred His wrath, as they all had, were doomed to suffer His punishments.

Tom and Dylan were laughing at some sports joke, and she smiled with them, though she had no idea what was so funny. She felt sad again, looking at her boy, the fear abating for a moment. Everything seemed to be falling apart, and she wished it was six years ago and Dylan was four, and that damn New Year's Eve party had never happened.

Weekends were boring.

Dylan would have preferred to attend school seven days a week. It was a long bus ride to Willcox, but it was worth it because other kids were there. He had friends at school, other boys he could play with. Here at home, he was pretty much stuck with his parents, and while he loved them and all, they weren't that much fun to hang around, and he usually spent a lot of time by himself.

There *were* other kids in Magdalena and the surrounding area, but not that many and none his own age.

Often, when he tired of playing computer games and his dad was too busy to throw the ball around and there was nothing worthwhile on TV and he wasn't in the mood to watch a DVD, Dylan ended up hiking by himself near the M mountain. He didn't know if the mountain had a real name, but that was what the people in town called it, and he had actually gone up to the M before and walked around the giant letter. He'd even sat in the middle of it. From down by his house, the M looked like it was made of white powder, like the stuff they used to mark off a football field or draw the lines between bases, but when you got up close, it was actually made up of boulders painted white and arranged in the shape of the letter.

The trails on the mountain branched off in seemingly infinite directions, and he wasn't sure if some of them were animal paths or if they were all manmade. Sometimes he saw other people hiking, couples mostly, adults, but he liked it better when he was by himself and there was no one else in sight.

Like today.

Dylan walked up a narrow switchback trail he'd never been on before. There were hoofprints on the hardpacked dirt, though no shoeprints other than his own, as far as he could tell. He should have brought some bottled water—his mom was always on him about that—but the day was pretty cool and he didn't plan to be gone that long.

From up ahead, behind a large outcropping of rock that looked almost like a miniature castle, Dylan heard what sounded like two kids talking. One of them laughed at something the other one said, and Dylan's heart sped up with what could have been excitement, could have been apprehension. For this had the potential to go either way. The kids might be happy to have someone new to play with and welcome him to their hideout, or they might resent the fact that he'd discovered their secret spot and start throwing rocks at him.

He approached cautiously, not sure whether to announce his presence.

The boulders that made up the outcropping were larger than they'd appeared from further back, and he could see spaces between them that looked almost like passageways. *Cool*, he thought.

"Hey!" Dylan called out. "Is anyone there?"

He knew there was, and figured he could judge by the response he received whether he should continue on. But the kids ignored him, kept talking and laughing amongst themselves, and he realized that he could not make out a single word they were saying. That was odd. This close, he should have been able to hear them more clearly, and he wondered if the reason neither of them had responded to his shout out was because they couldn't hear *him*. Sound did strange things when you were up here.

The path ended at the edge of the outcropping, and he stood next to a pillar-like boulder, yelling into the space between it and the cliffside. "Hello!"

The other kids did not respond, although they both burst out laughing before continuing with their conversation. They were messing with him, Dylan thought, and the idea so annoyed him that he picked up a couple of pebbles from the ground and slid between the rocks as quietly as he could, intending to scare those brats within an inch of their lives. If he'd had the ability to do a deep voice, he would have pretended to be an adult, but since that option was out, he thought he'd throw the pebbles up at the cliff, above where they were, and fool them into thinking there was an avalanche.

It was a good plan, and he stopped, peeked out from between the boulders at a flat open space surrounded by tall rock, and saw—

—no one.

The kids were laughing. He could hear their voices coming from the small area directly in front of him, but there was no sign of anyone around. He stepped out, looked in each direction, thinking that his ears had been playing tricks on him, that maybe they'd detected his presence and were hiding between other boulders, waiting to jump out at him. But, no, despite the voices, he was the only one here.

Except…

Except at the other end of the flat space there were two mounds of mud, each about two feet high.

That was weird, he thought. How could there be mud here? It hadn't rained recently, and there were no ponds or streams nearby.

The mound on the right shifted, a section of mud sliding off to reveal what appeared to be the decaying body of a bobcat beneath. The dead animal's blackened mouth opened and closed, and Dylan saw that the movement matched the nonsensical words spoken by one of the voices.

Mud fell from the mound on the left, exposing a dead bird encased in the center of the wet dirt, and the bird's rotted head jiggled up and down in time to the second voice's responding laughter.

He'd been confused when he'd stepped out from between the rocks, but now he was confused and *scared*. Swiveling around, intending to retreat and run back the way he'd come, Dylan was confronted by a pack of small creatures hopping out from the passageway through which he'd arrived. They resembled tiny kangaroos more than anything else, tiny kangaroos with rat faces and lizard skin, and they screamed angrily at him in high-pitched voices far too loud for their size.

Behind him, the animal corpses in melting mud laughed uproariously.

Dylan started to cry. He still had the pebbles in his hand, and he threw them one-by-one at the small creatures hopping toward him, but he missed every time, and one of the little monsters jumped directly in front of him, screeching. Even through his tears, he could see the look of hatred on the tiny rat face, see the sharp thin fangs in the wide-open mouth. Sobbing in fear and frustration, he called out "Mom!" at the top of his lungs.

It was an instinctive reaction, a plea for help that had no hope of being answered. His mom was not here, and she would not be able to hear him from this far away. No one in town could hear him, and he suddenly realized that he could die up here and it would be weeks before anyone found his body.

Turning, he ran across the open area, between the laughing mounds of mud, and attempted to climb the boulders at the opposite end. The rocks were high with no footholds, and he scrambled in vain, trying to get up and out. There were no other paths save the one that had led him here, and his attempts to climb grew more frantic as he heard the approaching screams of those hopping creatures.

"Mom!" he cried again.

One of them leaped onto his back, claws digging into his skin and holding on. The pain was unbearable and overwhelming, unlike anything he'd ever experienced. It felt as though he was being cut with razors, and he flailed about, hitting at his back, trying to get it off, lurching from side to side, screaming so loudly that his throat burned.

Someone somewhere was calling his name, but he couldn't focus on that because more of those hopping monsters were jumping onto him, and he instinctively turned around, shoving his back against the boulder, trying to squish them, trying to kill them, trying to get them off, but they held on and dug in, slicing open his flesh, and he saw more of them coming, hopping happily across the open space toward him, fangs bared.

One of them either bit or clawed open his right ankle, and he collapsed on the ground, that leg no longer able to support him.

He knew he was going to die. He was still screaming from the pain, still crying from the fear, but inside himself, beneath it all, was a strange stillness that allowed him for his last few moments of life to see everything as though it was happening to someone else. He heard his name called again and knew this time that it came from the rotted bobcat encased in mud.

Next to it, in the other mound of mud, the corpse of the bird laughed like a boy.

And then there was nothing but pain.

SIXTEEN

J ILL POURED HERSELF A CUP OF GREEN TEA, POPPED IN AN OLD
Tori Amos CD, took out a pencil and opened up her sketchbook.

She hadn't felt much like painting since meeting Ross, although she did not think the two had anything to do with each other; the timing was completely coincidental as far as she was concerned. She'd continued to sketch, however, and she paused for a moment to glance over her recent work, frowning as she turned the pages. Now that she looked at them, the subjects of her drawings were all sort of…gruesome.

There was a detailed rendering of an eviscerated lizard she had found on her doorstep; a depiction of a dead child inspired by a recent news story; a close-up of a bloody eyeball; several examples of grotesquely deformed genitalia, and a fantastical landscape populated by hairy monsters recalled from childhood nightmares.

Unusual, to say the least, but Jill had never been one to censor or second guess herself, and, turning to a blank page, she started to sketch something new. An instinctive artist, she liked to draw whatever came to her, without thinking about it or planning it out, and this time she found herself penciling in a dark room filled with cobwebs and farming implements. She worked from the outside in, the opposite of her usual method, sketching the room, its walls and roof, leaving an empty white space at the center. Whatever was supposed to fill that hole was the focal point of the drawing, was the reason she had started the sketch, but now that she was here, she was afraid to continue on. She had no idea what she would draw if she kept going, but she was afraid to find out, and she quickly flipped the page, starting instead on a purposefully benign picture: the mountains visible through the window behind her house.

The CD ended, and for several seconds the house was silent save for the scratching of her pencil on paper. Then, from the kitchen, came the familiar sound of paws padding across linoleum, accompanied by the equally familiar jangle of dogtag on collar.

"Puka?" Jill said. She stopped drawing, put down her pad and pencil, and hurried out to the kitchen.

Where the back door was open.

And Puka, her golden retriever, was walking in a circle in the middle of the floor.

She almost didn't recognize him. Most of his fur had fallen out, and what remained were spiky tufts. One of his eyes had been burned out of his head, leaving only a blackened cauterized socket, and the other rolled around uncontrollably, while, beneath it, bone showed through an exposed nasal cavity.

"Puka!" she cried, rushing to the dog and falling to her knees next to him. How had this happened? And when? She hadn't seen her missing pet since he'd swooped in and taken the crow that had crashed into her window, but he'd looked fine then. Had some psycho been torturing him? Had he been involved in a series of unique and unfortunate accidents?

She tried to hug him, but he backed away from her, growled, then sped out the door.

How the dog could see with one eye gone and the other rolling around randomly in its socket she had no idea, but he did not bump into the cupboard or the wall, and he sped surefootedly through the brush away from the house as she frantically called his name. "Puka! Puka!"

She almost called someone—Ross was the first person she thought about, interestingly—but the dog was already out of sight, and no one would be able to find him and bring him back. There were tears in her eyes as she realized that this might be the last time she ever saw Puka. In the shape he was in, the odds that he would be able to survive on his own in the wild were virtually nil.

How did he get to be in the shape he was in? she wondered. What had happened to him?

And how had he gotten into the house? That door had been closed and locked since yesterday afternoon. If she hadn't opened it, who had?

Jill suddenly wished she *had* called someone. What if the same sicko who'd tortured Puka had brought him back home and purposely placed him in the kitchen?

Even if it were possible, she was sure the person wasn't in the house. She'd walked past every room, and she would have seen him or heard him. Still, just in case, she took a cleaver from the knife rack and opened every closet and cupboard in the house, even those too small for someone to hide inside. As she'd known, the rooms were all empty, there was no one there, and she locked the doors, taking a moment to peek out each of the windows to make sure she saw no one unfamiliar anywhere near the house. Most of her neighbors were out, but Shan Cooper was home—she saw his battered El Camino in the carport—and she gave him a quick call to find out if he'd seen anything unusual. He hadn't (he sounded as though he'd either just woken up or was drunk), but she warned him that there was a possible dognapper in the area and told him to keep his eyes open.

Shan had several bulldogs that he let run wild, and he was outraged at the prospect. "I see anyone I don't know, I'll shoot the bastard's balls off. That'll show 'em."

"It's probably not anything," she said, trying to calm him down.

"I'll shoot 'em!"

It might have been a mistake to call Shan—she wouldn't be surprised to hear the echoing reports of his shotgun throughout the afternoon as he blasted away at shadows and imaginary sightings—but at least she felt a little less alone. Jill walked back to where she'd left her pad and pencil, planning to continue where she'd left off. But she couldn't get back into a landscape mode, and when she flipped the page and looked again at her first drawing, she didn't like the empty space in the center of the picture.

Putting the sketchpad away, she decided to start work early today. She logged onto the telemarketing command center, signed in, called up the script and first list of numbers to dial, clipped on her headset and got down to business.

But in her mind she kept seeing the nearly bald Puka, one eye gone, one eye wild, walking around in a circle in the center of the kitchen, and as she tried to convince people to protect their identities and buy credit card insurance she felt cold.

❧

Ross arrived at Jill's house over twenty minutes late.

She'd invited him for dinner, and he'd promised to be there by six, but things had come up. Shortly before five, he'd gotten an email from National Floor Mats. As Alex had predicted, he'd been offered a work-for-hire job, helping put together a needs assessment for the company's proposed expansion, and while the consulting position was only for six months, the pay was decent and, as his friend had pointed out, it would boost his resume with more current credentials, He'd immediately emailed back his acceptance, then called Alex to thank him for his help.

By the time he got off the phone, it was nearly six. On the way to her place, already running late, he'd encountered an improbable accident: a fenderbender involving a very masculine looking woman in a beat-up pickup truck, and that internet mogul's model wife, who was driving a Cadillac SUV. The vehicles were blocking the narrow road, and the two women were standing toe-to-toe in the dirt, lit by headlights, arguing and one push away from a fight. It was all Ross could do to get them to calm down, exchange insurance information and finally agree to move on.

"You're a witness!" the model yelled at Ross as she got into her SUV. "I'm calling you for my court case!"

The pickup driver shook her head. "Crazy stupid bitch."

Ross got back in his own car.

To top it off, his cell phone was dead—again—so he couldn't even call Jill and tell her that he would be late.

As a result, dinner was ready and lukewarm by the time he got to her house. He expected Jill to be mad at him, and wouldn't have blamed her if she was, but she didn't seem to mind his tardiness and greeted him with a big kiss. She seemed a little on edge as she led him into the kitchen, and he found out why when they started eating and she told him about the reappearance of her dog.

"Here in the kitchen?" Ross said incredulously.

"And then he took off." Jill took a bite of her stir-fried chicken, was silent for a moment. "I still don't know how the door got open. It was closed. And locked. Puka certainly couldn't open it."

"Did you call the police? *Are* there police around here to call?"

"No and no."

Ross frowned. "What happens if there's a crime? You have to be able to call someone."

"The county sheriff, I guess. They're the ones looking for Dylan Ingram. You heard about that, didn't you?"

Ross nodded grimly. "His mom's one of Lita's friends."

"Do you think he's…?"

"I don't know what happened to him. Hopefully, they'll find him and he'll be okay. I guess the searchers told his mom that last year they rescued a boy who'd gotten lost in the desert and was out there by himself for over a week. In the summer. So if he's just lost, there's a good chance he's still okay."

"*If* he's just lost."

The implication of that hung in the air.

Jill sighed. "I'm not sure I like it here anymore. I'm not sure I feel safe."

"You can come back with me tonight."

"It's not just tonight. And it's not just this house. It's… Magdalena."

His pulse was racing. Was this his cue? Should he invite her to come back with him to Phoenix, suggest that they move in together? Probably not. It was too early, too fast. But while he hadn't planned to leave anytime soon, eventually he'd be returning to the real world, and if he could get her to come with him, that would be amazing.

The moment passed.

"I'm sorry," she said. "I'm just jittery after what happened."

"Understandable."

Jill smiled. "So how are things in your neck of the woods?"

He would have told her the truth, would have described those monsters being hatched from chickens' eggs, but she was in a fragile state and he didn't want to alarm her any more than she already was. So he lied and told her everything was fine, then switched the subject to the meal they were eating, which was outrageously delicious. She told him how it was a recipe adapted from something she'd seen on *Iron Chef*, talked about her love of food, described her latest pastry concoction: a jigsaw-puzzle cookie that could be used up to four times without breaking.

They shared one of the jigsaw cookies for dessert—a four-piece puzzle that looked like the statue of liberty, and that they took apart and put together again before eating—and though he thought she'd mellowed out a bit, he could tell from Jill's body language as they walked out to the living room afterward that she was still nervous. She tried to smile. "I was going to give you a break, and just stay in tonight and watch a movie. I even picked it out—" She held up a DVD of *Monty Python and the Holy Grail*.

"Good choice," he said admiringly.

"—but I want to get out of the house. Do you mind if we take a walk?"

"I've been looking forward to it," he told her.

"Really?"

"Well...I've been *expecting* it. That's almost the same, right?"

She laughed, a real laugh, and slapped him lightly on the shoulder. "Get walking, buddy."

They didn't head back toward town this time. Instead, Jill led him down a road that led in the opposite direction, further into the desert. They both had flashlights but didn't really need them;

the moon was out, the sky was clear and the rocky land before them was bathed in a bluish glow.

"My mom called this afternoon," Jill said as they strolled. "I almost told her what happened, but at the last minute, I didn't. I didn't want to worry her. Isn't that weird, though? I was going to tell my mom because I wanted her help. Here I am, an adult, and for some reason, I still think that my mom, who isn't even here, who lives two hundred miles away, can somehow save me, can tell me what to do to solve my problems." She shook her head. "Maybe I'm not an adult."

"I know you've mentioned your mom before," he said, "but what about your dad? Is he...?"

"He's alive."

"But you're not close."

They walked for a moment without speaking. Finally, Jill took a deep breath. "When I was in high school, I worked at this clothing store in the mall. The other girls warned me the very first day about things I might encounter. They'd recently found a small webcam in one of the dressing rooms and the guy had been arrested. They also told me about this one pervert who would call up and make obscene phone calls. I'd been there around a month, I guess, when it happened to me. This man called up, and I answered the phone. 'Do you like big cocks?' he asked. 'Do you like to suck big dirty cocks?'

"It was my dad. I recognized his voice. I hung up right away, but I never answered the phone again. I always made sure someone else did it. I didn't turn him in, either. I didn't tell anyone, not even my mom, even though I wanted to.

"About a month later, he called the store again when I wasn't there, and I guess someone told the police, and they were able to trace back the call." She exhaled deeply. "They arrested my dad, and my mom divorced him, and I don't know what happened to him after that, and I don't care."

Ross didn't know what to say.

"The thing is, he knew I worked at that store. He knew I'd just gotten a job there. And I always wondered if he knew it was me when I answered the phone, if he *wanted* to say those things to *me*."

"Jesus."

"So, no, my dad and I aren't close."

There was nothing to be said after that, and they continued on in silence. The night was chilly, but he knew that was not what was making her shiver, and he put his arm around Jill's shoulder, drawing her to him. Her hand snaked around his waist, and they walked that way for awhile.

Ahead, on the road before them, was a big black lump. Training their lights on the object, they saw that it was a cow.

Only it had...*changed*.

Jill's hand clutched his arm tightly as they beheld the sight. While the animal appeared at first glance to be dead, it was not. It was moving. Possessing no legs, it was pulling its bulk across the dirt by inching forward like a grossly overweight and wrongly shaped worm. The two of them stayed where they were, coming no closer, watching in horror as it struggled to cross the road. The cow was making noise, but the sound that issued from its wide open mouth was closer to a squeal than a moo. Its head, misshapen and elongated, flopped wildly from side to side as it lurched forward.

Ross was the first to speak. "What *happened?*"

"What's *happening?*" Jill responded, and he understood that she was referring not just to the monstrosity in front of them but to everything that seemed to be occurring lately. His skin prickled.

The cow cried out, reached the side of the road and rolled into a low ditch. In the stillness of the night air, they could hear its bulk rustling the weeds and brush as it pushed itself into the desert.

"Let's turn around," Jill said, sickened.

He didn't argue, and they headed back the way they'd come, both of them glancing over their shoulders periodically to make sure something *else* wasn't on the road and following behind. He thought of the chickens and the eggs and wondered what could possibly be causing such horrors. He was an engineer, so he knew the idea was stupid, but he'd seen a lot of science fiction films and his gut theory was radiation. There was no radioactive agent on earth that could cause such a variety of selective deformities in such a short amount of time—and the Palo Verde nuclear power plant was west of Phoenix, on the way to California, the nearest military base, Fort Huachuca, about fifty miles away in Sierra Vista—but the human brain never let facts get in the way of fears. "Maybe there's some sort of secret government lab out here," he said aloud, looking over at Jill in the darkness to try and gauge her reaction. "Maybe there's been a leak and something's spreading out and contaminating the environment."

"Maybe," she said, but sounded doubtful.

"What do you think's going on?"

"I don't know, but I don't think there's a...*scientific* explanation," she said.

For some reason, the image of that black flying thing crossed his mind. "What do you mean?"

"My friend Cissy tried to get me to go to church with her on Sunday. She said God was punishing Magdalena for its sins."

"And you believe her?"

"I *didn't*," Jill said.

"And now?"

"I don't think God's punishing Magdalena. I don't think there's a curse on the town. But something's going on that I don't think anyone has an explanation for."

Ross thought again of that thing in the sky.

"I'm not superstitious, but I'm open-minded, and when I see things like *that*..." She gestured behind them, leaving her thought unfinished.

He had no response.

They walked quickly back to her house, keeping a close watch on the road for anything else that might jump, slink or crawl in front of them. They made it back safely, and Jill walked from room to room, turning on all the lights. Whatever romantic mood had been generated earlier was long gone, but they had sex anyway, a quick desperate coupling on the living room floor, the only sounds in the otherwise quiet house an occasional grunt and the frantic slapping of skin. Afterward, he asked again if she wanted to stay with him for the night—or if she wanted him to stay with her—but Jill shook her head and told him she was okay, although she did ask him to wait outside until she'd locked all the doors and was safely in bed. He patrolled the house and the yard, made sure everything was all right, then tapped twice on her bedroom window with their pre-arranged signal before getting into his car and heading out. The other neighbors all seemed to be home—their lights were on at least—and that made him feel a little better, but he called her when he arrived back at the shack, just to make sure she was all right.

She was. She was in bed and reading, the TV on in the background, and he said goodnight to her once again before getting undressed and crawling into bed himself.

Closing his eyes, he tried not to hear the chickens outside, and tried to pretend to himself that their clucking didn't sound like laughter.

SEVENTEEN

CAMERON HAD COME INSIDE THE HOUSE FOR LUNCH AND WAS eating a melted cheese and bacon sandwich when the phone rang. He considered not answering—was there really anyone he wanted to talk to right now?—but he picked up the phone anyway, and it was Jack Judd. His friend did not sound so friendly today, and when the other rancher announced that he was coming over, along with Cal Denholm, Jim Haack and Joe Portis, Cameron knew the reason why.

He wolfed down the rest of his sandwich, took a fortifying swig of Coors and went out to the porch to call Jorge. His foreman came over, but didn't hurry the way he usually did. He kind of sauntered up, in a way that seemed almost deliberately disrespectful. Come to think of it, Jorge had been acting uppity for several days now, not showing the proper respect. On this ranch, that sort of behavior required punishment, so as soon as he stepped onto the porch, Cameron punched Jorge hard in the stomach. The other man doubled over, gasping for breath. "When I call you," Cameron said in a low angry voice, leaning forward so he could be heard more clearly, "you come. Do you understand, *maricon?*"

"Si," Jorge said, straightening up, but even that word was spoken in a snide, insolent manner.

Cameron would have beat the shit out of the fucking wetback then and there, but Jack and the others were coming, and he needed help. "Get all the men together," he ordered. "Now. I want them out here guarding the smokehouse. Jack and Cal and Joe are coming over and I think they might want to *do* something. You have to stop them if they try."

For once, the two of them were on the same page. Jorge's insolence disappeared, replaced by a determination so fierce that it took Cameron aback. He was glad to see such resolve, but it frightened him a little, and he wondered for the first time if that Catholic priest was right, if maybe they should bury the body instead of keeping it in the smokehouse. The feeling passed as quickly as it had arrived, though, and Jorge nodded his compliance before heading toward the barn, shouting orders in Spanish.

Cameron went back into the house to finish off his beer, then stood on the porch, waiting. He could track the arrival of the other ranchers by the moving cloud of dust kicked up by their trucks, and he walked down the steps to meet the men as they got out of their vehicles, slamming the doors.

It was Jack who spoke first. "Six more head last night, Cameron. Half my herd is gone."

"I know. Same thing's happening to me."

"We're going broke here!"

"I told you, we need to find out—"

Joe interrupted him. "We all know what's causing it, Cameron. It's that *thing*."

"You don't know that."

"Bullshit!" Joe said.

"Even my men are scared," Jack continued. "I'm losing as many hands as cattle. Two more ran off yesterday."

All of them had lost workers, it turned out.

Cameron said nothing. Looking toward the smokehouse at his own men gathered there, he realized that there were several hands he didn't recognize. Jorge was talking to one of them, and he was pretty sure it was Cal's foreman.

Their workers were coming to his ranch.

He wasn't sure what to do. He didn't need any more hands, and he sure as hell wasn't going to pay any wages for additional men.

Jack must have seen where he was looking. Squinting, he peered at the area in front of the smokehouse. "Holy shit. Is that Pepe? And Julio?"

"I guess they're not that scared," Cameron said drily.

"You're stealing our workers!"

"I'm not stealing anything. I didn't even know they were there until now, and I don't want 'em. Take 'em back, they're all yours."

Cal spoke for the first time. His voice was low and grim. "I don't know what the fuck's going on, but our workers are defecting to you, our cattle are dying—"

"Mine are, too," Cameron pointed out.

"—and we're losing money by the minute. At the same time, Lee Roberts—who had what? five or six head?—now has twenty. I don't know where he got the money, but I saw the stock supplier's truck over at his place, and when I asked him what was what, he said that he was expanding his herd and that he also had two out-of-season foals. Fucking Birkenstock Shane with his organic pea patch of land has made a deal with some sort of new age winery to supply grapes. All these little pissants are suddenly making money hand over fist."

"And our herds are dropping like flies!" Joe said.

"They're not just dying," Jack said quietly, and all of them knew what he was talking about. Cameron thought of those bright red moths.

Joe glared at him. "So fuck you, Cameron. I don't give a shit what you say. We need to destroy that thing."

He'd been getting more alarmed and had actually been thinking the same thing. But he wasn't about to concede the point to Joe Portis. Glancing back at the smokehouse and the men positioned protectively around it, his reservations disappeared. Somewhere in his brain, he thought dully that there was something wrong with that. All of his fears had suddenly been wiped clean, and that was not normal, not right. But he knew as well that it was evidence of tremendous power, power that could be harnessed and used—if he could only figure out how to do so.

He turned toward the other ranchers with renewed determination. "You're not touching it," he said.

Joe took a step forward. "The shit we're not!"

Like a dictator general, Cameron held up his hand, snapped his fingers and pointed forward. Jorge and the men behind him started forward, threateningly. "The shit you are."

Jack tried to appeal to reason. "It's putting us in the poorhouse. You, too. It's knocking everything out of whack. It was a mistake to keep it. We should have burned it or buried it that first night."

"But we didn't."

"But we should."

"Things'll turn around," Cameron promised. "It's ours. We just need to figure out how to make it work for us instead of against us."

"Meanwhile, our livelihoods are heading down the crapper."
Jack shook his head. "We were doing fine. We don't need anything
working for us."

"We do now."

"We just need things to go back the way they were."

Cameron smiled thinly. "Not going to happen." Jorge had
moved next to him, and he could sense the others close behind.

There were several more minutes of argument, but he wasn't
going to budge, they knew he wasn't going to budge, and they knew
there was nothing they could do about it. Eventually, Jack, Jim, Joe
and Cal got back in their trucks and took off, purposely spinning
their wheels in the dirt before they left, angrily trying to stir up
as much dust as possible. Cameron had won, and he felt good,
but when he turned back and saw the disrespectful expression
on Jorge's face, the smokehouse with its padlocked door behind
him, that feeling leeched away, and he was left with nothing but a
looming dread.

That night, he heard noises coming from the smokehouse. He
was asleep and in bed, but a muffled knocking woke him up. Even
through the closed windows, he could hear the irregular pounding,
and Cameron knew before he pulled aside the curtains and gazed
down at the yard, that it was coming from the smokehouse.

It was impossible, but it was not surprising, and though his
heart was pounding, Cameron put on his pants and slipped into
his boots, trudging downstairs and then outside. The noise was
louder here but not appreciably so. It still sounded muffled, but its
source was very apparent, and he could not help imagining that
oversized corpse rocking back and forth inside the smokehouse,
hitting the walls.

Cameron shivered but not from the cold. Surrounding the
smokehouse were all of his men and then some—even more than

had been here in the afternoon, he thought. A handful were on their knees and facing the small building, like worshippers before a shrine, while several others were crossing themselves and muttering prayers. Even more than the noises from within, it was the sight of all those men in the moonlight that made him uneasy.

Maybe Jack and the others were right. Maybe they should burn it.

Jorge stepped in front of him, and Cameron jumped. He hadn't even seen him walk up.

Was that a smile on the foreman's face?

It was too dark to tell.

"I think you should go inside, Senor Holt. I will take care of this."

It was less a solicitous suggestion than a thinly veiled demand. Cameron wanted to punch Jorge in the gut and order that greasy motherfucker to just do as he was told and not try to use his little pea brain to make decisions on his own. But everything out here made him nervous: it was nearly midnight, noise was still coming from inside the smokehouse, there were far too many ranch hands gathered around. "Make sure you *do* take care of it," Cameron said, trying to save face, and he turned on his heels and strode away, back into the house, where he locked the door, got in bed, closed his eyes and tried desperately to fall asleep, hoping against hope that he would not awaken until morning.

EIGHTEEN

DARLA WAS UP WELL BEFORE DAWN, THOUGH SHE HADN'T fallen asleep until long after midnight. She knew the truth ahead of time, but, as she had the last four mornings, she got out of bed to check anyway, walking down the hall to Dylan's room—where his bed was empty and his night light was off.

He was still gone.

Behind her, she heard a noise, and she turned quickly, hope overpowering reason for a brief fraction of a second until reality crashed into her.

It was only Tom.

"Go back to sleep," he told her.

"I'm not tired."

"You're *always* tired."

She glared at him. "And why do you think that is, hmm? What reason could there possibly be?"

He turned away, heading back into the bedroom. "Get some sleep."

"How can you sleep when Dylan is *gone?*"

He swiveled around. "What are you saying? Are you saying I don't care about Dylan?"

"It's your fault!" Darla screamed.

Tom stared at her. "How is it my fault?"

"You're the one who wanted to live out here! I didn't! I told you: no hospital, no fire department, no police..."

"So you think—"

"There's not even a full-time police department looking for him! There's sheriff's deputies and rangers from...where? Willcox? Benson? Tucson? They don't know Dylan! They don't care about him!"

"They're looking as hard as they can. We all are. Everyone's doing as much as they can."

"It's not enough!"

"I know that!" he shouted back at her. "Don't you think I know that?" He stepped toward her, pointer finger extended. "It's *your* fault for telling him he could hike out there. I never said he could! He's ten years old, for God's sake. Who lets a ten-year-old traipse around the desert on his own? You were too lazy to watch him, so you let him just wander through the wilderness..."

Darla burst into tears. "That's not fair!"

"You're just like your mother."

"Go to hell!" She stomped down the hall, out to the kitchen, and was grateful when he didn't follow her. It was still dark outside, the coming day little more than a white line at the edge of the eastern horizon, and she made some coffee and sat at the kitchen table sipping it, wondering where Dylan could be, praying that he was still alive.

Tom woke up and came out for breakfast sometime after seven. Ordinarily, she made breakfast for them both, but today she didn't, and he didn't ask her to. He poured himself some cereal while Darla walked out to the living room, where she sat down on the couch and picked up the needlepoint pillow she'd been working on as an effort to distract her from her pain and keep her calm.

She'd completed the purple petals of an orchid when there was a knock at the door. Gasping, she dropped her needlepoint. Tom emerged from the kitchen. Through the front window, she could see a sheriff's SUV parked in front of the house. "Don't open it!" she screamed.

Tom opened the door.

Darla was already crying.

"Mr. and Mrs. Ingram?" A sheriff and his deputy stepped into the living room.

"No!" Darla wailed.

"I'm afraid I have some bad news."

Tom was crying now, too. Great hiccupping sobs wracked his body, and his shoulders slumped as though he were a human-shaped balloon that had just lost half of its air. She wanted to go to him, but she couldn't move, and she heard through a wall of white noise that they had found Dylan's body on a trail halfway up the mountain.

One of them needed to identify the body.

"Where is the body?" she heard Tom ask.

The body?

"Dylan!" she yelled. "He's not 'the body!' He's Dylan!" Now she did jump up and go to Tom. She hit him, pounding on his shoulders with her fists. "He's your son! He's Dylan! He's not 'the body!'"

Tom grabbed her wrists to keep her from hitting him, and when Darla saw the devastation on his face, she stopped her assault, all the energy draining out of her. Slumping against him, she sobbed.

"Where is he?" Tom asked, and she heard his voice through his chest, deeper than it sounded through the air.

The sheriff's voice was thin and tinny by contrast, far away from her. "They're taking him to the morgue in Sierra Vista."

"Can't we see him before?" Tom asked. "In the ambulance or whatever?"

There was a pause. "It's better if you see him in the morgue."

She didn't like that answer. It made her think thoughts she didn't want to think, and her mind started running down all the reasons it might be "better" for them to see Dylan in the morgue. Every scenario she could come up with involved injury, dismemberment and mutilation, things that could be cleaned up a little before viewing, and her sobbing shifted into overdrive as she imagined her son's last moments of life filled with terrible suffering. *He died alone,* she thought. *In pain.* And she was filled with a despair so black and bleak that if she could have stopped living at that moment, she would have done so.

But she didn't die, and she let Tom take over, and she went with him to the truck, and they drove all the way to Sierra Vista.

When they were finally let in to see Dylan, naked, covered with a sheet, lying on a silver table, it was far worse than she thought it was going to be. He hadn't just had an accident; he'd been *attacked.*

And partially eaten.

As she'd expected, they'd washed him and tried to clean him up, but in a way that made it worse because the damage was clearly visible for all to see. The coroner tried to keep them from the worst of it, unveiling only her son's head and letting the rest of him remain covered. But his face was half torn off, one eye missing, his throat slashed open, and at the sight of him, Tom started wailing, sounding to her like one of those Middle Eastern mothers ululating over the loss of a son. She herself was numb, and even as she identified the body—

the body

—as that of her son, Dylan Ingram, she was ordering to coroner to uncover him rather than pull the sheet back up over his head. She wanted to see. She wanted to know what had happened to her boy.

His chest had been clawed open on the right side, and chunks of his arms and legs had been eaten away. There were fingers and toes missing, bite marks all over his flesh, and though his belly button was gone, the little birthmark above it was still visible.

It was the birthmark that sent her over the edge. She remembered looking at it as she diapered him, as she kissed his little baby tummy, as she rubbed him with lotion. She understood, in a way she hadn't until that moment, all that she had lost, all that would never be, and she broke down, throwing herself on top of him.

She remembered someone pulling her off, remembered someone taking her away, remembered voices yelling, voices soothing, but that was all she remembered because afterward there was only darkness.

NINETEEN

LITA WROTE OUT A RECEIPT FOR THE SIX JARS OF HONEY SHE'D delivered, then handed it to Ben, thanking him for the sale, and walked past the other customers and out the door of the grocery store without looking back.

She didn't relax until she was in the truck and driving past the gas station, onto the street. This was not the first time she'd gone to town and found everyone acting weird. It was nothing specific, nothing she could put her finger on, but she knew her neighbors, knew when they were behaving differently, and lately they'd been…well, behaving differently. Just like Ben. He and the other customers in his store this morning had exchanged meaningful glances when she'd said certain things, things that, as far as she could tell, had no relation to her or each other. They thought she hadn't noticed, but she had, and it made her feel more than a little uncomfortable. It was as though they all had some secret they were keeping from her, knowledge that they shared but were actively trying to keep from her.

Her friends had been acting that way, too. She could understand Darla being distraught after all that had happened, but she had been acting strange *before* her son had disappeared. JoAnn and Lurlene, as well.

Lita drove past the Ingrams' house, saw Tom's pickup in the carport. Darla had left town to stay with her mother in Oro Valley, but Tom had stayed, ostensibly to work, and she felt a deep profound sadness for her friend. Dylan had been a great kid, and Darla was a wonderful mother, completely devoted to him. How was she going to cope with his loss? How was she ever going to adjust to a life without him?

Lita couldn't imagine.

But she didn't like the fact that Tom was still here. He should be with his wife. Darla needed all the support she could get. A tragedy like this could take a huge toll on a marriage, and the thought that her friend might lose her husband as well as her son made Lita feel even more depressed than she already was.

Her mind wandered again to the increasingly odd behavior of…well, almost everyone she knew. Something was going on, and Lita had no idea what it was. She wondered why she was being kept out of the loop. Did it involve her? The more she thought about it, the more bothered she became. She thought of just coming out and asking JoAnn and Lurlene what was going on but was pretty sure she wouldn't get a straight answer.

Not only curious now but genuinely annoyed, she decided to put pressure on the weakest link, and instead of heading home, Lita turned back around and drove to the laundromat, parking on the street in front instead of in the lot behind the building. There were loads in two of the big washers, but no one waiting for them to finish, their owners apparently having gone elsewhere rather than sit in one of the uncomfortable plastic chairs arranged against the opposite wall. Lurlene was the only one in the laundromat, seated in the back at her desk, reading a romance novel.

"Hey, stranger," Lurlene said. "Your washer go out?"

"No—"

"Dryer?"

"No, I was at the market and thought I'd just stop by and say hi."

The two of them shot the breeze for a few moments, but to Lita, the conversation seemed slightly strained. It was probably due to her more than Lurlene, but there were questions she needed answered, and she brought the talk around to her market visit again, and explained how Ben and his customers had all seemed wary around her, as though afraid of giving away some secret they had sworn not to reveal.

"Huh," Lurlene said. "That's weird."

"I get the same feeling when I talk to you now, too. You and Darla and JoAnn."

"Well, Darla—"

"I know," Lita said. "But this started before that." She faced her friend head-on. "What's going on around here?"

Lurlene tried to look as though she didn't know what Lita was talking about. "Going on?"

"Lurlene…"

"Really. I don't know." She smiled, as though this was all a big joke or misunderstanding, but the smile was tight.

"Spill it. We both know you can't keep a secret and I'll wear you down eventually. You might as well come out with it now."

Lurlene seemed about to argue, but then gave up. Reluctantly, she pulled out her phone. "I snapped a picture of it." She pressed the power switch, then frowned. "Oh, I forgot. My phone's not working."

"Mine isn't either," Lita said. "I'm not sure anyone's is."

Lurlene looked as though she'd just figured something out. Something that scared her.

"Lurlene," Lita said firmly.

Now that she'd committed herself to coming clean, the laundromat owner seemed less tense, and the expression on her face was one of relief, as though she'd been wanting to talk about this with someone but had not been able to do so. "First of all, no one's tryin' to keep anything from you," Lurlene said. "I just assumed you knew. Prob'ly everyone else did, too. I thought *everyone* knew. It's just that no one ever brings it up or mentions it."

"Mentions what?"

"The angel."

Lita wasn't sure she heard right. "The *what?*"

"It was an angel. Even Father Ramos said it was."

"An angel? I don't believe in angels."

"I didn't either. Until I saw it."

Lita was even more confused than she was skeptical. "Slow down, slow down. Start from the beginning. What are you talking about?"

Lurlene took a deep breath. "New Year's Eve. The party at Cameron's. You and Dave left before midnight, so you missed it all, but you know what happens, you know how it goes. Jim Haack's kids' band was playin' "Bloody Mary Mornin'"—I guess they hadn't practiced any New Year's Eve music—and it's almost time, and Cameron gets up there, takes the mike, and says he's gonna count it down. So everyone takes out their guns— Cameron, too, and my Danny, too—and Cameron starts out with 'Ten, nine, eight...'" And everyone's pointin' their guns up, and the rest of us are coverin' our ears, and then he gets to 'one' and shouts out 'Happy New Year' and everyone starts firin' into the sky. You know, I always worried about one of them bullets fallin' back down and hittin' someone—"

"Me, too," Lita said. "That's one of the reasons we left early."

"But what happened this time was that they *hit* something. Everyone's all whoopin' it up and shootin' into the air, and right then this *thing* fell down, came crashin' out of the sky and landed behind everyone there in the yard, prob'ly would've crushed some people if they weren't all gathered around the stage."

"That was the angel?"

"It didn't look much like an angel, to tell you the truth. It wasn't a woman dressed all in white, it was more like...like a demon, actually. It was about twice as big as a person and kind of dark green. It did have wings, but they weren't feathers, like you usually think of angels. They weren't like bat wings, either. They were thin, kinda like construction paper, and you could see through them where they were torn by bullet holes. There were holes in the body and head, too. It must've been flying *right* above us when everyone started shooting."

"What made you think it was an angel?"

"Like I said, it didn't *look* like an angel. It was all dark and slimy looking. And that face..." Lurlene shivered. "I took a picture of it on my phone, but my phone ain't working, so I can't show you. I think a lotta people took pictures. I was scared, and I kept lookin' up to see if there were more of 'em, but that seemed to be the only one. It was all dead and bleeding, and its blood was red but, like, *bright* red, glow-in-the-dark red. I never seen anythin' like it.

"We were all quiet. No one said nothin'. Not even those Haack kids. And then I noticed that there was sort of a light around the body. I don't know if it was there before, because I didn't notice it, but it was there now and it was gettin' stronger, and all of a sudden

I felt…good. Happy. Everyone did. We were all laughin' and smilin' at each other, and it was like…like…I don't know. I felt like I did on Christmas when I was a kid. Sort of excited and happy all at the same time. I knew right then that it was an angel, *knew* it, and Father Ramos said that, too, and a whole buncha people started prayin'. The Catholics started doin' that crossin' thing they do over their hearts. I ain't religious, so I didn't know what to do, but I knew it was an angel and thought I should try to pray, too, but then I looked at all that blood soakin' into the dirt of Cameron's yard, and I thought, *We killed it.* It was an angel and we killed it, and when God found out, He was gonna be pissed. I think a lotta people had the same thought at the same time, because everyone started lookin' around at each other, kinda frightened, and then Cameron, who was still at the microphone, said, 'We need to hide the body.'

"There weren't no arguing or nothin'. We all felt the same way. We knew it was what we had to do. I don't…I don't think there was even any talk about who would do what. Some of us just stepped back, and some moved forward, and some of Cameron's farmhands went over to the barn to get blankets and such, gloves or what have you, and Cameron told the other ranchers and everyone to put the body in his smokehouse."

"Cameron *ordered* them? And they *obeyed* him? Cal Denholm? And Joe Portis?"

"He wasn't exactly orderin' them. He was just sayin' what everyone already kind of knew, although, lookin' back on it now, he was prob'ly schemin' to keep that angel for himself, knowin' how he is. For all I know, he's tryin' right now to use it to help himself get more land or money or whatever. But that night, everyone was just ashamed that they'd shot it out of the sky, ashamed and scared and…and horrified, I guess, and we all just wanted to hide that angel's body and pretend it hadn't happened. Even Father

Ramos. Even Vern Hastings and his crazy little churchies. So the farmhands brought out stuff to cover it up and pick it up with, and about ten or twelve guys brought it over to that smokehouse and put it inside. It looked real heavy, and it was still kinda bleedin' but they got it in, and then afterward, a whole buncha people chipped in and got shovels and buried all the blood in the dirt, and then they closed and locked the smokehouse door, and that was it."

Lurlene exhaled heavily. "Boy, it feels good to talk about that."

"Maybe everyone should be talking about it."

"Everyone *should*," Lurlene agreed. "But they won't. That angel has…some kinda power, I think. And no one wants God to find out that we killed it. So everyone's just pretendin' it didn't happen." She looked at Lita. "I guess that's what you picked up on, why you kinda felt outta the loop."

One of the washers had long since turned off, and Shelley Martin came back into the laundromat from wherever she'd gone and started taking her laundry out of the machine, putting it into an adjacent dryer.

Lita leaned in closer so Lurlene could hear her above the noise. "Was she there?" Lita whispered, motioning toward Shelley.

Lurlene nodded. "Yep."

Lita didn't know Shelley well, but she'd seen her around and knew her by sight. She'd always thought Shelley was extremely pretty, but today the other woman looked tired, haggard and far older than her years. *That angel has…some kinda power*, Lurlene said, and Lita wondered if everyone who had been there that night had been affected by that power. It would certainly explain Darla's and JoAnn's recent odd behavior.

She was glad she and Dave had decided to leave early.

Although, Dave and Ross had been acting kind of strange themselves lately. And Ross hadn't been there at all.

191

She started examining her own thoughts and actions to see if she'd been behaving differently than normal.

Lurlene tapped her on the arm, and Lita nearly jumped. "You all right?" her friend asked.

"Yeah. I'm fine."

"You kinda spaced out there for a minute."

Lita looked at her. "Do you really think that was an angel?"

Lurlene's expression was deadly serious. "I *know* it."

"Do you think…I mean, there're some weird things happening around here lately. Do you think…?"

"Do I think it's because we killed that angel?" Lurlene nodded. "Yes, I do. Is there anything we can do about it?" She shrugged. "According to Father Ramos, pray."

"Do you believe that?"

"Not really." Lurlene met her eyes. "But I'm doing it anyway."

Lita felt uneasy on the drive home. She wasn't sure how much of what Lurlene had told her she bought, but she believed most of it, believed that something had been shot down on New Year's Eve, even if it wasn't an angel, and believed that its body was in Cameron Holt's smokehouse. She recalled the black creature that had flown low over their truck on the way back from the party that night and shivered at the memory.

She decided to tell Dave and Ross what she'd learned, and when she arrived home, she gathered them together in the kitchen. "Do you know about what happened at the New Year's Eve party?" she asked.

They both looked blank. "No. What?" Dave said.

She told them, repeating the story Lurlene had related to her. "They think it's an angel."

"Who thinks it's an angel?" Ross asked.

"Everyone, apparently." She addressed Dave. "I think it's that thing that nearly made us go into the ditch on the way home. Remember? The black flying thing that swooped over us?"

"Of course I remember. But that sure as hell wasn't an angel."

Ross had a weird look on his face.

"Rossie?" she said.

"I think I saw it, too. On Christmas night."

Her heart was pounding. "Really?"

"Yeah, when you guys were gone. I was sitting out there at night, just looking up at the stars, and something flew over me, bigger than a bird but smaller than an airplane. I didn't know what it was, but it was black and silent, and it kind of spooked me, so I went inside."

The three of them were silent for a moment.

"Can something like that actually be real?" Dave wondered.

"I'm pretty sure it is," she said.

"What do you think it could be?"

None of them had an answer for that, and she thought about some of the things that had happened lately around Magdalena, some of the things she'd heard about, and she realized that the world was not as rational as she'd thought it was when she woke up this morning. And she knew that it never would be again.

TWENTY

MONDAY WAS FREE, NO WORK LINED UP, SO JACKASS McDaniels did what he always did on such days—he worked his mine.

Well, it wasn't really a mine. It was more of a big hole in the desert behind his house. But he'd been digging that hole for over a decade now, and it *looked* like a miniature version of an open-pit. Roughly circular, big enough in diameter to swallow his home twice over, and wider at the top than it was at the bottom, it went down a good sixty feet. A series of ladders and ledges allowed him to reach the pit floor. Although several layers of earth had been uncovered—striations on the sides made it look like a miniature Grand Canyon—he hadn't yet found what he was looking for.

Gold.

He knew what the geologists said, what other prospectors had told him. This wasn't gold country. This wasn't even copper country, although Clifton-Morenci was only an hour or so away and the Copper Queen lode in Bisbee had yielded high grade ore for nearly a century before petering out.

But he had faith. He didn't know why he was so sure when all signs pointed the other way, but he was and always had been, and it had kept him working on his mine for the past twelve years.

McDaniels had always been a rockhound. Collecting rocks and minerals had come natural to him, and as a youngster he'd been obsessed with lost mines of the old west, especially the Dutchman. He'd found more than his share of pyrite in the hills and mountains hereabout, and one day, as a teenager, he'd looked at his collection of pyrite and thought that if that fool's gold was real gold, he'd be a millionaire. So for a lot of years, when he'd had a regular job working for the Terry Brothers doing roofing and construction, he'd spent his vacations gallivanting around the state, looking for lost mines and the caches of gold that were supposed to still be there. Gradually, he came to realize that many of the desert ranges that were said to be home to those mines looked a lot like the Magdalena mountains, and he started to wonder if the land around here might not have some veins of gold running through it. No one had ever tried to look for gold around Magdalena and he decided to be the first.

He'd been at it ever since, and though he'd never found so much as a single flake in a piece of rose quartz, he'd continued on, growing ever more certain as the prospects of finding the precious metal grew increasingly more unlikely.

This morning, with no jobs scheduled, he'd come out here after breakfast with his pickaxe and his goggles, and he'd fired up the gas-powered sandblaster he kept at the bottom of the pit and started his mining operation. He'd been at it for nearly three hours, had sifted through a lot of loose rock and sand, and was about to quit for lunch, when a dazzling light hit his left eye. He was looking in a different direction, but it was bright enough to make him tear up and force him to close his eye against the glare, and he shifted position and saw that it was some sort of mirrored surface at the bottom of the pit reflecting back a powerful ray of the sun.

Although he knew right away that it wasn't just a "mirrored surface."

Dropping his tools, he ran over to the shiny object and picked it up, hefting it in his hand.

It was a gold nugget, as big as a Reese's Peanut Butter Cup.

McDaniels' heart began beating crazily. Was it possible? Could it be real?

Yes. He knew it was authentic without even testing it. Dusting off the nugget on his shirt, he held it up to examine it more carefully, acutely conscious of its weight in his hand. Were there more like this? Had he happened upon a deposit that would yield him not just ounces of gold but *pounds*?

He put the nugget in his pocket, feeling it press coldly against his thigh through the material. His brain was buzzing. What would he do if he was suddenly rich? Buy a house in Acapulco? Move to Switzerland? *Nah*, he thought. He'd stay right here. This was his home, these were his people. He might quit working or might not. He'd probably build himself a nicer house, but chances were that he'd just continue on with a slightly more comfortable version of the life he already had.

It occurred to him that nuggets were usually found through panning or sluicing, where rock had been worn down by water. Mines or pits usually exposed veins of gold that had to be smelted to separate the metal from the surrounding minerals. It was strange to find a nugget in a situation such as this.

Dropping to his knees, he started digging through the pile of rubble where he'd found the first nugget and, moments later, he uncovered another. Again, he dusted it off and held it up. Smaller than the first, the shape and size of a peanut shell, it gleamed brightly in the morning sunlight. Looking at the gold—*his* gold!— McDaniels smiled broadly. So much for the experts. They were wrong, he was right, and now he was going to be wealthier than he'd ever dared hope.

Thank God for his good fortune.

Although maybe he should be thanking the angel.

McDaniels put the second nugget in his pocket. He paused for a moment, thinking about the bullet-ridden body he'd helped carry into Cameron Holt's smokehouse. It might sound crazy, but in the past few weeks he'd noticed something that no one else seemed to have picked up on: the angel was good luck. It didn't matter that they'd shot it down, its mere presence here had brought unexpected windfalls to people in the community. Shane Garner had struck a big bucks deal with some winery, Xochi and Maria had won the lottery, he was finding gold on his property…

This was luck of biblical proportions.

Providence, as his mother used to say, was smiling on them.

Jackass McDaniels was not a religious man. Though he'd been raised to have a healthy fear of God, life had made him more practical and realistic. He hadn't seen too many examples of miracles performed by an invisible, all-knowing, all-powerful deity. In fact, most people he knew who prayed regularly *never* got what they wanted from the man in the sky. They were still poor and unhappy, and afflicted loved ones were never cured of the diseases they contracted.

But this was something different. This wasn't a made-up story but a concrete reality. The angel's physical body, whatever it was made out of, seemed to possess a measurable power. And, because it was an angel, that power was good.

McDaniels stood. But *was* it good? He'd heard things lately about other occurrences not quite so happy. And the Ingrams had lost their son, who'd been torn apart by wild animals. Were those a result of the angel as well? He wasn't sure, but he didn't think so. Those were just the ordinary problems of everyday life. The angel hadn't gotten rid of them, but she hadn't caused them.

Couldn't the same thing be said about the winning lottery ticket and his gold? After all, he'd always thought there was gold here; he'd been working his mine for years.

It didn't pay to examine the situation too carefully. Hell, he wasn't even sure the angel was a *she*. He thought about picking up that body and unconsciously wiped his hands on his Levi's, as though he could still feel the weird sliminess that had gotten on his section of blanket on the way to Cameron Holt's smokehouse.

No, it wouldn't do to think too hard about the angel. Best to just accept the gift for what it was and move forward.

He walked over to the opposite side of the pit, grabbed the shovel that was leaning against the wall, and used it to turn over a big scoop of earth. Several shiny gold nuggets stood out against the tan blandness.

Smiling, McDaniels bent down to pick them up.

There wasn't a lot to do on the bus ride from school when he didn't have any homework, especially for the last twenty minutes, when it was just the ranch kids: him, his brother Ray, that retard

Mitt Stevens, and the three cholo girls. So Bill Haack usually just slept.

But today he was too hyped-up to sleep, just as he'd been too hyped-up to pay attention in his classes.

Tumbleweed Connection had gotten a gig. An honest-to-shit paying gig.

He hadn't told the other members of the band—hadn't even told his brother—because he was trying to think of a way to explain to his parents that he was dropping out of school and following his dream without his old man beating the crap out of him. For the fiftieth time today, he unfolded and reread the email he'd printed out last night, the paper so worn from use that it looked like it was a year old instead of a day.

It was a legitimate offer from Desperados, a club in Nogales. Monday through Thursday for three months, fifty bucks a night. Plus whatever tips they got. They could even sell merchandise! They didn't *have* merchandise, but that was definitely something he needed to look into. He knew the money wasn't much, but this was a real place. Dierks Bentley had played here on his way up. So had Trace Adkins. It was a launching pad, and that's what he needed to stress when he talked to his dad.

Of course, that was going to be one tough conversation, which was why he'd already put it off twice. His dad had been acting like an even bigger asshole than usual since New Year's Eve. He'd brought his holster to the party and, like everyone else, had shot off his guns at the stroke of midnight to celebrate the arrival of the new year. Bill suspected that his old man thought *he'd* been the one to actually kill the angel, which was why he'd been so ornery lately. Bill could use that in an argument against him, if necessary, and he was fully prepared to do so, even though it would probably piss off the old bastard even more.

The bus dropped off the cholo girls in front of the dirt drive that led to Mr. Holt's ranch, then headed out to that crappy little farmhouse where Mitt Stevens lived, before taking him and Ray home. The two of them walked up the long driveway, past the corral to the house.

"What's up with you?" Ray asked. "Why're you so quiet? And why did you keep looking at that piece of paper all the way home?"

Bill stopped walking. He took the email out of his pocket, unfolded it and handed it to his brother. "We got an offer. Desperados in Nogales. They want to make us the house band!"

"Oh my God!" Ray grabbed the email, growing more excited as he read on.

"They need an answer by tomorrow, and I'm just trying to figure out how to tell Dad. Because this is a once-in-a-lifetime offer. We don't take it, they'll find someone else."

"We're taking it!"

"We're gonna have to quit school."

"Who gives a shit?"

"Dad will."

"Yeah, but he'll understand—"

"He won't understand anything. He has no clue how these things work. This is either take-it-or-leave-it, and if we don't step up, we're spending the rest of our lives in Magdalena. This is the big time, dude. You know how many famous people started out at Desperados?" Bill took his email back and started walking again.

"We'll just *tell* him. We won't *ask* him. You're seventeen; I'm sixteen. He can't tell us what to do."

Bill hoped his brother kept up that attitude. Because it wasn't going to be that easy.

They walked up to the house and inside. As he'd expected, the old man was sitting on the couch, half-drunk and watching a judge show. He'd been avoiding the cattle since they'd started dying, since they'd turned. Bill was pretty sure his dad was afraid of the animals, which was why he spent most of his time hiding in the house. That gave Bill a psychological advantage, and having the upper hand made him feel brave. He dropped his backpack on the floor and motioned for Ray to follow him.

"Dad?" he said.

The old man did not even look up from the TV. "What?"

He'd decided the best way to bring it up was just to blurt it out. "Tumbleweed Connection was offered a gig. At a club in Nogales. We're going to take it."

Unconcern had changed into confusion, but at least his dad looked away from the television. "What?"

"Me and Ray are going to have to quit school. It's a Monday through Thursday job, and it starts next week."

"Not for you it don't." Their dad stood, and the look in his eye was mean.

"But Dad—" Ray started to say.

"Shut up, Ray. You two aren't going, and that's final."

Bill stood his ground. "Yes we are," he said. "This is a real opportunity. It could be our big chance. A lot of famous musicians started out at Desperados—"

"You're not famous, and you're not musicians, and you're not going."

"Yes we are," Bill repeated, his face getting hot.

"Dad—" Ray began.

"I told you to shut up, Ray! This is between me and your brother."

"He's right," Bill said. "It is between us, and I'm telling him that I'm making the decision that we are going to quit school and take that gig."

"Not as long as you live in this house!"

"That's the point. We're not going to anymore."

His father glared at him. "Don't get smart with me, young man. You're not eighteen, and you need my permission, and I ain't giving it. So just shut up and do as I say or you're going to live to regret it."

"Fuck you!" Bill shouted. "We're going!"

It felt good to yell at his dad, and he wondered why he hadn't done it before. What had that miserable old shit ever accomplished in his life? Who was he to tell Bill, or even Ray, what to do?

Fists clenched, his dad advanced on him. "Don't you dare speak to me like that! I won't have that sort of language in this house!"

"Yeah? Well, if you're so good and pure, why did you shoot an angel? Huh? You think God hates me swearing more than he hates you killing his angels?"

His dad hit him. Not a slap, not a tap, but a roundhouse to the jaw that sent him reeling back and brought tears to his eyes. Recovering quickly, Bill kicked the old fuck in the nuts, and was gratified to see his dad double over, clutching his crotch and letting out a weak, ineffectual moan.

Ray was standing there, wide-eyed and shocked. "Go grab your stuff and pack," Bill told him. "We're getting out of here. Today."

"And we're taking the Jeep," he informed his dad, still doubled over and holding his damaged genitals. "You can have the truck."

Bill waited until Ray was down the hall and out of sight, and then kicked his dad in the head as hard as he could, knocking him down. "Fucking hillbilly."

He walked down to his own room to pack his clothes, guitar and amplifier, feeling good.

TWENTY ONE

WEDNESDAY NIGHT'S FINAL CONFESSION WASN'T OVER until ten, and Father Ramos locked the church doors immediately after the last parishioner, Elena Martinez, stepped outside, making sure no one else could come in. He was bone tired, and he was tempted to just lay down in the pew next to him, close his eyes and go to sleep. Ever since the angel fell, not only had occasional churchgoers become regular, but *all* of his flock had started coming to confession, many of them daily. It took a lot out of a man to deal with so much sin, to forgive so many transgressions when he himself was not pure.

He glanced back at the confessional, feeling uneasy. Hearing so many confessions had led him to notice a bizarre pattern that had emerged since the angel had fallen, a reversal of fortune among his parishioners that had to be connected to the event but that made no logical sense: people whose finances were in shambles had suddenly started doing well, while those who were well-off had suffered a run of financial misfortunes. A gorgeous young woman had been disfigured in an accident, while a frumpy matron had suddenly discovered beauty secrets that rendered her extraordinarily attractive. It was as though the polarities of luck had been flipped, and those who had been the beneficiaries of good fortune up until now had been cursed with bad luck, while the sad sacks who'd never had anything go right in their lives were suddenly having a run of spectacularly good luck.

At least that's the way it had started.

But now things were becoming more complex, the patterns more subtle. Certain individuals seemed to be getting caught in competing cross-currents of changing luck. Charley McGill, for example, had always been poor but happily married—yet now his wife had suddenly died, leaving him a substantial life insurance settlement. Jack Judd was a failure as a husband but a very successful rancher—now he had reconciled with his wife but his cattle were dying. It was a strange and complicated amalgam of alternating good luck and bad that seemed to be playing out all over town.

Father Ramos himself was caught in the middle. His fortunes had changed not at all.

No, that was not true. His church was consistently full these days. The overflowing congregation he had always wished for had been delivered to him by the fallen angel.

He kept thinking of the angel as "fallen" because it made him feel better, but that was not strictly true. The angel had not fallen. It had been shot down. The men of Magdalena had killed it in cold blood, and he was still awaiting the full consequences of that accidental murder.

The *full* consequences.

Because some consequences seemed to be occurring already. From what he had heard, and from what he had seen—

the eggs

—there were pockets of unexplainable events that could have no source other than the angel. He would include the veterinarian's disappearance and the Ingram boy's mysterious death among them. As well as the poltergeist that Ana and Miguelito Chavez claimed was haunting their trailer, and the influx of snakes that had taken over the Garcezes' property.

But as far as he could tell, there was nothing consistent about these incidents. Proximity to the body, involvement in the angel's killing, none of these factors seemed to in any way determine to whom things would happen. The occurrences appeared to be completely random, and if there was a pattern to them, it was one that was known only to God.

Except Father Ramos did not think God's attention was on Magdalena yet. The Lord knew everything, so obviously He knew that the angel had been killed, but maybe He was busy elsewhere because the knowledge had not been acted upon. Once God focused the full force of His wrath on Magdalena, there wouldn't be just crumbling marriages and missing children. There would be wholesale destruction. Vengeance from above.

And that was what Father Ramos feared.

The chapel needed to be swept, the pews polished, the confessional cleaned, but all that could wait until morning. He was beyond tired, and after he put out the candles and checked all of the doors, he intended to turn in immediately and let his worries be washed away by sleep. Yawning, he started up the aisle.

"*Hector.*"

Father Ramos had not heard the voice since that first night, though he had been dreading its return every second of every day, and he jumped at the sound of it. Once again, it came from everywhere and nowhere, was all around him, and with a cry of terror he fell to his knees, clasping his hands in prayer, closing his eyes tightly.

The laughter came, that terrible sibilant laughter, mocking not only his actions but his very existence, and, wide awake now, he sent up an entreaty to God, begging that his life be spared though he knew the Lord did not condone cowardice such as his.

As before, he heard the sound of shuffling, as though something large had entered the chapel and was lumbering up the aisle. Last time, he had turned to see what was coming, and there'd been nothing there. He opened his eyes, hoping for the same result.

But this time there *was* something.

A creature of dirt, a bastardization of God's creation, not man but monster, fully eight feet high and as wide as two humans, had entered the chapel from the vestry and was shambling toward him. It had no arms or legs, only slightly delineated sections of its bulk that roughly corresponded to limbs, and it advanced in an almost waddling manner that did not require the independent movement of feet. The head, however, was less rudimentary, and despite the fact that its features were formed by the placement of small rocks and indentations of mud, it looked less like the primitive face of a child's snowman than that of a perfectly rendered classical sculpture. Its expression was one of sly malevolence.

The cold had come again, not merely a change in air temperature but a complete transformation of the environment, as though the church had been dropped into a new and different atmosphere.

"*Hector.*"

208

The voice bounced around the chapel, echoing from wall to wall, from ceiling to floor. He did not think it came from the shambling monster, but the two were obviously connected, their strings pulled by the same puppeteer.

The Lord God.

"Forgive me," Father Ramos babbled, his hands still clasped in prayer. He closed his eyes. If he was to die here and now, he wanted to do so in a state of forgiveness. "I am and always have been Your humble servant. I know I have done wrong and will accept Your judgment gratefully..." The words, spoken increasingly fast, flowed into each other. The creature, he was certain, had been dispatched to take his life, and he needed to unburden himself before he died.

He continued praying, and he sensed the presence of the monster next to him...but nothing happened. He did not open his eyes, afraid to find out what was going on, but beneath the by-now-rote prayer, his brain was spinning. If the monster had not been sent to kill him, why *was* it here? It certainly had a purpose and a reason for being.

For the first time, he thought that perhaps the angel had not been sent from God.

No. That was blasphemy. God would punish him for doubting.

It wasn't blasphemy, though, was it? He knew that the creature they shot down was an angel, but maybe the only reason he was so certain was because the thought had been planted in his head. Maybe the blasphemy was believing that that grotesquerie was one of God's servants.

He closed his eyes more tightly, his head hurting. There was no possibility here that was good.

"*Hector.*"

He decided to answer the voice rather than try to hide from it. "Yes?" he said tentatively. "What do you want?"

An image seared itself into his brain: the angel, dead and rotting in Cameron Holt's smokehouse. Its decay and deterioration had been greatly accelerated, and its dark green skin, now almost black, seemed to have melted, looking like heavy chocolate syrup that had been poured over a deformed and twisted body. He understood instantly that he was meant to protect that form, that it was being resurrected, was in the process of *becoming* and was in a fragile state.

Father Ramos opened his eyes, feeling as though his brain had been jolted with a shot of electricity. Before him, the creature collapsed in front of the altar, devolving into its base components: mud, dirt, sand, rocks.

The chapel was silent.

Whatever had been here was gone, and he stood shakily, staring at the mess in front of him, afraid to touch it, afraid to go near it.

He understood now that the angel had to be protected…but he didn't want to protect it. *Someone* had spoken to him, *someone* had put that image in his head, but he was less sure than ever that it was God, and he realized for the first time that it was not the possibility of God's wrath that most frightened him but the angel itself. Whatever the angel might be, it was causing havoc, and he shuddered to think about what it might do once it was resurrected and became…the thing it was becoming.

The impulse to flee Magdalena returned, but Father Ramos knew he would not do that. As terrified as he might be, it was his sacred duty to look after his flock, to see to both their safety and salvation. Besides, he was a part of this. He had been there that night and while he had not shot a gun, he had done nothing to stop those who had.

Tired, scared, emotionally drained, he put out the remaining candles, walked past the pile of mud, giving it a wide berth, and locked himself into his quarters.

Where he took off his collar and cassock, put on his pajamas and went immediately to sleep.

And dreamed of a world where flying demons filled the sky.

TWENTY TWO

ROSS DECIDED NOT TO GO TO THE FARMER'S MARKET. It wasn't as though he was needed. In fact, the ranch's egg and honey stocks were both so low at the moment that it made little sense for Lita and Dave to sell there, though they wanted to keep up the routine and maintain contact with customers. But Jill wasn't going this time. She hadn't baked any cookies or pastries this week, so she had nothing to sell, and if she wasn't going to be there, he didn't want to be either.

"Dick suck mushroom! Pickaninny pie!"

There was that, too. The girl. Ross didn't want to see her. Was *afraid* to see her, though he was not sure why.

So while Lita and Dave drove off to town, Ross stayed behind to feed the chickens and see if there were eggs to collect. He did not find out whether any eggs had been laid, however, because when he went outside and peered through the wire fence, he saw, in the center of the yard, a gigantic chicken, a foot taller than any of the others surrounding it, walking in an erratic circle, squawking hoarsely, its head twisting strangely atop its unusually long neck. The sight made him shiver. And when the bird's eye met his own, holding his gaze even as the scrawny neck rotated unnaturally beneath it, Ross turned away, heading back to the shack.

He'd wait for Dave to come back before trying to feed any animals.

He turned on the television to drown out the infernal squawking. On the *Today* show, there was a story about a new poll that had been conducted regarding religious beliefs. A majority of Americans reported that they believed in angels, and a significant number thought they were personally protected by a guardian angel.

He changed the channel to CNN, where they were covering a shooting at a North Carolina high school, a subject more comfortably normal.

He could still hear the chicken outside, and turned up the volume. Did he actually believe that an angel had been shot out of the sky here in Magdalena? No. But *something* had certainly been shot down—and he was pretty sure he'd seen it himself Christmas night. But what was it and why was it here and how was it causing all of this weird shit to happen? He didn't know. It was a problem unsolvable by his rational, unimaginative mind. And it scared the hell out of him.

Maybe, he thought, it was time to move on. He had some money now, and a job (sort of). Maybe he should thank Lita and Dave for their hospitality and hightail it back to Phoenix.

But he couldn't just leave them like that.

And what about Jill?

For someone living out in the middle of nowhere in a shack on his cousin's property, his life was definitely getting complicated.

Ross was on his laptop, checking on the status of various resumes he'd posted on jobhunting sites, when he heard his name being called from outside. He jumped in his seat, startled, and for a brief fraction of a second thought: *Chicken!* But then he recognized Jill's voice and hurried out to meet her.

She was standing in front of the shack, drinking water from a plastic sports bottle.

He looked around for her Econoline, but didn't see it. "You *walked* here?" he asked incredulously.

"Sure," she said, pushing the cap down on her bottle.

"It's, like, five miles."

"So?"

He shook his head. "You're incredible."

"Would you care to join me? It's nice weather for a walk," she suggested.

"You always think it's nice weather for a walk."

"You don't think it is?"

"I guess," he conceded.

"So, do you want to come with me?"

"Where?"

"Around. Here and there. Hither and yon. It's addicting, walking. If you give it a chance."

"You're talking to someone who faked sick notes from his mother in order to get out of playing P.E."

"Nevertheless."

"Sure," he said. "Just let me lock up." Heading back toward the shack, he turned around. "Do you need to use the bathroom or anything? Would you like something to eat?"

She shook her head. "No. But you might want to get yourself a water bottle."

"It's not that hot."

"But it's dry. And I'm not sharing."

Ross went inside, turned off his laptop, got a can of Coke out of the refrigerator and locked the door behind him as he left.

"Coke?" she said. "Really?"

"You drink what you want; I'll drink what I want."

He thought they'd be walking back toward town, but at the head of the driveway, she turned left instead of right, and he followed her lead as they strolled along the road, through the desert, toward some of the bigger ranches. He had to admit, it felt good to be outside in the open air. He *was* starting to get a taste for it, and though for his entire adult life, walking had merely been a way to get from room to car, from car to room, from room to room, he found that he was actually enjoying this little hike.

At least until Jill brought up the angel.

"I've been asking around," she said. "After you told me…what you told me. It's hard to get anyone to talk about it, but my friend Cissy did—she was there—and she said your story's pretty much on the money." Like Ross, Jill had stayed home on New Year's Eve and, like Ross, she'd heard nothing about what had happened at the party.

"Does she think it's an angel?"

"It seems like everyone does."

Ross stopped walking, turning toward her. "Maybe that's what it wants them to think. Maybe it put that idea in their minds."

"It's dead, isn't it?"

"But it's supposed to have some kind of power anyway. At least that's what people are saying. And with all of these deformed chickens and dead cattle and missing kids…"

"I don't think it's an angel either," she told him.

"But what is it? It's obviously *something*."

She turned away, started walking again. "I don't know."

Neither of them spoke for awhile, but the subject was on both of their minds, and the mood as they continued on was more sober than it had been a few minutes prior. Looking off to his right, Ross could see, far in the distance, a hulking barn that he was pretty sure belonged to Cameron Holt.

Somewhere over there, the dead body of that dark flying thing was rotting in Holt's smokehouse.

The idea made him uneasy. Ross stopped. "Let's head back," he said.

Jill nodded, not arguing, and they turned around, walking in silence back the way they'd come.

The mood brightened considerably as they approached the L-Bar D. Suddenly thirsty, Ross popped open the tab of the Coke can he'd been carrying and took a long drink. Jill squeezed water into her mouth, then squirted some at Ross. It felt as though they'd broken through some sort of gloom barrier, and he found himself wondering if that were possible or if the change in emotional temperature was all in his head.

Jill walked back with him to the shack, and though neither of them had said anything, he hoped that meant they were going to have sex. But instead she told him, "I need to get back."

"Now?" he said, disappointed.

"Yeah. I have some telemarketing work to catch up on. There's no rest for the obnoxious."

"You want me to drive you home?"

Jill shook her head. "That's okay. I'd rather walk." She gave him a quick kiss. "Maybe I'll call you. You could use some credit card insurance, couldn't you?"

"No. But I'd like to hear your spiel."

"I'll be calling when you least expect it." She refilled her water bottle from his sink, gave him another kiss, then walked outside, waving as she headed up the drive.

He watched her until the dirt lane curved behind a palo verde tree and she disappeared.

A few moments later, Lita and Dave returned in the pickup. Ross had a partial erection left over from his unfulfilled hopes, and he pushed it down before walking out to greet them. "So how'd it go?" he asked, though he already had an idea since they were back so early.

"We sold out pretty quickly," Dave said, putting the best face on things.

"It was a nightmare," Lita told him. "There were hardly any customers, and only about half of the usual sellers were there. Some of the ones who did show up were selling really weird things: pig milk and snake jerky and I don't know what else. Paul Coburn was there trying to sell balloons! He was just standing by himself next to the tamale lady. He looked like a homeless guy. I don't think he's bathed or changed his clothes in a week. He was all dirty and nasty, and he just stood there with his balloons, staring at everyone."

"It was pretty creepy," Dave admitted.

"Hattie's daughter just kept repeating this nasty mushroom poem, and someone finally told her to shut up, and Hattie started screaming like Debbie the Pet Lady. It was crazy." She shook her head. "Even if we *hadn't* sold out, I think we would've left."

She grew quiet.

"What is it?" Ross pressed.

"Anna Mae and Del came by." Her voice cracked. "Del was leading *her* around. She didn't know who we were."

"So *she* has Alzheimer's now?"

"I think so."

"How's that even possible?"

"How is *any* of this possible?" Dave sighed.

"You think it's that...angel?"

"What else could it be?"

"We need to get a look at this thing for ourselves," Ross said. He nodded at Dave. "Do you think you could get us in there to take a peek?"

"I don't know. I could try."

"See if you can. We need to know what we're up against."

Who could they call? Ross wondered as the pickup truck bounced over the uneven road on the way to Cameron Holt's. Police? Sheriff? FBI? What government agency could they alert to what was happening in Magdalena? And what could they say to make an outsider believe? Because the angel story certainly wouldn't fly in the real world.

Ross was in the passenger seat, Dave driving, Lita between them, and he was overwhelmed by the impossibility of getting help from any kind of authority. He was not a hero, not a go-getter, not a take-charge kind of guy. From his school days to his job at Air Research, he'd always been a cog in the machine, far more comfortable completing assignments than giving orders, and the fact that he was investigating this under his own initiative, with the implied intent of subsequent action, made him extremely apprehensive.

Dave had called Cameron Holt, who said they could come over. But Dave hadn't been completely forthcoming. He'd offered to deliver eggs to Holt's ranch since Holt had not shown up to the farmer's market, even though the dwindling store of untainted eggs was nowhere near large enough to meet the rancher's usual order. Holt had fallen for the ruse, and now the three of them needed to figure out a way to at least get a look at the "angel."

Ross wondered if he could sneak a peek while Dave and Lita were selling the carton of eggs to Holt. If the rancher was distracted, he might be able to spy through a window or a hole in the wall or, if he were really lucky, open the door of the smokehouse and look in. The problem was, he didn't know if he'd recognize a smokehouse if he saw one, and if there happened to be a bunch of sheds and shacks on the property, he might not be able to find the right building before being caught.

As it turned out, he didn't need to worry.

They approached the house and barn, pulling to a stop before the skeletal remains of three cows that had been arranged in the shape of a triangle. Before them, through the windshield, at least a dozen workers were bowing down in front of a wooden structure that had to be the smokehouse.

"Jesus," Dave breathed. "It looks like they're worshipping it."

It did indeed, and that gave Ross an idea. "We'll pretend that *we're* worshippers. We'll say the angel called to us and we came to pay our respects—"

"Pay our respects?" Lita said.

"You know what I mean. We came to see it. We're believers like them..."

"I don't know, Rossie."

"I think it's a good idea," Dave said admiringly. "The only question is: will they believe it? And what'll they do if they don't?"

It was a good question. Some of the men were pretty rough looking, and more than a few of them had tools clutched in their hands, tools that could easily double as weapons. What if *it,* the thing in the shed, told the worshippers that they were frauds? How would the men react?

Ross realized how completely he had bought into the idea that this dead body, this corpse of a creature that had been shot out of the sky, possessed some sort of sentience, and the frightening thing was that he knew Lita and Dave had, too. The entire town had.

"So what do we do?" Lita was whispering.

"Get out," Ross said. "We'll play it by ear." He didn't like the fact that none of the kneeling men had turned to look at them. They had to have heard the pickup driving up and stopping. At least one of them should have evinced some curiosity about who had arrived.

And where was Holt? The rancher should have come out to meet them, but so far there was no sign of him.

They got out of the cab and closed the doors, walking around the dead cattle and into the yard. Ross looked around, checking the corral and the open door of the barn for signs of other people. The lack of response by those bowing down before the smokehouse worried him, and he had the feeling that his "We're-worshippers-too" speech wouldn't go over too well. They might try just walking up to the building, but he was pretty sure they'd be attacked if they did.

"*Over here.*"

The three of them turned at the sound of the voice. It was Cameron Holt, and he was standing on the porch of the house. His clothes were wrinkled, as though he'd slept in them, and the salt-and-pepper stubble on his face indicated that he hadn't shaved for several days. Ross caught Dave's look and silently registered his own shock at the rancher's appearance.

"Where's m' eggs?" Holt growled.

"In the truck," Dave said. "Hold on."

Turning to watch him head back to the pickup, Ross saw that the workers who'd been kneeling on the ground had stood and were now facing their direction. A chill touched his spine. This would be the part in a horror movie where they were either taken prisoner or killed.

One of the men separated himself from the pack and walked over. Ross recognized him as the man who'd accompanied Holt to the farmer's market.

"Ola, Jorge," Lita said.

He nodded at her, unsmiling, but did not respond as he stopped at the edge of the porch.

Dave returned with a flat of two dozen eggs, all they could scrounge from their dwindling stores. "Six dollars," he said, walking up to the porch.

Jorge took the eggs while Holt took out his wallet. "Jesus H," the rancher said. "That's all you got?"

Dave nodded. "I'm afraid so."

"And the three of you drove all the way out here for a lousy six bucks?"

Lita stepped up. "Actually," she said, "We heard about the… angel, and we were wondering if we could see it." She gestured toward the smokehouse.

"No," Holt said, not meeting her eyes as he handed Dave six ones.

"I just thought—"

"You got your money. Now get off my property," the rancher said angrily.

Jorge shook his head. "No. They may look."

Holt seemed to flinch, and, for a brief second, actually looked frightened. Then he waved a disgusted hand toward the smokehouse. "Fine. Let 'em look." It had not been his decision, but

222

he pretended that it was, and Ross realized that the relationship between employer and employee was not what it initially appeared.

Jorge handed Holt the eggs, then gestured for the three of them to follow him. They walked across the hard dirt toward the smokehouse, the other ranch hands parting to make way. He expected the foreman to let them peek through a small window or a knothole in one of the boards, but instead he pulled a key from his pocket and unlocked the door to the shed, pulling it open. Behind them, Ross could feel the other workers leaning forward for a better view.

The interior of the smokehouse was dark, and for the first few seconds, they could see nothing. Then the door was opened wider, letting in light, and the contours of the square room became visible. Aside from what looked like a series of clotheslines strung crossways four to five feet above the floor, everything had been shoved against the far wall: a table, a butcher block and what looked like an air-conditioning unit but was obviously the device used to create smoke for the drying of meat.

In the center of the room lay the creature.

The monster.

Ross sucked in his breath. As black as coal and curled into a fetal position, the corpse was rotting. There were holes in its body, not just bullet holes but larger cavities exposed by the pulling away of decaying flesh. Skin seemed to be dripping from the frame, as though made of rubber and melting, but, remarkably, the decomposing body gave off no smell. It was smaller than Ross had expected, only slightly larger than a man, but perhaps that was because, in death, it had shrunk in on itself. The wings, obviously the biggest part of the creature, were folded up and tucked underneath it. The shape of the face, almost triangular, resembled that of an ant, although the wild malevolence of its expression was

223

not one that had ever been found on an insect. The eyes, round, wide open and completely white, were accentuated and made cruel by stark pointed clownlike eyebrows. The mouth, filled with sharp needleteeth, was frozen in a silent scream. Here, too, the skin appeared to be melting, but the effect was to pull the face tauter and exaggerate the characteristics already there.

Ross stared at the creature. It definitely wasn't an angel…but his brain was telling him that it was. Which was probably what had happened to all of the people at the New Year's Eve bash. Fortunately, he was self-aware enough that he *knew* he was being influenced, and that distance and sense of removal allowed him to understand what was happening. He glanced over at Lita and Dave, pretty sure that they were each having a similar experience. The expression on Lita's face was one of fear.

Ross focused again on the rotting body in the center of the floor. There was something extremely primitive about the creature. It didn't look like a dinosaur, although it definitely seemed like something that could have lived at the same time. If that were so, however, where had it been hiding in the millennia since? Why had no one seen it until now?

And were there any more of them?

As usual, he had more questions than answers, but the one thing that was incontrovertible was that, even in death, this creature—

angel

—was possessed of tremendous power.

Behind him, he heard the murmured sound of men in prayer.

And then Jorge closed the door, ending their glimpse of the creature.

Ross felt like someone just waking from a dream. His thoughts were fuzzy, and it took him several seconds to get his bearings. As rationally minded as he was, he was already running down possible reasons for what he'd experienced: there was a property within the wood that blocked the power exuded by the body as lead did radiation; the creature had to be seen for the effect to work...

What he could not confront in such a logical manner, at least not yet, was the big question: what was it?

Lita was the one who spoke for all of them. "Thank you," she told Jorge. Her tone of voice made it sound as though she were a convert, as though one look at the—

angel

—creature had made her want to bow down in front of the smokehouse with the ranch hands. He was pretty sure she didn't really feel that way—he certainly didn't—but it was probably a good tack to take if they wanted to get out of there safely. Who knew how those fanatics would react to a dose of reality?

Jorge nodded solemnly as he locked the door. Cameron Holt was already back in the house, nowhere to be seen, and with Dave leading the way, the three of them walked silently between the rows of workers toward the truck. Ross wondered if Jorge and the others had some expectation of them, if, after looking into the smokehouse, they were supposed to do something to advance the...*angel's*...cause. But no one said anything to them, and they were allowed to get back into the pickup and drive away.

Ross heard Lita exhale loudly as they pulled onto the road. He felt the same, a great release of tension, as though he'd been anxiously holding his breath and was only now able to breathe normally.

"What was *that*?" Dave said.

"For a moment, even *I* thought it was an angel," Ross admitted.

"But there was that whole...*thing*. All those men worshipping it. And Jorge calling the shots instead of Cameron. What the fuck is going on there?"

"I don't know," Lita said quietly. "But it scared me."

The same was true for all of them, and they drove the rest of the way in silence.

Back at the L-Bar D, Lita got out of the truck and went directly into the house. Dave waited a moment before joining her. "How could that dead body in Cameron's smokehouse affect my chickens and bees over here?" he asked.

As if in answer, a swarm of bees flew out from one of the white boxes housing the honeycombs and hovered in the air before it, arranging themselves in what looked like a sketchy circle.

"And who can we call about this?" Dave wondered, echoing Ross' own thoughts. "I mean, it's not exactly the jurisdiction of the sheriff or the forest service, and what would they do if they *did* come out to check on it?" He shook his head. "We need to call... what? A witch? A witchdoctor? Who?"

"I have no idea," Ross said.

Dave started toward the house. "I'm going to call around, tell everyone what we saw, see if they know any more than we do."

Ross walked over to the shack and went inside. He tried calling Jill to tell her what he'd seen, but either she wasn't home or wasn't answering, and he hung up, not wanting to leave a message. This was something that needed to be discussed, and he decided to call back later, maybe at the usual time. He put the phone back in its cradle. He hadn't realized until now that there *was* a usual time, but sometime within the past week, nightly phonecalls had become a habit with them—and had become the part of his day to which he most looked forward.

Jill called *him* less than a half-hour later, to ask a computer question, and he described to her their visit to Cameron Holt's, the weird dynamic between the rancher and his workers, and the rotting *thing* in the smokehouse.

"So it's *not* an angel," Jill said.

"No, but…something about it makes you *think* it is when you're near it. I don't know how, don't know why, but it happens. We all felt it, and obviously we're not the only ones."

"Is it scary?" Jill asked.

"Not exactly. It's…weird."

"But it's scary when you think about it, isn't it? That all of these things are going on around it?"

"Yeah," Ross admitted. "It's scary. And I haven't been able to think about anything else since. Someone has to do something. We can't just let things go on the way they are. We have to get rid of it somehow."

"If that's even possible."

"Do you have any ideas?" he asked.

"Do you?"

"Fresh out."

She was silent for a moment, thinking. "You know, maybe Native Americans have encountered this before. Maybe they know what this is and how to deal with it. Odds are, this thing's been flying around this part of the country for some time. You saw it, right? And Dave and Lita? Well, I'm sure they have, too, over the years. And maybe they know something we don't. I'll go see Michael Song. He and his family sell leather goods and turquoise jewelry at the market—next to Dave and Lita, actually—and even if they don't know anything about this themselves, they might know someone who does."

"Like a…?"

227

"Shaman," she said. "Let's face it, religion's a lot better equipped to deal with something like this than science is. For the simple reason that it acknowledges the existence of the mystical.

"In fact, I'm going to talk to Father Ramos, too," she said. "The Catholic religion has cleansing rituals, rites meant to drive out evil spirits and repel demons."

"Father Ramos thinks it's an angel," Ross pointed out.

"I'm going to talk to him. You should come with me and tell him what you've seen."

"Okay," Ross said. He was a rationalist. He didn't believe in ghosties and ghoulies and gods and monsters. At the same time, he followed facts and evidence, and if the facts led him to some sort of paranormal explanation for everything that was going on, he wasn't so closed-minded that he would automatically reject that conclusion.

And right now the evidence pointed toward that body in the shed being one powerful supernatural entity.

He certainly didn't think Jill's shaman was going to solve all of their problems.

But it couldn't hurt.

TWENTY THREE

V ERN HASTINGS GLANCED AROUND AT THE SIX WOMEN AND four men gathered in his living room. He was the lay preacher of this congregation, and though several others had tried to join his church in the past two weeks, he knew that they did so purely out of fear. The true believers were the ones who had been with him from the beginning, and it was only these worshippers he allowed into his house to celebrate the seventh day.

Rose had placed a pitcher of water on the table, along with a stack of Dixie cups. As always, they had each been fasting for the past twenty-four hours, and the fast would continue until suppertime this evening, though in the interim they were allowed to partake of the cleansing purity of water. None of them did, each wanting to show their strength of will to the others, and Vern was glad. He was proud of his congregation. He had taught them well.

The grandfather clock in the hall chimed ten, and Vern began his sermon, which today was about children and the Lord's admonitions to them. He quoted Deuteronomy: "And they shall say to the elders of his city, 'This our son is stubborn and rebellious, he will not obey our voice; he is a glutton and a drunkard.' Then all the men of the city shall stone him to death with stones." He said this specifically for the sake of Tessa Collins. She was a glutton, and so was her son Wade, and if Vern had his druthers, they would both be taken to the edge of the city and stoned to death.

He liked Tessa's husband Andy, however, and he figured Andy might pick up on the hint and get his woman and his boy in shape before it was too late.

Vern continued talking about children, going over God's laws against disobedience, harlotry and girls' wearing of clothing associated with men. Though he and Rose had no children of their own—the Lord had not seen fit to bless them with offspring—there was no doubt in his mind that the two of them would have been far better parents than everyone else in this congregation. Not to mention the idolaters and heathens who populated the town and lands around them.

After he was finished speaking, they each prayed, then sang a song unto the Lord. There was a pause, and then Vern cleared his throat before addressing the most important subject before them: the angel. As he had for the last several Sundays, he recounted the events of New Year's Eve.

"There are no accidents," he continued. "There is nothing that happens that God does not know about or plan. He *knew* we would shoot down His angel in our drunken revelry. He *wanted* us to do so. But now He is waiting for our response. Yet again, He has sacrificed one of His own for us, a blood sacrifice, and now it is up to us to do the same, to offer up to Him a blood sacrifice of *our* own."

This was the moment he had been waiting for, and he opened the closet door behind him and pulled out the small cage that he used to house the jackrabbits he sometimes caught. In it was a baby he had taken from an Indian woman on Thursday. He placed the cage down on the carpet next to the coffeetable and stood there proudly as everyone looked at it.

He had seen the Indian woman standing next to one of the pumps at the gas station, holding her baby, obviously looking for a ride, and the idea came to him. He had no doubt that it was divinely inspired—there was no way he could have come up with such a plan on his own—and as smoothly as though he had rehearsed for days, he rolled down the window of his car and said easily, "Would you like a ride?"

She was suspicious for a moment, but she got in, and Vern drove at first in the direction she told him, until they were out of town, then he ignored her directions and took off down a dirt road that led into the desert toward the ruins of the old Peralta ranch. She was quiet, almost as though she knew what was coming, and she did not fight him as he stopped the car next to Wailing Woman Wash, got out, walked around to the passenger door, opened it and took the baby from her. He motioned for her to get out, and when she did, he placed the infant on her seat. She'd said nothing since getting into the car, and he knew that was the Lord's doing, because he was weak and would probably not have been able to go through with it had she pleaded for mercy or begged him to stop.

Grabbing her arm, he pulled her to the side of the road and threw her into the wash. He wasn't sure what he would have done at that point—stone her? strangle her?—but it didn't matter because she hit her head on a large rock when she fell and was immediately still. Blood, an astonishing amount, flowed out from the side of her head onto the sand.

Instantly, as though it was part of a plan—and it *was*: God's plan—a wild one-eyed dog came running out from between some brittlebush and began desperately chewing on the woman's exposed ankle. Several crows flew down from the branches of a nearby palo verde, and from high in the sky two turkey buzzards dropped down and landed on her back. None of the animals paid any attention to the others, and all tore into her flesh, feasting. He had no doubt that in several hours there would be nothing left but bone.

As he turned away, back toward the car, a coyote crossed the road, heading toward the woman in the wash.

Vern had taken the baby home with him, told Rose of his plan, and put the infant in the cage, in the closet, feeding it only water. It had remained there until now, until needed. Opening the wire gate, Vern withdrew the baby and placed it atop the table, where it lay on its back, unmoving. Too weak to cry, the infant made low mewling noises.

Rose handed him a knife—her curved filleting knife from the kitchen—and he held it up. "Who would like to do the honors?"

He knew none of them would be brave enough to carry out the Lord's will and was merely trying to shame them, to make them uncomfortably aware of their own cowardice, but to his surprise old Etta Rawls raised her hand. "I will," she announced.

He was proud of her—as was the Lord—but he smiled, shaking his head. "I thank you, Etta, but on second thought, I believe it would be better if I did the deed myself."

For a brief moment, looking down at the brown-skinned infant, Vern thought that maybe God would not consider this a real sacrifice because it was not someone who mattered. It was just some papoose he had stolen. For the sacrifice to count, it should be one of them, a white person, someone important. But then he remembered that he was doing this for the entire Magdalena community and not just for his congregation. This baby *was* a member of that community, so in the end it *did* count.

Besides, the angel they'd killed could not have been a very important one. If it had been, God would already have taken His wrath out on them. The fact that He was waiting, that He was offering them a chance of forgiveness and redemption, meant that this was the right thing to do.

He held the knife aloft, offering a prayer. "Dear Lord, we are sorry for what we have done. Forgive us our sins, forgive us our pride, and let this sacrifice pay our debt to You so that we may once again bask in the glory of Your goodness. In Jesus' name we pray. Amen."

Vern brought the knife down, feeling an odd satisfaction as the blade overcame a quick spongy resistance and pierced the skin, sinking easily into the flesh. Pain made the baby find its strength, and it cried out as the knife sliced into its midsection, but the cry was cut off almost before it could start as the child started to choke. Blood was everywhere, not spurting but flowing, running over the sides of the small body onto the table and streaming onto the rug. He pushed down harder, through organ, through bone, and within seconds the infant was dead, pinned to the table like a lab specimen.

Blood continued to pour out of the body. Rose was trying to move the Dixie cups out of the way, but Vern stopped her. Improvising, he picked up one of the cups and put it under the red waterfall cascading over the side of the table. "Drink!" he ordered, and took a small sip before passing it to Rose next to him. She did the same, then passed it on, until everyone had partaken and the cup was back in his hands. He felt like vomiting—he wasn't sure he would *ever* be able to wash that putrid taste out of his mouth—but he remained stoic, and said, "We will now give this child a proper Christian burial and hope the Lord hears our pleas."

Rose ran off to the kitchen to get something to clean up the mess, and Vern withdrew the knife, putting it down on the table before picking up the small body and placing it back in the cage. He'd take the cage outside and bury the baby in the yard. They would all help him.

And, if they were lucky, the Lord would take back His angel and all would be forgiven.

Jeri Noblit delivered the mail in town, and, after lunch, went out as she usually did to deliver to the scattered homes on the ranch route. For Christmas, Don had gotten a satellite radio installed it in her car, and she was beyond grateful. Reception had always been hit and miss out here—mostly miss—and it was nice to be able to hear continuous music as she drove. She was especially partial to the Outlaw Country station, and it definitely made the long drives between the various ranches more palatable. Not to mention the initial trip out to the highway to collect the mail from the postal delivery truck.

She actually enjoyed her job now.

The red flag was up on Dave and Lita's mailbox—bills to be sent out, most likely—and she pulled next to the box, pushed the flag down, removed outgoing mail and replaced it with incoming: a couple of ads and what looked like an official envelope with a Las Vegas postmark (something to do with Dave's parents, no doubt). The next stop was Mose Holiman's trailer, and it was so far out that she considered skipping it today. But though there was only one piece of mail for Mose, it was from the government, so it was probably important, and as inconvenient as it was, Jeri drove the ten miles out to his place. After all, it was her job.

On the way back, she intended to swing by Cameron Holt's ranch and drop off his mail. The past few times she'd been by, there'd been no problem, but last week Cameron had been standing by his mailbox with a shotgun, waiting for her, and when she'd rolled down the window to hand him his mail, he'd pointed the shotgun at her and told her to get the hell off his land. She'd been tempted to just throw his mail on the ground and take off, but she was honestly afraid that he might shoot at her as she was driving away. There was something off about him, something crazed, and she'd reacted instinctively, pretending she didn't hear him, putting his mail in the box and driving calmly off as though nothing was amiss.

She hadn't told Don what had happened—he just would've gotten himself worked up and that wouldn't have done anybody any good—but now every time she came by, she worried that Cameron was going to be out there again.

She'd always hated that man, and now she was afraid of him, too.

As impossible as it might seem today, she knew that at one time Cameron Holt had been someone's baby, someone's cute little boy. He'd probably watched cartoons and played with toys, and maybe when he'd had a nightmare, his mommy had gone into his bedroom to reassure him. "I started out as a child," Bill Cosby had said on one of her mom's old records that Jeri had listened to as a kid, and that was the truth of it. *Everyone* started out as a child, and it was only on the way to adulthood that paths diverged, that some turned out to be saints, some turned out to be assholes and the vast majority of people ended up somewhere in-between.

She navigated by landmark and knew she had reached the eastern end of Cameron's vast holdings when she saw the familiar water tank and adjacent rusted tractor. But there was something new here today, and she slowed down, peering through the windshield.

What the hell was that?

She stopped the car. Scarecrows had been put up in Cameron Holt's field.

Even at a casual glance, there seemed something disturbing about them. That field had been fallow for as long as she could remember—Cameron was a rancher not a farmer—and the figures were not spaced throughout the pasture but were lined up in a row along the edge of the fence, facing the highway. They were not uniform, but were of different shapes and sizes, wearing different types of clothes.

They looked real.

Jeri didn't want to think about that.

She rolled the car forward slowly, until she was even with the first of the figures.

She remembered, years ago, when she was in high school, renting a video with a couple of her friends, a horror movie about a deranged farmer who killed people and installed their bodies in his cornfield as scarecrows.

Why was that even in her head? That obviously wasn't what was going on here.

Was it?

The scarecrows, she could see now, were made of clay or mud. She looked out the window at the one nearest her. This close, the detail of the face was clearly visible, so meticulously wrought that it resembled an actual person. The hands, too, she noticed, were realistically shaped from the mud, like a sculpture. She got out of the car for a closer look. She could even see an expression on the brown grainy face: anger.

How could mud be posted on a pole? Jeri wondered. The figures couldn't be nailed there, and she saw no ropes or twine. What was holding them up?

She stepped up to the fence, staring over it at the raised figure. She still didn't understand the purpose of these scarecrows. There weren't any crops to protect, and there weren't even many birds to scare away. What was the point? Why had Cameron put them up? She glanced down the row, and a chill passed through her.

Had the second one been facing straight ahead a moment ago, looking toward the road?

Because its head was now turned in her direction.

They were *all* turned toward her, she noticed, and, heart pounding, she backed slowly toward the car, keeping her eyes on the row of scarecrows, alert for any sign of movement. Her rear bumped against the car door, and she quickly fumbled for the handle, opening the door, hurrying inside and locking it.

She knew about the thing in Cameron's smokehouse, the *angel,* as everyone called it, and she wondered if it was in any way connected with these eerie effigies. People told her that the angel had great power, even though it was dead, and several individuals on her route had been the victims of mysterious circumstance. It hadn't affected her or Don, but then again she was afraid to look at things too closely. It was said that the angel turned good luck bad and bad luck good, and it was true that weird things along those lines had been happening since New Year's eve. Roscoe Evanrude's celebrated mineral spring had run dry overnight, while Jackass McDaniels' ridiculous mine had yielded gold. Dave and Lita's hens had stopped laying, while Mary Mitchum's long-dead apple tree was suddenly full of blossoms.

Jeri started the car, put it into gear. Ahead, a man was walking toward her down the road, a man holding a large bunch of balloons that were sagging above his head, half-deflated. An odd sight at any time, it was downright creepy under the circumstances. *Where had he come from?* she wondered.

The man, she saw as she approached, was Paul Coburn, that rich nerd with the bimbo wife who'd decided to slum it in Magdalena for some strange reason. He was filthy, wearing torn raggedly clothes, but he was smiling at her. On the satellite radio, Johnny Cash was singing about "Ghost Riders in the Sky." Jeri maneuvered around the balloon man, not making eye contact, speeding up as soon as she passed him.

Glancing in her rearview mirror, she saw a gap in the line of scarecrows.

One of them had come off its pole.

She floored the gas pedal, fishtailing for a second before the tires caught, and sped away, topping seventy on the narrow dirt road as she hauled ass toward town. She flew past Cameron's drive and the dented mailbox at its head without stopping.

New rule, she decided. She was no longer going to deliver the ranch route. If Cameron and the other ranchers wanted to pick up their mail, they could come to her house. She'd set up afternoon hours for them. If the postal service didn't like it, they could find someone else to do her job. But she was *not* driving out here again.

She did not look any more in her rearview mirror, and she did not slow down until she reached Margo Hynde's place at the edge of town.

The setting sun was already half-hidden behind a hill, and Tax Stuart glanced nervously toward the east. He still had another forty minutes until the landfill closed, and by that time it would be dark.

He didn't like working here when it was dark.

He turned up the CD player in the weigh-station booth. Long shadows were forming between the piles of refuse and in the pit, and while the brush pile had been burned and the fire was out, smoke still hung heavy over that section of the dump, making the area even gloomier.

He was thinking of changing the landfill's hours so he wouldn't have to be here when the sun went down. He knew it was childish and irrational, but though this fear had only started recently, it had become a growing concern, and for the past week he'd dreaded coming to work each morning, knowing what awaited him at the end of the day. If he could afford to do so, he'd hire another worker, have *him* close up, but unless the population around here drastically increased, that wasn't going to happen.

Tax looked to the left, hoping to spot the telltale dust cloud that meant someone else was coming to dump trash or yard waste at the landfill.

Nothing.

Looking to the right, he saw that the shadows had grown and lengthened from even a few moments previously. The entire far side of the pit was now so engulfed in murk that he could barely see it. Closer in, near the mounds of rubbish that had been dumped this week, shadows within the shadows moved. They had to be rats, but not all of them *looked* like rats, and he was afraid to go out and check for fear of what he might find.

The CD ended. From somewhere nearby, there was a high birdlike whistle, and for the first few seconds, he thought it *was* a bird. But the phrase went on too long, a song not a fragment, and it actually seemed to have a tune. There was no one here but him, and, frowning, he peered through the sliding window to see if he could determine the source. He saw nothing, and he opened the door behind him to peer out the back but saw nothing unusual there, either. The whistling continued, the sound becoming increasingly disconcerting.

He thought of that thing they'd accidentally shot out of the sky on New Year's Eve, shivering at the recollection of it. He knew what Father Ramos and everyone said it was, but he'd helped carry it into the smokehouse, and if that thing was an angel, it was an angel from Hell. He'd always been one to laugh at those liberal pansies in places like New York and Los Angeles, where politicians passed laws against shooting off guns to ring in the new year, but he wished now that there'd been such a law on the books here in Cochise County. Maybe not everyone would've abided by it, but some of them would have, and one might have been the guy who shot the fatal bullet.

It was that angel creature that was the reason he was so spooked out here now when it started to get dark. He'd *dreamed* about that thing, and those nightmares had left him feeling like a five-year-old boy coming out of an R-rated horror movie. He'd been going to mass every Sunday morning and Wednesday evening since it happened, praying for his soul the way Father Ramos told him he should, but God wasn't giving him much strength these days.

Tax saw movement out of the corner of his eye and turned back toward the window.

Where a small shriveled hand was reaching up and placing a dirty coin on the narrow shelf in front of the sliding glass.

He cried out in surprise and fear, immediately backing up, his heart hammering crazily in his chest. The whistling was louder now, and it was obviously coming from the thing in front of the booth. Whatever it was, it was too short to reach the window, and he was glad that the shelf was there to block it from his sight. That shriveled little hand was creepy enough by itself, and he did *not* want to see what it was attached to.

The hand withdrew, leaving the coin, and the whistling lessened in volume as whatever it was moved away. Tax was breathing hard, and he quickly turned around, realizing he had not locked the door behind him. Leaning over quickly, he did so, just as there was a faint knock on the thin wood.

He held his breath as though trying to fool the thing into believing he wasn't there. He had never been so scared in his life.

The knock came again, slightly stronger this time, and with it, the whistling, muffled by the closed door.

Had he heard that tune before? It seemed to him that he had.

Tax took out his cell phone, but it had been acting up lately, and of course this was one of those times when it was on the blink. In fact, it didn't even turn on at all; the battery appeared to be dead.

He heard a new noise, and was surprised to find that it was coming from his own mouth as he hummed along to the whistled tune. He stopped humming and clapped a hand over his mouth the way a cartoon character would. *It knows I'm here,* he thought wildly.

Obviously.

That's why it was trying to get in.

There was a fusillade of pounding on the door, and a small fist broke through the cheap wood—the same shriveled little hand that had left the coin on the shelf. Thinking fast, Tax kicked the door open and made a run for it, dashing out even as the creature connected to that horrible hand tried to disengage itself from the door. He didn't look back, not wanting to see, but made a beeline for his Jeep, only a few yards away on the side of the shack.

The whistling was loud, filling the air around him, and if he hadn't had to get to his vehicle so quickly, he would have plugged his ears with his fingers. But there was no time for wasted movement or extraneous thought, and he reached the Jeep, pulled the key out of his pocket, jumped in and started that mother up.

He wished he'd driven his pickup today—he'd feel a hell of a lot safer locked inside a cab than out in the open air—but this provided easy access and quick maneuverability, and he backed up, spun the car around—

—and saw what was after him.

It was a creature of the dump, with discarded wig hair and torn mismatched clothes. The size of a small child, it appeared to be female and was holding a tattered purse by its frayed strap. Beneath the castoff trappings, the face and body were brown and wrinkled with the dehydrated look of beef jerky. It pointed at him.

And the Jeep's engine died.

Tax tried frantically to restart the vehicle, turning the key in the ignition, as the little creature waddled toward him on unsteady legs, still pointing.

Could there be more of them? He didn't know, didn't even have any idea what it *was*, but judging by the way it moved, he was pretty sure he could outrun it, and rather than continue trying to start the Jeep as the monster continued to approach, he decided to make a run for it. Pulling out the key, he leapt out and sped toward the road as fast as his feet would carry him.

From overhead, a crow swooped down, whistling the tune that was still issuing from the wrinkled mouth of the waddling creature. Other birds charged out of the sky, coming from nowhere, all of them whistling that maddening melody. One of them clawed the top of his head, another pecked the back of his neck, still others attacked his back. Crying out in pain, he tried to keep going but was engulfed in a whirling fury of feather and wing, talon and beak. Attempting to bat the birds away, he tripped over an unseen rock or piece of refuse and fell hard on his side, still trying to fend off the avian attack. Pecked and clawed relentlessly, it was all he could do to protect his face. He rolled over, turtling up duck-and-cover style.

And then the birds were gone.

He pulled his hands off his head, looked up to make sure it was safe—

And stared into the shriveled face of his whistling pursuer. This close, he could see the deepset empty eyesockets, the snakelike holes where a nose should be, the grim line of the lipless mouth. The wig was gone, and so was the purse, but he recognized the raggedy clothes as belonging to one of Linda Ferber's kids. It lent the monster the appearance of an evil dwarf, and for all he knew, that's exactly what it was. He tried to get up and run away, but that skinny arm reached out to hold him down, and the same tiny hand that had left the coin on the shelf grabbed a hank of his hair.

He was humming again, he realized, and for a few seconds, before the hand shoved his head down and smashed it into a rock, both the humming and whistling were in perfect harmony.

TWENTY FOUR

ROSS TOOK A SHOWER IN THE MORNING BEFORE EATING breakfast and going out to feed the chickens, but halfway through, water began splashing against his ankles. The drain was stopped up, and he washed his hair quickly before the pool at his feet overflowed the lip edge of the stall. He got out, dried off, and a few moments later, when he turned on the hot water in the sink in preparation for a shave, that drain was clogged, too. Deciding to skip the shave, he put on his clothes and walked across the yard to tell Lita and Dave—*my landlords*, he thought with a smile—but they were having their own plumbing issues. Dave was using a plunger on the kitchen sink, and Lita called out from the bathroom that the toilet was still overflowing.

"I don't mean to pile on," Ross said, "but my drains are all plugged up, too."

Dave had worked up a sweat, and he put down the plunger and wiped the perspiration from his forehead with the back of his arm. "That's it. We're calling someone."

Jackass McDaniels was at the ranch a mere twenty minutes later, the back of his truck packed with a sump pump and various types of drain-clearing equipment. "I was thinkin' on the way over that maybe your septic tank's full," he said, getting out of the cab.

Dave shook his head. "It's not that. Each drain is backed up, individually." He took the handyman on a tour of the house and guest house, Ross and Lita tagging along, and after McDaniels checked the septic tank just to make sure that wasn't the problem, he brought in a coiled wire snake connected to an electric motor that he plugged into a kitchen wall socket. "We'll start in here," he said. "It's closest to the main line."

The three of them stepped back as McDaniels put on a pair of rubber gloves, inserted the coiled cable into the drain as far as he could push it, then turned on the motor. A terrible clanking filled the room; it sounded as though the pipes were being torn apart. But the snake, fed by the handyman's gloved hands, continued to unspool down the drain. The clanking became more muffled and then there was a loud wet pop.

The stench that came from the sink was nearly overpowering and reminded Ross of the terrible smell in the root cellar. McDaniels flipped a switch on the motor to reverse direction, then shut it off and withdrew the snake. Tangled up in the coils was what looked like a mass of bright green string, but within seconds after hitting the air, the green filaments coalesced into a disgusting gray goop that dripped thickly onto the sink in bloblike patches.

Lita's eyes were big. "What the hell is *that?*"

"I don't know," McDaniels said, "but that's what was clogging up your drain."

Ross took a step forward to look at the gelatinous glop. He had no idea what it was or how it had come from that tangle of strange green threads, but he was pretty sure he knew its source.

McDaniels turned on the water, washing everything down the sink, and leaving the tap on to make sure the drain was clear. It was.

"Next," he said.

In the bathroom, the toilet water was already black and thick like oil after being plunged, and the handyman told them to wait while he got something out of his truck. "That snake'll crack your porcelain all to hell. We need something a little more delicate for this job."

Lita was staring at the obsidian-colored water. "What do you think's down there?"

"What was that back *there?*" Dave asked, cocking his thumb toward the kitchen.

Ross didn't say anything, but he thought about the chickens and the bees, the simultaneously clogged pipes, and wondered if the ground beneath them was contaminated, if that monster in the shed had somehow tainted the earth for miles around and the poison was seeping up through the thin spots and causing havoc.

McDaniels returned with a handheld device from which protruded a long thin probe. "I think this'll work," he said. It did, and this time there was nothing unusual to see when he withdrew the tool.

It was another story in Ross' shower, where the water had not gone down and there were tiny creatures *swimming* in the water. Buglike, shocking pink, the size of paperclips and almost as flat, they had appendages that approximated human arms and legs, and looked like miniature Olympians breaststroking their way around the pool. The creatures had clearly come up through the drain, though no new ones were emerging at the moment, but their presence gave McDaniels pause, and he hesitated before inserting the snake.

The handyman glanced back at Dave, Lita and Ross. "If any of you have any idea what's goin' on here, you better fill me in, cuz I'm completely lost."

"Not exactly," Ross said. "Not *specifically*. But I'm pretty sure of the original source."

The three of them told McDaniels what they'd seen at Cameron Holt's place. The description of the monster matched his recollection from New Year's Eve, but the handyman seemed surprised by the account of Holt's workers all worshipping the shed. Even more surprising to him was the description of Holt's odd subservience. "That sure as hell don't sound like the Cameron Holt I've come to know and hate."

"It's because of…"

"The angel's influence?" McDaniels said.

"I'm not sure I'd call it that," Dave admitted.

"To be honest, it's brought me nuthin' but good luck."

"That's not what it's brought everyone," Lita said.

"I know. I heard." He looked toward the pooled water in the shower and the little pink creatures swimming in it.

"You know, I'm not religious," Dave said. "I don't believe any of that happy horseshit. But I'll give you this: that thing has power. Dead or alive."

"I've been thinkin' that, too," McDaniels told them. "But how's that even possible?"

"The way I figure, it's like nuclear waste. You know how those spent fuel rods are all used up but still radioactive and will be for another thousand or something years? It's the same situation."

Lita nodded in agreement.

"The only thing is," Ross said, "it's not consistent; it's not predictable. Logically, the people closest to the body should be the most affected. But it doesn't seem to work that way. It's random. Even the effects vary in a non-patterned way."

"My cousin the engineer," Lita said, smiling.

"It's something we have to consider," Dave admitted.

Lita put a hand on the handyman's shoulder. She nodded toward the shower. "I understand if you don't want to—"

He pulled away, offended. "Don't want to what? Do my job?"

"It's just those *things* in the water..."

But he'd put on his gloves and was already shoving the cable down the drain. He plugged in the motor, started it up and fed the snake into the pipe. Black gunk bubbled up, obscuring the swimmers and filling the room with a foul odor far worse than that of the kitchen sink in the Big House. Seconds later, the water began to drain, and in moments the shower stall was empty save for a thin layer of black silt on the tiles. McDaniels turned on the shower and washed the residue down the drain, letting the water run for a few minutes to make sure everything was clear. Turning off the water, he shook his head. "I just don't understand where this stuff's coming from," he said. "This ain't an open system. You got a septic tank, and all your drain pipes lead to the main line, which goes there." He took a deep breath. "I don't even want to *think* about what's in that septic tank."

Ross stared at the shower nervously, then looked over at the sink and the toilet. He felt uneasy. What if he was shaving and something came out of the sink? Or, even worse, if he was taking a dump...

He pushed the thought from his mind.

"You want me to call Fred Hanson, have him come out here and vacuum out your tank? Just in case?"

249

Both Dave and Lita nodded. "Sounds like a good idea," Dave said.

"I'll ask him if he's come across anything else like this lately. Anybody's likely to know, it's Fred."

"In the meantime?" Lita asked him.

"Keep your eyes open." He gestured toward the toilet. "And, I was you, do your business quickly."

He picked up his equipment and headed outside, the three of them following. "So how much do we owe you?" Dave asked.

"I don't know. Ten bucks?"

"Ten dollars? Come on, I know it's more than that."

"I told you, that angel's been good to me. I'm gonna have more money than I know what to do with. And if you can't use your good fortune to help out your friends..." He held up a hand as Dave took out his wallet. "In fact, this one's on the house. I know Fred'll charge you up the yingyang for scoopin' out your poop hole, so just consider this one a freebie."

"Hold on a second," Lita said. She ran into the house and hurried back moments later with two jars of honey. "Here. We'll barter instead of pay."

McDaniels grinned. "You know I won't turn down free honey."

"Then it's a deal," Dave said. "You want some more? Because—"

"No, this is plenty. Thankya." The handyman lifted his snake motor onto the back of the pickup.

"You're a good man," Lita said.

The handyman smiled widely. "I am, ain't I?" He finished packing up and walked around to the driver's side of the cab. "I'll call Fred as soon as I get back."

"Thanks again," Dave said. "Appreciate it."

Ross announced that he was going to feed the chickens and check for eggs, and both Dave and Lita said they'd come with him.

To the surprise of all, the birds were acting perfectly normal, and, just as surprising, they collected nearly three dozen eggs—all of which appeared to be normal as well. Dave went to check on his bees, and Ross followed Lita over to where the goat and her horse were penned up. Again, there was nothing unusual to be seen. It was as if the past few weeks had never happened.

"Honey!" Dave announced from the other side of the house. "We have honey!"

"Maybe whatever it was seeped into our pipes instead," Lita speculated. "Maybe the ground's clean now."

It made no logical sense, but then nothing made much sense these days, which meant it was just as valid an explanation as anything else. For some reason, Ross was reminded of a Dr. Seuss book, *The Cat in the Hat Comes Back,* where a red ring around a bathtub transfers from object to object until it ends up contaminating all of the snow outside of the children's house.

"I think that's yours," Lita told him.

Ross was confused. "What?"

She pointed to the shack. "The phone. I think it's yours."

He heard the ringing now and hurried over. He wasn't sure how long it had been going on, but whoever was calling did not hang up, and he grabbed the handset. "Hello?" he said breathlessly.

It was Jill, calling to tell him that she hadn't found out anything. She had talked to Michael Song and to Father Ramos, but neither of them had any insights—or at least none they were willing to share. Father Ramos, in particular, seemed guarded, almost as though he was hiding something, she said, and while that was definitely out of character for him, a lot of people were behaving in ways that they ordinarily wouldn't.

Was *he* behaving oddly? Ross wondered. He didn't think so, but then everyone probably thought they were acting normally.

251

He thought of the inappropriate dreams he'd had about Lita.

"So no one seems to know what that thing is," Jill said. "You didn't happen to get a picture of it, did you?"

He hadn't even thought of that. *Stupid.* He'd had his phone with him and could have easily snapped a photo. "No," he said. "I wish I had."

"But you'd recognize it if you saw it again, right?"

It had been curled up in a fetal position, so he wasn't exactly sure what its body looked like, but there was no way on earth he could ever forget that face. "I'd recognize it."

"Could you draw it?"

"I don't think so. I'm not really...I don't know how..." He took a deep breath. "I can't draw."

"Could you describe it so I could draw it? Like a police sketch? You describe the nose, the eyes, whatever, then you look at my drawing and tell me if I have to make something a little bigger or move something to the right..."

"Sure, I can do that."

"All right, then. If I can come up with what you think is a pretty fair approximation, we can scan it into your computer—you have a scanner, don't you?"

"What kind of an engineer would I be if I didn't?"

"We can scan it into your computer and then show it around to, I don't know, anthropologists or parapsychologists or comparative religion experts or something, and see if anyone recognizes it and knows what's going on."

"That's not a bad idea," he said admiringly.

"I'm surprised you didn't think of it."

"Well, I..."

"It's probably part of the same behavioral pattern that keeps men from asking directions. You guys just want to stumble along by yourselves and try to figure things out on your own, even when there's a whole world out there waiting to help you."

"I was going to say it was a lack of imagination on my part, but I like your explanation better."

"So when do you want to do it?"

"How about tomorrow?" Ross said. "This is actually supposed to be my first day of work and it's half-gone already."

"Oh, that's right."

"I have a bunch of emails to read and specs to sort through, and I want to make a good impression. My friend Alex kind of went out on a limb for me."

"I understand. Do what you have to do. Call you tonight?"
"I'll be waiting," he said.

"With bated breath?"

"With my pants around my ankles."

She laughed. "That's what I like to hear."

They hung up, and he actually did turn on his computer, but there was the sound of a loud engine in the yard, and he looked out the window to see what looked like a miniature tanker truck pull up in front of the Big House. It had to be Jackass McDaniels' friend Fred, the septic tank servicer, and, unable to stifle his curiosity, Ross went outside to see what was going on.

McDaniels must have already filled in his friend about what had happened this morning, because the big bearded man in the flannel shirt who was standing with one foot on the ground and one foot on the bottom porch step was already regaling Dave and Lita with stories of unusual things he'd come across in the past few weeks.

"...and I heard a thumping from the tank in back of my truck. I pulled over, thinking I'd accidentally left the pump on, and this thing looked like a big ol' snake with a pink triangle head came flying out of that opening in the top there. Scared the shit out of me! For a second, it looked like it was going to fly away, but then it kind of dissolved into little strings that looked like spaghetti, and they fell back on the tank, slid down the sides and wiggled off into the dirt. Like I said, I didn't suck up anything like that from their septic tank, and I *know* I tightened the lid on that opening." The man saw Ross and nodded in his direction. "Hey."

"My cousin Ross," Lita said.

"Glad to meet you." He grinned. "I won't make you shake hands. Knowing the work I do, not many people want to anyway."

"So, did you come across anything else?" Dave asked.

"Lotta small stuff. Nothing major like that. But yesterday, something kind of weird happened. I'd cleaned out three systems and headed over to the leech field to empty the truck. Only after I hooked up the line and reversed the pump flow to drain it out… there was nothing there. My tank was empty. Somewhere between that last house and the leech field, all that effluent just…disappeared. I don't know how, don't know where, but it was gone. All of it."

"So you heard Jackass' story," Lita said. "How much are you going to charge us?"

"A flat one hundred if there's nothing unusual. Any weird shit—pardon the pun—and it's double."

Lita and Dave looked at one another, a nod passing between them.

"All right," Dave said. "Do it."

Ross stayed around to watch. He really should have been working on his project for the floor mat company—he didn't want to start off by making a bad impression, not after being unemployed for so long—but he thought about the bright green string that came out of the kitchen sink when McDaniels cleared the drain, and the tiny pink creatures in his shower water, and wanted to see what would come out of the septic tank.

It was a nearly hour-long process, and for a long while, they knew nothing. Some gray-black sludge leaked out around the edge of the thick pump line inserted into the top of the buried septic tank, and when Fred shone a light into the tank itself, the sewage inside looked the same, but it was not until the tank was drained, and Fred climbed up on his truck to examine the contents from above, that he determined there was nothing out of the ordinary.

"A hundred bucks," he announced.

Dave wrote out a check, and they watched him drive off, as though waiting for that triangle-headed snake or some other impossible creature to fly out of the truck on its way down the drive. It wasn't until he had driven past the palo verde tree and disappeared that they all turned away.

"Finally!" Lita said, the relief audible in her voice as she hurried into the house. "Now I can go to the bathroom."

TWENTY FIVE

I T WAS AFTER MIDNIGHT, BUT CAMERON WAS WIDE AWAKE, sitting in his locked bedroom on the edge of the bed and drinking Jim Beam out of the bottle. Every few minutes, he would get up, walk nervously over to the door and press an ear against the wood, listening.

Something was out there.

Something big.

Something slimy.

He had not seen it yet, but he'd heard it, making a wet slurping sound as it moved down the hall, and it was what kept him from falling asleep. He had no idea what it was, but he could imagine it eating through the door to his bedroom, *slinking* across the floor and killing him in his bed in an agonizing and unnatural way.

Cameron sidled over to the closed window, parting the curtain just enough to peek through the glass and see the yard below. The smokehouse was still locked—and that *thing* inside it was dead anyway—but he had no doubt whatsoever that it was the source of this horror. It was the source of everything that had been happening since New Year's Eve, and when morning came and the sun was up, he was going to go out there, set fire to that bullet-ridden body and put a stop to it all. He didn't care what anyone else said; this was his property and his decision. Fuck the superstitious assholes around here. This wasn't one of those church fairy tales. This was real, and he needed to put a stop to it before things got even worse.

He saw movement out of the corner of his eye and flattened against the wall, away from the window, afraid of being seen. From somewhere outside came a sound that could have been the cry of a woman. It rose in pitch and volume, as though about to turn into a scream, then lowered into laughter that became a terrifying guttural chuckle. He waited until the noise had subsided, then hurried into the center of the room and back to the bed, finishing off the last of the bottle and letting it fall from his hand onto the floor.

Despite Jorge's iron hand, several of Cameron's men had run away, back to Mexico, maybe, and even some of the wetbacks who'd defected to his place from other ranches had changed their minds and left. The place was noticeably shorthanded, and if half of his cattle hadn't died, there wouldn't be enough workers here to take care of the herd. As it was, he was not sure how much work the remaining hands were doing. Jorge seemed to have them busy with other projects, mostly in and around the smokehouse, and Cameron knew the reason why.

That thing was calling the shots.

Even though it was dead.

And if he didn't put a stop to it now, well… who knew what would happen?

Why in the hell had he put the body into his smokehouse to begin with? What had he been thinking? Maybe he *hadn't* been thinking. Maybe *it* had been thinking for him. Because all of his original reasons had turned out to be nonsensical. He'd wanted to hide the body so no one would find out what had happened: but half of the town had been at the party and those who hadn't had soon learned about it from someone who had been. He wanted to somehow harness the energy he'd sensed in that horribly alien form: but he had no idea how to do that, and he'd discovered almost immediately that the power was affecting *him* rather than the other way around.

So what had kept him from acting sooner?

He wasn't sure. But his life and livelihood had turned to shit since New Year's Eve, and if Cameron had any hope of turning things around, he had to take action now before it was too late.

There was that *slurping* sound outside his bedroom door.

Unless it was too late already.

From somewhere on the ranch, someone screamed. It did not sound close by—not the barn, not the corral, not the barracks— but seemed to originate farther out, in the open grazing area. There was only the one scream, then silence, and Cameron imagined that one of the wetbacks had attempted to sneak off and had been stopped by… By what? Jorge wielding a machete? A hideously deformed cow with crazed red eyes and vampire fangs? Nothing he could conjure up seemed too farfetched.

Eventually, somehow, he fell asleep. He'd been trying to stay awake, and he didn't know when he had dozed off, but he awoke in his bed, and outside the sun was up. His head was pounding, and his mouth tasted like an iguana had just taken a dump in it, but he was no longer afraid, and he unlocked and opened the door, striding down the hall to the stairs. He half-expected to see slime coating the floor, dripping from the walls and ceiling, but the hallway looked the same as always, and he took the steps two at a time, intending to get some matches from the kitchen, then some gasoline from the garage. He was going to torch the smokehouse and that demon inside it before anyone could stop him, and then this nightmare would finally be over.

He grabbed the box of matches from the top of the refrigerator and went outside.

His men, seemingly all of them—or all that were left—were standing in a Hands-Across-America line blocking the front of the smokehouse, as though they already knew what he planned to do and were determined to stop him. The wetbacks stared intently as he marched down the front steps and across the dirt, Jorge, in the middle, following his progress with particular interest.

To the right of the men, alone in the dirt at the edge of the drive, stood an unkempt man holding the strings of several barely aloft balloons. The balloon man was whistling a tune that was at once eerie and familiar, and it took Cameron a moment to realize why he recognized the melody—it was the tune the cat had been whistling in the vet's office.

Holding onto what scant courage he had left, Cameron ignored them all and walked purposefully over to the garage, where he pulled open the door and went inside, picking up a half-full can of gasoline. His men were obviously under the control of that *thing*— he himself had felt the first faint stirrings of trepidation, which told him that he'd better act quickly while he still had the will—and his plan was to either go around them or rush through them, douse the smokehouse with gas and toss a match. If any of them tried to put out the fire, he would stop them. Somehow. His goal was to burn the shed and the body inside it, no matter what.

Carrying the gas can, he walked out of the garage—

And saw the line of ranch hands blocking his way.

In astonishingly quick time, they had moved en masse from the front of the smokehouse to the front of the garage. Jorge was at the fore, no longer part of the line, and it was he who pointed to the gas can. "What is that for?"

"You know," Cameron said, and tried to move past him.

Jorge blocked his way. "No, sir. You cannot."

"This is my house, goddamnit, my property, and I'll do what I want with it! You cholos don't fucking decide what happens here, I do!"

"No."

Cameron lashed out, hitting Jorge across the face. The foreman did not fight back but merely smiled, blood seeping between his teeth. The sight was both sickening and frightening.

Behind the other men and off to the right, the balloon man was whistling that maddening tune.

"I need to do this," Cameron said, and even to himself it sounded as though he was begging.

"No, sir," Jorge repeated softly. "You cannot."

Cameron pushed the foreman aside and found himself grabbed and held by two men he didn't even recognize. *Joe's workers? Jack's?* The others separated, formed parenthesis to either side of them. Jorge reached out and quickly took the gas can from his right hand. Someone else grabbed the book of matches from his left.

In the dirt behind Jorge was a body, and when the foreman stepped aside to put the gas can down, Cameron saw that it was Rudolpho, the kid he'd Sanduskyed, only he was dead and lying on the ground, and between his legs sprouted an enormous erection.

His skin was an odd amber color, and though there were scrapes and cuts in it, there was no blood.

His must have been the scream Cameron had heard last night, but he didn't even have time to think about it because while the two men continued to hold his arms, Jorge unbuckled Cameron's belt, unbuttoned his pants and yanked them down around his ankles. He was turned around, dragged backward, then shoved down onto the dead Rudolpho's crotch. The corpse's stiff penis was obviously supposed to penetrate him, but it missed at first, just poking skin. Then he was wiggled around, readjusted, and shoved down again, and this time the cock found its mark. He screamed as he was entered, feeling the dry hard organ rammed inside him. It broke as he was pushed all the way down on it, and the agonizing penetration grew twenty times more painful as his insides were jolted sideways. Something obviously ruptured within him, because along with the mind-blowing pain came a dribble of warm liquid that had to be blood.

The men let him go, and Cameron was left to fend for himself as, crying in anguish, he tried to pull away from the corpse and get off the broken erection that seemed to be stuck inside him. Finally, he succeeded in releasing himself, and whimpering like a beaten puppy, he pulled up his pants and hobbled back into the house, shutting and locking the door behind him before collapsing on the floor.

TWENTY SIX

I N THE DREAM, FATHER RAMOS WAS IN A SMALL DARK ROOM that he didn't recognize but that he knew was Cameron Holt's smokehouse. He was not alone. There were others there—Holt's foreman Jorge, parishioners of his like Cissy Heath, even that lunatic Vern Hastings—and they were all gathered before the angel, which was unmoving but *glowing*. It was curled into a fetal position, and although it had been killed, there was life within it yet. That life was responsible not only for the shimmering radiance but for the creation of the shell-like layer that had formed from fused sections of the body and started to encase the blackened figure.

It resembled nothing so much as a chrysalis, and Father Ramos understood that it was in the process of *becoming*.

This was why God had not punished them. His angel was not really dead but was transforming into something else.

An avenger?

Father Ramos would not have been surprised, and he was filled with dread at the thought of what might happen when the metamorphosis was complete. His eyes focused on the silently screaming mouth, filled with sharp needle-like teeth, and he shivered as he imagined those teeth ripping into flesh and tearing apart the people who had shot their guns into the sky.

And those who had let it happen.

Like himself.

Father Ramos awoke, suffused with a feeling of foreboding. He was supposed to perform an early morning mass and then hear confessions, but a much stronger impulse gripped him, and he put on his clothes and, without showering, shaving or eating, drove over to Cameron Holt's ranch. Jorge was waiting for him by the cattle guard, and as they looked at each other, an understanding passed between them. Jorge had had the same dream, he realized, and all of the others he'd seen probably had as well.

"Go," Jorge said, gesturing back up the drive toward the house and smokehouse. Though the chain was down this time, the way was blocked by recently installed metal posts that had been cemented into the ground and prevented any vehicles from going through. Father Ramos thought of the last time he'd been here, when his goal had been to give the angel a proper burial in the hopes that it would put an end to all that was happening, and he understood why the posts had been put up. He was probably not the only person who wanted to bury, burn or destroy the body, and he recognized Cameron Holt's desire to protect it because he now felt the same way. The dream last night had awakened something within him, and though he was still frightened of the angel—and

264

feared God's wrath—he knew that the way to salvation lay not in trying to cover up the past but in embracing the future.

He stopped the car. "I can't—" Father Ramos began, but Jorge interrupted him.

"Park here," he said. "Walk."

Father Ramos backed up and pulled onto the side of the drive next to the barbed-wire fence connected to the cattle guard. Getting out of the car, he locked the doors, then nodded to Jorge, who said, "I will be there. We all will be there. Go."

It had not been merely a dream, the priest realized. It had been a summons. The angel wanted him here, wanted to *see* him, and his legs felt weak as he started up the drive.

Although he hadn't noticed it at first, the lane ahead was congested with overgrown vegetation. That was weird. The surrounding land seemed perfectly normal, but the sides of the drive were choked with weeds and brush that, Father Ramos saw as he drew closer, did not resemble anything that grew in this part of the state. Or on land. Between strands of what appeared to be tall brown seaweed waving in the slight breeze as though gently undulating in ocean currents, was a bright white coral formation standing like a bleached mockery of the nearby saguaros. Next to that were graceful ferns, and thick clumps of ivy that appeared to have grown over statues—

bodies

—of people.

It was all part of God's plan, Father Ramos told himself. His was not to ask why. God knew what He was doing.

Still, it was with trepidation that he continued on, stepping around a protruding bush, walking over a series of vines crossing the drive. Catching movement out of the corner of his eye, he looked to the left and saw a long-necked vulture with a face that was all beak pecking out the eyes of a still-wriggling lizard the size of a medium dog. Further back in the brush, the pale delicate features of what looked like a mutated human child stared back at him.

He hurried on.

Ahead was the house, and the barn. Between them, a group of men stood, sat and kneeled before the smokehouse. Around the men, like a fence or barrier, was a ring of dead cattle. He pushed his way through the thin spidery branches of a strange low-growing bush and hastened up the remaining stretch of drive. From many of the men came the low mumbled sounds of prayer, and when he stepped within the ring of cattle, Father Ramos, too, began to pray, offering up a spontaneous thanks to the Trinity, to Mary, to the angel, for allowing him to be here.

This close, the angel's power was nearly overwhelming. He did not remember feeling this intensity of energy and force on New Year's Eve, but he felt it now, and it reminded him of what he'd experienced in the chapel when he'd heard the voice call his name.

"Hector."

He glanced up, startled. Had anyone else heard that? No one appeared to have moved, no one was looking up at the smokehouse or over at him, so he could only conclude that the voice was in his head.

But had he imagined it or was the angel actually speaking to him?

"Father."

He turned around to see Cissy Heath, Juanita Huerta and Iris Tomas walk between two of the dead steers and head toward him. Farther up the drive behind them, just emerging from the overgrown brush, was a scowling Vern Hastings, accompanied by Jorge. They were the people from his dream, and as he met the eyes of the new arrivals, he knew that he'd been right: they'd had the same dream, too.

Where was Holt? he wondered. The rancher had not been in the dream and he was not here now, and Father Ramos wondered if something had happened to him.

If God had taken His revenge.

Jorge stepped forward, past the supplicants, pulled a key from his pocket and opened the smokehouse door. He motioned for Father Ramos and the others to step inside. The ranch hands all remained where they were as the five other people from his dream walked into the darkened shed.

The interior looked just as he knew it would, and they all took up position in the same locations they had in the dream. In the center of the room, the chrysalis-like form of the angel's body seemed much darker and felt much more threatening than he expected. He knew he should pray to it, but he was afraid to address the angel directly, and the alien wildness of the face terrified him to the core of his being.

And yet...

He knew he had to protect it.

He was not sure when it had started or how it was occurring, but the angel was *communicating* with him, with all of them, not talking to them, not sending thoughts telepathically, but allowing knowledge to *seep* into them, as though by osmosis. He stared at those hateful features, and while he did not feel the love he knew he should have, he understood that God wanted His angel protected until he?...she?...*it*...had completed its transformation. Exactly *what* it would be after that transformation was complete, Father Ramos did not know, but it was his job to make sure that the process was not disturbed, that it was allowed to happen without interruption. He glanced around at the others in the room, meeting their eyes one by one, and an understanding passed between them.

Outside, he finally saw Cameron Holt. Naked and filthy, the rancher was running around the corral behind the smokehouse, as though chasing a horse that wasn't there. He wasn't saying anything but was breathing loud enough that they could hear him from this far away. On his face was an expression of mindless determination. He stopped, pissed, then continued running.

Father Ramos crossed himself.

When he returned to the church, it was full. Everyone who had come for the early mass had remained, waiting, and he was glad, because the angel had given him a voice, and he strode up the aisle to the dais and raised his hands high. "Brothers and Sisters!"

He sounded more like an evangelical tent revivalist than a Catholic priest, but the angel of the Lord was guiding him, and he continued on, telling his congregation that they needed to be ever vigilant, that there were those who would try to take this miracle from them, that it was their responsibility to make sure the angel remained safe from harm. He met the gazes of those the angel had touched—for better or worse—and knew that they understood.

"It is God's will," he concluded.

And, as one, the flock before him chanted, "Amen!"

TWENTY SEVEN

Ross had just gone over some reports that National Floor Mats had had him analyze, firing off an email to his fellow team members suggesting they get a few more estimates before committing to any new equipment, when Jill showed up on his doorstep. Once again, she'd walked all the way from her house, and she arrived unannounced, opening the screen door and coming in without knocking. "Hello," she said.

"Hey!' he greeted her, surprised.

"Busy?"

"I was. But I just finished."

"Good." Jill smiled, wandering over to the window. "Nice weather for a walk," she hinted.

It *was* a nice day, around 75 degrees, the blue sky dotted with occasional *Simpsons* clouds. "Apparently so," he said, watching as she took a drink from the water bottle she was carrying.

"I thought you might want to join me."

"So we're going to pretend nothing's going on, huh? That's the tack we're taking?"

"No," she said. "But you can't obsess about it twenty-four seven. Everyone needs a little breathing room. Besides…" She tapped three pencils that were in her shirt pocket. "I figure we can start the sketch when we get back."

"Okay," he said. "Let's walk."

He was surprised at how much he'd grown to enjoy these little excursions. "You're a good influence on me," he told her as they hiked up the drive out to the road. "I've exercised more since I've met you than I have in…I don't know how long."

She patted his stomach. "I can tell."

Laughing, she ran away as he tried to catch her.

They walked west for about ten minutes, until they encountered something that looked like a skinned seal by the side of the road. Ants were crawling all over the dead animal, and the sobering sight caused them to turn around. Neither of them knew what the creature was—or *had* been—and they speculated on its identity as they headed back to the L-Bar D, though they were both utterly certain of its ultimate origin.

The creature in Cameron Holt's smokehouse.

Ross started describing the monster while they were still walking, and his description was specific and vivid enough that she was able to quickly sketch out a rough draft the moment they returned. It was unnervingly close, and he suggested a few minor changes to the face and the body's position, watching as she erased and redrew.

She held it up for him to see, and Ross nodded, feeling cold. "That's it."

Jill looked at the sketch, saying nothing. There was an odd look on her face, an unreadable expression that prompted him to ask, "Is something wrong?"

"No," she said, but the answer was tentative and not at all sure.

"Jill?"

"Let me try something else," she said, and took another sheet of paper, this time drawing the monster with upright body and outstretched wings, the way it would have appeared before being shot. She drew quickly, the image obviously clear in her mind, and while he had never seen the creature alive, he was certain that this is what it had looked like. Even though she had changed the expression on that terrible face, closing the mouth and focusing the eyes straight ahead, he knew that the depiction was accurate. He thought of the black flying thing that had passed overhead on Christmas night, and imagined it looking exactly like this.

"Oh my God," he said. "That's amazing."

She glanced at the picture, shuddered visibly, then handed it over to him. "Let's get this out there," she said. "See if someone knows what it is."

Ross scanned both sketches into his computer, and they spent the rest of the afternoon looking up pictures of mythological creatures, as well as animals, extinct and not, and emailing Jill's drawings to zoologists, anthropologists, folklore experts, ecological organizations, and anyone else they could think of who might be able to identify the creature. They received no immediate responses, but Ross hoped that within a day or so someone might come up with an identification. Even if it was for a fictional being.

Although his fear was that no one would, that they would end up being completely on their own.

There was a knock on the screen. "Rossie? Are you two decent in there?"

He laughed, despite himself. "Come in."

Lita grinned. "Would you like to stay for dinner?" she asked Jill.

Ross glanced at his watch, surprised. "It's that late already?"

"Yep."

"Sure," Jill said. "If it's not too much trouble."

"I made jambalaya, so there's plenty of food. All we have to do is pull another chair up to the table."

"Thank you. Yes," Jill said.

While eating, the two of them explained to Lita and Dave what they'd been doing all afternoon. In the middle of the meal, Ross rushed back to the shack to get Jill's drawings, and their hosts marveled at the accuracy of the depiction. Lita examined the "before" picture. "I'll bet that's what we did see flying over us on the way home."

Dave didn't seem to want to look at the sketch too long. "Do you think this'll work?" he asked skeptically.

"We hope so," Jill said.

"No," Ross confessed, and surprised himself by the admission. They all looked at him. "Whatever's happening here, I think it's unique," he said. "I'm not sure anyone's going to be able to help us."

"But some people might have ideas," Jill said hopefully. "I mean, the more minds we get thinking on this the better, right?"

"Right," Ross said, but he wasn't sure he believed it.

Lita stood up from the table, although she'd barely touched her food. "My friend Lurlene took a picture of it," she said, walking across the kitchen. "That night. New Year's Eve. Other people probably did, too, but Lurlene did for sure. She tried to show me the other day, but her phone wasn't working. If we could get one of her pictures, or if she could tell us who else might have some, you could upload it and show people those."

Lita picked up the wall phone next to the refrigerator, started dialing, and Ross allowed himself a small ray of hope.

"Hello?" Lita said. "Lurlene, it's me—" She stopped talking, and a strange expression passed over her face. Slowly, she pulled the receiver away from her ear. "She hung up on me."

No one suggested that it hadn't been intentional, and Lita placed the handset back in its cradle, making no effort to redial. She headed back to the table, where they resumed eating in silence.

After dinner, they thanked Lita and Dave, then walked across the yard. The sun was starting to go down, and Ross knew that even if she left right at this second, it would be dark before she got home. The thought of her walking through the desert alone at night made him uneasy.

"I should probably drive you back," Ross said.

"Or…I could stay the night."

He smiled. "Or that."

"You know, *Giant*'s on TCM."

He nodded, smiled, hoping he didn't look too blank.

Apparently, he did. "You've never seen it, have you?" she asked.

He shook his head.

"And you're not exactly sure what it is, are you?"

He shook his head again.

Jill smiled, patting his hand as they strolled back to the shack. "You're in for a treat."

She was right. The movie was long and epic, but it moved, and he sat through the entire thing, spellbound. He was fascinated especially by Elizabeth Taylor. He knew her only through red carpet appearances and television interviews he'd seen before her death, and it was impossible to reconcile the cloying phoniness of

273

that latter-day media monster with the beautiful, totally believable actress in the film.

Halfway through, there was an intermission, just as there'd been when the movie was shown theatrically, and Jill took a bathroom break while Ross went over to the kitchen area to get a drink of water. On the way, he saw her drawings where he'd put them on the table next to his computer, and he turned them over, not wanting to think about the monster any more tonight.

It was dark outside, but the drapes were still open, and he closed them before Jill returned from the bathroom. It felt weird having her stay here when Lita and Dave were just across the yard, like having a girl sleep overnight in his bedroom while his parents were home. There was the same awkwardness and the same forbidden thrill, and he hoped she wouldn't be too loud. Later.

Jill came back from the bathroom just as the intermission was ending, and they watched the second half of the movie, which he didn't like quite as much. The film ended, and as the TCM host began talking about the making of *Giant*, Jill scooted closer to him on the couch. They kissed, their bodies pressing together.

Several minutes passed before she pulled away, sliding off the couch, kneeling on the floor and smiling. "I know what you want," she said, and started unbuckling his pants.

He half-heartedly pushed her hands away. "You don't have to…"

"I *want* to," she told him, and took out his growing penis, holding it in her hand and lowering her head to meet it. He closed his eyes as she teased him with her tongue, flicking it lightly around the tip before taking him all the way in. The soft warm wetness of her mouth engulfed him completely, and she began sucking greedily, hungrily, speeding up to bring him almost to the brink of climax, then slowing down or stopping when she sensed it was about to happen, allowing him to grow soft again before resuming her efforts. It was an excruciating tease, and it ended when, instead of slowing down, she sped up, and he came in her mouth, spurting jet after jet of semen down her throat. She held him there, waiting patiently until he was finished, then slid her mouth up and off, licking the last drop from the tip.

"Wow," he said breathlessly.

She smiled up at him.

His penis shrank, but not as much as it usually did, and it began to stiffen again almost immediately when she stood, taking off her clothes. That had never happened to him before, especially after such a powerful orgasm, and he took his clothes off as well, both of them moving over to the bed.

She lay down on the mattress, on her side in a classic cheesecake pose.

"I want you to lick my hole," she said.

He'd fully intended to reciprocate, and he nodded happily. "Of course, madame."

"My *ass*hole," she whispered.

He'd never done that before, and the idea made him a little uncomfortable, but he met her eyes, and she rolled onto her stomach, inviting him. His gaze moved down to the rounded curves of her buttocks. He was still hard, was growing harder, and he knelt down behind her, nosing into the crack of her soft bottom. His tongue found the tightly clenched opening, and he began working it, feeling her stiffen beneath him, her breathing growing harsher the longer he licked. Pushing herself back against his open mouth, her butt cheeks tightening on the sides of his face, she let out a small cry before finally pulling away, gasping.

Jill was breathing heavily. "Do you think you can…?"

He rose to his knees, looked down at his quivering erection. "Yeah."

She got up on all fours, and he saw a wet spot on the bedspread where she'd been lying.

She screamed as he entered her from behind, and he put his hand over her mouth to keep her quiet as he plunged forcefully into her, feeling the hard exhalation of air on his palm after each vigorous thrust. She came, bucking against him, then came again. And again. And again...

After they were done, they took a shower together. Giggling, Jill peed on his hand as he washed her well-used vagina. She was as playful in the water as she was intense in bed, and he thought about how lucky he was to have found someone so fun and uninhibited with whom he could actually see himself having a long-term relationship. They were compatible emotionally, intellectually *and* sexually, and in his experience that was a rare thing.

Unless...

Unless this relationship was a result of that creature in the smokehouse.

It occurred to him that he had not met Jill until after New Year's, and his love life had been on a downward trajectory for the past half-decade before meeting her. If it was true, as everyone was saying, that the monster (he *refused* to think of it as an angel) had changed everyone's luck, making the rich poor and the poor rich, the miserable content and the happy unhappy, then maybe it was responsible for whatever he had with Jill.

The idea depressed him, but he could not dismiss it, and though he was not suspicious of her, he was suddenly suspicious of what they had, and, a little too abruptly, he told her he was tired and suggested they go to sleep.

He dreamed, and it was a nightmare he had had before. Once again, he was on a flat featureless plain that stretched endlessly in all directions. There were monsters in the air, monsters on the ground, all of them after him, and he was running as fast as he could, trying desperately to stay alive in this hellish world.

He had just flattened on the ground to avoid the clutches of a swooping vulture-like creature when he was awakened by Jill, pushing his shoulder and whispering frantically in his ear. "Wake up! Ross! Wake up!"

Sitting quickly up in bed, he tried to open his eyes, which seemed stuck together. He pulled his eyelids apart. It was dark out, he saw, and he was aware of an odd whistling sound. "Huh?" he mumbled groggily.

"Do you hear that? That whistling? That song?"

He heard the fear in her voice, and that helped wake him up.

"What is it?" she whispered, huddling close.

There was indeed something eerie about the sound, which seemed to be coming not just from outside but through a specific window, the one on the east wall. Getting out of bed, he walked uneasily to the window, hesitating a moment before pulling the curtain aside.

The chickens were lined up in the yard, and they were whistling.

Dave had told him that he and Lita had a hundred chickens on the ranch, and most, if not all of them, were standing next to each other, wing to wing, in rows that stretched back dozens deep, staring at his window and whistling in unison. The sight was not merely unnatural but genuinely frightening, and, instantly, Ross let the curtain drop, his heart pounding.

The whistling continued unabated. It was a tune he thought he'd heard before, though he couldn't say where, and while thankfully he could not see through the curtains, the image of the perfectly aligned hens remained imprinted on his mind. He could still see their stiff and unmoving necks, their partially open beaks, their eyes glittering in the moonlight.

"What are they doing?" Jill whispered in his ear. She was right behind him, and he could feel her trembling body against his own.

"I don't know," he admitted.

"Should we call Dave and Lita?"

He shook his head. "Let them sleep. The chickens aren't actually *doing* anything, they're—"

"They're whistling!"

"But they're not causing any harm…"

"Ross, we don't know *what* they're doing. And you saw them. It's creepy. I can't get that tune out of my head, either."

His plan had been to ignore the birds, go back to sleep and hope they would be dispersed by morning. The windows were closed, the door was locked, and they were safe inside the shack. It might be hard to fall asleep again with all of the noise, but even if the chickens remained where they were, they would definitely seem a lot less scary in the light of day. Jill wasn't about to let him do that, though. So, gathering his courage and casting about for something to throw at the birds, he made his way toward the front door. In the wastebasket, he found a broken surge protector that he'd thrown away two days ago, and he picked it up, letting it dangle by the cord. It wouldn't do much damage, not to that many chickens, but it would startle them, and maybe that would be enough to get them to stop.

Afraid of being heard, he soundlessly opened the wooden door, then carefully opened the screen and, in bare feet and underwear, stepped out into the chill night air. It was all he could do not to loudly suck in his breath as he encountered the sudden drop in temperature, but he remained quiet as he padded over to the corner of the shack and peeked around the side.

The chickens were not looking at the window.

They were looking at him.

And they were still whistling.

Holding the surge protector by the plug and swinging it once in a circle above his head, he threw the object, letting it fly. It landed in the middle of the flock, and, as though a spell had been broken, the hens scattered, flying up, clucking wildly. Ross breathed a sigh of relief and hurried back inside, closing and locking the door behind him. Jill was already at the window, peeking out, and he moved next to her.

The moon must have gone behind a cloud, because the yard seemed darker, but even in the gloom he could tell that there was something off about many of the birds. Some were huge, some were peculiarly shaped, and some did not look like chickens at all. He knew Jill had to be seeing it, too, but neither of them said anything, and he pulled the curtains shut and walked over to the bed.

"It's over," he said. "Let's get some sleep."

Ross awoke in the morning to the smell of smoke. The windows in the shack were closed, but the burning odor was almost overpowering and made him cough when he breathed in too deeply. Leaping out of bed, his first thought that the Big House was on fire, but when he yanked aside the curtains and looked outside, he saw Lita and Dave standing before a pyre in the yard.

A burning pile of dead chickens.

His coughing and movement had awakened Jill, and, instantly alert, she asked what was going on as they both pulled on their pants.

"Hurry up," he said, and quickly slipped his sockless feet into a pair of tennis shoes, not bothering to tie them before hurrying outside.

She was in a shirt and her own shoes, only seconds behind him.

Dave was standing before the fire, leaning on a rake. His face was obscured by the thick black smoke given off by the burning bodies, but Lita, a few steps back and holding a gas can, could be seen clearly, and her expression was one of grim determination. There were dozens of chickens burning in the pile, but there were dozens more scattered about the yard, their bodies unmoving. Dave reached for one with his rake, pulled it across the dirt into the fire.

"What happened?" Ross asked.

Dave answered. "We found one in our bedroom when we woke up—"

"In our *bed!*" Lita corrected him.

"It was down by our feet, all dead and bloody, kind of a *Godfather* thing. I don't know how it got into the house; the doors were locked and the windows were closed."

"You didn't hear me scream?" Lita asked.

Both Ross and Jill shook their heads.

"I got a plastic bag, and picked it up and brought it outside," Dave said, "And all these other ones were dead. Except for one weird big giant one I'd never seen before that was kind of walking around in circles making strange noises."

"I've seen that one," Ross told him.

"I got the rake and killed it, and then I scooped all of these into a pile, got out the gasoline, told Lita to get some matches, and..." He trailed off. "Honestly, you didn't hear any of this?"

"We were tired," Ross said. "From last night." Before they got the wrong impression, he added quickly, "The chickens woke us up around—" He looked over at Jill. "What time was it? I didn't even notice."

"Two-thirty."

"Two-thirty. They were all lined up in rows, like some sort of military brigade, right outside my window there, and they were whistling. A song. You didn't hear *that?*"

Confused, both Lita and Dave shook their heads.

Jill began humming the song the chickens had been whistling, and just hearing the tune again caused gooseflesh to ripple over Ross' skin. "Yeah. That's it."

Lita was frowning. "I think I might've heard that before. Somewhere."

Ross coughed, the smoke starting to get to him. He and Lita both moved around the pyre to the opposite side, closer to Dave and Lita. "Are all the hens dead?" Ross asked.

"I don't know," Dave said. "This doesn't look like all of them, but I don't see any others around. Maybe they're hiding. Or maybe they ran away." He was silent for a moment, staring into the pile of burning bird bodies. "I'll tell you one thing. If I *do* find any more of them—"

"You're going to…?"

"Yeah."

No one objected, not even animal-loving Lita, and Ross found that he was relieved that there would be no more chickens on the ranch. They'd made him feel uneasy for some time, and though Lita and Dave were probably planning to buy more with their newfound money, at least these ones would be gone.

They were all coughing now, as an erratic morning breeze pushed the smoke in first one direction then another. The stench was disgusting, and Jill, gagging, had to spit so she wouldn't throw up.

"You guys go back to the house," Dave told them. "Get yourself some coffee or breakfast. I'll take care of this."

Lita, carrying the gas can, started toward the Big House, motioning for Jill to come with her.

"Do you need any help?" Ross asked Dave. "Is there anything you need me to do?"

"No, I've got it. I'll meet you guys back inside when this is done."

Ross followed the women into the house, where Lita kept the doors and windows closed to keep out the smoke and put on a pot of coffee. No one felt like eating, not with that horrible smell lingering in their nostrils, so they sat around the table, talking about what had happened, waiting for Dave to come inside.

Ross looked out the window at the black smoke that had now chimneyed into a plume that rose straight and high into the air, and could probably be seen for miles. He thought of how grateful he'd been to Lita and Dave when he'd first arrived, how happy he had been, after months of stress and insecurity, to actually have security in his life and a place to live.

Now it was all going to hell. And, as rational and unimaginative as he'd always considered himself to be, he knew that it was because of that *thing* rotting in Cameron Holt's smokehouse.

Something needed to be done about it.

But though they continued to talk about it even after the fire was out and Dave was in the kitchen with them, none of them had any idea what that something was.

TWENTY EIGHT

THE SUN HAD ONLY JUST COME UP, BUT TAD WAS ALREADY OFF to his new job with a roofing company in Benson, and Mariah was safely on the bus to school. Alone in the house, Cissy Heath knelt on the floor of the kitchen before the cross on the wall, praying. She prayed each morning, not for material success, not even for health or long life.

For forgiveness.

Even now, she wondered what sort of judgment would be passed on her. She'd been a cock jockey in her younger days, had ridden any pole she could fit in her hole, but she'd returned to the church in the 1990s and had led a blameless God-fearing life since then.

Now, through His angel, she was in the direct service of the Lord. Which ought to count for something. Then again, Tad had been one of the men shooting off guns to celebrate New Year's Eve, so it was also possible that any gains she'd made were balanced out and she was right back where she started.

Finishing her prayer, she remained kneeling, eyes closed. She was trying for calmness, inner peace, but there was an old fragment of song lyric trapped in her head, going around and around, and she couldn't for the life of her remember the name of the tune or who had sung it. After the song segment that was tormenting her, there was a line about the "flat Sargasso Sea," which made her think it might be "Rock Lobster" by The B-52s, but she knew that wasn't it.

The title was on the tip of her brain.

Flat Sargasso Sea.

It was…it was…

"Mimi on the Beach." By Jane Siberry.

Yes.

The entire song came flooding back to her—melody and lyrics—and while relief accompanied the knowledge, another emotion was stirred by the recollection: sadness. The song made her sad. She remembered when it had come out, remembered how young she'd been, how much future was still ahead of her, how many possibilities the world had held. Her life could have gone in a thousand different directions, and while she was proud of who she was today, the truth was that this was not where she would be—or *who* she would be—if she had her choice.

She suddenly felt depressed. Where was Jane Siberry? she wondered. Was she still recording music? Where was Selina Choy, who'd been her freshman roommate back then? Was Selina still alive?

Every path her thoughts took ran to darkness and Cissy opened her eyes and looked up at the cross on the wall, then around at the shabbiness of her small kitchen. She loved her husband and her daughter, and she truly did believe, but every so often she wondered what things would be like if she *hadn't* gone back to the church. A nagging notion in the back of her mind told her that she might be happier.

Which was why she needed to pray.

She shouldn't have such thoughts.

Closing her eyes tightly, she offered up another prayer for forgiveness, finishing with three Hail Marys, and told herself that she felt better.

Cissy had had breakfast with Tad and Mariah, but mouthing prayers had made her thirsty, and she stood, opening up the refrigerator and pouring herself another glass of orange juice. She set herself in front of the sink, drinking it, staring out at the vacant lot behind the grocery store.

Last night, she'd dreamed again that she was in the smokehouse, only this time she had been alone with the angel and it had... *unfurled.*

Its new form had been terrible, far worse than its original appearance. It was jet black rather than dark green, and its formerly thin wings were thick and spiky. Demonic. Just like its body, which now had clawed feet, two extra insectile arms and stood twice as tall as a man. But it was the look of insanity and hatred on its wild monstrous face that frightened her to the core of her being.

The end was coming soon, she knew, very soon, and the angel would reward those who deserved it and punish those who didn't. She was afraid of that judgment, and she wondered if it wouldn't be better to just avoid it, to escape it, to opt out.

To kill herself.

Kill herself.

The idea was somehow calming.

The church had always taught her that suicide was a sin, but when she thought of the angel and the way it had looked when it revealed its new self—

when it had unfurled

—killing herself seemed like a viable option.

Cissy had heard about the good fortune the angel had brought some people, the bad fortune that had befallen others, the luck that had changed, and she'd wondered why nothing like that had happened to her or her family. It occurred to her that that was what was happening now. For the truth was that she had been happy and satisfied until today, until this moment. Her past had been something she had been ashamed of and regretted. All of a sudden, it was something she missed, something she had lost, and she wondered if the change in *her* fortunes involved her happiness.

Maybe, maybe not. The reasons didn't matter. The fact was that the future was no longer something she had the confidence to face. She loved God, but she was afraid of His angel, and taking herself out of the equation seemed like the easiest and best solution to the problem.

The only question was: what to do about Tad and Mariah? It would be wrong to leave them alone; there was no way she could do that. It would be better for all of them if she killed her husband and daughter first, *then* took her own life. That way, they would be together.

She smiled to herself, feeling calm and reassured. Finishing her orange juice, she walked over to Tad's gun case and chose a rifle. Mariah wouldn't be home for another eight hours, Tad for ten, maybe twelve, but it didn't hurt to be prepared. She would load the rifle, set up a chair in front of the door and wait. She'd shoot Mariah when she walked through the doorway—in the face, so it would be quick—then she'd do the same to Tad when he returned, and then she would kill herself.

Maybe, if she was lucky, the angel wouldn't get them then.

Jeri finished her route early, unnerved by the amount of mail that had remained uncollected in various boxes. It wasn't her place to check up on people—her job was just to deliver the mail—but after seeing the letters, catalogs and bills she'd delivered yesterday and the day before piling up untouched, she had been sorely tempted to get out of the car and knock on doors to make sure everyone was all right.

Only...

Only she didn't really want to. She was *afraid* to know the truth because she suspected that more than one of the mail recipients was not sick or on vacation or incapacitated but...

Dead.

Yes, dead. That was her fear, and she didn't want it confirmed. So she forced packages and envelopes into overstuffed boxes with no room to hold them and forced the doors closed, wondering what she would do tomorrow if the mail was still not collected.

She had stopped delivering to the ranches several days ago, but from various points on her route she could still see Cameron Holt's scarecrows, and even at a distance those things freaked her out. She'd told Don about them, had even driven out with him to so he could see for himself, and he had indeed thought they were freaky. But he didn't seem to feel the threat that she did, and she wasn't sure he totally believed her story about the scarecrows *looking* at her, about one of them actually climbing off its pole. Like everyone else, he knew that a lot of weird things had been happening around Magdalena since New Year's Eve. But he was one of those people who seemed to have been affected *positively*. She had been terrorized by those damn scarecrows, beset by complaints from postal customers, and now half of the people on her route weren't even picking up their mail.

Dead

She hadn't even been in the mood to have sex for the past two weeks.

But Don was in great spirits these days. More people had dropped off equipment to be repaired at his shop than ever before, and he'd almost earned enough money to buy that new outboard motor he wanted. Strangely enough, despite his good mood, he hadn't tried to make love to her, hadn't asked for sex or even *hinted* about it, and Jeri wondered if he was seeing someone else. That would certainly account for his change in attitude.

The thought made her depressed and, on a whim, she drove to Don's repair shop instead of heading home. He wasn't there; the place was locked up. He wasn't at the house, either, and Jeri's heart dropped in her chest. She tried calling him on his cell phone, but she had no bars, so, leaving the ranch mail in the car, she hurried inside to use the land line. She was able to reach him, but he must have had his phone turned off because all she got was a message. She hung up, feeling worried and frustrated.

For a moment, she seriously considered getting back in the car and driving around, looking for him. But she knew how paranoid that was and thought it would be better to give him the benefit of the doubt, to wait and then ask him where he'd been this morning when she saw him.

Besides, she had to take out that ranch mail in case one of the recipients came by to pick it up.

Like Cameron Holt.

She shivered.

Getting a quick drink of water from the kitchen, Jeri walked back outside—

Where there was a scarecrow standing in her yard.

She jumped, screamed, and immediately rushed back inside, slamming the door behind her. She had seen the scarecrow for only a second, but it was the closest she had ever been to one of them, and she had noticed the specificity of its mud features, the broadness of its nose, the slightly mismatched eyes, the high cheeks, the hint of an overbite in the mouth. Leaning with her back against the door, breathing hard, she wondered who had sculpted that face and how, who had made those oversized clothes—

Thump!

Thump!

Thump!

There was pounding on the door behind her, strong enough that she could feel it through the wood, and she let out a scream that would have done Linnea Quigley proud. Jumping away from the door, she dashed over to the phone and dialed 911, an automatic response, though she knew there was no police, fire or sheriff in town and the call would go through to Willcox.

Behind her the door crashed open.

She should have called a neighbor. Not daring to look behind her, scrambling to get out of the way in case the scarecrow was right on her heels, Jeri ran through the den to the back door. It took several agonizing seconds to get it unlocked and open—seconds in which she was sure the scarecrow was going to grab her—but then she was outside, in the back yard.

Where three scarecrows blocked her way.

Sobbing, she sank to the ground, even while a part of her brain was exhorting her to fight back, call for help, run away, duck, dodge, find a way out. She closed her eyes, hearing rustling movements louder than her own cries, then feeling strong rough fingers of hardened dirt tighten around both arms and pick her up. Screaming now, but unable to resist the urge, she opened her eyes, staring into two deep black holes in a brown mud face, straw hair sticking out far enough to poke into her forehead.

She had never seen any of the scarecrows actually move, but as she was twisted sideways, as one of them grabbed her legs, as the one holding her arms opened its mouth to reveal teeth made from jagged chunks of rock and broken pieces of bottle glass, she finally did, and the sight terrified her into silence.

Her last thought was a complete non sequitur: *Who's going to deliver the mail now?*

Vern Hastings made himself a ham sandwich for lunch, using the curved knife he'd utilized for the sacrifice to smear mustard on the toasted bread. The knife had been washed several times since then, but it he liked to think that there was still some DNA on the blade.

Putting the knife down, he bit into the sandwich, chewing slowly to enjoy the taste.

Rose walked into the kitchen. "You're eating a sandwich? I thought we were going to—"

Vern picked up the knife and stabbed his wife in the throat. Blood gushed out, but it gushed out cleanly, and a ring of yellow was still visible along the upper edge of the wound where mustard from the knife had wiped off on the skin. Collapsing on the floor, she grabbed her neck with both hands, desperately trying to stem the flow, but blood continued to pour down her neck and seep through her fingers.

Vern calmly took another bite as she thrashed about, made loud gasping gurgling sounds, then twitched once and lay still.

He thought about who would replace Rose during services, who would assist him. Old Etta Rawls, maybe. Definitely not that fat pig Tessa Collins. In fact, it might be time for Tessa to be punished for her gluttony.

He would be happy to do the honors.

Popping the last bite of sandwich into his mouth, Vern looked down at the mess Rose had made. Blood was everywhere, and the last thing he wanted to do was clean it up. There was no one else to do it, however, and, sighing heavily, he went out to the laundry room to get a bucket and rag, resenting the angel for making him kill his wife.

TWENTY NINE

STUPID! JILL BERATED HERSELF. *STUPID!* BOTH HER EMAIL AND answering machine were full of messages. She hadn't made any telemarketing calls—or even checked in with the company—for nearly two days, though she'd promised to put in at least six hours during that period. Listening to the messages, she discovered that two different supervisors—one from her group and one from the tier above him—had attempted to contact her to make sure nothing had happened.

The stress was on, and before calling back she tried to come up with a reasonable excuse, an explanation that sounded legit and would account for her not checking in, but would not make it sound as though she'd purposely blown off work. She finally decided to go with the generic "family crisis," and since she was such a bad liar, she responded by email. Immediately afterward, she clipped on her headset, logged onto the command center, signed in and started making calls from the list she was given.

She called for six hours straight, without a drink, food or bathroom break, and it was midafternoon before she finally signed out, logged off and removed her headset. She was dead tired, but she'd made up her time. It had also been an impressive stretch and, hopefully, that would counteract her unexpected period of inactivity.

Wearily, she glanced down at the open sketchbook on the table in front of her. She tended to doodle when she talked on the phone, and sometimes her subconscious came up with images and ideas that she expanded on in her work. This time, however, there were only endless drawings of the monster, standing and lying in various positions, its body in assorted stages of decomposition and…metamorphosis. The doodles were much more detailed than her usual random scratchings, and they caused her to look over at the new canvases she had leaned against the wall. On each of them, she had painted the same creature—which was why it had been so easy for her to depict what Ross had described—and she wondered again how she could have so perfectly imagined exactly the same beast that Ross had seen before hearing any details of its appearance.

Where the ideas for the paintings had come from, and why she had done so many, she did not know—and that frightened her.

Feeling nervous, she walked over to the paintings, pulling forward the ones in front so she could see those behind them. Ten! She'd painted ten of them over the past few days. Jill had not realized that she'd done so many. She had never worked so fast in her life, and the fact that such prolificacy had gone entirely unnoticed by her was disconcerting. Especially considering the subject matter.

"*Jill.*"

In the silence of the house, she clearly heard her name spoken aloud, though where the voice was coming from she couldn't say. It sounded strangely high-pitched, like someone speaking on helium, and it was accompanied by a truly obnoxious odor, a combination of rot and fecal matter that made her think of a decaying corpse.

"*Jill.*"

It came again, and this time it sounded as though it was coming from outside. Frowning, she walked over to the window.

Puka was on the other side of the glass, looking in at her, and she jerked back, crying out. The dog was standing on his hind legs, front paws against the window. His fur was gone, as was much of his flesh. Dirt, burrs and twigs were stuck with dried blood to red musculature and white bone. In the burned face, that one crazy eye still rolled around, while sharpened teeth grinned hungrily beneath the exposed nasal cavity.

The mouth opened, closed.

"*Jill.*"

Screaming, she ran around the butcher's block, through the kitchen to the back door, intending to dash over to Shan Cooper's and take refuge inside his house. But Puka was already rounding the corner, walking on its hind legs (it was now an *it*, not a *he),* the way a person would, and she could see that wild rolling eye and that terrible white grin even from this far away.

Dogs were not designed to walk upright, so Puka's steps were slow and awkward, and Jill ran in the opposite direction, screaming. "Help! Help!"

She sped through the side yard to the front of the house, running into the middle of the cul-de-sac while simultaneously checking out her neighbors' driveways. Shan Cooper's El Camino was gone, as was the Porters' Explorer. But Tim's pickup was in the

Russells' carport, and she headed directly across the street as fast as her legs would carry her. Gina's Kia was not there, but she and Tim never drove together, so the odds were that Tim was home.

He wasn't.

She stood, screaming and crying on the Russell's front porch, banging on their door, jabbing the button for the bell, but there was no response, and when she turned around, she saw Puka crossing through the center of the cul-de-sac, still standing erect.

"*Jill!*" the dog called out. Its voice was louder now, though just as high-pitched. She could hear it all the way over here, above her own frantic crying.

Desperate, Jill ran around the edge of the circle back to her own house. There was no sidewalk, but there was a dirt trail, and she passed over two driveway entrances on the way to her own, when she suddenly knew what she had to do.

The dog was already turning around in its disturbing, awkward way.

She ran up to her front door. Had she locked it or not? Not! She opened the door, grabbed her purse from the spot next to the couch where she'd dropped it, and was already fumbling for her keys as she carried the purse back outside and hurried over to her van. It, too, was unlocked—thankfully—and she got in and locked the doors as she rummaged through her purse, finally finding the Econoline's keys. Glancing at the side and rearview mirrors, she didn't see Puka, which meant that the dog was either in back of the van or in her blind spot, and she shoved the key in the ignition, started the engine and threw the vehicle into reverse.

There was a crash and a bump, and as much as she had once cared for Puka, she hoped that she had run the dog over. Tires squealing, she backed the van all the way over to the Russells' house across the street, feeling a sense of relief as welcome as it was horrific when she saw the bloody body crumpled at the edge of her own driveway. Just to be on the safe side, she shifted from Reverse to Forward and ran over the dog again. Then did it one more time for good measure.

She didn't want to see the result of her efforts, but she had to make sure Puka was gone for good, so she got out of the van and walked back. What had once been a dog and had then become a monster was now a flattened mess of blood, guts and bone on the edge of the road. She got close enough to verify but not close enough to see details, then hurried back in the house, locking the door behind her. She wasn't about to pick up the body, but she couldn't just leave it there, and when Shan or one of her other neighbors came home, she'd have him take care of it.

She considered calling Ross and asking him to come over, but didn't want to throw this on him right now, not with everything else he had to worry about.

She'd tell him tonight when he called.

There was a knock at her front door, and her heart leapt in her chest.

"Anyone home?"

It was Ross! Grateful, she ran to the door and yanked it open.

"Nice day for a…walk," he said, frowning as he took in her rattled, disheveled appearance. "What happened? What is it?"

Unable to stop herself, she burst into tears, throwing her arms around him and hugging tightly. She made him close the door and lock it, and on the way to the couch told him about Puka. Immediately, he turned around and went outside to look at what was left of the dog. She could see the expression of horror on his face when he saw the flattened, bloody remains and knew he was far out of his comfort zone, but when he offered to pick up and dispose of the body, she gratefully allowed him to do so. Part of

her wanted the dog buried—she owed Puka at least that much—
but the animal was not what it had been, was not the pet she had
known, and she did not raise any objection when Ross used her
shovel to scoop it into a Hefty bag and then threw the bag into the
covered garbage can at the side of the house.

Afterward, she made him wash off the shovel with Lysol and
leave it lying flat on the ground at the side of the house to dry.

"Done," Ross announced, coming back inside, and he
scrubbed his hands with Comet in the kitchen sink in order to get
off whatever germs might have been on his skin.

Jill was not a drinker, but in the cupboard she had a bottle of
scotch left over from her old boyfriend that she'd brought with her
to Magdalena and kept on hand in case she ever entertained and
guests wanted some. It hadn't happened yet, but she could really
use some extra courage right now, and she poured herself a shot.
Ross declined an offer for one of his own, so she drank his, too. He
was considerably less rattled than she was, but then he hadn't seen
Puka in action.

She was putting away the bottle when she saw Ross looking at
the paintings against the wall. "When did you do these?" he asked.

"The past few days."

Frowning, he started looking through them. He pulled one
canvas out from the back and placed it next to one in the front,
rearranging all of them until, in a few minutes, they were lined up
in a semi-circle around the room.

Jill saw the progression immediately. She hadn't noticed it
before because her eye had always been on the creature, not the
background, but now she saw that there was a *story* going on
around the central figure.

"When did you paint this one?" Ross asked.

She could barely speak. Her voice when it came out was a whispered croak. "The day before yesterday, I think." In this picture, the monster was curled up inside of what looked like a translucent egg on the floor of a darkened room. Inside the egg, one clawed hand was pointing to the right.

And at the edge of the painting, between the wall of the room and the edge of the canvas, a small, skinned Puka, standing on hind legs and nearly invisible amidst a depiction of dead cattle, was heading off in that direction.

She didn't remember painting the dog at all. She remembered painting the cocooned monster, but, if asked, she would have sworn on her mother's life that the background had been a solid brown or blue.

Only none of the backgrounds were solid colors. They were all *scenes,* though that was not something she had noticed even this afternoon when she had been sorting through the works herself. Looking at them now, in the order in which Ross had placed them, Jill saw the evolution of the beast from a dead body enveloped in an egg to a fearsome monster standing tall and looming over the smoldering ruins of Magdalena. Somehow, in her paintings, she had predicted not only the return of her dog but the burning of Dave and Lita's chickens, which were visible in the corner of the very first canvas. Seeing that, it made her wonder if the other events depicted would come true. There was a line of angry well-armed men with elongated animal shadows walking through the desert, a street littered with the mutilated bodies of women, a field of wildly overgrown and unsettlingly colorful vegetation, and those smoking ruins, out of which were crawling creatures that looked like they'd come from the depths of hell.

She tried to tell herself that it was all coincidence, that none of it meant anything, but she did not voice that thought to Ross because she knew it was not true.

Were they all hers? Or had something been working *through* her?

She was afraid to even consider that line of reasoning.

"Did you really come here for a walk?" she asked, clumsily trying to change the subject.

After a pause and a long look into her eyes, he let her. "Sort of, I guess. I mean, I drove here, and I definitely would have been willing to take a walk, but mostly I just wanted to see you." He looked into her eyes. "You don't want to go for a walk *now*, do you?"

"After what happened, you mean?" She thought about it. "I think I do. I usually walk when I need to relax or de-stress or want time to think. It helps me. You don't mind, do you?"

"No. Like I said, I'm up for it." He took her arm in an exaggeratedly courtly fashion. "Shall we?"

It occurred to her that the last time they'd walked together they'd seen that skinned-seal thing covered with ants, and, the time before that, the deformed wormlike cow inching its way across the dirt. Then they were out the door and starting up the road, and it felt so good to be out of her house and away from her yard, that she pushed all reservations aside. Besides, it was daytime. What could happen in the daytime?

Puka.

She pushed *all* reservations aside.

They walked in silence, but it was a comfortable silence. She didn't feel like talking right now, and Ross seemed to sense that. She was grateful to him for it, and she untwined her arm from his and simply held his hand. The weather was cool but not cold, and his warm hand felt nice in hers. Although the sun was out, billowing white clouds were rolling upward in the east. If this was summer, she would have thought they were monsoon thunderheads, but this time of year, she didn't know what to make of them. They were beautiful, though, like something out of *Arizona Highways,* and she thought that maybe she would like to paint a picture of clouds sometime.

They encountered nothing unusual on their stroll, and instead of staying on the road, she led him onto a trail that wound partially up the mountain before circling back to her neighborhood. There was something reassuring about everything being the way it was supposed to be out here. The brush was normal, the rocks were rocks, they even saw a jackrabbit and a lizard and there was nothing the matter with them. It had the effect of making what had happened with Puka seem small. In fact, looking out at the vastness of the desert, even the angel and its spooky influence on everything around it seemed small.

By the time they arrived back at her house, the sun was starting to go down. Jill was feeling much better, much braver, much more herself. There were no lights on in any of the rooms and the windows were dark, but that didn't faze her. She did shoot a quick uneasy glance at the garbage can at the side of the house, but then she walked inside, turning on first the living room light, then the kitchen. She poured both Ross and herself glasses of water, and when they were through drinking, she gave him a wet kiss on the cheek. "Thank you," she said. "I'm glad you came over."

He gave her a kiss not on the cheek, and then they were embracing, their bodies pressing together, their tongues entwined. They moved to the bedroom, quickly shedding clothes.

There was no reason for foreplay. He was hard, she was wet, and they just did it.

Afterward, they put their clothes back on. Ross offered to stay, but the walk had calmed her down, her fear had faded, and she told him that she'd be fine. Besides, she needed to make at least an hour or two more of calls. She smiled tiredly. "Dinner and after-dinner pitches. Everyone's favorite."

"So you're one of those..."

"Yes," she said. "Yes, I am."

"Are you sure you'll be okay?" he asked.

She put a hand on his arm. "I'm sure."

It was just as well, Ross admitted, because he had work to do as well. "If I can go through everything that's piled up and send off some suggestions by early tomorrow morning, I'll be in good shape."

Jill gave him a quick kiss, though she was slightly annoyed that he'd given in so easily. She'd been sincere in saying that she needed to work this evening and that he could go, but it would have meant something if he had insisted on staying. It was unfair of her, she knew. He was only doing what she'd told him to do. But, nevertheless, she felt disappointed.

Together, they walked out to the living room. Outside, through the windows, the darkening clouds were building up. The eastern half of the sky was a deep gray wall that looked distinctly threatening. "I think it's going to rain," Ross said.

An hour ago, she would not have thought that likely, but now it seemed inevitable. *Maybe you* should *stay,* she almost told him. Instead, she said, "You'd better get going before it starts coming down."

They parted with one last kiss, and although she closed and locked the door behind him, she watched him go through the front window. It was dark enough now for him to put on his headlights, and as he pulled away, she thought that his taillights against the blackness of the building clouds looked like the eyes of some gigantic feral creature staring back at her.

THIRTY

T HE STORM HIT AT MIDNIGHT.

Ross was awakened by the thunder. It didn't sound like any thunder he'd ever heard before, and he lay in bed listening to it over the rattle of rain on the roof. Immediately before each peal, lightning flashed, and for brief irregular seconds it seemed as though some hidden cameraman was taking flash pictures of the room.

The truth was, the thunder reminded him of the roar of some monstrous beast. Rather than a loud echoing whipcrack, the traditional noise of air heated and expanded by electrical discharge, the sound was throaty, animalistic, building to a crescendo rather than starting big and fading. It did not seem possible that such a sound could be formed by mere weather, and he imagined some massive creature hiding in the night, behind the clouds, ready to tear apart Magdalena…Arizona…the United States…the world. It was a ridiculous thought, but none the less frightening for that, and he remained in bed, waiting for the flashes, listening for the roars, knowing in his heart that at the root of it was that thing in the shed, that fiend they were calling an angel, that dead monstrosity that was metamorphosing into…something else.

Staring at the horrorshow window with its runny rain backlit by periodic lightning, he tried to think of what could be done. But he had been trying to think of that for days—as had Lita, as had Dave, as had Jill—and nothing had come to him. He was not a person who thought outside of the box, and even under ideal circumstances his imagination was what could be charitably called compromised. In a situation like this, where the box was an octagon made out of flypaper and cheese, he was next to useless.

Still, he told himself that even illogical problems had logical solutions, and he tried itemizing in his head everything he knew, everything he'd seen, heard and suspected, hoping that an idea would occur to him.

It didn't.

He fell asleep thinking of one of Jill's paintings, the one with the chrysalis in the shed and the skinned dog in the corner, walking on its hind legs.

He dreamed that Lita was lying naked atop that black chrysalis, and Jill was lying on top of her, and little sparks of blue lightning were shooting up from the dark egg beneath them and illuminating their faces with expressions of ecstasy.

⚮

Not only was this type of thunderstorm out of season, but it was by far the largest one they had ever experienced. Lita and Dave were sitting up in bed when the thunder and lightning started. They'd been awake already, had heard first the wind, then the rain, but it was not the storm they were discussing, nor was it the angel and its ramifications. They were talking about Dave's parents. The subject had come up on its own, and, for the first time since the accident, he was crying. He had never been the most emotionally demonstrative guy, and she wasn't surprised that he had not cried at the funeral. Detached numbness was the biggest response she figured he'd show. But she was surprised tonight when he had started talking about his childhood home in Sonoita, and she was even more surprised when he had started welling up. Surprised, touched and ultimately pleased. She had always been of the opinion that emotions were better let out than held in. It was much healthier, and she was relieved to see Dave opening himself up this way.

"I miss my mom," he said into her shoulder, great sobs wracking his body. "I miss my dad."

In the back of her mind was the idea that this emotional unburdening was not all his doing, just as somewhere in her brain she was thinking that this thunderstorm was...not quite right. But she refused to allow her thoughts to go that deep. She held him close, and chose to believe that a perfectly normal storm had triggered perfectly normal memories and emotions in her perfectly normal husband.

Outside, the storm grew more frenzied. If they'd still had chickens, Lita would have been worried about them. She was worried about her horse, but he had access to the barn and had been through many monsoons. He knew what to do. The bees were another matter. The wind seemed strong out there, seemed to be growing proportionally as the lightning grew brighter and the thunder grew louder. If the hives were knocked over...

She said nothing about it, not wanting Dave to go outside and check—which she knew he would.

Dave pulled away, wiping his eyes, embarrassed that he had been crying. But she would not allow him to be embarrassed, and she took his hands in hers, moved them away from his face and looked into his eyes. "I love you," she said.

He smiled through his tears. "I love you, too."

The phone rang.

They both jumped.

There was a slight lull in the ruckus outside, and, except for the sound of the rain, the house was quiet. The phone rang again. Lita looked over at the closest extension, on the nightstand on Dave's side of the bed. Her first reaction was to not answer. But it might be important. So she told Dave to grab the phone, afraid to do it herself, and she held her breath, watching his face as he picked up the receiver and said, "Hello?" There was a long pause. "It's for you," he said, handing it to her, and she could tell from the expression on his face that it was not Ross, not one of her friends, but something serious.

Lita breathed deeply, knowing she didn't want to hear what the person on the other end of the line wanted to tell her, but taking the phone anyway. "Hello?"

She listened as the woman on the other end of the line identified herself as Dr. Warren from Albuquerque General Hospital and informed her in tones of practiced sympathy that her mother had been in an automobile accident. She'd been hit head-on by the drunk driver of an SUV—

just like Dave's parents

—and had been rushed to the hospital by ambulance, where emergency surgery had been performed.

There was a pause.

Her mother, Dr. Warren said, was dead.

Lita did not hear any more. The phone dropped from her hand onto the bed, and as the thunder and lightning resumed with a wild fury, she screamed out her anguish in an involuntary cry of pain that came from the deepest part of her soul and felt as though it was never going to end.

Jill was baking cookies when the rain started.

She hadn't been able to sleep, and though she'd gone to bed shortly after nine, she was up again by eleven, restless and wide awake. Drawing usually helped her relax, but the pencil felt heavy in her hand, and after ten awkward minutes with her sketchbook, she tossed it aside.

What she really felt like doing was making cookies, and despite the lateness of the hour, she went out to the kitchen, put on her apron, got a mixing bowl out of the cupboard; eggs, milk and butter from the refrigerator, and yeast, flour, sugar and salt from the pantry. She hadn't made cookies for over a week, hadn't gone to the farmer's market last Thursday, and even though it was nearly midnight, she felt good getting back to baking.

After mixing and rolling out the dough, she decided to make cookies in the shapes of angels. *Real* angels. They were on everyone's mind lately, and maybe seeing some of the traditional variety would make people realize that that thing they'd shot down *wasn't* one. Using a knife, she carved out an angel freehand: a long-haired woman in a billowy dress, hands raised in benediction. She carved out three more, placed them on a baking sheet and put the baking sheet in the oven.

Outside, it began to rain, the sound of it on the roof reminding her of an onomatopoeic Dr. Seuss book from her childhood. *Dibble dibble dop dop.* She'd been planning to whip up a few colors of frosting with which to paint her cookies, but she paused. There were no shades on the kitchen window, and she stared out at the darkness, remembering when she'd found the heavily damaged Puka walking in circles on the floor where she was standing.

Now he was in a garbage can at the side of the house.

Lightning flashed, and she saw the desert behind her house illuminated for a brief second. There was too much darkness, too many shadows, and as thunder roared above her, she wished that she had put in drapes or shutters or shades, something to block the view, to keep the night out of the house. Lightning flashed again, and something in the sky caught her attention. As much as she wanted to look away from the window, she moved closer, leaning over the sink, waiting for the next lightning flash. It came, and the burst of electricity illuminated the heart of the storm.

Was there a face in the cloud?

She waited again.

Yes.

But the next time it was gone, and it did not reappear, though she stood watching for the next five minutes.

Glancing at the timer to see how long it would be before she could take out the cookies, she heard, in the lull between peals of thunder, an insistent tapping coming from the oven. Some sort of propane leak? She hurried over. For the millionth time, she wished she had an electric stove and oven. But the house had come with a propane hookup, and she couldn't afford to—

She stopped three feet in front of the appliance.

One of the angel cookies was upright, standing behind the oven window, tapping on the inside of the glass and trying to get out.

She was too scared to even scream. Her first impulse was to run away, to get the hell out of the house and drive to Ross' place or the home of one of her friends, but she realized almost instantly that in this situation, she had the means to fight back.

Keeping her eye on that six-inch figure in the oven window, Jill took two steps forward. Turning the knob from "Bake" to "Broil," she cranked the temperature up all the way. Almost instantly, the tapping grew more frantic. The angel was pushed aside as one of the other cookies took its place, its little baked dough arms bending at the elbow, its fists smacking against the thick glass. This cookie was darker than the first, brown in patches, and there was a desperation to its movements that almost made her feel sorry for it. But, despite outward appearances, it was not alive, and she waited and watched as it cooked in the heat, darkening further before finally burning. It had fallen over, and smoke was coming out of the oven, but she was not about to turn the appliance off until that thing was a crispy crumble, and she grabbed a chair, stood on it and pulled the battery out of the smoke alarm before it went off.

The smoke was getting so thick that it was getting hard to breathe. She opened the window a crack, but she was afraid to open the door, and she suffered for another few minutes before putting on her heat protective gloves, opening the oven door and taking the cookie sheet out of the oven. She ran across the kitchen, threw it into the sink and, on the off chance that one of the cookies was still moving, turned on the water and tried to soak it. A gush of steam whooshed up, and, seconds later, when she could see, Jill discovered to her relief that blackened crumbs were all that was left of the angels.

The storm outside had gotten crazy. Lightning and thunder were nearly constant, and powerful wind was forcing water into the kitchen through the small space of open window. This was flash flood weather, and she would have turned on the outside lights to see if any water was running through her property if she hadn't been afraid that she might see something else.

Turning around, she faced her mixing bowl on the table, where half of the dough she'd made was still resting. Not knowing what to do with it, only knowing that she was not going to bake it, she considered putting it in a plastic bag and dumping it in the garbage. But, on the off chance that the dough could become animated even without baking, she took the bowl to the sink, filled it with water, diluted its contents and dumped the runny mixture down the drain, letting the faucet run for a couple of minutes afterward to make sure it was gone.

There was no way she'd be sleeping tonight, and she definitely wasn't going to bake anything, so she went back out to the living room and once again picked up her sketchbook. Even out here it was hazy and smelled like burnt cookie, but she was not about to open any doors or windows, so she turned on her swamp cooler for the first time since September, hoping its stale summer air would help dissipate the smoke, and settled down to draw.

She couldn't draw, though.

And she remained on the couch with the pad on her lap, pencil in hand, listening to the storm, waiting.

"Hector."

Father Ramos jerked awake at the sound of the voice. Lightning flashed, and in that brief second, he saw a figure in the corner of his room, a thing of darkness and dirt, a travesty that was neither dead nor alive but somehow both. Thunder followed instantly, only the thunder sounded like a giant's growl, and in its aftermath, the thing in the corner moved forward, closer to the bed.

Father Ramos threw off the covers and scrambled off the opposite side of the mattress. Like Ebenezer Scrooge, he feared this apparition more than any other, though he knew not why.

"Hector."

Hugging the wall, he tried to calculate whether he could make it to the door before the hulking figure blocked it off, but it was nearly impossible to determine with the quickflash bursts of lightning in the otherwise total darkness. The thing was closer to the other side of the bed, though, and that put it slightly farther away from the door than he was.

Taking a chance, Father Ramos ran for the doorway, made it through, and shut the door behind him, hoping against hope that those dirt hands would not have the manual dexterity to turn the knob.

Keeping a wary eye out for other surprises, he hurried toward the safety of the chapel, turning lights on along the way. *Would* the chapel be safe? he wondered. He had been accosted there before.

"Hector."

The voice was in his head, not in the air.

Entering the chapel, he saw immediately that it was empty. He *should* be safe here. After all, he was doing God's will.

But he *wasn't* doing God's will.

Father Ramos shut his eyes tightly, trying to will away the headache that was squeezing his brain.

313

He locked the door behind him and started down the aisle toward the front entrance in order to make sure it was locked. Halfway there, he slowed. Then stopped. On the wooden floor was his shadow…only it was not his shadow. Stretching out in front of him was the elongated silhouette of what looked like a hunchbacked ape with the neck of a giraffe. The sight would have been comical if it had not seemed so *wrong,* and Father Ramos took one step to the left, one to the right, trying to see if it was the angle of the light that was distorting his shadow.

It was not.

Someone—

something

—was knocking on the double doors in front of him, the sound not particularly loud, but obvious in its regularity against the randomness of the storm, and he hurried over to make sure they were bolted. His twisted shadow rose from the floor to the door at his approach, confronting him, but he ignored it, checking the doors, grateful to confirm that they were indeed locked.

The knocking continued unabated.

"Hector. Let me in."

Jumpy, he turned around, certain that he would see that mud man behind him, but the chapel remained empty save for himself, and he walked slowly back up the aisle toward the altar, glancing from left to right, alert for any sign of movement, ready for anything. But nothing appeared, and though the knocking continued, and the voice—

"Hector. Let me in."

—occasionally spoke to him, he ignored them both.

Kneeling before the crucifix at the front of the church, bowing his head, he prayed for guidance.

∽

Cameron Holt jerked awake just as the gunshot that would have taken his life was fired. The sound of the shot morphed into thunder, and he sat up in bed, inspired by the nightmare, suddenly knowing what he had to do.

Lightning flashed, and the thunder that followed was so loud that it shook the house. He hobbled over to the window, wincing in pain with every step. As he'd hoped, Jorge was standing sentry in front of the smokehouse. Cameron saw no other men with him. Whether they had run off, were sleeping or were dead made no difference to him. The important thing was that Jorge was alone, and before that situation changed, Cameron hurried into the hall and down the stairs, moving as fast as he could, though it took every ounce of determination he had not to cry out in anguish.

Once downstairs, he went directly to his gun case and pulled out his favorite weapon, his Dirty Harry gun, the .357 Magnum he'd bought because of the Clint Eastwood movie and that he'd never been able to use in the way he wanted to. Ammunition was in the drawer below, and he sorted through the boxes of bullets and magazines until he found what he needed.

He walked outside.

It was raining hard, and he probably should have put on a raincoat or, at the very least, a hat, but he walked out barefoot in his long johns. Jorge was standing before the door of the smokehouse. Guarding it, Cameron supposed. For some reason, the cholo was facing the barn, not the house, not the drive, and for that he was grateful. He seemed tense, his body language that of an animal awaiting a predator attack. In the flash of lightning, Cameron saw glistening rain pouring down the foreman's jacket and could not help smiling. Now Jorge really *was* a wetback.

315

The sound of the storm hid the noise of his own awkward movements, but Cameron approached cautiously, aware that even a slight turn of the head by the other man could destroy any advantage he had.

Both hands were holding the Magnum.

He was soaking wet, and the mud beneath his feet made him think of walking through shit. Reaching the edge of the smokehouse, he stopped. He was close but not too close, and he raised the gun. "Jorge!" he shouted.

The foreman turned around.

And Cameron blew his head off.

There was a sound from the smokehouse, an inhuman wail loud enough to be heard even over the clap of thunder that exploded at precisely that second. The thunder faded away, but the wailing continued, a keening that grew louder and higher as Jorge's body fell into the mud. Cameron covered his ears with the index finger of his left hand and the butt of the Magnum held in his right, the sound boring painfully into his brain before growing thinner and then fading away as it moved beyond the range of human hearing.

Instantly, the storm stopped. It was as though a faucet had been turned off, and while clouds continued to blot out the moon and stars, no rain came down, no lightning flashed, no thunder pealed.

Cameron peered through the darkness. Without the aid of the lightning, he could barely see the smokehouse through the gloom. But this was his big chance, and if he was going to dispose of the body of that *thing* inside, he needed to do so quickly.

He was afraid to go into the shed, however, afraid even to touch the outside of the door. Burning down the building was still his best option, he thought, but had all the rain inoculated it against fire? Still looking toward the smokehouse entrance, he tried gathering his courage…only he had no courage to gather. For all he knew, that wailing was continuing, moving now beyond the range of dogs' hearing, a call by the monster to others of its kind.

Cameron backed away from the building before some mysterious power struck him down, or his mind was taken over as Jorge's had been, or a group of ranch hands emerged from the barn to attack him.

The barn.

Cameron frowned. Why had Jorge been staring at the barn?

He decided to see for himself, and, making a wide circle around the front of the smokehouse, still holding tightly to the gun, he limped through the dimness toward the structure. After the tumult of the storm, the calm was eerie. There were no animal or insect sounds, not even the chirping of crickets or cicadas. But he thought he heard his own name, spoken low, and he looked around the darkened yard, wishing he had brought a flashlight.

"Cameron!"

It *was* his name, spoken louder this time, and he realized that it was coming from the corral.

That was where Jorge had been looking, not the barn.

Either his eyes were getting used to the dark, or the weak diffused porchlight from the house just happened to fall at the right angle, because when he glanced toward the corral, he thought he saw movement. Hobbling as quickly as he could through the still-squishy mud, he was almost immediately able to make out the lines of the fence. In the center of the open space beyond, in sharp contrast against the pale dirt, he saw figures. Men. Three of them. One said his name again, and all three seemed to be waving their hands, though whether they were beckoning him closer or warning him away, he could not yet tell. His grip on the gun tightened.

Three steps further, and he could see who they were. Cal Denholm. Jim Haack. Joe Portis. He was shocked, though he probably shouldn't have been. The other ranchers had obviously snuck onto his property under the cover of night and storm, no doubt intending to do destroy the body in the smokehouse, and he was filled with an optimism and sense of hope that he hadn't experienced since before all of this started. Did they know that Jorge was dead? They had to have heard the shot, though the storm was it its height at the time and the sound could have blended in with the thunder. Without Jorge to guard the smokehouse, they would have a clear crack at the monster, and if they had enough gasoline or turpentine, they might even be able to set the building on fire despite all of the rain. Excited, Cameron made his way toward the corral gate—

And a steer blocked his way.

For a moment, he thought it was an accident, a coincidence, but then the animal stopped, turning to look at him, and he saw the awareness on its face. Another steer walked purposely over from the direction of the barn. There was a slight greenish glow about the animal, as though it were a radioactive character in a cartoon, and in that instant he understood the situation. The other ranchers were *not* trying to sneak over to the smokehouse. They had tried that, but they had been caught, and they had been herded into the pen by…cattle.

Cameron backed up slowly, ready to fire if need be. Behind the first steer, Jim was waving his hands in a pantomime that he did not understand. Cal was whispering something he could not quite hear.

Another steer had appeared from somewhere. Cameron glanced around, looking for more, but saw no others. For all he knew, these three were all that was left of his herd.

Lightning struck nearby, and he jumped at the decibel-busting thunder that instantly followed.

It was as though the thunder and lightning had jarred something loose in his brain. The situation before him was suddenly clarified, and he looked back toward the smokehouse, which appeared to be lit from inside, lines of light seeping out from between cracks in the wood.

Now he remembered. He was supposed to *protect* the angel.

How could he have gotten so far off track?

It didn't matter. He was once again on course, with the program, and he looked into the eyes of the steer blocking his way. The animal stepped aside to let him pass.

"Thank God," Cal said. "You've got to get us out of here. These fucking—" He stopped, seeing something in Cameron's eyes. There was fear in his voice. "You're not going to let us go, are you?"

Lightning flashed. Thunder cracked overhead.

"No." Cameron said, raising the gun.

"You don't want to do this…"

"Don't worry," he promised. "I'll take you out clean."

And he did.

THIRTY ONE

WHEN ROSS AWOKE, JUST BEFORE DAWN, HIS LAPTOP WAS open on the table, the screen shining brightly. He didn't remember leaving it on, didn't even remember seeing it when the storm woke him up in the middle of the night, but, then, he'd been tired.

Walking over to turn off the laptop, something nagged at him, something that was wrong.

Wait a minute.

Why was the screen bright?

His tired brain was just beginning to sort through and process the information it was receiving, and he realized that even if he had left the laptop on, the screensaver would have kicked in. Then, a half hour after displaying a photo of sunrise at the Grand Canyon, the laptop would have gone into sleep mode, and the screen would have gone dark.

He approached the table warily, leaning over the back of the chair to see what was being displayed. It was a list of email messages that had been sent since last night, and to his amazement there was an entire page of them. Sitting down and reading over the subject lines, he saw that they were from various companies in the aerospace industry.

All of them were offering him jobs.

He blinked, thinking for a moment that he was dreaming.

He wasn't. It was astounding, this sudden wealth of opportunities, and he scrolled down the list, reading each message, overcome by the offers, any one of which he would be grateful to accept. He noted the locations—San Diego, Long Beach, Denver, Dallas, Houston—and the proposed salaries: a hundred and twenty, a hundred, a hundred and forty, a hundred and ten...

Stunned, he sat there as the sun rose in the east. He'd heard that the economy was starting to rebound, but this was so ridiculously over the top as to be unbelievable. These offers were solid. Guaranteed. He had his pick of twenty-four positions, and all he had to do was decide which one he wanted. It was a dream come true, the answer to his prayers, every positive cliché he could come up with. He smiled. Suddenly, he was no longer of this place, and the problems that had been consuming him up to now seemed small and unimportant. Magdalena was about to be history, and he would never have to worry about weird storms or metamorphosing monsters ever again.

Only...

This was *one* of the problems. He knew it even as he tried to deny it. Like other people who had come into contact with that... thing, his luck had changed, the polarities of his fortunes had reversed, and he wondered if that was a survival technique on the part of the monster, a defense mechanism, a way to distract people from what should be their real focus. Because he *was* distracted. He didn't want to be, knew he shouldn't be, but his brain was already sifting through the pros and cons of various cities, weighing the positions and their compensation packages. In his mind, he had moved on, and Magdalena and everything that had happened here was rapidly fading into the past.

Jill.

The thought of her grounded him instantly in the here and now.

Lita.

This *wasn't* just an interlude, a memory best forgotten. The past two-and-a-half months had been an important transitional period in his life. Lita and Dave were lifesavers, there for him when no one else had been, and Jill was someone who, for perhaps the first time, he could see spending his future with. No matter what occurred after, his time in Magdalena had been valuable and significant, and what had happened here would send ripples, good and bad, throughout the rest of his days.

First things first. He needed to talk to Lita, Dave and Jill, and tell them about the offers. He was hoping he could convince Jill to come with him—which, after that freaky incident with her ex-dog, shouldn't be too hard—but he thought that he should also try to get Lita and Dave to get away from Magdalena. His cousin and her husband weren't going to find a solution to what was happening here; they were going to get sucked into the vortex. He saw that now. Instead of vanquishing the monster, they would become two more of its victims. They had new money. They could afford to go elsewhere, even if only for awhile, until this all blew over.

If it blew over.

He thought of Jill's paintings and their apocalyptic visions.

Quickly, Ross got dressed, opening the door and looking toward the Big House to see if Lita and Dave were awake.

The ground between the shack and the house was covered with bright red flowers. They had popped up overnight, and they were growing in the yard, in the hard dirt of the drive, in the garden. Dazed, he stepped outside, onto the porch, to get a more panoramic view. They were everywhere. The entire surrounding desert was a sea of red.

And the flowers had faces.

His heart was thumping so loudly he could hear it in his head. His legs were shaking. Seeing that cocooned body in Holt's shed had been utterly terrifying, a feeling he did not think could be surpassed, but the scope of this took his breath away. In his wildest dreams, he would not have thought it possible for flowers to be scary, but the little crimson faces surrounded by sunbeam petals frightened him on a primal level he did not understand. They looked like something out of a video game, but they were not smiling and looking at him, not swaying from side to side or dancing in place. They stared straight ahead, *thinking*, and the mere fact that the plants were sentient was so wrong that his entire body was covered in gooseflesh.

The flowers were whistling a song, he suddenly realized, in unison, and it was the same tune he and Jill had heard from the chickens in the middle of the night.

Another noise cut through the cool morning air. The sound of a door slamming. Ross looked to the right, back toward the house, to see Lita running across the yard toward him, barefoot and wearing a bathrobe, apparently oblivious to the carpet of flowers through which she was running. He knew instantly that something terrible had happened—even if it had not shown in her face, it was there in her body language—and he stepped off the porch to meet her, feeling the soft give of the flowers beneath his shoes. The sensation was repulsive, like stepping on worms.

"Oh, Rossie!" she cried, throwing her arms around him.

"What is it?"

"My mom died!"

"Aunt Kate?" Of course it was Aunt Kate. What a stupid thing to say.

Lita was sobbing. "I have to go, Rossie. I have to plan the funeral, I have to…I don't know what I have to do, but there's only me, and it's all my responsibility."

He held her.

"I want you to come with me."

He hesitated for only a second. "I think we should all go. Me, you and Dave." Pulling back a little, he glanced around at the flowers. "Jill, too. I think we need to get out of here."

Lita nodded, numb but understanding, even in her grief recognizing the enormity of what was going on around them. For the first time she seemed to notice the flowers and, grimacing, she climbed onto his porch, lifting up first her right foot, then her left, in order to look at the soles and make sure that contact with those red abominations had not affected her skin.

"Wear my slippers," he said, going inside to retrieve them. "Then go back and get dressed." He brought the slippers out, handing them to her. "They're probably a little big for you, but it's better than walking in your bare feet through…" He motioned toward the flowers.

"Thanks."

"So where is your mom? And what happened?"

She sniffled. "Albuquerque General. It was a drunk driver."

"Just like—"

"Yeah." She shivered even as she wiped tears from her eyes. "We got the call last night, in the middle of that storm. I've been up ever since. Dave fell asleep about ten minutes ago."

"I'll drive, then. You're both tired. Go back in, get what you need to get, wake up Dave, make whatever arrangements you have to make, and let's get out of here as quickly as we can."

Lita frowned, turning her head. "What's that music? Are those…are those flowers *whistling?*"

"Yes," he told her. "So do what you need to do, and let's go."

After watching to make sure she got safely back to the house, Ross went inside and called Jill. She was obviously still asleep—it took her five rings to answer the phone—and when she spoke, she sounded frazzled. But he told her they were leaving Magdalena and they wanted her to come with them.

"Leaving?" she said. "What does that mean? For good?"

"I don't know."

But he did know. Although he hadn't planned on bringing anything with him other than his laptop and the clothes on his back, Ross suddenly realized that he was leaving Magdalena and not coming back. It was time to cut and run. Wasn't that the phrase politicians used? It was always meant as a pejorative, but sometimes bailing was the best policy. You needed to know when to hold 'em and when to fold 'em, and right now it was time to cut, run, leave, flee and put Magdalena in his rearview mirror.

"Yes," he said. "For good. And I want you to come with me." He quickly explained to her about the rash of job offers, and Lita's mother's death. "After what happened yesterday with your dog, and everything else that's going on, it's not safe to be here anymore. We need to be realistic. We can't fight this. We can't do anything about it. All we can do is leave. You said yourself that you can do your telemarketing anywhere. Well, do it somewhere else. Maybe it'll be safe to come back later, maybe not, but for right now, I think the best thing to do is to get as far away from Magdalena as quickly as possible."

He expected an argument, expected to have to do more to convince her, but to his surprise, she said, "Okay."

"Okay?"

"Okay. I'll get some clothes together, some other essentials..."

"And we'll pick you up at your place."

"I'll drive myself. I'll meet you downtown by the gas station. A half hour?"

"Sounds good."

There was a pause. "Are there any...red flowers around Dave and Lita's?"

"Millions of them. And they all have faces."

"Just making sure. I'll meet you by the gas station. Love you," she told him.

It was the first time either of them had said it, but it sounded natural, sounded right, and, just as easily, he replied, "Love you, too."

Hanging up, Ross looked around the room, quickly deciding what to take and what to leave. There was a chance he might come back for the rest of his stuff later, but for the moment he was assuming that he would never return. So he only needed the essentials. And those were? Laptop and clothes. He packed a small box of CDs for the trip as well, but left everything else, since all of it was easily replaceable.

Dashing as quickly as he could over the flowers, he packed his laptop and suitcase in the trunk, put the CD box on the floor between the two front seats, and ran over to the Big House, where Lita and Dave were ready to go. He hadn't told them yet that he was leaving for good and decided to have that conversation on the road. They shouldn't come back either, but it would waste time to have that discussion here and now, and he figured he'd be in a better position to argue his point once they were away from the ranch.

"I called Jackass," Dave was saying. "He'll take care of the animals and bees for us, feed Mickey while we're gone."

"Okay," Lita said. She was crying again.

"Let's go, then," Ross suggested. "Before…" He trailed off.

Before what?

He didn't know. But he was gripped by the strong feeling—the *certainty*—that if they did not leave quickly, they would not be able to leave at all. Irrational, he knew, but what wasn't these days?

He could tell from their grimaces that Lita and Dave were both as repelled by the sensation of walking over the flowers as he was, but they made it to the car, put their suitcase and toiletries in the trunk, and got in, Dave riding shotgun, Lita in the back. No one said a word as Ross started the engine and circled around the head of the drive before setting out for the road, rolling over the densely growing flowers. He half-expected to hear screaming, cries of pain as the plants were crushed beneath the wheels, but there was only that maddening song, only the whistling, and luckily the closed windows and the sound of the car's engine kept its intrusiveness to a minimum.

He drove slowly at first, almost gingerly, as though the tires were going over glass or nails and might pop at any second, but gradually he grew used to the sensation, and while he couldn't see the road, he knew where it was, and by the time they approached the downtown, the car was humming along at a good forty miles an hour.

There were no red flowers here. He was not sure where they had stopped, if they had gradually thinned out or if there'd been a line of demarcation, but by the time they passed the empty beauty salon, the road was clear. And not just the road. The yards, the vacant lots, the open areas of dirt were all free from those terrible blooms.

Maybe, he thought, the further they moved away from Holt's ranch and the monster in the smokehouse, the fewer the flowers. But Jill's house was on the other side of the town, past this point, and she said that the plants had popped up in her area, so obviously that theory was completely wrong.

It didn't make any sense.

None of this made any sense.

Looking to the right before turning left onto the main street, he saw that the chimney-shaped mountain, the one with the M, was almost entirely red.

Jill had said that she'd meet them at the gas station in a half-hour. It had already been twenty minutes, but when Ross drove into the grocery store parking lot, there was no sign of her. He glanced down at the gas gauge. He had a third of a tank, enough to get them to Willcox, maybe Deming, but definitely not as far as Las Cruces. Pulling next to one of the two pumps, he decided to fill up for the trip while waiting for Jill to arrive. There was no one in the cashier's booth, however, and the pumps were so old that they had no automated card readers, so he could not charge the purchase. He was about to go into the store to find out if someone could help him, when he noticed a crowd gathering in the street.

And coming toward the gas station.

He probably shouldn't have been as concerned as he was; for all he knew, they were also worried about what was happening and were coming over in an effort to find some answers. But his gut told him something different, and he backed against the car, opening the driver's door, ready at a second's notice to get in and take off.

A good twenty people, mostly men but several women as well, were approaching the parking lot from the direction of the church. Others were emerging from buildings along the way to join the crowd.

Where the hell was Jill?

"That's Vern," Dave announced from within the car.

"It is!" Lita said.

"Who's— " Ross began.

"The one with the knife."

In the front line of the advancing crowd, a hard-looking, hatchet-faced man was holding a long knife in his right hand. Ross got quickly back into the car, locking the door and turning on the engine.

Goddamn it, Jill!

The group of locals, now numbering closer to thirty, stopped to the left of the car, next to the cashier's booth. Ross scanned the gathering for other weapons—in his mind, the Magdalenans were horrorshow villagers carrying rifles, pitchforks, shovels, ropes, staffs—but Vern's knife seemed to be the only one in evidence.

"I think we'd better go," Dave said.

Ross nodded, but made no effort to leave. He was waiting for Jill, and while she was no doubt smart enough to find them if they waited by the side of the road outside of town, he was worried that something might have happened and that he might need to go after her. He considered calling her cell, but at the moment driving might require her full attention. Besides, cell phones usually didn't work around here these days.

He looked to the left.

The crowd was getting ugly.

So to speak.

For some of the people in the rear of the crowd seemed to have…changed. The individuals were moving, shifting, but here he saw a pig nose, there some teeth that looked like tusks. Overlarge eyes bored into him from within a face covered by far too much hair.

It was not only the people in the back, though. Ben Stanard, the old man from the market, was now not so old. He was meaner looking than he had been before, but appeared years younger. And the big-breasted bimbo married to the internet guy was no longer so big-breasted. Her formerly pretty face was haggard and drawn, and her chest was as flat as a boy's. She was standing not next to her husband but next to the mushroom lady from the farmer's market, whose red face was twisted with rage.

Everyone seemed angry, though not at anything in particular. It was the type of mob, Ross thought, that would require only one incendiary word to graduate to a riot.

They needed to get out of here. Now. If only…

He saw Jill's van turn on to the street.

Filled with relief, Ross put the car in gear, honked his horn and swerved around the growing mob. Jill had seen him, and instead of pulling into the gas station, she remained on the street, waiting. She motioned for him to pull in front of her, and he did so, turning right, heading out of town.

There were still no red flowers, but there were people on the street, and he drove slowly so as not to hit them, Jill's van following closely behind. Many of those they passed ignored the vehicles, but some individuals stared, openly hostile. Ross thought of Jill's painting depicting a line of armed and angry men with long animal shadows, the street littered with bodies of mutilated women.

And of course that painting of a monster looming over the smoldering ruins of Magdalena was never far from his mind.

He wondered what the thing in Cameron Holt's smokehouse looked like right now.

Ross slowed the car as they reached the end of town. Standing forlornly in front of an empty adobe house, looking lost, was Father Ramos. The priest stood next to an overturned red tricycle, his collar open and partially ripped, a dark bruise on his cheek. Ross pulled over, concerned. Stopping before the house, he got out, shooting Jill a look through the van's windshield as he moved around to open the back door of the car. "Hop in, Father."

The priest stared at him blankly. "They won't listen to me," he said, perplexed. "I tried to get them to stop, but..." His voice trailed off.

Ross felt a chill caress his spine. "Stop what?"

The priest shook his head. "It all got away from me."

"Get in the car," Ross said gently. "We're leaving. We're getting out of here. We'll take you with us."

Father Ramos hesitated. "This is my flock. I'm responsible—"

"Not any more, Father. And you know it. You need to come with us. We need to get out of here. It's dangerous to stay."

It was obvious that the priest didn't want to leave, but while he'd probably be wracked with guilt later, he was dazed enough to be pliable, and, at the urging of all of them, he reluctantly got in the back seat of the car next to Lita.

Apparently, they were not the only ones to feel that it was time to leave, because other vehicles were also on the road heading in the same direction. It was a virtual caravan out of town, and Ross was glad to see it. The more people who left Magdalena, the better. They'd be safe.

But the ones who remained...

He didn't know what would happen to them and tried not to think about it.

When the monster hatched…

He *really* didn't want to think about that.

Father Ramos, atypically, did not seem to be in the mood to talk, and none of them pressed him. He looked as though he'd gotten into a fight, and Ross wondered what had happened, but unless and until the priest wanted to share, neither he, Lita nor Dave had any right to demand answers.

"I think it's time we told someone about this," Dave said as they were travelling toward the highway. "Sheriff, national guard… someone."

Ross looked over at him. "You think they'll believe that—"

"We tell them there's been looting, a riot, civil unrest. Magdalena has no police force. They'll have to come out to investigate."

"Not a bad plan," Ross said admiringly.

"And when they go out there, they'll find…what they find."

"I'm going to tell the diocese."

They were all surprised to hear Father Ramos' voice—Ross had not even been sure he'd been paying attention to the conversation— and not only was it a relief to discover that the priest was alert and aware of what was going on, but it was reassuring to think that the Catholic church would be getting involved. As heathenish as he might be, deep down Ross thought that Jill was right: this was something that might require a religious solution.

"It is not an angel," Father Ramos said. "I know that now."

"What is it?" Lita asked.

"That is what we need to discover."

There were lineups at nearly all of the gas stations in Willcox, mostly Magdalena refugees. While Ross filled up at a Shell, Lita and Dave got out to talk to some of their friends and acquaintances and compare notes. Jill had pulled up to the pump behind them, and Ross set the clip on his gas nozzle and walked over to her.

333

They hadn't spoken since their short conversation on the phone this morning, and the first thing he said was, "Are you all right?"

She nodded, smiling tiredly.

"Did you have any trouble?"

"Not getting out. It took me awhile to pack everything I needed, but that was no big deal. Last night, though…" She exhaled deeply.

"What happened?" Ross heard his nozzle click as the gas tank filled up, but he made no effort to take it out.

"There was that storm?"

"Yeah, it woke me up."

"Well, I was already up, and I was baking cookies. I thought I'd make angel cookies." She smiled wryly. "It seemed appropriate. Anyway, my cookies…came alive. I don't know any other way to describe it. They were in the oven, and they were trying to get out, and I had to burn them up."

"Jesus."

"I stayed awake all night after that. So I'm really tired. But after that, and once I saw those red flowers—" She shivered at the recollection. "—I knew it was time to get out."

The hose was between them, but he stepped over it and gave her a hug.

"What do you think's going to happen back there?" Jill asked.

"Dave had a good idea. We're going to call the county sheriff, maybe the National Guard, tell them there's civil unrest in Magdalena. Riots. They'll go out to investigate. And Father Ramos is going straight to the leaders of the diocese…"

"What do you think is going to happen?" she repeated.

He met her gaze. "I don't know."

Jill's pump clicked off, and while she attended to that, he returned to his own car, withdrawing the nozzle and placing it back on the hook. Father Ramos had walked over to visit with some of his parishioners in other cars, and he returned to inform Ross that one of the families had offered to take him to Tucson, where he intended to inform officials of the church about what was going on. "I should have done this immediately, on New Year's Day," he said. "It's my fault that I did not."

"You're doing it now," Ross told him. "That counts for something."

"Thank you for the ride." The priest took Ross' right hand in both of his, clasping it with genuine warmth. "Bless you."

Lita and Dave returned. "I talked to Armando Rascon," Dave said. "He was already planning to go to the sheriff and tell him what's going on in Magdalena. I convinced Jed and Marla Weaver to go there, too. We can't afford to get bogged down, so instead of going with them, I'll just call 911 on the way. I don't know why I didn't do it already. Stupid!" Lita put a hand on his shoulder. He patted it. "Anyway, the law should be heading over there pretty soon. I'm going to tell them about New Year's Eve. They won't believe me, but when I tell them there's a dead body in Cameron Holt's smokehouse, they'll have to check it out."

"What do you think will happen?" Ross asked. In his mind, he saw a group of sheriff's deputies kneeling before the smokehouse in prayer or eaten by pig people or overwhelmed by a mob of villagers.

Dave shrugged. "All we can do is hope for the best."

"Father!" a man's voice shouted from two islands over. "Are you ready?"

"I'm coming!" Father Ramos called out.

Lita turned to face him. "Are you leaving us?"

"I must. I am going to Tucson."

Bursting into tears, Lita threw her arms around the priest, giving him a big hug.

"I will pray for your mother," he said gently. "And for all of you."

Lita would not let him go, but sobbed into his shoulder. Dave had to pull her away, and he nodded at Father Ramos. "If I ever *did* go to church," he said, "I'd go to yours."

The priest smiled wryly. "You might be the only one there now."

"What did happen back in Magdalena?" Ross asked.

Father Ramos shook his head, a dark look passing over his face. It was clear that he still wasn't ready to talk about it, and Ross backed off.

"Goodbye," the priest said. "And God bless you. I pray that we will meet again under happier circumstances." Waving, he headed between cars toward a white SUV.

Ross felt a hand on his.

"So where are you going from here?" Jill asked.

"Albuquerque. Lita has to make the arrangements."

"I'm thinking I'll go back to Mesa, to my mom's."

Ross nodded. "I think that's a good idea."

"Meet me when you're done in Albuquerque?"

"I plan to."

They worked out the arrangements while Lita and Dave got back in the car, and he agreed to call her tonight, from wherever he ended up.

"No matter how late," she told him.

"No matter how late," he promised.

She kissed him on one cheek, on the other, on the forehead, on the mouth. "Be careful," she said.

THIRTY TWO

I T HAD BEEN A LONG TIME SINCE ROSS HAD SEEN HIS AUNT Kate, and she looked older than he remembered. Her body had been cleaned up after the accident for easier identification, but even though she was dead, he could tell that she had aged a lot since he had last seen her. He was reminded that this was his mom's *younger* sister, and the thought made him depressed. How much time, he wondered, did his mom have left?

Ross hadn't wanted to see the body at all, but Lita had insisted. He was family, and she wanted him there, so he did it for her sake. In the back of his mind—and in the back of hers, no doubt—was the idea that her mother's death was connected to that *thing* in Magdalena. Lita's luck had changed, as had so many other people's, and though he still had no idea how the chrysalis-enveloped body of a monster that had been shot out of the sky could enact such widespread and far-reaching damage, he did not doubt that it was possible.

But why?

Revenge?

That seemed plausible, and he marveled at how far his worldview had shifted, and how quickly and easily he had adjusted.

They were staying in adjoining rooms at a Holiday Inn on the western outskirts of Albuquerque. They'd driven nonstop and had checked in after midnight, grabbing a quick five hours of sleep before going to the hospital. After identifying the body, they headed over to a Denny's for breakfast, where they sat around the table, drinking coffee and orange juice as Lita tried to decide what sort of funeral her mother should have. As far as she knew, her mom did not have a will, but she didn't yet feel strong enough to go over to the house and start looking through her mom's belongings. Lita's dad had also been notified, but apparently he had not arrived yet, even though he lived in Farmington, which was a good deal closer than Magdalena. Left unspoken was the thought that something might have happened to him, too.

Although they'd traded off, Ross had done most of the driving, and he was still tired. There were things Lita and Dave had to do, and though she wanted Ross along, he convinced them to drop him off at the motel so he could catch up on his sleep. They could pick him up later, after lunch.

Only he couldn't sleep. He was exhausted, but his mind would not rest, and as hard as he tried, he could not force himself to nod off. So after twenty minutes of lying there with his eyes closed and his brain churning, he got up to phone Jill. He'd made a quick call to her last night while Dave was driving and they were on the road, and he'd promised to let her know this morning what was going on. His cell phone worked fine here in New Mexico, and while he hadn't checked his messages last night, he did now, and was surprised to see how many were waiting for him. Most were from the various firms offering him work, and he listened to each and every one of them before finally dialing Jill.

She was at her mom's house, she was fine, and nothing unusual had happened overnight, although this morning she'd tried calling a friend of hers who'd remained in Magdalena and the call had not been able to go through. She'd then dialed the Cochise County sheriff's department, but when she'd asked if anyone had been sent out to investigate the situation in Magdalena, the dispatcher had become curt, taking down her name and phone number and telling her only that someone would contact her later.

Ross reported that they, too, were all right, if tired from lack of sleep. He told her that they'd identified Lita's mother's body, and that Lita and Dave were now trying to track down Lita's father before settling on funeral arrangements. He paused, cleared his throat. "And I think I'm going to take the job in San Diego."

"I can go there," Jill said after waiting a beat.

"Do you—"

"Want to? Yes, I do."

The emotions that were stirred up within him—relief, gratitude, joy—were all good, and despite the nightmare going on around him, for a few seconds he actually felt happy. Maybe they'd even be able to rent an apartment by the beach while they looked for something more permanent. He'd have to call National Floor Mats first, and bow out of the temp project for which they'd hired him, but he also might be able to find a place for Alex at his new company as a way to pay his friend back.

Then a beep announced that he had a call waiting, a number he didn't immediately recognize, and he asked Jill to wait a moment while he checked to see what it was.

It was his brother Rick.

Their dad had had a heart attack.

Ross didn't wait for the other shoe to drop. "Is he...?"

"No. He's in ICU, but he's alive, and they think he's going to pull through."

"I'll get there as quick as I can." Already he was thinking that he could leave his car with Lita and Dave, and take a plane to Phoenix.

"No," Rick said, and there was an awkward pause.

"No what?"

"He doesn't want you to come. He doesn't want you there. Mom doesn't, either."

"Damn it, Rick."

"It's not me. And I'm not making it up. Dad said specifically, 'Don't tell Ross. I don't want him here.'"

"When exactly did this happen?"

"Day before yesterday."

"And you're just telling me now? Jesus, Rick!"

"I'm only calling you now because Kevin told me to. If it was up to me..."

"What a surprise." Ross took a deep breath. "I'm coming there anyway. What hospital's he at?"

"He wasn't joking. And it's not one of those I-don't-want-you-to-see-me-this-way things. He really doesn't want you to come." There was another awkward pause. "Mom doesn't want you there, either."

"What?"

"I'm telling you the truth, Ross."

"Why?"

"I don't know."

"Fuck them, then. And fuck you, too." He hung up, not sure himself whether he was hurt or angry.

It was only when he heard a faint "*Hello?*" from the phone's small speaker that he realized Jill was still on the other line.

"Sorry," he apologized, and told her what had happened. "If it wasn't for Rick's son nagging him, the asshole probably wouldn't have called me at all. I still wouldn't know about it!"

"What are you going to do?"

"Call my mom, I guess. See what she says."

Jill was silent for a moment. "You know this might be—"

"I know," he interrupted, but he didn't want to think about that. If the blackened corpse in Cameron Holt's shed could stretch out its tentacles to touch relatives, there was no hope at all.

"Call me later," Jill said.

"I will," he promised.

Ross spent the rest of the morning on the phone, although the aggregated calls confused rather than clarified. It was made plain to him by both his mother and his sister that his presence would *not* be welcome at the hospital, and while he tried not to blame his family too much, he could not help it.

Lita and Dave arrived with a McDonald's lunch, and he found that he was starting to resent them. If they had not invited him to stay at their ranch, none of this would have happened to him.

But that was unfair. It still would have happened to them, and to make up for his selfish thoughts, he offered to accompany them to his Aunt Kate's house after they finished their lunch. Lita's dad was still a no-show, and if they hadn't heard from him by this evening, she was going to go to the police and file a missing persons report.

He didn't tell them about his dad's heart attack, at least not right away, but later in the afternoon, searching through a pile of bills at the house, looking for evidence of a will, he let them know what had happened.

Lita hit his shoulder. "And you're just telling us now?"

"They made it pretty clear that I was not welcome."

"Rossie! He's your dad!"

"I know, but…"

"You have to go," Lita told him. "You'll regret it if…" Her voice trailed off, her eyes tearing up.

He wasn't sure that he would regret it. All of a sudden, he felt very tired. Not just physically tired—though that, too—but emotionally exhausted. He was sick of all this, and right now what he wanted more than anything else in the world was to pick Jill up in Mesa, drive to San Diego, have a beer while he stared out at the beach, and forget that the past few months had ever happened.

Lita wiped her eyes. "We can handle things here," she said, putting an arm around Dave. "And we have a car now. Mom's car. So you can go if you want."

He did want to go. But not to the hospital to see his dad. Just… away.

"That's okay," he said.

"Rossie!"

Twenty minutes later, he was packed and checked out and saying his goodbyes in the parking lot. Everything of Lita and Dave's that they'd brought with them had been transferred from his trunk to the trunk of her mom's car, and he gave his cousin a big hug. "Call me when you decide on the details of the funeral," he said. "I'll be here."

"You have your own—"

He pulled back, looked into her eyes. "I'll be here."

She started crying again. "Thank you."

His left arm still around her, he stretched out his right to shake hands with Dave. "Take care of her."

"You know I will."

"I won't get there till late, but I'll call tomorrow morning," he told them.

"You be careful, Rossie," Lita said.

"We'll all be careful."

THIRTY THREE

Two weeks had passed, though it seemed more like two days. Or maybe a month. Time *was* relative, and while it seemed impossible for so much to have happened in such a short period, the days themselves had flown by.

Jill's own life had been mercifully free of complications since leaving Magdalena, but the drama in Ross' life had shifted into overdrive. An attempt to visit his father in the hospital had somehow erupted into an all-out family feud, and his mother had not even allowed him to stay overnight at their house, forcing him into a motel. He had gone to the funeral of Lita's mom, but no one else from his immediate family had, and their absence reflected on him and made him persona non grata with the other extended relations who showed up. Lita's dad was still missing, and though the police were in on it now, no one had any idea what had happened to him.

Thank God for the new job. Ross had started work in his new position three days ago, and he seemed to like it. He wasn't happy, exactly, not with everything else that was swirling around him, but he was in his element, and she knew that it had been the right move for him. She'd never stopped working, and between bouts of unpacking, she clocked in and made her calls. Quick research had shown her that San Diego had a thriving arts community, and while she'd left most of her paints and supplies back in Magdalena, she'd brought enough with her in the van to start working on some projects should the mood strike.

So far, it hadn't.

Ross arrived home from work shortly before six, and, Ozzie and Harriet-style, she greeted him with a kiss as soon as he walked through the doorway. She'd just finished two solid hours of grueling soul-sucking hard sell and was desperate to get out of the house. Here at the end of the continent, it stayed light later—until the sun sank completely below the edge of the horizon—and that was one of the things she definitely intended to take advantage of. "Nice weather for a walk," she hinted.

Laughing, he put down his briefcase. "Let me change my shoes."

They strolled along the sidewalk at the edge of the beach, venturing onto the sand when the sidewalk ended. There were other walkers out, several joggers, and even some surfers in the water, though it wasn't *that* warm. Jill missed the desert, but she had to admit that this was nice.

They watched the sunset, hand-in-hand, and it was so beautiful that she wished she'd brought a camera.

She hadn't planned anything for dinner, so on the way back they stopped at a stand whose driftwood-inspired sign read, "Surfside Tacos." She ordered three shrimp tacos, Ross three mahi-mahi, and they sat at a plastic table outside the small shack, sharing their food and drinking Coronas.

It should have been a perfect evening, but in back of everything was Magdalena, and when they walked home in the dark and a streetlight illuminated a statue of an angel in front of a nursery, she felt Ross' grip on her hand tighten. Neither of them mentioned it, but they were silent the rest of the way to the house.

It was only when they were in bed and about to go to sleep that Ross said, "What do you think's happening back there?"

"Maybe it's over," Jill said hopefully, but she didn't believe it and neither did he, and no more was said as, individually, they drifted off.

She awoke in the middle of the night from a dream about Magdalena.

She had returned with her van to pick up the rest of her belongings, but all of the houses on her cul-de-sac had been burned to the ground. Most of the town was in ruins, and the only building that appeared to be untouched was the church. It was no longer a church, however, at least not any kind that she recognized, and although it had been broad daylight only seconds before, now it was night, and she saw eerie green light spilling out from the windows of the building, heard the sounds of raucous celebration from within. Walking over, she opened the front doors and peered inside. Townspeople, some she recognized and others she didn't, were cavorting about the chapel in a bacchanalian frenzy, all of them naked, most of them covered in blood. On the altar was a giant black egg as big as a Volkswagen.

No.

The egg was not black. The thing *inside* it was black. The egg itself was clear, and as she tried to make out details of the folded creature encased within the transparent shell, a single red eye blinked open—and stared at her with hatred and complete understanding.

She did not wake Ross up to tell him about the nightmare, nor did she mention it in the morning before he left for work, but its imagery haunted her throughout the day, and she ended up drawing a picture of it in her sketchbook.

Her telemarketing schedule was five hours today—from eleven to one and then again from five to eight—but she couldn't bring herself to do it, so she sent an email to her group supervisor, begging off, pretending that she had laryngitis. Digging through the hall cupboard for the biggest towel she could find, she grabbed a bottled water out of the refrigerator and walked down the street to the beach, sitting alone on the sand staring out to sea. The sky was overcast, the water gray, her mood melancholy. The happiness and sense of renewal she'd felt since coming with Ross to San Diego was gone, and the phrase that kept repeating in her brain was chilling: *Our luck has changed.*

The cool breeze that ruffled her hair felt like something more than wind.

Ross came home early from work, in a bad mood—
Our luck has changed.
—and when Jill asked him what was wrong, he wouldn't tell her. That was new. Until now, they had shared everything, had been completely honest with each other. She pointed this out, throwing in that she had also moved to a completely different

state with him after dating for only a few weeks, and he apologized instantly. "Sorry," he said. "It's just…"

"Just what?"

"France rejected our new guidance system. That was supposed to be our big new market, and it's why the company brought in all us new hires. They were certain it was going to fly." He smiled wryly. "So to speak. But now there's talk about a round of cutbacks, and since it's last hired, first fired…" He shook his head. "I should've taken that job in Denver."

"You still can, if worst comes to worst."

"Those jobs are filled already."

"But you have a new job on your resume, and—"

"Magdalena got me this job."

She looked at him. "What?"

"You know it's true. I was unemployed, unemployable in this terrible economy, and then I saw that monster in the shed and suddenly I had job offers galore. That's not going to happen again."

Our luck has changed.

She put a hand on his arm. "Maybe it won't happen."

"Yeah," he said. "Maybe."

They tried to make love that night, but he couldn't get hard and she couldn't get wet, and eventually they gave it up and went to bed.

Things should have looked better in the morning, but sleep hadn't helped, and after Ross left for work, Jill signed in and started disrupting people's breakfasts with her phone calls.

By lunchtime she was tired and cranky, and she was grateful when the doorbell rang, giving her an excuse to take a break. Putting down her headset, she walked through the living room, opened the front door…

And no one was there.

"Hello?" she said, stepping out and looking from the left to the right. There was no one in the small front yard or in the street. Trying to convince herself that it was kids playing a prank, she closed the door and locked it.

From somewhere in the house behind her came the light clicking sound of paws on floor, accompanied by the jangle of dog tags.

Jill was suddenly cold.

Puka?

No, it couldn't be. He was dead and flattened and back in Arizona. Ross had thrown him in the garbage, and his body was either still there, rotting, or had been taken to the dump.

He was not padding around their rented beach house here in San Diego.

Something growled from down the hall.

That was it. She was out of here. Jill grabbed her purse, locked the front door and strode directly to the van. Parking in front of a 7-11 down the street, she took out her cell phone to call Ross. He wasn't going to want to hear this, but he needed to know about it. His phone went straight to voicemail, but instead of leaving a message she clicked off and drove down to the complex of steel-and-glass buildings where he worked.

At least, that's what she started to do.

But somewhere along the way, her goal changed. Why was she hurrying to warn Ross when *she* was the one being pursued? What she needed to do was get as far from here as quickly as possible and hide. Go someplace where no one would find her. Ross would be safe once she was safe—nothing was after *him*—and if she could ditch this whatever-it-was now, she would be free from it forever.

Jill was aware that her thoughts were not as clear as they should be, that something was wrong with her logic, but it didn't seem important, was a trivial objection in the back of her mind. What was important right now was getting away from their house and out of San Diego, and she found a freeway heading east, took it and continued out of the city into the countryside. Buildings grew more spaced out, offramps farther apart. The freeway shed two lanes, became a highway, and somewhere in the mountains, she turned off on a side road. She had no idea where she was, but that was an advantage. It would make her more difficult to track.

It occurred to her that this reaction was wrong, that she was doing precisely what she *shouldn't* do, but she pushed those thoughts aside. Passing a gas station, some tourist cabins and an occasional farm, she followed the road as it wound upward through high chaparral, twisting and turning. Ahead, she saw the twinkling blue of a large reservoir. Ringed with pine trees, it was beautiful, and she stopped at a roadside pullout, got out of the van and stared for several minutes at the shimmering water, enraptured.

She decided that she would like to paint this scene. Ordinarily, she was not one for landscapes, but something about this place spoke to her.

Did she have any art supplies still in the van? A quick search determined that she did not, but that was easily remedied. She'd seen a sign a ways back on the road announcing at least two upcoming towns. Even assuming that neither community had an art supply store, all she had to do was find a Target, a Wal-Mart or even a CVS. Any of those places would carry simple school supplies, and they were bound to have construction paper and watercolors, which were really the only things that she needed at the moment. Then she would come back here and paint. Maybe from this spot, maybe from another, maybe from several. And if she could not find a place nearby to stay for the night, she would sleep in her van.

Why? Jill wondered.

It was not a question worth answering. It was what she wanted to do, what she needed to do, and what she would do.

Jill knew she should call Ross and tell him where she was, but she didn't dare because she didn't want *it* to know. This way was safer, and she would stay here until…until…until she didn't need to anymore.

She got back into the van.

And continued up the road to the next town, where she bought her paints and paper before heading back to the reservoir.

THIRTY FOUR

DAVE HAD BEEN AFTER HER TO GO BACK TO MAGDALENA, IF only to check on their property and their animals—"We can't stay away forever," he said—but although Lita worried about the fate of her horse and wondered if Jackass was even still taking care of the ranch for them, she agreed with Ross: she would only go back when it was proved to her that that monster was gone.

Unfortunately, she had not been able to contact any of her friends in Magdalena to find out what was happening. For all she knew, they had left, too. But if that were the case, their cell phones and email should have worked—and they didn't. Her gut told her that things were worse now than they had been when she'd left, though there was no way to know one way or the other.

Her dad was still missing, and it was getting harder and harder to tell herself that there was nothing sinister in that. No one had any clue as to his whereabouts, the police were apparently stymied in their investigation, and it took every last ounce of hope and optimism she had in order to convince herself that he was not dead.

And that it was not connected to the angel.

The monster.

Dave, too, had been trying to get ahold of people back in Magdalena, and when he finally did get through to Jackass, the news was not good. The handyman said that over half the population of the town and surrounding area had fled, and that of the ones who remained, many were holed up, survivalist style, in barricaded houses filled with guns and supplies.

Some had *changed*.

They talked for a few moments, before Dave handed the phone to Lita.

"What about our place?" she asked after a quick greeting. "How's Mickey?"

There was a short pause, while Jackass obviously tried to decide what and how much he should say. He opted for the vague and simple, "He ain't Mickey no more."

Lita felt as though she'd been kicked in the chest, as though she'd had a hole punched through her heart, but she quickly decided that she didn't want to know the details. She was silent for a moment. "Get out of there," she told him finally.

"As soon as I get the rest of my gold, I'm off for better climes," he promised.

"You should go now."

"I'm bein' left alone so far. As long as my luck holds out…"

"Luck changes," she said. "That's what it does."

"I know. And at the first sign, I'm outta here." He sounded apologetic. "But there's a lot a gold, Lita. And after all this time of everyone thinkin' I'm crazy..."

"You don't still think that angel's protecting you, do you?"

"No, but a lot of people are protectin' the angel now. At least that's what I hear." For the first time, there was a hint of fear in his voice. "They're waitin' for it to *arise.*"

A chill caressed her spine. "Did the sheriff ever come out there?" she asked. "Or any priests or anyone from the Catholic church?"

"Not to my knowledge."

She'd been afraid of that, though she didn't see how it was possible. *Several* people had gone to the sheriff's office, Ross and Dave had both phoned, and the sheriff *had* to send someone out to at least take a look at what was happening in Magdalena.

Of course...

It was powerful. She remembered the mob that had been gathering in front of the market before they left town, seeing in her mind the man with the pig nose, the suddenly youthful Ben Stanard. Anything that could do that could certainly exert a little influence over local law enforcement.

In a way, that was what scared her the most: how easy it was for the institutions of society to break down, how quickly Magdalena could be so completely cut off from the rest of the world. It made her realize that things like this could be happening all the time in small out-of-the-way locales without anyone in the wider world being the wiser.

"Get out of there," she told the handyman again.

"I will," he said. "Soon."

After that call, she and Dave were both depressed. They were glad to be away from Magdalena but felt guilty that they'd run away without doing anything to stop the horrors that were occurring there. It was the uncertainty of the future, however, that weighed heaviest upon them. His parents were dead, her mom was dead, her dad was missing…what would come next? How far did those tentacles reach?

Dave was no longer suggesting that they return to Magdalena, but neither of them wanted to live indefinitely in her mom's house here in Albuquerque, either. Their lives were on hold, everything was up in the air, and it left them feeling completely unsettled.

They had finished sorting through most of her mom's belongings, separating the things they were going to sell from those having sentimental value that Lita wanted to save. Originally, she'd planned to have a big garage sale, but they decided to do what they'd done with Dave's parents' possessions and have someone come in and buy the whole estate, so until they figured out where they were going to live, she needed to find a cheap storage unit to hold everything she planned to keep.

Her eyes alighted on a small unicorn of curlicued glass that was lying on top of a box of knickknacks. She remembered when she bought that unicorn for her mom at a glass-blower's shop in Scottsdale. She'd been ten, and her dad had brought her back to the shop after dropping her mom and her aunt off at Los Arcos Mall. She'd given the object to her mom for Christmas, and Lita was both touched and surprised that she'd kept it all these years.

She picked up the unicorn, her eyes tearing up.

Maybe their luck would change again, Lita thought.

Although she wasn't sure if she really wanted that. She didn't want anyone she knew to die, but at the same time, there were a thousand different ways that their lives could be affected by a slight change of fortune. Their car could have a dead battery, which would make them stay home instead of going to the grocery store as planned, and because they didn't go to the store, they would be home when a robber tried to break into her mom's house, and, upon seeing them, the robber could break out his gun and start shooting...

Her mind instantly came up with a dozen such scenarios, but Lita immediately pushed them all from her mind, not wanting to consider any of them.

"I have to go to the bathroom," she told Dave. "I'll be back in a minute."

She tripped on the way. She was not a clumsy person; in fact, she had always been athletic and very well coordinated. But she stumbled over a wrinkle in the hallway carpeting, and instead of instantly righting herself, the way she would ordinarily, her left foot, already in mid-step, smashed into the back of her right ankle, and she pitched forward, arms flailing. In the brief second before her forehead connected with the corner of the table that her mother, for some inexplicable reason, had placed in the hallway, a single thought flashed through her mind:

Her luck had run out.

Dave called Ross from the hospital and told him what had happened.

"She's still unconscious, but she's stable. You don't need to come out here," he added quickly.

"I'm coming."

"No. I don't want you to. *Lita* wouldn't want you to."

"Why?"

"Something...might happen." There was no need to go into more detail. He knew that Ross knew what he was talking about. "You and Jill just stay there."

"Jill's gone," Ross said.

"What do you mean she's gone?"

"I came home from work yesterday and she wasn't here. She didn't come back last night, and I haven't heard from her." There was a pause. "I think she might've gone back to Magdalena."

"Have you tried—"

"I've tried everything."

"It could be something else. Are you guys having problems? You know, she might not be used to California..."

"She wouldn't just run off without telling me. Not if it was something normal. Besides, her van's gone, but she didn't take any of her stuff. Not even clothes."

"Did you tell the police? Maybe she's been kidnapped." Dave knew he was reaching for rational answers, but he didn't want to go where he knew this was headed.

"It's that monster in Magdalena," Ross said. "We both know it."

Yes, he did know it. Not logically, in his head, but where it counted, in his gut. He recalled the power he had felt in Cameron's smokehouse, thought of Father Ramos describing how the angel would be reborn. It seemed highly unlikely that whatever it was would be contained in Magdalena.

Why had they left in the first place without first destroying that thing?

And what the hell *was* it?

Dave looked over at Lita's unmoving form and was suddenly filled with rage, an emotion that felt purifyingly welcome after the numbness of the past six hours. "I'm going back," he vowed. "I'm going to get rid of that angel, and put an end to this once and for all."

"No," Ross said, and Dave heard an authority and seriousness of purpose in the other man's voice that he hadn't before. "You stay with Lita. *I'll* go back."

"Ross—"

"I know what to do. I can get it done."

"We'll both go."

"No," Ross repeated. "Lita needs you. Stay with her."

He spoke a thought that had been floating around in the back of his mind but until now had remained unspoken. "What if I *do* something to her? What if it makes me tear out the tubes she's hooked up to...or...or smother her with a pillow, or...?

"That's not going to happen, Dave. And you're safer in Albuquerque than you would be in Magdalena. You both are."

It was true, but he felt cowardly for even thinking it. "You can't go after that thing yourself. It won't let you. Jorge and his men are there, and who knows what defenses it's built up since we left? You need me."

"I don't. I told you, I have a plan. And I won't be doing it all myself. You just take care of my cousin."

Dave's mind was suddenly filled with an extraordinarily clear and extremely unwelcome vision. "Tell me the truth," he said. "Did you fuck her?"

Ross was brought up short. "What?"

"Lita. Did you fuck her? I know you wanted to."

"That's crazy!" The emotion in the denial was not as outraged as the words were. In fact, Dave thought, it wasn't really a denial.

"Did you?" he pressed.

"Of course not!" *Was he protesting too much?* "This is exactly what I mean. It's getting to you already. In New Mexico. Do you know what would happen if you went back?"

He took a deep breath. Ross was right. "This is exactly what *I* mean," he said. "What if I do something to hurt her?"

"Do what you need to do, then. Stay away from the hospital if it makes you feel better. But you two need to keep away from Magdalena."

Unwelcome images were still flashing through his brain—

Lita on her knees in front of her naked, erect cousin

—but Dave ignored them. "We shouldn't have left," he said. "We should have stayed and taken care of things."

"We should have," Ross agreed. "But maybe it wasn't our decision to leave in the first place. Maybe we just thought it was."

"Then what makes you think you can fight it now?"

"I don't know. But I do. I'm going back there, and I'm going to kill that monster again, and this time there won't be any resurrection."

Dave believed him, and he looked again at Lita's unmoving form and for the first time in a long while felt the faint stirrings of an unfamiliar emotion: hope.

THIRTY FIVE

Intending to take out his suitcase, Ross opened the door of the closet and found himself looking at Jill's clothes, still on their hangers in all of their multicolored splendor.

He stared at them, wondering if she was dead.

No!

As terrible as the thought was, he had to admit to himself that it was a possibility, and though a fire had already been lit beneath him about returning to Magdalena, this fanned those flames into a conflagration. Quickly, he dragged out his suitcase, pulled a couple of shirts out of the closet, grabbed some socks and underwear from the dresser.

He'd told Dave that he knew what he needed to do, and he did. Despite his false bravado, he wasn't sure if he could arrange it, wasn't even sure it would work, but the basic idea was sound, and the fact that it used the monster's own powers against it gave him a feeling of satisfaction. Karma was a bitch.

Even if it didn't exist.

He thought about Lita, lying unconscious in a New Mexico hospital, and that made him hurry even faster.

Did you fuck her?

Dave's question had hit him hard. His answer had been honest—he *hadn't* had sex with his cousin—but he couldn't deny that he had thought about it, and the knowledge made him feel both guilty and disgusted with himself.

Although he was fairly certain that *those* thoughts would not have occurred to him had not that creature been shot out of the sky.

Ross tried to recall exactly what he had seen Christmas night, when that thing had flown over the ranch, tried to reconstruct in his mind the feelings he had experienced at that moment, but so much had happened since then that his memories and attitudes were all jumbled together. Although he couldn't say for sure what it had looked like when it was alive, he clearly recalled the way it had appeared in the shed, curled into a fetal position, rotting, its flesh melting, its terrifying face filled with a horrible malevolence, and he felt once again the strength of the power that had enveloped him, that had made him believe for a few moments that it really *was* an angel.

It had influenced him there, and its effects were still following him, not merely following him but spreading, touching those he touched, and he understood now that the only way to put a stop to it was to destroy the body once and for all. He had tried calling the Cochise County sheriff's department to determine whether any efforts had been made to do that, had tried calling the Tucson diocese of the Catholic church and asking for Father Ramos, to see if *they* were doing anything, but both inquiries led nowhere. As

THE INFLUENCE

far as he could ascertain, the sheriff's office had sent no one out to investigate, and Father Ramos appeared to be persona non grata with the church.

Wanting some intel on the ground, he had gotten Jackass McDaniel's number from Dave, and when the handyman answered the phone, he told Ross that he was packing, getting ready to leave. "I'm done here," he said. "I'm out."

"What happened?" Ross asked, a sinking feeling in the pit of his stomach.

"What *hasn't* happened?"

"I mean, what made you decide to leave now?"

"My gold turned to shit." His voice rose. "My *gold* turned to *shit*. All the nuggets I dug out are now little pieces a smelly dog crap."

"I'm coming back," Ross said.

"Oh no. Don't do that." He could hear the concern in McDaniels' voice.

"I'm going to get rid of that thing."

"The angel?"

"Yeah."

"Other people've already tried," McDaniels said. "But it protects itself. Everyone who's gone after it's gotten killed, one way or another." He paused. "You ain't gettin' through, either."

"Have you seen it?"

"Oh yeah. I went out there with Hec the other day. He was a sharpshooter in Iraq, and his wife, Hannah, was kinda *attacked* by somethin' in her garden, so he had the same thought you did, cut it off at the head. We went out to Holt's place, but the road's all dug up and I think booby trapped, so we snuck in through the east side, through Shel Dilson's land—Shel's family's gone; they took off around the same time you did—and we found it, the angel. It's

bigger now. Holt's shed's not there anymore, and that thing's out in the open, and we saw it." McDaniels took a deep breath. "It's… different. It's turned into somethin' else, somethin' new."

Ross thought of Jill's paintings. "Like an egg?" he asked.

"Yeah. And I think it's ready to hatch."

"You said your friend was a sharpshooter. Did he miss?"

"He didn't even try to shoot at it. It was too damn scary. We just slunk off. Holt was there, though. We saw him. Him and a bunch a guards. They're watchin' out for it, makin' sure nothin' disturbs it until it's out."

"Well, I'm coming over there," Ross said.

"When?"

"Now."

"You sound sure a yourself, like you know somethin' the rest of us don't."

"I have a plan," Ross admitted.

McDaniels was silent for a moment. "Could you use another hand?"

"Of course! But I don't want to trick you into thinking—"

"You're not trickin' me into shit. This is my home. I don't wanna leave it. I was only goin' cuz I thought I had to. But if you got a plan, I'm in. We need to stop this sucker now while we still can, before it hatches all the way."

"That's what I thought, too."

"How long's it gonna take you to get here?"

"I'll be there tomorrow."

"Where are you?"

"San Diego."

"Hell, I made that run in six."

Ross smiled. "I need to stop somewhere first. I'll be there in the morning."

"Get here as quick as you can," McDaniels' said.

Ross had called in sick today, and, luckily for him, it was a Friday. Which meant he had the weekend. It was flaky, calling in sick on the first week of a new job, especially with the possibility of layoffs looming, but if he could get back by Monday, he knew he could sell this as a legitimate illness. Since he was a healthy guy who seldom if ever actually got sick, this would probably be his only absence for a long time, and after several months of good work, any doubts that might be raised by this aberration would be put to rest.

Ross left a note for Jill, in case she came back. He didn't expect her to return, but on the off chance that she did, he let her know where he was going and told her to stay in San Diego.

He drove to Phoenix, arriving just before nightfall. He'd skipped lunch and was starving, but before getting something to eat, he headed over to his brother's house, parking in the driveway next to Rick's leased Acura. Maybe he should have called first, but that would have involved argument and negotiation, and Ross thought it better to just show up and speak to his brother directly.

He rang the bell, hoping Rick would answer and not his wife. He got lucky. "Hey," Ross said as his brother opened the door.

A look of confusion passed over Rick's face. "What are you doing here?"

"I came to see you."

"About what?" Rick crowded the doorway, apparently afraid that Ross might try to sneak into the house.

"How's Dad?"

"He's home. Doing okay, I guess. Mom fell the other day, tripped over something in the garage and broke her hip."

"Jesus! Why didn't anyone call me?"

Rick shrugged, and Ross wanted to hit him, but he knew that it wasn't really his brother's fault. Or wasn't *all* his brother's fault.

He decided to stick to the script. "Listen, I need to talk to Kevin."

Rick was instantly suspicious. "Kevin? What for?"

"I just need to ask him something. Where is he?"

"I'll give you his phone number, but I can't—"

"That's fine," Ross said. "What is it?" He already had his phone out. He typed in the number as his brother recited it, then immediately walked away, back toward the car, leaving Rick standing confusedly in the doorway.

"What are you—"

Ross closed the door behind him, cutting his brother off as he put the car into gear and backed out of the driveway. Pretending to drive away, he stopped and parked halfway down the block, using the number he'd been given to call his nephew, hoping that Kevin would answer.

He did.

"Kevin," Ross said. "This is Uncle Ross."

"Hey," the boy said suspiciously.

He didn't want to jump right in. "Thanks for telling your dad to call me about Grandpa. I appreciate it."

"Yeah, well, I thought it was wrong the way they were treating you. You should hear what they say behind your back."

"I know, I know. And, like I said, I appreciate it. But...I was wondering if we could get together. I sort of need to talk to you about something."

"You can tell me now."

"I'd rather do it in person. Where do you live? I could come over right now if you're free."

The suspicion was back. "What's this about?"

"I'd rather not tell you over the phone."

He was about to play his ace and remind Kevin that *he* was the one who had bailed him out in Austin, who had paid for his dad's plane ticket out to Texas and sprung for a good portion of the fees for the lawyer who had gotten him off the arson charge. But Kevin must have been thinking the same thing, because suddenly he said, "Okay. I'll tell you how to get here."

Ross rummaged through his glove compartment for a pen and a scrap of paper, finally writing down his nephew's address and directions to the apartment on the back of an Auto Club map. "I'll be there in fifteen minutes," he said.

He was there in ten.

On the whole, Ross tried not to be too judgmental, but as he pulled up to Kevin's apartment complex on a trash-strewn street and saw broken overturned chairs on the dead lawn in front of the building, he thought that if he ever had a son, he would never let him live in a dump like this. Locking his car, Ross walked up to Apartment A, which, luckily, was on the first floor, and knocked on the door.

After a long moment, he knocked again.

And again.

Finally, the door was opened. Kevin stood there, eyes at half-mast, a small smile on his face. "Unc! How's it going, man?"

The last time Ross had seen his nephew, Kevin had had short spiky hair dyed an unnatural blond. Now his hair was long and stringy and back to its natural brown. As always, he was wearing faded jeans and a torn t-shirt. Past Kevin, on the couch, a dirty young man of approximately the same age was typing on the keypad of his phone. The apartment smelled so strongly of marijuana that even the air fresheners placed on seemingly every flat surface in the room could not cover up the scent.

"I need to talk to you alone," Ross told his nephew.

"I'm cool," the roommate said. "Anything you tell him, you can say in front of me. I don't mind."

Ignoring the roommate, Ross pulled his nephew outside and closed the door. He took a deep breath. Here now, faced with explaining the situation, he didn't know where to begin. "I need a favor," he said.

"Anything, dude, anything."

He decided just to come out with it. "I need you to start a fire for me."

Kevin backed up, suddenly suspicious. "Is this a test? Did my dad put you up to this?"

"No. It's legit. And I'm deadly serious."

Something in Ross' tone of voice must have conveyed the truth of his words because Kevin stopped his retreat, squinting at him. "What's going on?" he asked guardedly.

"I know this is going to sound crazy," Ross said. "But bear with me. Just hear me out." He started from the beginning, with his move to Magdalena to live on his cousin's ranch. He described what had happened on New Year's Eve, and the gradually escalating weirdness around the town and the outlying countryside, finally telling of his trip to view the body of the creature in the shed. There were a lot of things he left out, but one thing he emphasized was the way that the creature's presence had changed everyone's luck. For good and bad. "People were finding gold and winning the lottery, or their kids disappeared and were found dead. Dave and Lita's ranch was doing good, then their chickens stopped laying and their bees stopped making honey. Dave had a great relationship with his parents and was in need of cash, and both his parents were killed, leaving him money."

"I never saw any of this on the news."

"No, you wouldn't. And that's part of it, but..." Ross tried to put into words what he was trying to convey. "You know, I'd been out of work for well over a year, no job prospects at all. I'd used up all my money, was thinking of walking away from my condo because I couldn't make the payments. Then someone *bought* my condo. And suddenly I had a *ton* of job offers.

"The reason I'm telling you this is because I want you to set that creature's body on fire. I want it destroyed. And, not to offend you or anything, but you were a terrible arsonist. That's why you got caught. And didn't even burn anything. Although the *attempted* arson is probably what got you off. If you had succeeded, you'd probably still be in jail.

"But what I'm hoping is that *your* luck will change when you come with me to Magdalena, and you'll be a great arsonist. You'll know exactly what to do and how to set fire to this thing, and when you're done, there'll be nothing left but ashes. But even if that doesn't happen, you're still the only one I know who knows *anything* about setting fires, and right now, I think that's the only way to take this thing out. It was shot out of the sky, dead as a rock, but it started to influence everything around it, and now, apparently, some sort of cocoon has formed around it to protect it while it transforms into something else, like a caterpillar turning into a butterfly. We need to get to it before it becomes whatever it's becoming. We need to take it out once and for all."

"I don't know why I should believe that," Kevin said. "But you're the straightest dude I know. And you bailed me out and were there for me when I needed it, so I owe you, Unc."

Ross smiled thinly. "Yes, you do."

"Honestly? I don't think we're gonna find what you say we're gonna find out there, but I'll go with you to check it out. And if it turns out that you need it…I'll burn something for you. I'll burn anything you need."

Ross didn't like the way he said that. Not just the words but the tone made him uneasy, and he worried that he might be pushing his nephew back down the wrong path, like a person giving a an alcoholic his first drink after a long stretch of sobriety. But he needed Kevin, and this was the only solution he could come up with that seemed like it might have even a slight chance to succeed.

"I'm heading out tomorrow morning. Do you think you can be ready by six? You don't have a job or anything you have to go to?"

"No, dude, I'm cool. But isn't six a little early?"

"I'm hoping it's not a little late."

Kevin nodded. "Okay. I'm in. You gonna pick me up here?"

"Sure."

Kevin thought for a moment. "I may need to grab a few things up if we're gonna do this."

"Do you need me to take you there?"

"No, it's all right. I have a couple of other…*errands* to run." He smiled mysteriously, and Ross had the feeling he didn't want to know what those "errands" were. "I'll meet you here in the morning."

"Do you need anything from me?" Ross asked. "Matches or anything?"

Kevin laughed. "Don't worry, dude. I have it all covered." This might very well be the stupidest thing he'd ever done, Ross thought as he drove out of his nephew's bad neighborhood toward a nicer area of the Valley where he could find a decent place to stay for the night. But at least he was doing something, and that alone made him feel better. Who was it who said all it took for evil to triumph was for good people to do nothing? He was out of that cycle now, he was acting, and if it turned out that he wasn't part of the solution, at least he wasn't part of the problem.

At the motel, Ross tried for the millionth time to call Jill's cell phone, receiving only the familiar busy signal. He tried their house, then called her parents, but no one answered in San Diego, and Jill's mother refused to talk to him and hung up.

Ross then called McDaniels, unsure if he would answer, unsure if he would still be in town—

unsure if he would still be alive

—but the handyman answered the phone on the first ring, almost as though he had been waiting for the call. Ross breathed an inward sight of relief. He explained to McDaniels that he and his nephew Kevin were coming to Magdalena in the morning and that Kevin was an expert in fire and arson. "We're going to burn that thing up until it's nothing but ashes, and then we'll scatter those ashes to the wind. There won't be a molecule left of it to harm a fly."

The other man didn't sound convinced. "Cameron's ranch is guarded. There's no way you'll be able to get to it. And don't you think the angel'll *know* that you're comin' and what you plan to do? If it don't know already?"

"I'm trusting my nephew," Ross said. "Besides, I made it out there before. Jorge even opened the doors and showed it to us. I think...I think maybe it counts on being able to influence or control whoever comes near it, to kind of override the people it comes in contact with."

"Well, how you gonna make sure that don't happen?"

"Hatred," Ross said. "That'll keep me going."

"Well, there's plenty a that to go around."

Ross didn't respond. McDaniels' questions had him worried. He hated to admit it, but almost none of the handyman's qualms had occurred to him, and he wondered what else he might be missing.

He was going off half-cocked here, not thinking things through, which was totally out of character. He was a planner, a details guy, an almost obsessively logical thinker. He wasn't someone who just had an idea and, on the spur of the moment, acted on it.

Maybe the monster *did* know he was coming.

And was playing with him.

"Is your friend still there?" Ross asked. "The sharpshooter?"

"Far as I know."

"We may need him. You think he'd be willing to help us out?"

McDaniels thought for a moment. "I don't know, to be honest. We were gonna try and shoot it. But when we got there and saw it, all of us pussied out. Can't say that won't happen again."

"Do you think you can get him to try?"

"I'll give it a shot." He let out a surprised chuckle. "A shot. That's kind of a joke, ain't it?"

"Yeah," Ross said.

By his calculations, driving the maximum speed limit on the highway, ignoring the speed limit once he got on the road to Magdalena, he and Kevin should be there about nine or nine-thirty, ten at the very latest. He and McDaniels made arrangements to meet at the bar downtown, assuming it was safe, and by the side of the road at the edge of town if it was not; the determination to be made by the handyman, who promised to try and convince his friend Hec to come along.

Ross hung up feeling more anxious than he had before he called. What until this moment he'd considered a pretty good plan was now looking more like a half-assed Hail Mary, and he wished he had more time to flesh out the details. But he thought of Jill, thought of Lita, thought of his Aunt Kate and everyone else whose innocent lives had been ended or overturned as a result of this monster, and he knew that he needed to act now.

What was it that McDaniels had said?

I think it's ready to hatch.

If he waited any longer, it might be too late, and he saw in his mind Jill's final painting: that terrible demon standing amidst the smoldering ruins of Magdalena.

He barely slept that night, and, wanting to get an even earlier start than originally planned, called Kevin at four-thirty in the morning to wake him up. But it turned out that Kevin was already awake for reasons of his own, and Ross picked him up shortly after five. They packed three boxes of mysterious materials in the trunk, grabbed some coffee and donuts from what might have been the last Winchell's still in existence, and hit the highway, heading south.

Kevin was a captive audience, and Ross filled him in on more details as they drove. He had several hours to argue his case, and while he realized how fantastical it all seemed, he did not get the impression that his nephew thought he was making it up out of whole cloth. Maybe Kevin didn't believe all of it, but there was enough detail and specificity that at least some of it seemed to ring true.

Or Kevin was starting to sense something himself.

The road had been dirt for awhile now, and ahead on the horizon they could see the tips of the mountains that bordered the southern edge of town. Now that he was nearly there, Ross' stomach tightened. He had never been so frightened in his life. It wasn't the quick fright of a movie jump scare or the tension of someone walking into a dark house wondering if something else was in there. No, this was more the dread a convicted man might feel stepping up to the gallows, the unwavering *certainty* that something horrible was going to happen and that there was nothing that could stop it.

The car rolled over a rise, and the chimney-shaped mountain, the one with the M on it, became clearly visible. The town below sparkled in the sun, and maybe if a person didn't know better, all might have seemed perfectly normal. But Ross had been here before, and there were shadows where there should not have been, great swaths of land that looked as though they were recovering from a fire.

What *was* that creature? he wondered for the hundredth time. Where had it lived? Did it have a lair? What had it fed on? How had it not been noticed before? There were so many questions left unanswered, questions that would probably *never* be answered, and his logical brain rebelled against the unresolved chaos of it all.

He was of the belief that the creature was ancient, had been living on this land for centuries, perhaps millennia. It occurred to him that the monster's luck had finally run out when it had been accidentally caught in that hail of celebratory bullets, and in a sort of ripple effect, once it had fallen to earth, once its luck had changed, it had started changing the luck of everyone around it.

Ross half-expected to see other creatures flying above the town—its brethren, waiting for its metamorphosis to complete—but the skies were unnervingly clear as they approached, no birds, no clouds, only endless pale blue.

Next to him, in the passenger seat, Kevin looked nervous. "Unc. Mind if I spark one up?"

"No," Ross said. "I mean, no, don't do it. Yes, I do mind. I need you clear-headed for this." He glanced curiously at his nephew. "You don't…feel any different, do you?" he asked. "I mean, you haven't been hit with any brilliant new ideas about how to go about this, have you?"

Kevin smiled tightly. "Not yet."

They kept driving.

Ross slowed the car as they came to the outskirts of the town, looking carefully around for anything amiss. There was no sign of McDaniels—which could be good, could be bad—and, feeling the tension in his arms, he drove past the ruined adobe house where they had picked up Father Ramos on their way out. Ahead, in front of Magdalena's handful of small businesses, the street was empty.

No, not quite. In the center of the road stood a grimy little girl, wearing a torn granny dress and a wrinkled yellow blouse covered with dried blood stains. Ross recognized her immediately, and the skin prickled on the back of his neck. It was the girl from the farmer's market, the daughter of the mushroom seller. He looked around the street, searching for the mom, but saw no sign of her.

His eyes still on the child, who had not moved a muscle, Ross pulled carefully up in front of the bar, pulling behind the only other vehicle he saw on the street: Jackass McDaniels' dented red pickup truck.

The door to the establishment was closed, and Ross honked the horn, hoping to see McDaniels come out.

The door remained closed.

"I don't like this," he muttered.

Kevin said nothing. Whatever doubts his nephew might have had, Ross could tell that they had fled in the face of the overwhelming sense of dread that hung over the virtually abandoned town. Kevin, too, was keeping his eye on the little girl. The fact that he wasn't suggesting that they help her, or go over and ask her what was wrong, was a pretty good indication that he thought she was as spooky as Ross did.

Ross honked the horn again, then unbuckled his shoulder harness. "You wait here," he told his nephew. "I'm going in to check. If you see anything weird, honk the horn and I'll be right out."

"Don't you have a gun or anything?" Kevin asked nervously.

He had no weapons at all. The truth was that the idea hadn't even occurred to him, although whether that was a result of his own stupidity or that demon's influence, he would probably never know. "No," he said. "But honk the horn and I'll come out."

His hands were trembling as he got out of the car. His knees felt weak, too, but he walked around the front of the vehicle over to the closed door of the small building, took a deep breath, and opened it.

It was dark inside, but he walked in anyway.

The handyman was sitting alone at the bar, drinking a beer, a rifle on the countertop in front of him. "I'm assumin' that's you, pardner," he said without turning around.

"It's me," Ross said.

McDaniels swiveled on his seat. "I thought you was Hec. Arrived a little early, did you?"

"We left early." He sat down next to McDaniels. "So your friend's coming?"

"Saw him last night. Said he would." The handyman shrugged. "Hard to tell these days." Ross couldn't tell if he was drunk or not, but, as early as it was, he could probably use a beer, too. Or something stronger.

Outside, the horn honked once, twice, three times.

Without waiting to see if McDaniels was going to follow him, Ross rushed back outside.

The farmer's market girl was walking down the middle of the street toward them, chanting.

"Butt fuck dick suck! Dirty pussy pie!"

Kevin had gotten out of the car and was standing next to the open driver's side door, his arm stretched out to the steering wheel, ready to honk the horn again. He stopped when he saw his uncle. "She just started walking and saying that."

"Butt fuck dick suck! Dirty pussy pie!" The girl met his eyes, thrusting her chin out belligerently.

"Where's your mother?" Ross asked her.

She had nearly reached the car. He didn't know what to do, so he moved in front of her, blocking her way. "Stop," he said. She was only a few feet in front of him.

"Butt fuck dick suck! Dirty pussy pie!" She leaned forward, whispering. "Stick a needle in your eye. Hope you die."

He jerked back at just the right minute as the filthy child tried to stab his eye with a needle that she was pinching between her thumb and forefinger. She missed, the needle scraping his cheek instead and drawing blood. Reflexively, he lashed out, hitting her in the face.

McDaniels had come out of the bar behind him, rifle butt snug against his shoulder as he sighted down the barrel, ready to shoot. He put the weapon down when he saw who it was.

The girl had fallen to the ground but was not crying as she stood back up. She fixed Ross with a cold stare. "Hope you fucking die."

He grabbed her arm and pushed her back in the direction from which she'd come. "Get out of here," he ordered.

He half-expected her to leap at him again, to fight back, but she wandered up the street toward the church, chanting. "Butt fuck dick suck! Dirty pussy pie! Butt fuck dick suck! Dirty pussy pie!"

Past her, walking forlornly back and forth at the end of the street, near the front of the church, was an equally dirty man holding a handful of strings connected to dead balloons that dragged behind him on the ground.

"Holy shit!" Kevin said. "You weren't lying!"

"No," Ross admitted. "But I wish I was."

"So what do we do now?"

Ross glanced over at McDaniels. "Wait," he said, and the handyman nodded. "Wait and see if anyone else is going to join us."

THIRTY SIX

TODAY'S THE DAY.

The words were imprinted on his mind but Cameron Holt had no idea what they meant. Was the True Angel finally going to emerge from its cocoon? He knew the time was getting close; the cocoon had grown larger than the smokehouse that had originally held it, and the black outline of the new angel was clearly visible through the transparent sheath that covered its evolving form.

Was today the day his troops would finally be called upon to defend their savior? Was this the day Magdalena would finally fall?

Or was today the day he would die?

It almost didn't matter. He was ready for all of those eventualities, and he rolled off the cold body of the dead woman whose ass he'd been reaming, and pushed her off the side of the bed onto the floor, next to the other one. He was sore but sated, and he got out of bed, put on his underwear and dress, and walked downstairs, where he took his shotgun from its place on the kitchen table. April, the red flower that had grown out of the drain in the sink, whistled her little tune.

He hummed the song back to her, and she smiled at him.

Outside, he stood on the porch and fired the gun in the air to get everyone's attention. As soon as the sound of the blast faded away, he shouted the words that he had been given: "Today's the day!"

The cattle came first, or what was left of them: three hungry steers with permanent smiles and bright green gnats flying around their heads, wandering up one by one. The wetbacks and the churchies were all one big group, and they emerged together in various states of undress from their new home in the barn, all of them carrying weapons of one sort or another, ready to defend the angel to the death. There weren't as many of them as there had been the last time he'd checked, and he wondered if the missing had been killed, eaten or run off.

It didn't matter. They still had more than enough defenders to repel any intruders.

After the barn dwellers came the *others,* creatures that might once have been human or might have sprung fully deformed from the ground at the angel's behest. He had no control over these, they answered exclusively to the angel, communicating on a frequency he could not hear, but he spoke to them anyway. He spoke to *everyone.* Standing on his porch, he told them that something big was going to happen. He didn't know what it was, but they needed to be prepared for anything. "Today's the day!" he said again.

Immediately, the *others* started running off in different directions. They weren't running away, he knew. They were following orders other than his, taking up position in places where they would be most useful, probably intending to make sure that, if anyone *was* coming, they did not make it this far. Or perhaps setting up a perimeter to keep out undesirables because the True Angel was about to emerge.

Cameron hazarded a look toward the spot where the smokehouse used to be.

He still didn't like to look at the angel. One reason was that he was not sure if he was *allowed* to gaze upon it, and he didn't want to be punished for some stupid mistake he'd made during the interim once the angel was whole again. The other reason was, well…

Because it scared him.

He wanted to love the angel the way he knew everyone else did—

the way Jorge had

—but on a primal level he didn't understand and couldn't change if he wanted, the angel frightened him. No, not just frightened him. Repulsed him. It was akin to the feeling he'd had when he was camping and woke to see a big hairy spider bouncing up and down on its spindly legs, inches from his face, while his arms were stuck at his sides within his sleeping bag. There was something profoundly alien and unknowable about the angel, and looking at it now, all folded up in its cocoon, its open, silently screaming mouth morphed into a cruel black-toothed smile, its one visible red eye staring, staring, staring, Cameron was suffused with an unnamable fear that went far beyond the fear of death. Turning his attention back to the cattle and people in front of him, he was suddenly overcome with the conviction that today his luck was going to change again. For the last time.

The head churchie came up on the porch to say a few words to those assembled, but Cameron still couldn't stand the prick, even if they were temporarily on the same side, and he wasn't about to share a stage with the man and let everyone think they were equals. Without a word, he turned and strode back into the house, heading straight for the kitchen where, in the sink, April whistled her little song.

Cameron put his shotgun on the table, opened up the refrigerator, took out shotgun shells, a handgun and several rounds of ammunition. Just in case, he took out his Daddy's old pistol. Humming along to the flower's tune, he started loading.

THIRTY SEVEN

Lita was not herself. She was…a camera. A camera that floated over Magdalena, zooming in every so often to examine a particular area or particular person in closer detail.

She saw the ranch, their ranch, and the red flowers were gone but their corpses littered the landscape like dog droppings, little brown clumps of squishy smelly rot. Mickey was not in his pen but was running wild, a crazed look on his face as he chased a line of bright red moths that led him deeper into the desert. Every so often, he would catch one of the bugs, eat it, and for a brief fraction of a second, his entire body would flash a different color.

Then she was in town, where she saw JoAnn. Her friend was kneeling in front of a bonfire in her back yard, wearing a heavy coat and shivering as though she was freezing. Next to her on the ground was a pile of dead cats and dogs, neighbors' pets that she had obviously killed, and every few minutes she would pick one up and throw it in the fire, holding her hands up, palms out, in order to absorb the extra heat generated by the burning animals.

Next, she found herself looking at Vern Hastings and Ben Stanard. The self-anointed preacher and the grocery store owner were locked inside Ben's store, knives in hand, preparing to sacrifice a woman Lita didn't recognize, on the butcher table behind the refrigerated meat display cases in the back.

Looking down on the town again, she thought she saw Ross in front of the bar across the street from the market. But then she was inside Anna Mae and Del Ford's house. The old couple, now both suffering from something apparently far worse than Alzheimer's, were naked and drooling, crawling like babies on their hands and knees over a floor covered with feces.

Then…

She was at Cameron Holt's, standing in front of his house, staring at the spot where the smokehouse used to be. The small building was gone, only its foundation left, and on that foundation, the dead body of the monster was encased in a transparent egg-shaped shell twice as tall as a person. Within, the monster was no longer dead. Its red eye was wide awake and staring, and the coiled tension in its folded wings and scrunched-up legs made it clear that it was ready to emerge from its hibernation. She had never seen anything so awful, yet she knew that this partial look was nothing compared to the horror she would see once the creature was out in full view. She was filled with a feeling of complete and utter despair.

But she saw Ross again, in front of the bar, and Jackass was with him, and someone else. *They* hadn't given up, and they not only looked like they had a plan, they appeared convinced that the plan would work. Feeling better, Lita drifted up and away, her view pulling back above the town, above the clouds, into the darkness beyond.

And, slowly, with a groan, she opened her eyes.

Lita awoke, and Dave was there when it happened. He was holding her hand, and it twitched in his, and he looked into her face and saw her eyes open. He was not by nature an overly emotional person, but he burst into tears when he saw that she was once again conscious, and he realized at that moment that despite what he had told Ross, despite what he had told the hospital staff, despite what he had told himself, he had been preparing himself for Lita never recovering.

Even as he leaned forward to kiss her, still sobbing, Dave was pushing the red button on the side of the bed to call for a nurse, pressing it over and over and over again. After what seemed like forever but might have only been minutes, a nurse arrived, and while she wasn't in as much of a hurry as Dave would have liked, that changed instantly once she saw that Lita was awake. "Stay there," she told him. "I'll get a doctor."

Stay there? Where was he going to go?

Moments later, the nurse returned with a young female doctor. Not one he recognized, but that didn't mean anything. As far as he could tell, Lita hadn't been visited by the same doctor twice in the last two days.

He was asked to move back, and the doctor examined Lita's eyes, shining a penlight into her pupils, before checking her reflexes as she asked a series of formalized questions that were meant to test her memory and mental acuity. Several minutes of this resulted in the doctor patting Lita's hand and smiling in his direction. "Things are looking good," she said. "I'm going to schedule an MRI, we're going to run a few more tests, but I think she's going to be fine."

"You don't have to just tell him. You can talk to me," Lita said. "I'm right here."

The doctor chuckled. "*You're* going to be fine."

She left, and the nurse followed, after explaining that an orderly would be in shortly to take Lita down the hall for the MRI.

The two of them were left alone. Dave moved forward again and took both of her hands in his.

"I've been out for two days?" Lita asked incredulously. That had been one of the things the doctor revealed during questioning.

Wiping his eyes, Dave nodded.

"Did you tell anybody else?" She looked around as though expecting to see gifts and flowers.

He shook his head. "I was going to, but…I never got around to it. I've been camped out here almost the entire time. I did call Ross when it first happened."

"But he's not here. He went back to Magdalena."

"Yeah." He nodded, then frowned. "How'd you know that?"

"I saw it."

"I wanted to go, too, but he said I should stay and take care of you, and of course he was right." Dave's frown deepened. "What do you mean, you saw it?"

"It was like a dream, I guess. But it wasn't a dream. I saw things when I was knocked out."

"Did you see anything useful?"

"Not really. I just saw things as they are. In real time, I think. But I remember them clearly, not like a dream, where, you know, it kind of gets fuzzy after you wake up and you start to forget."

Dave sighed. "Even if you did see something Ross could use, there's no way we could tell him about it anyway."

"Cell phones don't work in Magdalena," they said together, and Lita laughed. His eyes filled with tears as he realized how wonderful it was to hear her laugh again.

"I love you," he said.

She smiled at him, squeezed his hand. "I love you, too."

THIRTY EIGHT

Hec arrived just as it started to snow. He came on foot, carrying a high-powered rifle and wearing a backpack that undoubtedly contained ammunition.

The clouds had sped in out of nowhere, in a matter of minutes, like something out of a Godfrey Reggio movie. They were white rather than gray, but they brought cold with them, and as soon as they settled into place, the snow began.

"Jackass told me whatcha wanna do," Hec said without preamble. "I'm in."

A burly guy with a thick lumberjack beard, he didn't look like someone who had ever been in the military, let alone a sharpshooter, but looks could be deceiving, and Ross had no choice but to trust McDaniels on this.

"Basically, we need you for cover," Ross said. "We're going to try and destroy it by setting it on fire, but I understand that there are some people protecting it. That's where you come in. I don't want you to actually *kill* anyone, but I'm hoping you can keep people away from me and Kevin over there while we do what we have to do." He glanced at his nephew, who seemed to be watching the farmer's market girl and the balloon man at the end of the street, wondering if Kevin's luck as an arsonist was going to change and, if so, how long it was going to take to kick in.

The more he thought about it, the dumber his plan seemed and the more ill-prepared he realized they were.

"You two have been there recently," Ross said to McDaniels and his friend. "What do you suggest we do? What's the best way to go in? If I remember right, there's a long drive coming off the road, and it sort of ends at a big open space between Holt's house and barn. The smokehouse is right there between the two."

"Ain't no smokehouse no more," Hec said.

"I know, but that's where the monster is—"

"The angel?"

"It's no angel, but yeah. And what I'm trying to figure out is how we get there. However many people they have, I assume they'll be watching that road. We need to find some sort of back way or side way to get on to Holt's ranch."

The flakes were changing color as they fell from the sky, white to green to yellow to red, but they froze when they hit the ground, and within moments, the earth had begun to be covered with a thin sheen of ugly brown-colored ice.

"We'll figure it out on the way," Ross said. "We'd better get moving, or we won't be able to drive."

McDaniels and Hec got in the backseat with their rifles, and Kevin sat up front with him. Ross put the car into gear and started moving out slowly. The road was indeed starting to get slippery, and the snow, as it hit the windshield in one of its colored states, melted to gelatinous goop rather than water, but the wipers kept the glass relatively clear, and he was able to see where he was going.

He turned left at the corner where the beauty parlor used to be. A disturbing thought occurred to him. He was lucky to have escaped Magdalena the first time, especially with that mob gathering in front of the store. Did that mean that his luck had now changed and he would *not* be able to get out safely this time?

Ross tried not to obsess on the thought, but it worried him.

He'd also had no problem getting in to see the monster before, with Lita and Dave. Did that mean they would not be able to get anywhere near it today?

Such concerns were not unreasonable. If McDaniels was right and the thing was close to hatching, it stood to reason that its powers would be getting stronger.

Ross drove carefully, hands at ten and two on the wheel. "So how do you think we get in there? Where do we go?" The last time, he and Lita and Dave had pretended to be believers. He didn't think that ruse would work again.

"I say we go east," McDaniels said, "past the driveway, to where the road dips. There's a dry wash there, which'll give us some cover if we keep low. I'm not sure where on his ranch it ends up, but if it goes anywhere near the back of the barn, like I think it does, we can prob'ly get close where we need to be."

The barn. That was a good idea. It offered them a place to hide, and if they could find a way in there—and it was unoccupied—it would also be easily defensible.

Ross slowed the car. Ahead, through the snowflakes, he could see two very tall figures standing in the road before them. From here, they looked like scarecrows, although that didn't make any sense. "Uh, guys?" he said. "Are you seeing what I'm seeing?"

"I seen those before," Hec told him.

Unsure of what to do, Ross stopped the car, hoping to gain a few minutes. He needed time to think. Did he *have* time? He'd assumed the figures in the road ahead were stationary, but as he looked through the windshield, he saw that they appeared to be moving closer.

They were walking.

It knew they were here.

So much for the element of surprise.

He felt amazingly calm, considering, and though Ross would not have described himself as even remotely brave, they were in this, it had started, and he was going to see it through to the end, no matter what happened. "So," he said. "Any ideas? Should we back up and come at this thing from another angle?"

"Let me out," Kevin said. "I need to get a few things from the trunk."

"We could try shooting it," Hec said dubiously, "but I don't know as it'd do much good. Might just be a waste a ammo."

Kevin opened the passenger door and hurried outside in the snow. Reaching under the dash, Ross popped the trunk. With one eye on the slowly advancing figures up the road, he, Hec and McDaniels also got out. Kevin had opened two of his boxes and was rifling through them. "I wasn't sure why I packed some of this stuff, but now I know."

He withdrew a couple of cheap wine bottles with short lengths of rag stuffed into their uncorked openings. Quickly, smoothly, he withdrew the rags, unscrewed the lid of a plastic gasoline container, pulled out a hose extension and poured gasoline into the bottles without spilling a drop. He shoved the rags back in.

"Molotov cocktails. Primitive but effective." Kevin grinned, and for the first time Ross had reason to believe that their plan might actually work. "I know what to do, Unc. I just need you to do what I say. I need everyone to do what I say."

"Got it."

His nephew's luck *had* changed, and it was with a sense of relief that Ross took one of the bottles and a Bic lighter.

But if *Kevin's* luck had changed...

Ross didn't even want to go there.

"We'll wait until they're close," Kevin told his uncle. He motioned toward the other two men. "Why don't you get off to the side there and pick a place where you can fire on them?"

"I don't think it'll work," Hec said. "I don't think they can be killed."

"They aren't made out of Kevlar. Even if they can't be killed, you can probably knock the heads off their bodies or shoot out their legs. Those are some good rifles you guys have. They can definitely do damage."

"Good point," McDaniels said, moving into position.

"Here they come."

They were, in fact, made out of mud, Ross saw as the figures drew closer. And they were indeed scarecrows, though their lack of uniformity gave each one an alarming individuality. While he knew that mud wouldn't burn, the clothes the scarecrows were wearing would, and he hoped that would at least distract the figures long enough for McDaniels and Hec to blast the shit out of their legs and bring them down.

"Light your rag," Kevin said. "Throw on the count of three, and aim for the center of the chest. One...two...three!"

The bottles hit within a second of each other, shattering and engulfing the top half of each scarecrow in a whoosh of flame. The result was better than they could have hoped for. McDaniels and Hec need not have wasted their bullets, because even before their legs shattered in an explosion of dirt, the scarecrows were lurching about confusedly, turning blindly in different directions. Whatever sort of mud made up their forms definitely *was* flammable, and the mounting flames not only burned off the scarecrows' clothing but quickly engulfed their entire bodies. The one on the left tumbled into a ditch on the side of the road as bullets tore apart its leg. The one on the right toppled over where it stood, its lumpy form burning on the hardpacked dirt.

"Back in the car!" Ross ordered. "Let's get out of here!"

He was trying to think fast and on the fly, though that was not something he was good at. Kevin slammed the trunk shut and got into the front passenger seat, while Hec and McDaniels hopped back into the rear seat with their rifles. Ross drove around the downed burning scarecrow in the center of the road. The snow had stopped, he noticed, and he slowed the car. "What should we do now? It knows we're here. Maybe we should just take the direct route and go straight up the drive."

"We don't know that it knows," McDaniels said. "Those scarecrows coulda just been patrolling randomly, making sure people stay away. If we drive past the entrance to the ranch, the angel might just think we're passing by."

"Angels know everything," Hec said simply.

"It's not an angel," Ross repeated. "If anything, it's a demon."

"I'm just sayin' we should stick with the plan," McDaniels said. "The driveway's a lot easier for them to defend. We have more chance, I think, if we sneak through that wash. Although," he added, "maybe we should hurry it up a bit."

With the snow stopped, it was easier to see, and what had remained on the ground was already starting to melt into that gloopy mess. Ross drove quickly by the head of Holt's drive, and, though he deeply wanted to, he did not even look in that direction as they passed in a probably futile effort to pretend that the ranch was not their destination. The road dipped down soon after, and McDaniels told him to stop, this was it. Ross shut off the car, holding his breath, half-expecting to be attacked by...*something*. But nothing came after them, and after only a moment's hesitation, Ross opened his door and got out, the others following suit.

He walked immediately around to the trunk, popping it open. "What do you need?" he asked his nephew. McDaniels and his friend would be carrying their rifles and ammunition, so he and Kevin would have to take the arson supplies themselves. It seemed unfeasible to carry all of those boxes across open land for who knew how far, and he was hoping not all of it was needed.

Kevin opened each of the cartons, looked through them and made a quick determination. "You take that box there with the Coke bottles. It's pretty light. Think you can carry it?"

Ross lifted the carton. It was light, if slightly awkward to carry. "Sure."

Kevin was already rearranging items, moving things from one box to another. "I'll take this one," he said finally.

"Let's move out then."

There was a barbed wire fence surrounding Holt's property, but it remained level at the top, even where it went over the wash, which meant that one post hung in the air above the dry stream bed, leaving a space beneath the bottom strand of wire. McDaniels ducked under it, and Ross passed through his box to the handyman before going under himself. Hec followed after, and Kevin crouched over, clutching his carton of materials to his chest as he made his way under the fence.

Ross took his box back from McDaniels. "Lead the way," he said. "But keep an open eye."

The wash wasn't deep, but there was enough brush growing along the sides to keep them hidden from anyone who might be looking. Ross' concern was that whatever was waiting for them did not *need* to look, but he said nothing and tried to focus on the positive.

It was not a short walk. A half-hour later, they were still trudging through the sand, and it was ten minutes after that that McDaniels raised his hand, silently telling them to stop. The good news was that they had not been intercepted. No one or no *thing* had come after them. But when McDaniels poked his head above the edge of the wash and peered through the branches of a young palo verde tree, motioning for the rest of them to do the same, they saw a pen attached to Holt's barn filled with people running about on all fours like animals. They were naked and filthy, and even from this distance, Ross thought he recognized some of them.

McDaniels ducked back down. "The angel's right behind the barn there. But if we try to go past that pen, someone'll shout a warnin'. Even if they're not part of it, even if they're captured, they'll call out for us to save 'em, and everyone'll know we're here."

"We go past the barn," Hec told him, "double back around."

"It's out of our way, and we don't know what'll be waitin' for us at that point. Might be even worse."

"Well, we can't go through this way."

The wash continued on, heading out and away from the house and barn, and they decided to go on a bit further and see if they couldn't find a better way in.

"Unc?" Kevin said quietly.

"Yeah?" They were all whispering now.

"I need a hose. I need some water."

He frowned, confused. "To drink?"

"No. To put in those bottles." He nodded toward the carton Ross was carrying. "That's what makes them work."

He wished his nephew had said something earlier, but he only nodded and passed the word along.

"Hopefully there is one," was all McDaniels had to say.

The bed of the wash had gotten rocky, slowing their progress, and, ahead, a tree stump marked a change in the direction of the dry stream. They followed the turn—

And stopped.

Squatting in the sand, waiting for them, was a man with the head of a jackal. He was wearing muddy jeans and a flannel shirt that looked familiar, and Ross was pretty sure that he used to be Fred Hanson, the guy who'd cleaned out Lita and Dave's septic tank. Ross glanced over at McDaniels, whose blanched face told him that he'd recognized the man, too.

But that didn't stop McDaniels from raising his rifle. "Stop right there," he said. "Don't move, don't say a word. I hear a peep outta you, I'm takin' off your head."

The jackal man was not alone, Ross saw. Behind him, several small creatures cavorted in the wash, jumping from rock to rock. They looked like miniature rat-faced kangaroos, but it was difficult to see them clearly because they kept moving.

Hec was counting. "...three, four, five... I see five of 'em." His rifle, too was raised.

"What do we do now?" McDaniels asked Ross. "It's kind of a Mexican standoff here."

Then the jackal man roared like a lion and leaped forward, the creatures behind him scurrying in his wake, squealing in high-pitched voices and showing fangs.

This close, the report from McDaniel's rifle was deafening. Hec's followed instantly after, or maybe at the same time—it was hard to tell because he was firing over and over again. The jackal head exploded in a burst of blood, fur and flesh, and the little leaping monsters were blasted into nothing.

"They know where we are now," Kevin said, hefting his box.

"In for a penny, in for a pound." McDaniels pointed up the sloping side of the wash. "It's now or never. Let's do it."

That was the last word any of them spoke as they ran out of the dry stream bed, across an open area, and along the east side of the barn. In the lead now, Ross stopped and peeked around the corner of the building, looking toward the place where the smokehouse should have been. He quickly pulled back. There was an *army* out there. Literally dozens of men and women, seemingly all of them armed, some with farming implements, some with firearms, were stationed in front of, behind and to the sides of what looked like an enormous black egg the size of a small car, a situation so daunting as to seem nearly insurmountable.

As of yet, they did not appear to have been spotted, and no one was coming up behind them, so Ross gestured for the others to follow him and backtracked several yards. Crouching down along the side of the barn, his box in front of him, he explained what he'd seen. "We're outnumbered ten to one. Anybody have any ideas?"

Kevin nodded calmly. He was already opening his box. "I'll create a distraction. I'll set up an explosion in the barn. Everyone will come running, and that's when I'll go in and take out that… angel?…demon?…whatever it is. You guys just cover me."

"I don't have a gun," Ross said. "And wouldn't know how to shoot it if I did," he admitted.

Kevin smiled, pointing to the box in front of his uncle. "That's what those are for. And that's why we need some water." He picked up one of the two-liter Coke bottles. "There's Drano crystals in here. And aluminum foil. All you do is add water, shake and throw. Basically, it'll explode and spray acid all over. It won't start a fire, but it'll take care of anyone in its way."

Ross felt uncomfortable about actually hurting anyone. Cameron Holt had always been an asshole, but that didn't necessarily hold true for everyone here. And even assholes didn't deserve to *die*. These were just people who'd gotten sucked into the monster's orbit, maybe the people who'd been there New Year's Eve when it had been shot down. Chances were, if they could pull this off and destroy that black monstrosity, those individuals would revert back to normal once it was all over. They couldn't do that if they were dead. Or scarred by acid.

That jackal man—*Fred Hanson?*—was already on his conscience.

At the same time, he had no illusion that they weren't doing the right thing. Dead, that creature had caused enough horror to justify destroying it. If it was allowed to "hatch" as McDaniels put it, to become what it was becoming, who knew what damage it would cause, what people it would kill?

"So what's the plan?" he asked Kevin.

His nephew was unspooling a long length of wire. "I've got some det wire, here."

"Det wire?"

"Detonation wire. I'm going to use it to set a fire inside the barn. If I can get in there without anyone seeing me."

Hec was already off, heading around the back corner of the building, presumably to check if it was empty.

"I'm sure there's something flammable inside there. I'll pick a bale of hay or some old wood or a pile of newspapers, soak it with gas, spread things out so it'll shoot simultaneously to each area of the barn, pop in the end of the det wire, spool it out here, light it and haul ass. The whole place'll go up in an instant. That'll bring them running. We need to be in a position at that point to swoop in while they're distracted. I'll soak the angel demon with gas and gel, set it off, and we're done."

"What's gel?" Ross asked.

Kevin grinned. "Good stuff."

Hec came running back along the side of the barn. "I think it's clear," he said. "At least, I got in without seeing anyone or being seen. The door's wide open."

"Any hay in there?" Kevin asked.

"Mountains of it."

"We're in."

Ross was impressed by the fact that his nephew had suddenly become such an expert in firestarting, but he worried that the opposite might occur, too, especially in such close proximity to the monster. What if Hec's sharpshooting skills suddenly deserted him? What if McDaniels couldn't aim for shit?

It didn't matter. They had no choice. This was the only plan they had.

"Before we do anything, we need to find water," Kevin said, pushing the hair out of his eyes.

"There'll be water in the corral," McDaniels said. "For the horses and cattle. Might be a spring or a pipe-fed barrel, but it'll be damn near impossible to get to. You'll have to go through the people you're gonna use it on to do it."

"There must be, like, a hose near the house, right?"

"Usually," McDaniels said. "But I never worked on Holt's plumbing, so I don't know for sure."

"I'll take that chance," Ross said. He was pretty sure he had a water bottle in the car, and he wished he'd brought it, but his nephew hadn't said anything at the time.

"Once everyone takes off and runs to the barn, it's your job to keep them there. Inside, outside, doesn't matter. Just keep that angel demon free so I can set up shop. You have six of those bottles. Use them wisely. After the first explosion, it'll probably scare them enough to keep them back. It's pretty gnarly. But if it doesn't work out, and you run out of bottles before I'm done..." He turned toward Hec and McDaniels. "You two keep them in line."

"Try not to kill anyone," Ross emphasized.

"I'll do what I have to do," Hec said.

He sounded tough, sounded brave, but McDaniels had said that the last time they'd come here, they'd both ended up running away, too afraid to take any action. He hoped against hope that that wouldn't happen this time.

"Give me a few minutes," Kevin said, his hands full as he started toward the rear of the barn. "And maybe stay back from that wall. Just in case."

There was a tractor off to the left of the barn, and Ross hurried over, hiding behind it. From this angle, he could see the open area between the house and barn, and the army of defenders stationed around the metamorphosing body. McDaniels and Hec ran up next to him, rifles at the ready. Hec's gun apparently had a telescopic sight, and he looked through it, aiming at the house.

"There *is* a hose," he said. "Right by the front steps. Holy shit! There's Cameron, too." He started grinning. "Here, bud. Take a gander."

Ross accepted the rifle and, using the gun site like a spyglass, he trained it on the house. Father Ramos was standing with Cameron Holt on the front porch, and Ross was not merely shocked to see the priest, but filled with a disappointment so profound it was almost sorrow. They'd rescued Father Ramos, driven him away, but he had not escaped Magdalena, had not returned with the full power of the church behind him. He had instead come back of his own accord, seduced once again by the empty promise of the *angel*. He was a part of this now, and, like Holt, one of the monster's minions.

Cameron Holt, for some reason, was wearing a dress. That's what Hec had been grinning about, but even through the small lens of the gun site, Ross could see from the rancher's face that the man was mad.

He swiveled the rifle toward the crowd in front of the monster's body, seeing several people who looked familiar.

Was Jill here, too, somewhere?

He hoped not, but he had to admit that it was possible, and he would have continued looking, trying to find her, but time was passing quickly, and if all went according to plan, the barn would be going up in flames at any moment. He handed the rifle back.

And the barn exploded.

It didn't literally explode. Roof and walls didn't fly outward in a hail of shattered wood. But the conflagration that engulfed the structure did so in a blaze of glory, flames bursting out with an audible roar, the heat so intense that he could feel it here by the tractor. The fire had the desired effect, most of the gathered throng instinctively dashing over to investigate.

But not all of them did.

A significant number remained guarding the encased body, and Ross realized that it was up to the three of them to do something about that so Kevin could get access to the monster.

He just hoped his nephew had survived starting the fire.

"Come on!" Ross shouted.

402

They ran into the open. McDaniels kept his rifle trained on the front porch of the house, while Hec scrambled sideways, facing the remaining guards.

Kevin was nowhere in sight.

Father Ramos was bending over the front porch railing, vomiting, but Holt was starting to raise his shotgun. "Stop right there, asshole!" McDaniels ordered. "Or I'll blow your fucking head off!"

Some of the men who'd gone over to the barn to see what had happened looked like they were about to turn around.

Ross ran for the hose, turning the faucet on and pulling the hose out to the center of the yard as far as it would go. He'd dropped his box of Coke bottles, but it didn't matter. The caps were all sealed, and he quickly unscrewed one, pressed the flowing hose against the opening, screwed the cap back in and ran several yards toward the men and women shielding the body. "Get away from there!" he ordered, and threw the bottle.

It flipped end over end, exploding in the air just before the first line of guards, the bottle bursting spectacularly, spraying acid in all directions, hitting several people and causing them to scatter, screaming.

He didn't have time to view the results, but immediately hurried back to where water from the hose was already making a puddle in the dirt. A bullet hit the ground next to him, splashing up mud. Another whizzed by, more felt than seen, and, next to him, Hec took a shot. Nothing else was fired at him, and when he turned around to unscrew the cap of another bottle, Ross saw the body of a middle-aged man lying on the ground. There was no time to think about it, to agonize about it, to worry if something else was coming his way. He simply filled the bottle with water, sealed it, shook it, ran and threw.

This time, people scurried away before the explosion, and behind them, in the corral, he saw Kevin scrambling through the spaces between boards to get to the monster.

The monster.

It had captured his attention, lying on the open floor of what had once been Cameron Holt's smokehouse as though displayed on a stage. He had not seen it in this state, and, this close, he saw how thin the outer covering was, how completely transparent, almost as if the body had been encased in plastic wrap. The body itself was not the same one he had seen before. Rather than that melting, devolving mess, this creature was much bigger, much darker, much more clearly defined.

It was also very much alive.

A single red eye stared out at him.

He heard whistling.

Today's the day, he thought.

As he watched, the chrysalis cracked open, in the middle, and through the breach, a long black appendage emerged that could have been a tail, could have been a tentacle, could have been a feeler, could have been a very thin leg. The slimy extremity slid along the top of the encasement, searching for another opening or trying to *make* another opening. There was nothing frantic in its movement, no hurrying, and Ross watched, enthralled, as the black appendage calmly felt for a way to get the angel out of its cocoon.

It *was* an angel, he saw now. And it was beautiful. It had not been resurrected for any malevolent purpose. Resurrection couldn't be evil. *They* were the evil ones for trying to attack it. The angel should not be assaulted, it should be celebrated. Father Ramos had returned because he knew the truth, and now Ross himself knew the truth, and he would do everything in his power to—

No.

This wasn't right.

He closed his eyes, fought against the thoughts that were imposing themselves on his mind.

Kevin!

Had it gotten to Kevin, too?

No, it hadn't. Ross opened his eyes to see his nephew sprinting away from the emerging demon—for that's what it was, he had finally decided, a demon—and unspooling det wire behind him.

"Get back!" Kevin was shouting to anyone within hearing distance. "Get away!"

Ross and Hec heeded the advice, as did several men and women who had started to wander back from the burning barn. Whether they believed in the angel or not, they understood after what had happened to the barn that Kevin was about to do some serious damage, and their survival instinct kicked in, overriding everything else.

McDaniels still had his rifle trained on Cameron Holt, but as soon as Ross and Hec ran by, he joined them, all three speeding past the edge of the house and down a section of the drive before a thunderous clap and a blast of hot wind at their backs made them stop and turn around.

A massive blaze, taller than it was wide, with flames of different color flaring up and out, engulfed the black figure on the old smokehouse's foundation, including the searching tentacle. In the fire, the remainder of the chrysalis burned away, and for a brief moment, the thing inside rose to its feet, stretching out to full size. It had thick black wings, but they clung to the spiky body rather than extending. The head, even more triangular than before, and more geometric than antlike, displayed a horrific face bearing almost no resemblance to anything human, insect or animal. From within the multi-colored flames, red eyes looked upon them with hatred and a depth of knowledge so vast that its very gaze made Ross more terrified than he had ever been in his life.

Kevin knew what he was doing, however. Like a fire tornado, the blaze shot up, swirling around the figure, and the heat was so great that the skin began to melt. The monster screamed, but instead of a roar there was a whistle, a keening so high-pitched and powerful that Ross thought his eardrums were going to burst.

Then it was gone.

The burning monstrosity didn't collapse or shatter, it simply disappeared, winking out of existence as though it had never been there in the first place. The inferno surrounding it lost *all* color for a second, looked black-and-white, and then it was a normal fire, the kind that burned houses and forests, yellow and orange.

Stunned, confused—*was it really all over?*—the three of them started slowly back, McDaniels and Hec with their rifles at the ready, just in case.

A lone figure emerged from behind the tightly controlled blaze, walking toward them. "Over here!" Kevin shouted.

On the porch, a furious Cameron Holt raised his shotgun.

Hec's bullet took him down.

As he ran over to his nephew, Ross wondered if Hec's action had been necessary—the man was a sharpshooter, after all. Couldn't he have been more precise? Couldn't he have injured the rancher rather than killed him?—but he was grateful that Kevin was okay, and though he wasn't sure they had ever hugged before, they hugged now, and Kevin cried into his shoulder like a little boy.

On the porch, Father Ramos was on his knees, praying out loud for forgiveness.

Ross was crying, too, and the hug lasted for a long time, family clinging to family for support. Around them, rifles raised, McDaniels and Hec looked out for anything amiss.

Ross wondered if cellphones worked here now, and pulling away from his nephew with a final pat on the back, he took out his phone and punched in 911.

"Nine-one-one. What is your emergency?" a woman's voice on the other end of the line responded.

Unprepared, Ross didn't know what to say. "There's a fire at Cameron Holt's ranch outside of Magdalena," he finally got out.

"What is the address on that, sir?"

"I don't know, but you can't miss the smoke."

"I'm afraid I'll need—" Before the dispatcher could continue to question him, he clicked off.

"If the cops question you on shootin' Holt," McDaniels was telling his friend, "I'll swear it was self-defense."

Ross nodded. "We all will," he said.

Hec shrugged. "If it even comes to that. This thing ain't registered, so they might not figure out it's me. Lotta people hated Cameron. He had it comin'."

"But if someone else here reports it was you..."

Hec nodded toward the still-burning barn, where dazed townspeople were wandering around aimlessly, as though they'd just woken up after sleepwalking. "I ain't gonna worry about it."

They left the fires burning. It was a long trek back out to the car, and they hiked through not only strange dying foliage but past the inert bodies of animals that were not quite animals, many of which were deteriorating into a gelatinous mess.

By the time they reached Magdalena, they could hear faint sirens sounding from somewhere up the road to Willcox. The main street of the town still looked abandoned, though Ross thought he detected movement behind the windows of one of the adobe houses. In the parking lot of the market, deflated balloons hung from the crooked antenna of an old pickup truck. A lifeless dog lay in front of the gas pumps.

He thought of the lyrics to an old Simon and Garfunkel song: *Nothing but the dead and dying back in my little town.*

Facing the wrong way on the street, he parked in front of the bar and got out. All of them did.

The sirens drew closer.

Kevin tapped him on the shoulder, smiling wryly. "Unc?"

"Yeah?" Ross said.

"We're even."

THIRTY NINE

IRTY AND DISHEVELED AFTER SEVERAL DAYS OF LIVING OUT of her van, Jill returned to the house in San Diego to collect her belongings. And take a shower. The place was empty, Ross nowhere in sight, and for that she was grateful. She didn't want to face him right now.

It felt as though she'd awakened from a long dream. No. From a drunken blackout. She'd been acting like...not herself, and while she understood why, the fact that it had occurred at all was a complete embarrassment to her.

She found the note Ross had left, read it, and relaxed a little. She didn't have to rush; it looked like he wouldn't be back for awhile.

After taking a long leisurely shower and changing into some clean clothes, Jill went into the kitchen to make herself a sandwich. She walked around the house as she ate, mentally deciding what she should and shouldn't take with her. Finishing the sandwich and grabbing a water bottle out of the refrigerator, she started packing her clothes. Cleaning out her half of the dresser and placing her underwear in her open suitcase, she thought about Ross with bewilderment. She had actually moved with him here to California? Why? That wasn't the sort of thing she did.

He wasn't even her type.

Not that she *had* a type.

She wasn't *that* shallow.

But an engineer? That was out of character for her, and she wondered now what she could have been thinking. It wasn't a knock against Ross. He was a nice guy, and she liked him all right, but not enough to move in with him and follow him to another state.

No wonder her mom was mad at her.

She got a trash bag out of the kitchen and used it to bag up the dirty laundry that she fished out of the hamper. Luckily, she hadn't taken *everything* out of her house. In fact, most of it was still back in Magdalena. She smiled wryly. At least emergency evacuations were good for something.

She bagged up her toiletries, then started carrying things out to the van, placing the bags, boxes and suitcases next to the godawful paintings of that reservoir that she had wasted her time on. It took only four trips, and after the last one, she walked back inside, looking through each room to make sure she hadn't missed anything. Glancing over at the lone bookshelf on the wall above Ross' computer, Jill realized that the only books displayed were manuals and technical books on science and engineering.

How could she not have noticed that before?

She left her key on the kitchen counter. And a note, a short message stating simply that she was moving out. It didn't explain anything, but, then, she didn't know *how* to explain what she was going through. She didn't understand it herself.

She would call him later, she decided, once she'd figured out what to say. For now, she just wanted to go back to Mesa.

And see her mom.

FORTY

Ross returned to Magdalena the following weekend in a rented pickup. Lita and Dave were already back at the L Bar-D and in the process of cleaning up, Lita still taking it easy for the most part, following doctor's orders, limiting herself to housework so she could take frequent rest breaks as instructed, Dave hard at work outside, using a borrowed tractor to drag all the accumulated debris out to a spot in the field, where he intended to burn it. Word had spread that Lita's cousin Ross was the one who had come up with the plan to destroy the monster, and as a way to say thank you, several people, farmer's market customers mostly, had volunteered to help Lita and Dave fix up the ranch, and they were there with rakes and shovels, planting new plants, cleaning out the root cellar.

There would be a lot of the communal spirit in the coming weeks, he knew, as neighbor helped neighbor get back on track.

That was one of the things he liked about Magdalena.

The bees, miraculously, had survived. Some might have flown off and not returned, but most of them were back in the boxes, in their hives. The horse and goat were nowhere to be found, but somehow, in the midst of all this chaos, new chickens that Dave ordered had arrived, and they were in their yard, clucking happily and scratching in the dirt. It was both a relief and a welcome change to see the hens acting perfectly normal, and more than anything else, it made Ross feel that everything was going to be all right.

Lita had thrown her arms around him the minute he arrived, and he was grateful to be able to hug her back unreservedly, without a single improper thought crossing his mind. Everyone greeted him with gratitude and enthusiasm, and it felt like a homecoming, even though there were a couple of people he didn't even recognize.

He'd come back, basically, to pick up the rest of his belongings from the shack, and his original plan was to do it all in one day: speed over to Magdalena, pack up his stuff and hit the road. But Lita convinced him to stay the night, and after she helped him box up his effects, he assisted her in making sandwiches for everyone. They all ate lunch outside, on and around a picnic table that had been set up near the fruit trees, and he heard story after story about the horrors people had endured over the past month.

Ross and Lita stayed at the table after Dave and the others had gone.

"So was your job still there?" Lita asked. "After?"

"It was still there." He paused. "Jill wasn't."

"Oh, Rossie! What happened?"

He picked at the crumbs on his paper plate. "I don't know, really. She left a note saying she was leaving, but that was all the note said. It didn't tell me anything other than that. I've tried to call her several times, but she won't pick up. My guess? It was never real in the first place, her interest in me. It was real on my part. Still is," he said ruefully. "But I've never had good luck with women. For a brief time, I did. Now it's over."

"Maybe she'll think about it and come back," Lita said encouragingly.

"Maybe," he said, but he knew that wasn't true. He might still have feelings for Jill, but it seemed pretty obvious that whatever she had felt for him had died with the monster.

Ross stood. "I have a whole afternoon ahead of me here, and you're trying to get this place in order. You must have something for me to do."

He ended up performing his old chores, feeding the chickens and collecting eggs. It was relaxing this time, rather than stressful, and afterward he helped Dave and a guy named Don dig a hole to bury the bodies of deformed rodents that had been collected from around the ranch.

Once again, he took dinner in the Big House with Lita and Dave, filling them in with more detail on what had happened at the last, then he walked across the yard to spend one final night in the shack. He had no laptop, but the TV was still here, and he turned it on for white noise as he prepared to go to sleep.

He had no dreams.

Leaving the next morning made him sad. He had grown used to this place and these people. Magdalena felt like home to him, and though he now had the job that he wanted and a rental house near the beach, it was hard to reconcile the fact that if he ever returned, it would be as a visitor rather than a resident, and nothing would be the same.

"I only look forward," Jill told him once. "It's too sad to look back."

He understood what she meant.

"Call me," Lita said, hugging him and crying.

"I will," Ross promised.

He drove back to San Diego, stopping off in Yuma for coffee, gas and a bathroom break before making a marathon run across the desert in an effort to beat the heat. Back in California, he unpacked the pickup, took it back to Enterprise, and someone from the rental car agency drove him home. Tired, he lay down on the couch, intending to take a short nap before finding a place for all the boxes he'd brought back, but when he opened his eyes again, it was morning. He'd slept through not only the rest of the afternoon but the entire night, and he awoke hungry, though his body clock was off and he was not in the mood for breakfast. Tacos sounded good, and he wondered if that little stand on the beach, Surfside Tacos, was open this early.

He was still wearing yesterday's clothes, and he took them off, got in the shower and changed into clean underwear, pants and a shirt. Tacos still sounded good to him, and he put on some sneakers and walked outside, looking toward the beach.

It was about 75 degrees and clear, the ocean as blue as the sky.

He breathed deeply, thought of Jill, and smiled sadly to himself.

Nice weather for a walk.